RONAL

Ronald Frame was born in 1953 in Glasgow and educated there and at Oxford. His first published stories appeared when he was 17, but it was not until 1982, after a brief stint of teaching, that he began to write full time. The author of ten books, including A WOMAN OF JUDAH, SANDMOUTH PEOPLE, WATCHING MRS GORDON and UNDERWOOD AND AFTER, Ronald Frame is also the winner of several awards. His first novel, WINTER JOURNEY, was joint winner of the first Betty Trask Award in 1984, A LONG WEEKEND WITH MARCEL PROUST won a Scottish Arts Council Award, and PENELOPE'S HAT was shortlisted for the James Tait Black Memorial Prize and the McVitie's Scottish Book of the Year Award.

Ronald Frame has also written several television and Sony-nominated radio plays, as well as a memoir for radio called GHOST CITY. His first television play entitled PARIS, won both the Samuel Beckett Award and the Television Industries' panel's Most Promising Writer New to Television Award.

Ronald Frame

WALKING MY MISTRESS IN DEAUVILLE
A Novella and Nine Stories

Words of 'These Foolish Things' by E. Maschwitz © Copyright 1936 by Boosey & Co. Ltd. reprinted by kind permission of Boosey & Hawkes Music Publishers Ltd. for the world excluding the USA, Canada and Newfoundland.

Lines from 'Night and Day' by Cole Porter, in 'Mask and Shadow', © copyright 1957 Notable Music Co. Inc., USA & WB Music Corp. Warner Chappell Music Ltd., London W1Y 3FA/International Music Publications. Used by permission.

'Gregor's Garage' and 'The Siege' both appeared in volumes of 'Scottish Short Stories' (Harvill Collins).

'Privateers' was broadcast on BBC Radio 4.

'Walking my Mistress in Deauville' was published in *Cosmopolitan* and has been adapted as a play to be broadcast on BBC radio.

Lines from 'Witchcraft' by Coleman and Leigh, in 'Table Talk', © copyright 1932 Harms Inc., USA. Warner Chappell Music Ltd., London W1Y 3FA/International Music Publications. Used by permission.

The qutotations in 'Crossing the Alps' are taken from the Penguin Classics edition of Livy's *The War with Hannibal* (Books XXI–XXX), translated by Aubrey de Sélincourt.

Copyright © 1992 by Ronald Frame

The characters and situations in this book are entirely imaginary and bear no relation to any real person or actual happenings.

First published in Great Britain in 1992 by Hodder and Stoughton Ltd

Sceptre edition 1993

Sceptre is an imprint of Hodder and Stoughton Paperbacks, a division of Hodder and Stoughton Ltd

The right of Ronald Frame to be identified as the author of this work has been asserted by him in accordance with the Copyright, Designs and Patents Act 1988.

Printed and bound in Great Britain for Hodder and Stoughton Paperbacks, a division of Hodder and Stoughton Ltd, Mill Road, Dunton Green, Sevenoaks, Kent TN13 2YA. (Editorial Office: 47 Bedford Square, London WC1B 3DP) by Clays Ltd, St Ives plc. Typeset by Hewer Text Composition Services, Edinburgh.

British Library Cataloguing in Publication Data
Frame, Ronald
  Walking My Mistress in Deauville.
  I. Title
  823.914 [FS]

ISBN 0-340-57971-4

CONTENTS

To Dodo and the Texan, of course

MASK AND SHADOW

Seeing is deceiving.

Jean-Luc Godard, *Detective*

But time is always guilty. Someone must pay for
Our loss of happiness, our happiness itself.

W. H. Auden, 'Detective Story'

ONE

Our story, hers and mine, begins in a resort town on the south coast of England.

The year is 1957.

Spring was on the turn into early summer.

I had come to the town alone. My solitariness was the point. I had just broken up with a girl. I knew that when I went back to London we wouldn't get together again. I had that one certainty, but no more than that. I tried to keep my mind from straying back to our history together. I wanted it to be just that, history.

I'd needed to be somewhere different for a while. Anywhere would have done. I'd happened to notice a photograph of Castlebay's promenade in a newspaper. I'd never been to the town, so I decided to pay it a visit. Why not?

The streets criss-crossed on a gentle declivity of green hill between white cliffs. There were a couple of large hotels, the Beaufort and the Regency. Between them stretched the sedate arcades of shops, and various ornamental gardens fitted into curious-shaped plots of ground. There was a little theatre with a plaster frieze of actors' masks – alternately gleeful and despondent – ranged beneath the building's compact dome, and with an interior of green plush whose pile had been flattened by the years. On the esplanade brisk widows with tightly permed curls walked their lapdogs. They were closely watched by feisty ex-colonials in waistcoats and moustaches, men who had willed themselves to become those perfect archetypes.

An air of cliché hung over the resort, myself included, which was why I knew it to be all true enough, even my own moodiness – a sort of watered-down, not very well-thought-out existentialism. I'd decided I should have to be alone, to get over everything. But having come to a strange town I felt more alone than I probably needed to be. My own company had started to get me down; I had started to feel quite bored with myself.

On warm sunny days it wasn't so bad. The temperate sunshine was a polite veil drawn over sensation, smoothing everything out. I lazed about: on the shingle beach, on the esplanade benches, in the garden of the Beaufort Hotel where I could make a drink or a pot of tea last and last. I had a funny notion, which there seemed to be no accounting for, that I was waiting: waiting for something to happen. That wasn't faddish existentialism, I can say now, it was probably no more than old-fashioned fatalism. The feeling was inexplicable, but it was strong, stronger than my reason was able to be at that time. I just supposed that whatever would be would be, as the Doris Day song put it, and that because I felt as I did, the sensation must be true.

I tried to read, but I would quickly lose interest. The sort of fifties English novel stocked in the bookshops failed to convince me with their dependable structures and neatly balanced sentences. Real life had more clichés than fiction, yet I wasn't convinced by the articulate examples of bourgeois life who regularly obtruded between passages of tasteful description to motivate the plot. The tone of the books seemed 'Establishment' to me, and did existence actually point itself to such tidy moral solutions as the authors meant to persuade us?

I skimmed through newspapers instead, in the garden of the Beaufort Hotel or in the cocktail bar, postponing for as long as I could my departure and the walk back through roads of bungalows in sandy hydrangea gardens to the modest private hotel where I was staying. I flitted among the stories set in newsprint, and that was the most suitable butterfly activity for my long afternoons as they drifted into pleasantly forgetful alcoholic evenings.

At first I supposed she was a guest. The impression I had was of a *soignée* woman quite relaxed and in her element.

Nervous people can't cross their legs, can't coordinate their movements with conviction. She gave every indication of control, from her eyes and mouth to her ankles and feet. It wasn't usual to see a young woman drinking alone: older women did, but they had the riddles of their lives to try to put out of their minds. My solitary companion in the cocktail bar wasn't any older than myself. I naïvely took it for granted that her attractiveness and collectedness protected her from riddles.

Her sartorial taste struck me as similarly confident, and refined: single, striking colours for those dresses and two-pieces in our still rather dowdy times – cerise, emerald, citrus lemon. Her accessories had an expensive, original look about them: plain, dark court shoes, a black crocodile handbag, variously coloured suede or kid gloves which extended halfway along her forearms, sheeny stockings, assorted items of jewellery given only a single airing – large pearl studs, a gold and yellow sapphire brooch shaped like a shooting star, a blue chalcedony necklace, an ivory netsuke worn as a pendant on a black velvet choker, a bangle of linked gold Russian rings.

She acquitted herself with the sort of assurance I imagined a prerequisite of the frequenters of such premises. She sat back in her chair with the aplomb of a woman versed at taking life mostly in her stride. Nevertheless, while she didn't tap her feet or drum the pads of her fingers on the chair arm, yet I had the distinct notion that she too was someone waiting: waiting behind her cloudlet of cigarette smoke in a state of unresolved anticipation. Why was she here, why was she dependent on the doubtful ambience of a cocktail bar and the smiling but deferential *politesse* of Tommy the barman, stationed behind the counter with its padded leather front? A curious tautness built up among the three of us, the regulars, and the one or two others who might also be there. Maybe the warm somnolent weather aided the effect, and the sound of the breakers on the cliff-edge beneath the hotel's garden, and the exotic scratching of the dwarf palms against the glass of the windows. The last fires of the season burned in the grate: sweet-smelling logs perished into sparks that whistled up the chimney into mild, starry May skies.

While I naturally supposed she was a guest I felt it must be all too evident to her that I, with my gaucheness, was not. I didn't know why else she should have been drawn to look at me if it wasn't that my own interest was too obvious and unsubtle. I tried to gauge when she might not be looking, and to take advantage of the vertical reflecting surfaces in the room. Sometimes she caught me, sometimes she gamely deferred and looked away. Sometimes I found she wasn't looking at me at all, and then I was much more disappointed than relieved. Failing to be noticed, even in my gaucheness, was too much like being forgotten and relegated to the outer edges of the situation.

She knew my name.

'I know your name,' she told me the afternoon she stopped at my table.

I stared at her. She smiled to see my bafflement.

'How – ' I coughed a frog out of my throat. 'How did . . .?'

'Oh – ' She affected a look of deep wisdom, but continued to smile: a slightly lopsided smile.

A few minutes later, when I asked her again, she told me she had heard the receptionist call through to me one day when I was preparing to ring from the telephone box at the back of the foyer. I did use the box for my work, but the girl who had happened to call over that day – making a commotion about nothing much, only my enquiry about reversing charges – had used the wrong name, that of the person I was trying to contact, called Trenor.

My fellow *habituée* of the cocktail bar had used my correct name, Charles Swale. Her manner and the tone of her voice were confidential, almost intimate, but also quite assured. I didn't understand. I had intended to pass my time in the town as anonymously as possible. Who in the world would have known who *I* was anyway?

I'm not sure that I was able to understand any better, even when I'd returned to my hotel, the Llanberis House, and noticed the Guests' Book placed open on the table in the hall, with my name, address and room number all clearly visible to anyone who might walk in or out. I felt – I can't say why – that I didn't want to pursue the topic with her, that it shouldn't be allowed to matter.

I had already told her in the Beaufort where I was staying, after she must have discovered for herself, so she had that excuse for knowing where to find me on the next occasion when we met. She was standing in the hall when I came out of the Llanberis's dining-room after breakfast. She was a little wind-blown, and wore a white chiffon headscarf tucked into a leopard-skin jacket, buttoned up to the collar. She stood smiling from cheek to cheek, maybe at the evidence of my surprise. Faces were gawping down from the staircase landing at this most unlikely fellow guest. She removed a pair of very fine mauve kid gloves from her pocket and used them to indicate the general direction she meant to take on what she called her 'morning constitutional'.

'I expect,' she said, 'you could do with walking off your breakfast?' Frying smells were wafting from a back corridor, and she moved past me, towards the fresher draughts that were always seeping through the front half of the building from un-shut doors and ill-fitting windows. Her shoes, I noticed, were hardly the walking kind: reptile skin of some sort, high-heeled and mauve, to match the colour of the gloves. The inconsistencies only pleased me, however. I jumped at the prospect of a walk, at such an unlooked-for manner of filling my morning.

She stood smiling, more privately, at my response. In recollection she possesses a maturity and authority far beyond the plausible reach of myself. That may be what I want to believe, in the hope I can excuse myself for everything that follows. But I was far from supposing myself so inexperienced and lacking at the time. I had a naïf's absurd confidence that, sooner rather than later, I should prove my true worth and no one would have a moment's doubt. Why had she searched out the Llanberis at a time when I would still be there but when she would be an object of general attention herself, if it wasn't to make completely sure of finding me?

She had rented rooms, it transpired, and came to the big hotels for the activity. I smiled when she told me, and she asked me why, sounding puzzled.

'"Activity"?' I repeated, still smiling.

Instantly the skin of her face and neck reddened. I wondered what she had read into my tone of voice that it should have caused her either this embarrassment or irritation.

I only meant, I went on to explain too wordily, that they didn't seem the most exciting places, for the sort of clientèle they drew or the numbers of them.

'By the standards of the town they are,' she said. 'You're really living it up at the Beaufort!'

She was trying to sound jokey about it, unconcerned, as if she hadn't really had to struggle with her composure just a very few seconds before. The slightly left-of-centre smile returned to her face. I sensed her determination to lighten the moment.

'Do you know Castlebay?' I asked her. 'Have you been before?'

'No. I just had a picture of it in my head.'

'Is it like that? – how you imagined it?'

'With some places it doesn't matter,' she said. 'You can go to them, visit and look about, then leave them, and when you're away and it's far behind you . . . What you remember of it isn't what you actually saw but what you envisaged before you went. The image of the place.'

I nodded slowly. The remark had a prepared feel to it: or maybe she was simply expressing something she'd long thought about. Presumably she had the proof of it. But I didn't quite like to ask, to pry. Already, but without fully appreciating as much, I was being cautiously selective in the things I said to her – or which I wished to hear from her in return.

On our walks we focused on third parties, on observable

Castlebay. Our talk might have been inconsequential, but of course it wasn't, because we were establishing a safe and common ground between us. We didn't much deal in our histories, but I felt that was no great loss, nor can she have done. There was a fascination in only belonging to time current, in having this shadowless existence of surface, of here and now – and, more and more by optimistic implication, of tomorrow.

Custom and habit were established in no more than a week. We met every morning by prearrangement at a different spot – by the flower clock on the esplanade, or by the windows of Rowley and Sister's china shop, or by the green bench directly opposite the House Of Steps tea-rooms – and we filled the morning hours in the instinctive knowledge that we should wend our way quite naturally by whichever route back to the Beaufort Hotel, to the stepped garden firstly and then indoors to the cocktail bar.

When I think back, Tommy the barman is our good luck charm. He was there every time we walked into the cocoon of maroon velvet, lunchtime or evening. He watches over us in my memories of those hours we whiled away so pleasantly, so effortlessly. He is observant, strategically aware, but beyond a certain elementary point he is incurious. Rather, I choose to remember him as protective, overseeing our well-being in that toning burgundy fastness.

We were public spectacles, notwithstanding the smallness of numbers to be encountered in those last ten days of May. In theory, at any rate, we were exposing ourselves to watching eyes. It seemed important to me then that we were, as the lovers we technically became after a long afternoon's sweaty antics in my room at the Llanberis. Being together with Marina in a public place – being seen with her – was like a formal affirmation of a liaison that had started almost too easily to credit could be the case. I needed to believe in the latter by means of the former. I found I was able to view us as if I were another person watching from one of those leather-topped and button-upholstered, three-legged high stools ranged in front of the bar counter. I discovered I could look in at the story of ourselves, performed like some kind of playlet.

The words, my lines, were no problem to speak: I might have known them all my life. I didn't even have to concentrate on them, to have to try to remember.

We would sit at the bar and continue the game we played on our walks, imagining who certain people *really* were and what had brought them here.

Marina's explanations were more inventive than mine. She could always see scope for drama – and melodrama – where I did not.

Nothing was how it appeared to be, she was quite sure of that. At the least – the swaggering men were always cowards by her reckoning, the billing-and-cooing couples were putting on a show, the vinegary wives who said nothing in public were waiting to let rip in private, the elderly hoarded their own dark secrets of lust and betrayal long ago.

There was another world complementary to the obvious and declared one, she was wanting me to understand: its negative mandala image.

She smiled, laughed, and wouldn't explain *how* she knew. 'Inscrutable', I called her. But to me it was a pastime, a divertissement, and nothing more. I only wanted to be with her, to have her scramble up Castlebay for me like this, to have my expectations all turned on their heads: head over heels, arse over elbow. It was the natural condition of life, she showed me, and it didn't occur to me for a moment that its obscure, arcane precepts – its upside-down methodology – might have any bearing on the two of *us*, outsiders with privileged access to a company of hoaxers and self-deluders incorporating everybody except ourselves.

We were the same age, twenty-seven, which struck me as being a propitious coincidence.

She looked younger in certain kinds of soft light, but in harsh and direct sunlight her age was easier to believe.

Our birthdays in fact were only seven months apart. It always did feel a fortuitous bond to me, that we should both have been born within the same clough of historical time. I don't know if that is a legitimate reason or not for accepting yourself as fated to encounter a person: but in my own case it had the force which a proven logical truth would have had, so that arguing the matter is neither here nor there. The coincidence of our ages, I was persuaded, could hardly have been just that alone, a coincidence.

Seven weeks previously, in London, I had walked past a hotel in George Street and seen my girlfriend leaving the entrance to the restaurant, disentangling – but only slowly – her own arm from her male companion's as she walked out into the afternoon sunlight.

Joan didn't catch sight of me, but that was irrelevant. The point was that I had seen *her*. I enquired later – with tensely affected casualness – about her whereabouts at lunchtime, and she told me she'd gone up to Harrow to see her mother. I said nothing. I could see the man quite clearly in my mind, even better when I closed my eyes to concentrate. Perhaps his good looks were as galling to me as anything else, and the neatness of his suit, shirt, tie. Joan was forever trying to smarten me up, and although she managed it (comparatively) I knew I fell short of fulfilling all her hopes for me.

Over the next eight days I shadowed all her movements. She rendezvoused with the man another four times. On each occasion she had her alibi prepared for me. She could lie to me and smile so sweetly as she did so. I was fascinated and horrified simultaneously. I was like a rabbit caught by the blithely disguised wiles of a very practised snake.

When matters came to a head, all hell broke loose. The fur that flew was mine, yet I knew I was in the right. Joan protested her innocence much too much, and her eyes blinked far too little, considering the danger she was in. Things were said that put an end to our life together, which suddenly became the past, an irrecoverable past.

We were finished – I was determined about that, smarting with my humiliation – we were over and done with.

Later I became less easy and sure. I wasn't convinced any differently about the fact of Joan's infidelity to me, but I was pricked by guilt for having helped to cause the situation. Because I had failed her in this or that respect: because all along I had been too predictable and too dull for her. I wanted to believe that she might have had too much affection for just one lover. I was still hurt to the quick, however, that she could so purposely deceive – she could, after all, have got herself off the hook of her dilemma by saying nothing, by resisting the cold cunning it takes to lie.

I didn't feel that I could have done anything else but cut and leave. The luxury of deciding had been mine, elevated as I was on my moral high ground. I felt, merely, becalmed: sails emptied of wind: up a creek: beached: cast high and dry.

My days had nothing in them except thought: the same thoughts recycled, and in endless rotation, one after another after another, the snapping head of the next to the wriggling tail of the last. In the end they all negated each other, and I was left with only a soft squelchy mulch where the thoughts finally rotted down – a sensation of mental overactivity, but no distinct recollection at last of any precise argument or counter-argument. I fretted away to no end whatsoever; I taxed my brain to arrive at only a frenzy of indecision, a frantically paced inertia.

For the next five or six weeks I prepared myself to be shocked, ambushed into a diversion.

It ought to have been no surprise to me that it happened, with Marina, but I lacked sense and mental coordination at that time. I was a man in the East on Western time, or the other way about. I saw without, in the subtler aspect of the word, seeing.

I prefer to think that Marina recognised a fellow soul in torment. She was to tell me so little about her own former life, but when I very gently asked the question she didn't deny that she had recently been unhappy. I decided that the cause must have been amatory, as in my own case. At any rate, I chose to conclude, the other gender was implicated, and none too favourably or kindly. We had both been abused: in crude terms, she and I found ourselves similarly on the rebound. Our parabolas had been destined to cross. Our coming together possessed an inevitability, like the power of nature, like electrical charge.

Her voice was low and soft, and the lower and softer the more compelling it became. She never spoke quickly, but took great care shaping her vowels and clarifying consonants between her tongue and teeth. There was something of a foreigner's deliberateness in her delivery, but her accent was placeless and neutral – except very occasionally, when she slightly widened an 'o' or narrowed an 'a' and I vainly and disloyally tried to think of a source. But I had no clues, since all I'd been told – or required her to tell me – was that she'd lived here and there in central London all her adult life. I deduced she came from the Home Counties, but something lurked in that past more disquieting than lost love, and I hadn't the heart to see her pained to remember.

She may have been looking towards me, or – quite possibly – just past me, that first evening in the cocktail bar of the Beaufort Hotel. I was unaware then of any confusion: her head was turned on a diagonal of attention across the room, in the direction of myself where I was sitting, two or three feet away from the connecting door into the corridor. Large green eyes and a full mouth in a handsome tapering face. A small nose which turned up slightly, delightfully, at the tip, the sort called 'retroussé' which became so à la mode and desirable a few years later. A mouth demurely outlined with a restrained pale lipstick. Eyes – on a closer inspection, a few minutes later – made up with the craft of an experienced hand to appear un-made up. Hair worn unfashionably long in a chignon: wavy blonde-coloured hair contrasting with a vaguely Latin complexion I mistook for a suntan.

She was attractive, highly so. Maybe 'prettiness' requires more conventional softness than was there. Her features had a definiteness, a kind of insistence which was better suited to a magazine cover than any number of vapid English Roses would have been.

It was the eyes that held me: wide, not over-large but their prominence accentuated by the line of the clipped brows, the irises – even seen from the other side of the room – so circularly green in their whites, with intensity or with alarm.

TWO

A fortnight after we met we were married in a brief civil ceremony.

I didn't fancy the Register Office in Granby Street. I arranged, with her disbelieving headshakes and asymmetrical smiles for approval, that once we'd got hold of the paper verifications we needed, the knot should be tied in the middle of one afternoon in the cocktail bar of the Beaufort Hotel.

Asking her to marry me was a crazy impulse. But I was madly in love, and it was much of a piece with all the rest.

Our papers arrived, although for some reason – I forget how it came about – I didn't have a chance to see her birth certificate. The town clerk who officiated must have done, however. The off-duty barman and an under-manager stood duty as witnesses, and two of the waitresses appeared at the close of the formalities, one to throw rice and the other to scatter confetti over us. Her rings, which we had bought so hurriedly, were dutifully admired. The under-manager looked ill at ease with the mess on the vacuumed carpet, but he bravely smiled nevertheless.

Why did we marry?

I married Marina because she said 'yes' and because I was tired of good sense and caution. Already Joan represented for me the ways of the bourgeoisie, and I wanted to believe that marriage – the high point of Joan's type of existence – was a matter of superlative insignificance. Anyone could do it, and as easily as this: an institution was just words. Also, I wanted this craziness to last, and sanction (a quorum of signatures, and an ink blot) seemed to me a means towards longevity.

*

So. Now we were husband and wife. Mr and Mrs Swale.

I had only ever imagined it happening with the woman I had parted from with so much sourness, but that phase of my life was now instantly forgotten.

Marriage – the state of being a married man – could never have been imagined by me previously, I discovered. It was a comforting kind of numbness, mental and physical bound up together. Like permanent intoxication, but with none of the after-effects. An extreme heightening of awareness, or of certain aspects of it. Also, a condition of desensitisation, to everything that did not pertain to ourselves.

The pace of life moved up a gear. I was speeding somewhere, in Marina's company, although the speed and direction had been taken out of our control. I was used to people, colleagues, talking of adulthood's 'responsibilities', but those still weren't in the forefront of my mind even at this point. What I wanted to be was protective, even though it seemed to me I would be in the lee of the attention Marina must unwittingly attract to herself. No matter, she should always have the confidence of my devotion, my courage, my continuing to believe – what possible cause could I have not to? – only the very best of her.

I decided that we needed appropriate transport to get us away from Castlebay and back to London. I sold my old Austin A35 without telling her. Having the money in my wallet I could afford to be so reckless with, I hired a silver and grey Daimler Conquest – the smallest of the marque's models, the Century Saloon, but at nearly fifteen feet long and with two and a half litres of power, a Daimler was a Daimler – which I arranged to return to a garage in St John's Wood.

It was worth all that it cost to see the wry pleasure on Marina's face. I *could* have had a mint Riley 2.6, or a Humber Hawk, but I wanted the best that was available to me – to us. She must have appreciated that I'd done it wholly for her sake. She knew that by my standards it was not a little excessive – of course – but she surely understood the reason and looked grateful that I'd been so foolish.

The confetti was rather vulgar lying scattered on the cream hide upholstery and grey pile carpet, but the cabin smelt privileged, notwithstanding that I had only hired this exclusivity temporarily.

The car had a thirst, and after forty miles or so we were running low on petrol.

I turned off, at the first garage we came to. As we crossed the forecourt the tyres triggered a mechanism connected to a cable. A bell rang, loud and clear, inside the attendant's unoccupied wooden kiosk.

At the sound Marina jumped, nearly out of her skin. I turned to her and smiled. She was looking back over her shoulder, towards the house that was attached to the covered servicing bay.

I saw that one hand was trembling on her lap, the ring hand. I placed my own hand on her elbow. She jumped again. She swung round on the seat and stared at me. For a second or two it was as if she had forgotten who I was, what she was doing here, in this rented car on the forecourt of a garage somewhere between Farnham and Guildford.

The ringing stopped. Then, of course, she remembered. And remembered also that she had to make light of this – to me, very curious – embarrassment. She smiled, a chilled and nervous little smile that surely would have deceived nobody. I beamed back at her, meaning to reassure her with my own happiness. I wanted my joy to be contagious.

She looked away, towards the kiosk. Just behind me a sudden noise – knuckles rapping on the window glass – undid my own composure. Startled, I jumped in my seat. I forced myself to smile at the stubbly red countryman's face peering in at me. He crooked a hand to his ear, awaiting instructions.

North of Leatherhead the car started to judder intermittently and jolt. I concentrated on keeping my foot pressed harder down on the accelerator. But on several gradients in succession the car bucked like a mule. I convinced myself that the garage I'd leased it from must have 'seen me coming' from a mile off. I said something about the petrol, dirt in the carburettor. Marina had another opinion – wasn't it more likely to be a faulty condenser? Or one of the sparking plugs?

I stopped the car in a lay-by and got out. I wasn't expecting Marina to get out also, but she did. I lifted the bonnet lid, fixed the catch, and stooped forward to look. She too leaned forward. She pointed to a trailing wire. Watch your sleeve, I told her. At the same time I was realising she'd been correct in her surmise.

I rolled back my own sleeves and attended to the errant plug. I reconnected it, and checked the others. She watched all the while; she didn't speak, but I had a sense of her silent authority in the matter.

When I'd finished she rubbed at the oil marks on my arms with the handkerchief she took from my pocket. She dampened it in the water in the radiator and cleaned me up. Like a mother, I felt. If I'd been completely clean, I would have put my arms around her. I did try, using my wrists for support. She smiled at the attempt, but I noticed – I couldn't help noticing – how she was looking round over her shoulder, checking to see if any cars were about to pass us.

Back inside the Daimler, on the rear seat, she became loving, so tenderly pliable as I'd found her that first afternoon we made love, on my lumpy single bed at the Llanberis House Private Hotel. She gave herself up to me, complying with all my unspoken wishes. I let down her hair and sank my face into its softness. I breathed in the dreamy tangle of old scents and new, the soap and powder coating of her perfect skin. My fingers fumbled past her suspender straps, for the knicker elastic, for the mons Veneris which it had shocked and thrilled me that first afternoon to find so meticulously and closely shaved.

I found accommodation for us from a letting agency.

Our new home was in one of the quiet streets off Portland Place, a small flat which I supposed must be quite a bit smaller than what she had been used to, but she didn't say so. She couldn't have been more amiable about her situation. I just knew from the way she had of pulling in her skirt as she passed through one of the narrow doorways, the care she took with her elbows passing between pieces of furniture.

The flat was the best I thought I could afford, at a pinch and a scrape. We were in a good area, at the very top of the building. In the bathroom you could hear the communal water-tank, but even though we were up in the roof all our walls were straight.

It was a very sound, dignified building. Greater Sebastopol Street had a solid, expensive look to it. In those days of the later fifties, there was more residential occupancy, although we had our scattering of professionals round about – a firm of solicitors on the ground floor, a dentist next door, two doctors within hailing distance.

Socially it was a little off the familiar beaten tracks reported in newspapers. Dinner parties took place in the building, our fellow tenants entertaining their regular company, but it wasn't done on a Knightsbridge or Kensington scale. That seemed to be a relief to Marina. She would watch from the picture windows, with some interest but showing no signs of recognition for anyone she saw, breathing quite freely and sometimes drawing on a cigarette. I asked her several times if she would rather be living further up-town. She shook her head at that very positively. No. She was quite content to be where she was, I presumed she meant, content just to be with me, her husband.

The flat was let furnished. I had been persuaded by the condition and quality of the fittings. The taste was slightly dubious, admittedly. I noticed at once that there was something theatrical about the decor and appointments. Curiously I liked that, the unreal feel of it all. The velvet drapes and pelmets were too heavy for the rooms, but plushy and expensive-looking – and tied back like stage curtains. The furniture belonged in a French farce perhaps: gilt and cane Directoire in the little sitting-room, cream boudoir in the bedroom next door. There was an ormolu clock, and dainty firescreens of embroidery under glass; the chairs had tapestry seats and backs, there was a low velvet ottoman-pouffe in the bedroom; the china cabinet was pretend-Louis XV, with lozenge-leaded glass, and there were two table-candelabra of blue glass, each fitted with three mint white candles apiece, positioned on either side of the neat, scaled-down sideboard.

The compactness seemed, not confining, but intimate. There were only ourselves, and it was more than adequate for our purposes surely. I suppose I must have believed that we had our own mental geography to discover, a landscape to travel which made our physical considerations immaterial.

If I hadn't had the skyline in front of my eyes, as proof that we were Londoners, we might have been in, say, Bournemouth, or a Jewish suburb somewhere: or on a stage-set, in rooms that each ought to have had one wall less.

We also had a peppermint green telephone, a dramatic and vivid object provided for the hostess or the maid in a play to answer as a contrivance of the plot. It was the old bakelite sort one never sees now; the heavy receiver had shaped mouth and ear shells, the dialling wheel with outsized numerals was bulky and awkward to turn, the long black plaited flex was for ever complicating itself into knots. During our honeymoon it was our only contact with the life outside, other than what we could see from the windows of any activity down on the street or what we could pick up of conversations, at our remove, through the fabric of the building, through the walls and floors on their grid of joists and timbers.

The erotic of the everyday. The tread of pile carpet, the touch of smoothed wood and velvet, the aroma of polish. The close-fitting manner of the drawers in the tallboy and the wardrobe doors, the resisting tightness and then the easy click of the handles on the room doors, the welcoming temperature of the handles' gilt finish. The caressing hold of the armchairs, the cosy fit of the little bathtub in the bathroom, the pouting mouths of the faucets, the pleasant comfortable span of the tap wheels inside the grasp of your palm and fingers.

The elemental white cavity of bathroom. The airy containment of kitchen at the back, with an arsenal of honed steel on
the wall and the rounded squareness of cool refrigerator the
colour of clotted cream. Elsewhere a sense of enclosure by
hanging and fitted fabrics, by the ivory-painted half-panelling
and the nearly pristine fitted beige carpets. In one place Marina
spilled a little blood on the floor, between the bathroom and our
bedroom, but that for me only added to my sensual attachment
to the premises.

It was an ideal setting for my seduction and my submission.

She didn't bring much with her. But what she did bring was of
very fine quality.

A crocodile-skin suitcase. Matching vanity-case. Two leather
hat-boxes. A leather shoe portière lined with suede.

Her clothes were the high fashion of the current season.
The labels sewn into some of them were expensive names.
Her shoes were mostly plain court, in alligator and lizard, with
several pairs of low-heeled kid loafers for walking and wearing
in the flat. Her jewellery was very superior quality, and tasteful
and unshowy.

She was my high-quality wife. I could have gone anywhere with her, because any door would have opened for
us.

I had never thought to expect so much in my life.

Up among the rooftops we watched London shimmering in an
early but full-blown heatwave. At our eye level, heat gases
danced above the tiles. Beneath us the roads might have been
buckling.

We found coolness in the kitchen, filling the stone sink with
cold water and sinking in our forearms past the elbow, or else
gulping water from glasses and listening to the musical drips
in the tank through the wall.

We guessed the conditions wouldn't last long, so we gave

ourselves to the experience of it. I was now going out to
work for a portion of the day, but I sprinted home so that
I could share the weather with her. I suggested going to
Regent's Park, but she wasn't very keen on the idea. Too
many 'hot-looking' people, she said. We spent our afternoons
in the flat instead. Sometimes with half our clothes removed,
bed was naturally the next stage. That got us sweatier than
ever, so I'd follow her into the tub. When you leaned out of
the sitting-room window, you could almost scorch the flesh from
your elbows on the fiery lead. The tiles were like hot-plates.
The structure of the whole building heaved with its expansions
and contractions and it was like living inside some animate
organism.

Those were to prove themselves to be the best days of
my life, the easiest and quickest lived and the very least
considered.

She had dusky colouring and sensual Latin features, but was
English to the marrow. 'Don't ask me how,' she would say in
that gentle and curling voice, smiling to where I couldn't see
myself, beside her reflection in a mirror.

She knew the manner of her beauty obsessed me: its contrast
to the sorts I was used to. She never complimented herself,
but she must have known what her unique physical advantages
were. She didn't often discuss other women either, but I
watched how she appraised the faces and postures she saw
in the magazines that were her staple reading matter. Beauty
considering beauty, I told myself, there could be nothing more
natural – or for *me*, with the spectacle of her, a more desirable
state of affairs. How could she not have perceived so from my
own wide-eyed worship of her, in those first weeks especially?
During that time I imagined I might close my eyes to sleep
and wake up in the morning and find her gone, with our
chancing to meet and our marriage – equally bizarre – just
a dream.

Beauty was 'worshipped' in books, I knew, and not very
good books at that. But there was no other word for it,

to express so aptly that element of devotion and – with more time, as further weeks passed – of faith and belief. Any sacrifice would have been worth my making in the service of this harmony between us, this condition of human grace. Beyond ourselves there were no threats that I was conscious of, and yet I had an instinct – a superstition – that I had to continue devoting myself. It didn't matter how I did it – crossing town to buy her favourite chocolates or searching for a particular brand of bath salts or silk stockings: allowing her silence and space (what space was left over) in the flat – I did what I was happy to accept that I had to. My sense of self-virtue doubtless added to my pleasure, but my story at this point risks straying into the province of the psychoanalytical, where I am ill-equipped to follow.

I saw that other men watched her too – passers-by on the pavement, car drivers, our neighbours – and I observed the same determination on her part not to notice. Our competing male attention was as necessary and automatic an element to her as the air she stood at the window sipping into her mouth, which brought her down on to our quiet street in the evenings.

Whenever she glanced at her reflection walking past a shop window, there was no trace of furtiveness or of apology. She was quite matter-of-fact about it, but the action was fleetingly done, as if she knew quite well what to expect and was only performing a routine, ritual aside. It seemed to me that there was a kind of innocence about the deed. We were hardly angels, I suppose, but I don't now disown my original conjectures then. There was a truthfulness even in her reticence and vagueness: if she had wanted to tell me lies, then she could and would have done. But she meant to spare me, I plead for her, by telling me only what she thought she could, because it would return me no chagrin. Recriminations would have been the worst hurt, and she was presenting me with as little cause as possible.

I accepted that it was a very harmless conspiracy – of my curiosity and her own assumption of ignorance. I could conceive of no danger in it. Here we were taking the weeks, the high summer, more or less in our stride, with as ever a few intrusions from outside but only a few. I wasn't even thinking of 'always', of any future at all. We were quite uncircumscribed, notwithstanding the cramped flat: we were temporally free agents, living only for one another, for this here and now, both of us glad strangers to our own and the other's past.

I did discover that, before we met, she had been living no further than a couple of miles away from me, in Kensington. I presumed that she must have been sharing the house – 'house', she said later, not 'flat' – with whomever it was she didn't seem inclined to discuss, the house's owner by unspoken implication.

She didn't enquire directly about my own recent whereabouts.

The London she talked about consisted of restaurants, shops, the parks, public and personal places of rendezvous. But she never asked to go to these places. She didn't speak of how her life used to be; she never lifted the receiver of the telephone to call anybody.

Sometimes – when she thought I wasn't looking – she would sit just turning and turning the rings on her third finger, her eyes fixed on them in a stare and her thoughts very far from Sebastopol Street.

We liked different actors and film stars – she Anita Ekberg and Leslie Caron, I Farley Granger and Richard Burton – but I felt that was no real ground for incompatibility.

She preferred her oranges to my apples, while I would have picked plums to her peaches. But we both enjoyed fruit.

She loved sunshine on her skin, but also the contact of wind. I went more for moods – for dusty sunsets, for the sizzly fusty aftermath of a summer downpour. Either way, we were weather people.

She would choose a hot, sudsy bath in preference to a brisk, efficient shower, but we both had a healthy interest in our personal hygiene. She had to have a clean kitchen, and I was only too pleased to assist with damp cloths and brush and pan or mop.

She found tea more to her taste than coffee, but we had a compact: tea could have the daylight hours, if coffee might be the order of the evening after supper. She didn't drink more than one small cup after we'd eaten, but I felt that as I had arranged things it was an equal sacrifice to us both.

She liked to sleep on the left side of the bed, and I on the right, so that was very straightforward. When we made fast, conventional love it was tit for tat – I on top, then her – and that was fine, more than fine indeed.

At first she always systematically tidied her clothes once she had removed them, while I dropped mine where they fell. But even in this respect we changed our behaviour somewhat. She became a little less exact in her tidiness, while I trained myself to toss my things in a pile on the floor next to my side of the bed.

She claimed that she liked Gainsborough's tactful renderings, if not idealisations, of his sitters, and I went instead for Chardin's mellow-toned still lifes, his elevation of humble domestic utensils. It was all art, though. I suggested we go to galleries, but she wasn't so sure, so I bought her postcards from art shops and she propped them up around the kitchen: Gainsborough's upwardly mobile family groups, Ingres's *haute bourgeoise* women, even Manet's nude Olympia with black servant and jet cat.

She would turn off the Home Service News, silencing those serious, plummy newscasters' voices, but she bent an ear to those chirpier, more upbeat digests on the Light Programme of who was performing where in theatreland and which Hollywood movie actors were currently in town tonight.

She was rather cloudy about England's geography, except where Norwich and Ipswich and Bury St Edmunds were and the sequences of resorts on the south coast, which was next to which. She could tell me where this restaurant or that supper-club was to be found in the West End, but was in complete confusion about the polar direction in which any of the suburbs lay.

She told me that she'd been born in the early hours of the morning, which must explain (she said) why she felt she had more energy in the hours of darkness. But of the other circumstances of her birth, where and to whom, she still chose to divulge nothing, and I too weakly, too readily – thinking I was being chivalrous but only confirming the tractability and acquiescence she must already have read in my nature – rushed in precipitately to respect that reticence.

I absurdly offered to secure the services of a maid, but Marina turned that proposal down with an irresistibly skew-whiff but resolute smile.

It was as if, in domestic matters, she was having to re-educate herself. I had the impression that, for the first few weeks at any rate, she was remembering things she had forgotten. It was understandable that the controls on the refrigerator should have fazed her a little, or the stop-cock under the sink. But she was disconcerted also by the gas rings, by the temperature wheel that controlled the oven; she was even nonplussed by the design of the tin-opener in the drawer. I had to show her, very patiently, so that it shouldn't seem in any sense like a slight, how it was that *I* peeled a carrot or an apple with a grater: then it seemed to click, she shook her head, tut-tutted at herself – and smiled another of those charmingly lopsided smiles. I would have forgiven her anything at all: but I'm uncomfortable using that verb, 'forgive', which implies some wrong done – and done knowingly – by her to me. There was no wrong committed, unless it was my letting her perform those household tasks, and going along with the traditional chauvinist conspiracy. And how could I have believed for one moment that any of her errors and oversights domestically, so small and insignificant, were of her own actual volition?

We muddled away. We had each other: that was all that mattered to me. I did help about the flat all that I could, but Marina was clearly determined that I shouldn't have to do more than any other woman married to me would have expected me to do. If our vegetables were overcooked to a pulp and came to the plate with peely bits included, if eggs were inattentively boiled or scrambled too soft or too hard, if chops could somehow be burned outside and left rawly pink inside – what of it? I didn't care then, and it wasn't long – only months – before I grew tenderly nostalgic for it all. I wanted it all back, and to have been able to achieve that I should have agreed not to change one single thing.

When we made love I was oblivious to everything beyond ourselves and the experience of my own pleasure and, I naturally supposed, of hers.

I hope that I treated her with gentleness, with respect, with every consideration. But I hope also that I left her in no doubt of the vigour she summoned up in me.

The walls of the flat could have been cracking and splitting around us and I wouldn't have been aware.

The bed resembled a sled with its high cream and canework boards at either end, fancily turned and gilded. It was out of proportion to the smallness of the room, and filled it like a secondary stage inside the other. The white sheets rolled in drifts, like great snow-fields we skimmed over. In full afternoon sunlight the effect was blinding, and she sometimes asked me to close the curtains, please, as she lay with her head back on the pillow and one arm held across her eyes for shade, and her freshly shaved pudenda quite bare.

The sun shone directly through the plate-glass panels of the window from mid-morning until late afternoon, and had the intensity of a spotlight. Even with the panels opened and the passing of traffic on Langham Place and Oxford Street audible – like a soft and persistent wash of sound – the heat was stifling. It would have grilled us like coals if I hadn't done as she requested.

The heat and the burning clarity of linen snow is my abiding memory of those late mornings and long afternoons when we abandoned ourselves, when the world passed the two of us by.

At other times she would stand with cigarette in hand watching from the sitting-room or bedroom window, looking out across the spread of the city. She seemed to me lost in the pursuit of an object. And yet, I also knew, the view from the flat was, in that sprawl between the famous landmarks, of the vast impersonality of the place. It was the proverbial haystack, of elusive needles and purposes. What was she looking to find, my beautiful stay-at-home wife, or what loss was she having silently and painfully to acknowledge to herself?

She suggested we buy a portable record-player. One afternoon I returned home with one. I went out again and came back with a clutch of records. Sinatra, Ella, Eine Kleine Nachtmusik, the entire *Daphnis and Chloe*. That same day we listened to them all, and she played the bits she liked a second or third time; she was hungry for the sound of them.

I took pleasure in the effect. I stood and watched her lying across the sofa in a kind of matinée swoon which was none the less quite genuine. She saw me looking. She stared over at my foolish smile with incomprehension for several seconds as if she'd just woken and couldn't instantly recall . . . Then she started to smile, but just a little warily, as if she'd caught me spying behind a door she knew she wanted to keep closed to me.

After that the music became a central circumstance of our lives. Our collection of records increased. She mentioned this or that, and I would remember and find it when I went on unaccompanied expeditions trawling the shops on Regent Street or Charing Cross Road. (Apart from work purposes, I was seldom tempted to venture much further, not on those high days of our elasticated, seemingly perpetual honeymoon.) When we knew the flats beside and below us were bound to be empty, Marina turned the volume knob and filled the rooms of our home with music.

Doubtless the choice was obvious – to certain ears – and not very well informed, but all that is of significance to me is that we both learned through rapid custom to share the very same tastes. Hers and mine became indistinguishable. I got to know all the lyrical crescendos and diminuendos in 'La Valse' and 'Introduction and Allegro', and learned the words of Schwartz and Dietz and Van Heusen and Mercer by heart. She would join in when I was singing in the bath: I would be humming along with the melodies as she seated herself at the dressing-table and then started to hum herself, deliberately enough to have me hear and respond in my own counterpoint.

When daylight faded and a lamp or two went on in the flat, our reflections appeared in the glass of the windows. The two of us floated over the rooftops like cartoon libertines; we danced like party spectres – both of us, to my watching eyes, earnest and disengaged at the same time. How cumbrous all that substance and clutter outside seemed, how extraneous.

She would stand before a window, pulling up her hair, her eyes directed to the panorama. But I don't know how much of it registered with her. Maybe she was considering our reflections within the metal frame – herself, and me behind her, a silent observer. Music would be playing, from the turntable or the radio set, so that I didn't need to speak. She loved to hear the music, her music, a rich satiny soundtrack for everything that couldn't be said.

Like her, I came to believe that we didn't need others.

I thought too that no one could touch us there, that we were far out of harm's way, ranged so high above people's heads. The tides of traffic in Portland Place had nothing to do with us, less than a hundred yards away in Greater Sebastopol Street. Sounds glanced off us, the mechanical and the human. We had our own music on the record-player, and why did we need to hear the talk of others when we could make our own idle chatter? The sun was so warm in the flat during this second heatwave of the summer that we could have been in Nice or Lisbon or Beirut; we were placeless, in London in July, and yet not. I felt we *had* created our own metaphorical geography in conversation, a private landscape less of memory than desire: a verbal one, and so – I forgot – capable of just as much off-the-cuff invention as truth.

The afternoons were for 'Come Fly With Me', 'From This Moment On' and 'These Foolish Things'; the evenings were for Mozart's starry nights in Salzburg and Wien and for Ravel's orchestral evocations of the Basque country, for Debussy's quieter piano souvenirs of the southern Spanish cities.

That peppermint green telephone. Marina standing at the window, unfurling and then piling up her hair. London ranged before us, but kept at a distance, a diminishing temptation viewed from our eyrie. An American's voice singing of love on the gramophone turntable. Our solitude together.

Marina. The name spoke to me of sea, distance, horizon.

THREE

At that time of my life I had a job – one part-time job among several – which I find difficult to describe. I was neither a journalist nor a researcher, and yet I was a little of both.

I suppose I was a sort of news-runner. A favourite Anglophile American commentator living (mostly) in London employed me. The tasks I was paid for were: to scour the newspapers – the provincial press as well as the national dailies – in search of stories he could use in his syndicated columns and radio broadcasts; to collate the various versions of a story, do an amount of background probing (it usually entailed extracting a few quotable comments from the main protagonists or those closest to them), and then to write the pieces up. Trenor, my provider, would add a few touches of his own, but the material was essentially mine: hardly original, as I've indicated, but by the time it had been slanted for a new audience across the Atlantic it was less obvious as the newspaper story of a fortnight or a month ago. I have to admit that when the boredom of the enterprise got to me, I took the liberty of embellishing the base matter – ornamenting it rather more if I had culled the piece from some less obvious organ beyond London's ken.

I've altered the name, of course. 'Walter Trenor' took his reputation more or less intact to his death. For the first half of his adult life it was deserved, but not for the second. Early fame – fame if not fortune – went to his head and, I realised, addled some of his judgments. Or perhaps it was the drink, the Southern Bourbon, that was to blame. From being an interested but professionally *dégagé* spectator of English society, he graduated into an active participant. (Extremely active.) As a result of all the influences subtle and not so acting upon him, his opinions became increasingly partisan: or where they were more complex, they became ambivalent for the wrong reasons, in case he should offend sensitive parties.

Parties were the nub of it. He would have travelled to the ends of the land for the right sociable cause. His life had assumed the character of a semi-royal progress from country house to country house. He kept a flat in Mayfair, in Upper Grosvenor Street, but was less and less to be found there. Either he was country-bound, or he was out and about in London until all hours. There was no easy keeping tabs on him. He'd had a social secretary once – a euphemism, I'm sure – but she had found her job tying her too much to the telephone and railway timetables. (And maybe she had felt a little piqued never to be able to sample for herself the myriad delights he held before her in his reports, like irresistible fresh bait to the uncommonly named Miss Roach.)

I didn't think it was my function to track him down. He had developed the habit of working very hard in a few very short and sharp bursts of activity. Three of my articles would be tinkered with overnight, he'd tidy a couple of radio fireside talks over a liquid lunch before setting out to the bleakly practical recording studios in Euston Road to do all the takes that it required – while his eyes struggled to focus – in order to confect the finished, usually (somehow) seamless final product of both our labours. It was *my* work essentially, but I was a wholesale borrower, I knew quite well – a fairly shameless plagiarist of the common or garden news that is surely in the public domain – and I was paid, really very generously, for both my 'input' and a tacit oath of silence on the working habits of my famous patron.

He was a man of sophisticated cultural tastes, even if his fancy for the species of humankind whom he favoured struck me as wrong-headed and not worthy of someone I gauged to be an intellectual. He was an East Coaster, somewhat in the Henry James mould: a pastiche of an English gentleman, I might say, but it was effected with flawless good taste and in such a restrained manner that it came to seem a purer, less self-conscious variant of the Englishman's brand of Englishness. His accent was really no accent at all, because like Marina's it was so keenly disciplined to be neutral: a toned-down Boston brahmin, not too lockjaw and with fewer of those inbred class nuances of the true English gentleman. His English wardrobe steered clear of Prince of Wales checks and dapperly wasp-waisted suits and coloured waistcoats: instead he was faithful to blazers and neat flannel trousers without turn-ups and cashmere knitwear in essential, sedate hues. He didn't have any truck with shirt armlets and suspenders and the ritual of handkerchief concealment. When I first went to work for him, I admired his unfussiness, what I interpreted as comparative honesty and straightforwardness in one able to afford an existence in West One.

The flat was amply filled with furniture whose appearance suggested it might all have been inherited. Every object had a lived-with look – but the usual accompaniment, shabbiness, was avoided. The books were newish, and the subjects displayed a bias towards memoirs and illustrated panegyrics to the homes and histories of the country's great families; America was scarcely represented on the shelves at all, and a stranger would have had few grounds for supposing that a transatlantic transplantation had taken place. The many framed photographs showed Trenor in the company of a veritable gallery of famous English celebrities, the greater number of them titled.

Nor, clothes apart, did the man *appear* an American. I don't know what I would have been looking to find, to prove that he was. His features might have been regularly British, or German, or Dutch, even Swedish. He had acquired some bulk with his experience of gracious living. I foresaw that once his forties were behind him, in another five or six years, his face would turn florid, and the rest of his skin would stretch tightly and acquire the pale, sunless colouring – or lack of colouring – that is the corollary of a pampered and indulgent style of life. He would start to fret about his nails, for instance, or his feet, and resort to manicurists and pedicurists and masseurs. Although in all probability he would have kept most of his hair, he would begin to experiment with hair dyes, in a bid to keep the years in check, but befuddling the picture more and more absurdly as he became embroiled in preserving the lie of the dyeing, having to apply the darkening agent to more and more of his hair. It was all, I conceitedly dared to think then, supremely predictable.

*

I had to have a magpie attitude for my job. I sat in libraries perusing each week's publications. Doing it this way, I was able to save some time for myself: which meant for Marina, of course, and for the other (but occasional, and as yet un-met and uncorresponded-with) passion of my life, the novelist Dorothy Richardson, whose critical biography I had been attempting to write for the past four years. A publisher was paying me an annual 'retainer' fee in addition to the little sums I received when he asked me in hard-pressed moments to copy-edit the middle-brow novels that were really his stock-in-trade.

I think this accounts for all my sources of income: as news-gatherer, as intending literary biographer, and as sporadic (although becoming threateningly more regular) copy- and proofs-editor. I gave myself to the three, I ducked and wove among commissions and commands, and hoped not to spread myself too thinly. And always there was Marina, of whom it was all in aid. I tried my very best to hurry through the work, the sooner to get back to her – even though, as a literal point, she was invariably to be found no more than one room away from me, since I did all the work that I could do in the flat. When I was at home I worked at the little put-up table in the galley kitchen, a spindly affair which folded from the outside of the cupboard where the ironing-board and brooms and brush and dust-pan were kept. The table shook whenever I leaned on it, but I learned just how much pressure to exert to keep it upright and my papers in place. By perching on a stool and pushing myself against the edge of the table, I left Marina enough room to potter round about me. When she did come in to make us tea or prepare something for us to eat, she kept vigilantly silent. In fact she had the stealth of a cat in those circumstances, and I mightn't have known she was there sometimes if I hadn't been able to catch sight of her reflection in the glass of the windows – the image of her, my fine and beautiful wife, impressed above the rarefied heights of Hampstead and Highgate to the north, best of all worked into a golden or muscatel sunset. How still and tranquil life felt, and suddenly how fresh with a draught blowing relief after Marina had thoughtfully and soundlessly opened a panel of the window to cool us down. For aural company up there we only had occasional pigeons and, inevitably, the odd stray bleat of the car horn. We were alone and it was bliss, notwithstanding the fact that I had commitments where work was concerned, to earn the money that would provide for us both.

I didn't dislike my work. The editing was the most tedious part, and I knew I had to keep myself sharp-witted for it. Dorothy Richardson had been an enthusiasm since my schooldays – harmless then if precociously earnest, but now there was four years of retainer fee riding on it: yet my interest in her novels hadn't waned, or my regard, and I pursued every new lead in my planned exegesis with relish. The employment commissioned by Trenor was always engaging, because I was effectively left free to pick whichever stories I wished to pick. Additionally I was intrigued by the man and his social activities, and had all along been entertained by the simple but dramatic displacement offered between my own manner of life and his. His surroundings were as much a vacuum from outside life as our own on Sebastopol Street, but on a grander, more soundproofed scale. After my marriage I longed to let Marina see the apartment – I certainly told her all about it, like a West End Odysseus or Othello, like some mercenary warrior returned from the field – but I didn't know how, given her reluctance, I was going to set about favouring him with an introduction. I had informed Trenor of my altered state, but he had forgotten twice thereafter, and could only remember after *that* because one day I went to Upper Grosvenor Street wearing a hand-painted bow tie which Marina had given me, which he thought in fairly bizarre taste. (I could tell his opinion from his evasions: he wouldn't have been so vulgar as to express himself on the point.) I tried to persuade Marina that she should allow me to fish for an entrée, but she continued to be very much against it. I wanted to show her off – like the proud bridegroom I was – yet I wasn't so insensitive that I failed to recognise the accumulating pain on her face when I mentioned the matter. I could see that the prospect was, for her own reasons, actually quite hurtful to her. 'It's all right,' I could say at last. 'If you really don't want to – ' I thought it must be because the address intimidated her: even though her appearance would surely have enabled her to fit in anywhere at all. I thought it must be failure of social nerve. She was quite adamant, however. She tucked her fingers back into her palms and pressed flesh into flesh, she was so determined she wouldn't let me take her to Mayfair to be introduced. Yet she listened carefully to me, I realised, when I merely spoke about the flat and its decor, about Trenor and his social movements: not just *appearing* to listen to me, but certainly listening. I was happy to be able to repeat his inventories of party guests if she wanted to hear. It wasn't what I'd had in mind, sadly, so eager that a man of Walter Trenor's sophistication and contacts should have an opportunity to meet her – and for him to recognise either my singular good fortune or such advanced powers of discernment in myself as he could have had no grounds for guessing at.

Marina did ask me a little about my work, but I found myself telling her rather less than I would have anticipated beforehand. It may well have been that I was trying to balance what was mysterious in *her* with what might be, or what I could attempt to make similarly so, in myself.

I wasn't ashamed of my makepiece way of life. Rather, I preferred to keep some things private. Perhaps it was so that she could allow her imagination to construe something better than was the case. Or perhaps it was because I didn't want her to have to concentrate on the humdrum mechanics of our existence, my income and how we made do. I was chauvinist to the point of believing that as my wife she deserved nescience – the material responsibilities were mine, and the only source of my earnings could be my work.

That was all below-stairs stuff. I meant her to have the life of a lady. I wanted her not to wish that she was anywhere other than here at home, with me, in this blessed condition of matrimony.

'I think my favourite word,' she said, turning the pages of her magazine, 'is "serene".'

'Why "serene"?' I asked her.

'I imagine – oh, I don't know – a very content, very rarefied

– *countess* at the least. She's untouchable. She's so certain of herself.'

'Do you see the word often? Or hear it?'

'People at parties in magazines, that's how they're described. Clothes designers use it, and it's used about their work. Even the models can be, sometimes.'

'I think of pregnant women,' I said. 'And Serene Highnesses, with all that time on their hands and too little in their heads to think about.'

'Do you associate them? Those two – ' She thought of a term pointed enough, ironic enough for me. ' – as sisterhoods?'

'Serenity is a state of being,' I hurried on with. 'Placidity. Composure. Containment.'

'Do you think – ' She flicked the thickness of pages left with her thumbnail. ' – I might ever be serene?'

'Aren't you? Now?'

'Serene?'

'Well . . .'

'Could I be?'

I was flummoxed.

'Why ever not?'

'That's not really an answer,' she said, without looking up.

'If you feel you *can* be – these things – '

'Do *you* think I might become these things?'

'I – '

For a split second I hesitated.

She cut in before I could continue.

'You're not certain?'

'So long as one is honest,' I told her. It was a glib reply. I compounded the glibness by repeating myself. 'Just honest,' I said again.

She was frowning at me, I perceived with a dull shock. This wasn't what she had been expecting to hear. Now I couldn't simply pretend that it hadn't been what I'd meant to say, and that it didn't matter. It had been exactly my point, my more or less instantaneous – but instinctive – conclusion. If I were to shrug it off, more and not less damage would be caused. What we had begun with was a not so immodest wish, that she might merit serenity and that I should condone the ambition in her –

She seemed to me a little desultory afterwards. I tried to coax her into a happier frame of mind. She took some winkling out. She submitted eventually, and she did start to cheer up. 'Serenity' was still on her mind, though, and she may have recognised that – unlike our instant patch-up – it had to be utterly genuine to be significant, not just tactfully performed to negotiate the small fall-out from a fleeting domestic strain. Serenity had to be un-accidental and absolute.

Occasionally her past would surface. She would tell me something quite unexpected, usually *à propos* of something else.

We had a problem with insects on evenings when the lamps were switched on and the windows had been left with their panels opened out. To begin with, I would chase them flailing dish-towels and rolled newspapers. But she would shake her head at that. Her father, she said – her father about whom she had told me nothing except that he was (very much a past imperfect tense) a Suffolk man – used to go to any lengths not to kill an insect. She showed me how to catch wasps inside towels. She cupped her hands and gently but nimbly folded them around daddy-long-legs, taking great care they weren't bruised in the process. More subtly flies could be coaxed window-wards by opening or closing doors to create or eliminate draughts of air. Moths were more of a problem: they lay so flat on surfaces, and tore so easily, but she would put off the lights and lure them to a closed window using a pocket torch. It amazed me that she should concern herself to that extent. But she couldn't have thought to do any differently, I came to realise. Her father had instilled in her the practical lesson, and it was for life – in both senses.

I had soon realised that she didn't much like to leave the flat, and rarely did.

She took a little exercise, walking about our unhurried streets at quiet times of the day or evening, but she didn't care to venture further.

I was completely mystified. I had merely supposed that she would relish the attention that others were bound to pay her. She was slim, and healthy so far as I could tell, which meant she couldn't have been suffering physically as a consequence of her immobility. But I remained lost for an explanation. She said, quite charmingly and with the aid of her smiles, that really it wasn't worth our discussing, and she was very comfortable with things as they were, long might they continue to be so.

I couldn't convince myself, though. She had a wardrobeful of fine clothes, and she had several shelfloads of shoes. She had come equipped for a public life.

Could she possibly be ashamed of me?

I plagued myself with the thought of it, until she had to chide me – as charmingly as before, and with the aid of more smiles – that nothing could be further from the case and I was a fool, a proper twit, if I thought any such thing.

But why then? I tried to let my expressions ask the question for me.

No reply was forthcoming, however. She maintained her most polite silence. It was enough, she told me, to sit by an open window to breathe in the air: fresher air than she could find on the street. Anyway, she added, it was hot and stifling out of doors, she'd only come back more tired and bothered than she'd been before she left.

Maybe. Maybe, I thought, there's sound sense in what she's telling me. But I still couldn't convince myself entirely. The eccentricity seemed so out of keeping with – my touchstone – the appearance of her. How could she be content merely with me? Didn't she need to see and experience life going on all round about her? I supposed that was why we had come back to London, so that she might savour again something of the life she had known before. I hadn't sought to be in any way an impediment to her fulfilment and felicity. Here we were, and now it seemed she didn't want it, what I had presumed.

I wondered also at her sleeping late, and thought it must be owing to our nocturnal activities between the sheets, and – yes

– maybe to a certain tranquillity in her. It didn't bother me if
she preferred sleep to humdrum domestic matters, which I was
quite glad to have to occupy me when she was still unconscious
and before I left the flat for my 'work'. But I became less certain
of the situation when that lethargy she had on waking became a
daily habit: when she got up and dressed carefully and made up
her face only for the sake of that simple lunch which I as often as
she got ready for us, and for an afternoon – another afternoon
– spent moving about the flat. She'd sit for a while, glance at a
newspaper or speed-read a few pages of a book, get to her feet
and walk around, stand for a spell at a window, seat herself again
in another chair, repeat the whole process a second time, a third,
a fourth, always taking time at some point to return to the cream
and gilt dressing-table and the three images awaiting her in the
triptych of angled mirrors. Standing at the windows, she would
appear to be lost in reverie. London was spread before her, a
panorama across rooftops; at our height I could believe we lived
on a level with the domes and spires and the flags fluttering on
their poles. I never knew what she was seeing, or what she was
picturing to herself of the past out of the paraphernalia of the
present, the clutter of chimney-stacks and caretakers' washing
lines and the recent infestation of television aerials.

I longed for enlightenment, but still didn't even know how to
ask.

There was a question I had to ask myself: was she agora-
phobic?

I meant to bring up the subject with her, but – again – I never
did. I had an unaccountable conviction that, just because I was her
husband and she my wife, that didn't give me the right to broach
directly such personal and intimate questions. I may have been
afraid she would think I didn't understand, that she might take any
remark – any slanted hypothesis – as a criticism of her. She could
conclude I was having thoughts about her, so to speak, behind
her back: second thoughts. Or I might simply prove to be
wrong, and she would have cause to believe I read people by
information in psychology manuals which I only half digested.

I don't know if I *can* explain why I didn't ask her. I did not put the question to her. Her reclusiveness was a fact. What could agoraphobia be other than, as we learned to call it in later times, an attitude problem?

She would sit poring over maps which she unfolded on top of the only adequate flat surface we had for the purpose, a small semi-circular dining-table positioned against a wall in the sitting-room. The edges of the maps overhung, but she had developed a technique of laying them out, which involved some of the map being pushed back at an angle against the wall. That way she had the whole sweep of the geography in front of her, on whichever of three levels.

The maps had been among the contents of her luggage. Some were Ordnance Survey, one or two were of foreign countries. A couple of them featured plans of central London: one a clean copy, the other marked with crosses and with certain street names underlined. Perusing the maps was a solitary, excluding operation, but she must have liked it and seemed to require it. She would sit with her back turned to me. She never explained to me why she was doing it. I knew not to interrupt her then with distractions or with trivial questions which never received forthcoming answers.

Her concentration was total, whether she was on the familiar territory of central London or tracing the course of a rural B-road with her index finger. I didn't suppose that the Ordnance Survey maps – of Suffolk and West Sussex and the stretch of Hampshire coast where we'd met – were accidental choices. Her forehead crinkled and her eyes kept a steady focus on the details whenever she had a compulsion to remove one map or another from her suitcase and to retire with it to our dining-table.

It was an unusual custom for a newly married young woman, I couldn't help feeling. Unless she had some special cause for studying the terrain that she did? I offered to buy her other maps if she would tell me which, since I wouldn't have presumed to decide for her, but she told me – charmingly, smilingly – she had all that she needed for just now, thank you so much.

It was London to which she kept coming back. It was just outside, I wanted to tell her, on our doorstep. The street beneath, which would lead into another, and to others beyond that; the whole city was there, and accessible to us. But I didn't say so. One day, when she was lying in the bath and had forgotten to turn the tumble lock on her suitcase, I sneaked a look at those names she'd written in red and sometimes underlined, and among them I recognised the names of restaurants and night-spots. An area of central London approximately one and a half miles by the same was colonised by these red-inked markers: supper-clubs mostly but also discreet luncheon rendezvous. Quite a number of crosses – like those on a chart of buried treasure – indicated houses on the streets and squares of the West End, from Bryanston Square as far west as Holland Park's crescents and south to The Boltons and to Cheyne Walk in Chelsea.

I was puzzled, both by her interest and by her silence on the matter. I hated to think I could ever cause her to be irritated by me and possibly show petulance, which must make us both unhappy. However, I had the sixth sense to guess – most of the time – when that might be likely to happen, and also the tact to steer us both clear of such peril. I don't know if she was expecting me to ask more questions than I did, but I hoped I might be proving my worth to her by my very prudence and discernment. Did I convince either her or me? She would sit at the dining-table, holding herself a little rigidly, with her back arched, as if in anticipation of the remarks a new husband was bound to speak but couldn't bring himself to.

FOUR

I had never not tried encouraging her to go out. For a while, for some weeks, I seemed to make no progress. She continued to tell me she was very comfortable with things just as they were, just like this, thank you so much.

But at last – quite inexplicably, just as inexplicably as that familiar reluctance had formulated itself – my perseverance was rewarded.

In less than twenty-four hours she had shattered the skin of her cocoon, with no reason offered for her change of heart.

'We could go some place to eat, Charles,' she suddenly said, as if she had hit upon the plan by her own devising. 'Take ourselves off somewhere, couldn't we?'

For a few moments I was too taken aback to speak.

'Charles – ?'

'What's that?'

'I'm sorry? What's what?'

'What it was you said – '

She repeated the remark she'd just made, which I'd thought I must have misheard.

I agreed. I agreed to her proposal enough times to leave her in no doubt.

'So it's settled!' she said.

Her smile sank deep into her cheeks. She clasped her arms about herself.

'Certainly,' I replied. 'Certainly it is.'

'Except where – '

'*You* have to decide that, darling,' I told her.

The cost of it didn't matter to me, I knew I'd manage – somehow. The practicalities were of no consequence and they fell away, every possible reservation, to leave us at the centre of the story. Our story.

She proved to have the zeal of a convert, and it was all quite unforeseeable. That was only another element of her continuing mystery, and of her consistent charm and delight to me.

I took it for granted at first that she selected those dining spots we had started to frequent from either the restaurant reviews in magazines or the newspapers' name-dropping society columns.

She didn't tell me that she had eaten at any of them before. Since she didn't tell me, it didn't occur to me to ask her if in fact she had. But gradually I became prone to doubts, that she was actually more experienced than I'd thought.

For me it was a first taste of high living, and I was open-eyed. *She* was more informed: not blasé, and not at home, indeed she seemed on edge. But it did dawn on me that the geography of the premises wasn't always a surprise to her. She knew if there would be a hat-check girl or a male concierge to hand her coat to. She didn't have to enquire where the cloakrooms were. She was able to tell at once whether we were favoured customers or not when the *maître d'* consulted his reservations book and read off the number of the table and its location. When the menus were presented to us, her beady eye and index finger alighted on whichever dish was the house speciality.

It can't have been luck every time, even beginner's luck. I did eventually twig, but I suppose I must have supposed what I had at the outset, that she was remembering the information from an article she had read.

She didn't relax sufficiently to enable me to see these places as belonging to her history. We were in the same boat, I deduced: we had embarked on an adventure, a quest, and I could believe that what it had to do with was good food and a sprinkling of famous faces and our social manoeuvrability, she sometimes in the blue shantung dress with the Mattli label which was the star item of her wardrobe and myself in a dinner suit I'd persuaded my late father to part with.

Why should I have thought that the attention she gave to the clientèle – behind the cover of the menu and cigarette smoke and her own talk – meant that she was on the look-out for whoever might be recognisable to her: personally so, not because they were famous? Not all the restaurants were celebrity-spotting territory, such as the gossip columnists favoured. She was quite keyed up, sometimes on tenterhooks. The slowness with which she ate, chewing hard before swallowing, persuaded me of some complicated discomfort.

But she only shook her head when I vaguely enquired, and she made the effort to smile away my concern as unnecessary.

For my part, I was exhilarated just to be seen with her in those places. I refused to dwell on the cost. Nor did I concern myself with whether she had been a visitor to the premises previously, in another man's company. This was how we were now, I felt generous enough to assure myself: why might I have any need to think beyond our moment?

I see now that it wasn't really real. We didn't *talk*, and so we didn't take shape for one another. All we gave were the present and literal versions of ourselves.

To me the silence about the past was completely new, and quite the opposite of what had happened before with Joan, who had wanted to know everything, who oversaw how I dressed, how I ate, who would sit down on the edge of the bath and ask with unironic seriousness, could I please tell her what the separate bits of my genitalia were and how they each worked. Now we had wiped the slate completely clean. I was less curious, I think, than exercised by an embarrassment – about how easy it had been to come this far and so speedily: meeting, apparently by random chance, spending our time together, then getting married. All done in a proverbial whirlwind. I shied away from the thought that it had been a 'romance', remembering how Joan had cared for all the lush outer trappings of that story-book condition. Terms like 'love' also now frightened me. Two people could come together, it occurred to me, merely to enjoy all their time with one another, and why get unduly semantic and pedantic about the issue? Marriage shouldn't be blown up into the drama that it too often is – Joan's white satin and lace dream – as a *grand guignol* spectacle which covers so many social and moral conveniences.

And what of our gladness?

Compared with how I had been, I felt very settled and very content. Neither Marina nor I went in for the hyperbole of happiness. I didn't get breathless, nor she suffer hot flushes, and impassioned words didn't tumble just anyhow out of our mouths. We were being perfectly adult and mature about our lives, I could believe.

I can't say what she felt, if she was happy or not, because I don't know. I wasn't equipped to know. In the flat she was quite placid, as I aspired to be. She didn't ever show the obverse or as much as raise her voice about anything, I don't remember irritation, except perhaps once or twice a comment about my untidiness. It was as if she had learned from whatever she had been through previously and was determined this time to ignore any incidental niggles in our relationship.

Sometimes I had to remind myself that we *were* indeed married. It seemed so unlikely to me, but she didn't discuss it with me. Just a few times I caught her face in a moment of especially solemn repose, eyes lowered to her fingers, those of one hand ensuring that the rings, my rings, were placed on the third of the other, exactly so above the knuckle and just where she required them to be.

I don't remember planning ahead. I didn't picture how long this arrangement must last, either the domestic one in the flat or our personal one.

While I was a prober and pryer into other people's lives courtesy of newspaper stories, I wasn't so with our own. I swung between extremes – between prurience and ignorance. I could do so and cause only muffled stirrings of conscience. I was learning to wad myself against any inauspicious stringencies my judgment might still be capable of.

On some days she's easier to recall to mind than on others. Her appearance is easily overlaid by actresses' and models', who are quite definitively of their era. I can't imagine her in any earlier period than that one, which may have had to do with the modernity – not slavish fashionableness – of her clothes and her hair.

In the wardrobe, at the back, I once came across a tin of hair colourant. I didn't mention my find to her, but the next time I looked the tin had gone, and I never saw another. I couldn't have told if she dyed her hair or not, and she made the process of detection doubly difficult by visiting a salon in a hotel every Tuesday afternoon. But since her hair was so archetypically blonde, and since the colouring agent I found was a blonde bleach, I conclude in retrospect that she must have given herself that Bardot–Monroe look by deliberate choice. She wore a pair of Italian Persol sunglasses out of doors, even on dull days or when she was taking just a short breather; but in the flat – while spending the time she did at windows – she never put them on, so I was in a favoured position of seeing what others could not by daylight, those intensely green eyes, as vividly green as tigerstones. That small, sexily tilted nose. The full, well-defined mouth to which she would now apply lipstick closer in colour to orange than red, and a good many times a day even when there was only ourselves in the flat. Her chin was narrow, but she had a finely formed jawline which preserved her from the sly imputations of age.

I can't make my description of her read in any more specific detail. Perhaps what had drawn me to her in the first place was the unthreatening typicalness of her looks, an attractiveness which quite a few models and actresses exemplified. She had no blemishes, either because she'd never had any or because she'd elected to have them removed. It wouldn't have occurred to me that she might have done so if she hadn't once mentioned having previously gone to a dentist in Wigmore Street and paying him the equivalent of a down payment on a good house in return for his services. Her teeth *were* most irregularly regular, it struck me at that point: when she opened her mouth to laugh I saw no fillings, no discolouration anywhere, no shading on gums. Now I started to notice that when she read, the menus in restaurants or a magazine in our flat, her lower lip dropped slightly; she would place her elbows on the arms of the chair and hold up the reading matter in her hands so that the clarity of the jawline was shown to best effect, so that her strikingly green eyes were midway between horizontal and vertical, with her long fingers – nails manicured and clear-varnished – curling round the menu card or magazine cover and her forearms extended straight and taut at sixty degrees. Back at the Beaufort Hotel, or when she perused magazines now in the hairdressing salon, maybe it *was* being done more obviously to some end, to attract the attention of others, just as she had been able to entice mine at Tommy's bar? When she had only my own company at home, she behaved in exactly the same way as she did outside in restaurants, and I seriously considered if she wasn't obeying a habit by this stage gestated to instinct.

How did she know to give me all the sensual pleasure that she did? Where had she learned it? From books, or from other lovers?

How many other men had she known? I used to wonder. In her conversation I detected the shadows of men, even though she didn't talk about them. Was I a better lover than them, or only middling good? Or less than that? I couldn't decide about myself, I didn't have the confidence to guess, and she failed to express an opinion in a way that would have told me. She whispered in my ear, licked inside the concha, grazed the blades of my shoulders with her teeth. It would have been a very convincing performance of love, or of the sexual act, to any voyeur who might have chanced to see us. But we lived too high among the rooftops to risk having binoculars trained on us, even though she left the curtains open sometimes, and the window ajar.

She seemed knowing; or maybe her adeptness was intuitive, for the things that in giving *her* pleasure must satisfy me also. She started to take the initiative in bed, while allowing *me* to assume the credit, for my power and stamina.

She did the things so subtly. Yet her fingers never made a mistake. I went deep inside her and stayed there longer. I felt I was Casanova. She would look past me sometimes, and it wasn't until several weeks had gone by that I realised she was watching proceedings in the three panels of the dressing-table mirror. But with my bare buttocks high in the air or with her astride me in either direction, I didn't care, I didn't think to.

She seemed satisfied when we would be done at last. I don't know if she was happy: she seemed, rather, quietly and breathily content. I was elated, because I felt now like a savant. But in fact – what I expediently forgot, or had yet to realise fully – it was she who permitted me to feel that I was so clever and plausible as a lover. The cleverness was on every count her own.

I would watch her dressing in front of that dressing-table mirror. The standard lamp with the pink shade would be lit, casting a coral glow over that corner of the room.

Her brow would corrugate with concentration as she searched among the tubs and bottles for a certain talc, or for one perfume rather than any of the others, or for a particular lipstick. It was important to her to find exactly what it was she wanted.

In my recollection she is composed of insubstances: scents, colours, a coral aura. Humming the melody of a tune under her breath if she was quite easy in her mind. Not doing so if she wasn't.

She would examine the results of her labours in the three mirrors, turning her head this way and then the other. Sometimes she half smiled. There was an equal number of occasions when, instead, her mouth pursed at what she saw and she would start to unfasten her earrings or necklace or reach her hands further back to unhitch her dress.

Whether or not we went out depended on how she chanced to be feeling. If something displeased her about her appearance, or if she didn't seem inclined once dressed and seated at the dressing-table staring down at her hands, then we didn't go. She had the final say about it. Maybe I should have encouraged her more. If she was wanting me to be more forceful, she didn't reproach me. Maybe I was just as she had learned to expect that I would be.

While she was allowing herself to decide she would sit at the dressing-table and I would stand behind her, leaning against the wall with my arms crossed, wearing my dinner suit. On some evenings – evenings that later ran into night-time – she had me turn on the radio on top of the tallboy, as if she couldn't depend on the sureness of silence between us. I knew to tune to a channel with light music rather than serious, because atmosphere was vital. Outside nocturnal London awaited with its night-spots and supper-clubs, stucco-fronted Belgravia shone white, Mayfair was spliced by discreet streets between buildings of sparkling stone, and it was all as free and easy as a song.

But not always, not when she had something on which to vent her doubts. A blemish on her complexion. A hair-setting she didn't like. Lipstick she thought better of but wasn't able to remove. A scent that she decided wasn't the right one for some place she had contrived in her mind she would ask me to take her but to which we might not in the end go. A chipped fingernail.

I made an intriguing discovery, that some of the clothes in her wardrobe changed, that I wasn't seeing the same ones when I slipped into the bedroom and passed my hands along the rail. Some that I remembered from before weren't there; instead new dresses occupied their hangers.

The only possible deduction I could make was that she was selling the things she had tired of and was buying replacements for them. The new dresses weren't strictly that, though. I recognised that a few were in the style of two or three seasons ago, and in the material of most of them I could detect a crease somewhere or other, or my nostrils caught the trace of a perfume I had no recollection of.

I didn't see how I could blatantly ask without betraying the curiosity that had me sifting through the contents of her wardrobe. However I didn't stop myself from commenting on some of the dresses when she wore them to go out. She didn't so much as say 'You must have seen it before', but she implied it by offering me no information and by prettily smiling. The clothes were all very good quality. If she was buying them second-hand, I felt some guilt attached to me, that they couldn't be wholly new. Was this what she was protecting me from, the blame of hack poverty?

But when I did offer to buy her a genuinely new outfit, one I couldn't properly afford but which I was pledged to for my honour's sake, the smile – the awry smile – became gentle laughter.

'Charles, I've *lots* of clothes to wear.'

I nodded vigorously. 'But . . .'

'Don't you like me in them?'

'Of course I do.'

'Well, then?'

'Everyone likes something new. Brand new.'

'You don't buy new things for yourself, Charles.'

'Yes, but that's because . . .'

I didn't finish my answer. She would have guessed what it was.

'I've all that I need,' she said. 'Really.'

She had told me she'd inherited what money she had to her name. I had supposed that, in the way of these things, it would be a modest sum. It must have been sufficient in total to allow for the purchase of her dresses. She was using it, I imagined, so as not to disturb me and distract me from my work with concerns that must be a woman's. That, I persuaded myself, was what a good modern marriage was all about: the establishing of harmonies between the quite separate traditional domains of male and female.

'I was masturbating by hand when the door opened and in walked the Queen Mother . . .'

Some of the publisher's unsolicited manuscripts ruled themselves out from the very first paragraph. Ninety-nine out of a hundred got nowhere. A few could be worked on, and might or might not pass the test. Generally it was like panning for gold in ditchwater.

I had gone out to North Chelsea – so my author insisted on calling it – to discuss some finicky points of grammar and punctuation with one of the company's old reliables. Her novels didn't sell very well, but they collected modestly decent reviews which allowed her to justify the emotional self-martyrdom of her life, which she assured me over gin slings – quite failing to see my incredulity as she inched closer to me on the sofa – was necessary to the 'easy flow' of her 'creative juices'.

I managed to make my escape with my editorial credentials intact. Thankfully the block of flats was close to a bus route, and I was able to make a quick getaway.

I was on the bus – it was pitching and rolling along Cromwell Road – when I looked out the window and saw Marina hurrying along the opposite pavement. I wasn't in doubt for a moment that it *was* her, I recognised the clothes she was wearing and the Persol sunglasses.

I tore downstairs and jumped off as the bus slowed at a bottleneck of parked traffic.

I sprinted across the road. I called out, but she didn't hear. She couldn't have heard; she was fifty or sixty yards away from me. Her low heels gave her a turn of speed I couldn't remember from any of our walks in Castlebay.

I could have run to catch up with her. But I found I was trying to keep the same pace as her. In effect I was following her, but that only occurred to me later. Then I was to have the leisure to ask myself, had I been mistaken, only imagining that the woman had actually been Marina? But I knew that mackintosh, and the silk headscarf with the pattern of gold and silver keys, and the faux-tortoiseshell sunglasses. I had been certain all along who she was. What mystified me was her being there at all.

A man walking past her turned to look, to admire, and immediately I was jealous, helplessly possessive. I was so busy looking at him that I forgot to keep track of Marina's movements. I concentrated on fixing him with a dirty sneer, but he looked too genial or too thick-skinned for the insult to register.

She wasn't anywhere in sight when I reached the next corner. Beyond me on Cromwell Road there was only a high wall and, after that, railings next to the pavement. I could see no pedestrians except a uniformed nanny holding a child's hand and a couple of policemen on their beat surveying the traffic. The side-street was residential: in the distance a woman pushed a pram and an old man hobbled on a stick. That was all.

I had lost her.

I stood for a while, hoping she might emerge from whichever

house she'd gone into. But the only people to appear were a spry young man in a brown suit and brown derby, and – further off – an older woman dressed for more inclement weather than this in a chinstrap beaver hat.

The street – called 'Avenue' – was respectable but past its prime. Two long terraces of cracked white plaster confronted one another. Separate bells by the front doors announced the fates of what had been significant town houses in an earlier existence. On the frontages of some the paintwork was peeling.

I was perplexed by what I saw. The two sides of the street led in their symmetrical way towards a far gap, but in another sense it presented me with a dead-end.

As I stood there I was conscious of net curtains being crimped back at a window above me. The houses tried to dominate with height, with seven- or eight-step staircases rising from between substantial pediments. Behind area railings was a deep drop, with more stairs down and more windows and doors and doorbells. These well-dwellings, in themselves running the length of the two terraces, must have housed the population of a small village all told.

When I moved off I looked down into their paved areas, comparing the little differences of proprietorship that distinguished them: a flowering tub or an iron bench or a string of cold dripping for birds. At the fifth or sixth I slowed in my tracks. A piano was playing. I judged it wasn't a record when a phrase was repeated twice, with the same protracted emphasis. A woman's voice sang some of the words, then trailed away.

The tune was one of Marina's favourites, 'These Foolish Things'. Why? – why that of all tunes in a repertoire of American popular song? – and why at this particular moment, with myself outside on the street to hear? I closed my eyes, to hear the song better.

> A cigarette that bears a lipstick's traces,
> An airline ticket to romantic places –

It was a funny, hare-brained kind of game, this one. Here I was standing on an unknown street, a street I'd never set eyes

on before, somewhere west of Gloucester Road, in the middle of
an afternoon when I ought to have been working, letting a song
take wing inside my head because I supposed I'd just seen my
wife, four miles from our home.

A tinkling piano in the next apartment,
Those stumbling words that told you what my heart meant –

It was folly, but there was no helping it, and I couldn't have
known if I wanted to be helped or not.

You came, you saw, you conquered me.
When you did that to me,
I somehow knew that this had to be –

The tune carried on inside my head but the pianist had stopped
playing. I thought I heard voices talking. A woman's light laughter. But other sounds were reaching me now, interrupting the
ones beneath, behind the railings, adulterating them so that at
last they were lost to me.

I turned and walked away, back the way I had come, to the
corner of the street. I looked over my shoulder. There was still
no sign of her. Nothing. But of course not. I had let time, time
and the occasion, slip from me. Minutes perhaps. Still the tune
persisted, and the gramophone singer's light tenor voice from
home murmured in my head.

The sigh of midnight trains in empty stations;
Silk stockings thrown aside –

A breeze blew past me. I shivered inside my jacket. It was like
a sudden intimation of this summer's loss. September already.
The breeze blew out of a blue sky, but leaves rattled in a tree,
shaking with fright or defiance, at the inevitable.

She was there when I returned home, my disappearing wife.
She was waiting ready for me, with the gas fire turned on in

our chimneyless sitting-room and with my dry martini in her hand, freshly stirred and shaken for me. She kissed me tenderly, on the end of my nose, on one cheek, on the stubbly jawline beneath. I could smell a casserole cooking in the kitchen.

All the long afternoon since the thing had happened, I'd been burning to ask her if she was familiar with Cromwell Road, whom might she know there? But the questions on the very tip of my tongue to ask were nullified by her behaviour, because she was being so solicitous and because the casserole smelt so good and tasted even better.

'Where did you learn to cook like this?'

'You didn't think you'd married a complete naïve, did you?'

She giggled. She was at least one cocktail ahead of me. The day had been a fine one for her. She stood smiling – a little lopsidedly, as her wont was – into the back of her hand, her ring hand. Smiling and smiling.

It was the song that took me back.

After supper – the lamb casserole – that evening, I played some records on the portable Bush. When it was the turn of 'These Foolish Things' to drop on to the turntable, when the needle twitched into the groove and the first spoken words were spirited out of the speaker from that mythical New York of adjoining apartments and empty midnight stations, of lipstick traces and cigarettes and silk stockings thrown aside, my eyes fastened on her for a reaction. If she did react, it was only momentarily, seeming to hesitate as she pushed back her chair. She had her back to me for several seconds after that, so I lost whatever expression might have been on her face to work my conjectures from. She turned round with her glass raised to her lips and her eyes apparently smiling at something we must have said earlier.

I returned to Cromwell Road and to Chesters Avenue. I found the house, and the deep area beneath it. Tibetan bells hung by the door, spinning slowly in a draught and chiming lightly. I saw, and heard, no evidence of life from inside.

I was walking along the other side of the road when footsteps caused me to look over. A tall woman in colourful bohemian wear padded in sandals, a bit flat-footedly, to the area railings. We were much of an age, I guessed, although her style of dressing and her round-shouldered posture were unflattering. She unhitched the gate with her elbow, and started a descent of the steps. Her hands were full. She was carrying a bundle wrapped in a linen or cotton sheet over one arm, and a couple of round striped cardboard hat-boxes dangled from their strings in the other.

I listened to the door of the basement flat banging shut.

And that was all.

Three days later I noticed a couple of round striped hat-boxes placed on top of the wardrobe in our bedroom. I asked Marina if they were new.

'Not really,' she said.

'Newish?'

'I bought the hats a while ago.'

I hadn't realised, I said.

'Yes, but they weren't here,' she told me.

They weren't, I said, putting a question mark into my voice. She'd left them with somebody, she replied – and let a little silence follow, being no more specific about who the 'somebody' might be.

'Somebody,' I asked, 'in a shop?'

Her eyes narrowed fractionally.

'Not in a shop, no.' She shook her head. 'Why someone in a shop?'

I shrugged. 'I don't know.'

She looked away, behind her, to the drinks bottles on the sideboard. But she resisted the temptation. She glanced down at the glass of gin and tonic in her hand, one or two mouthfuls from empty.

'Somebody I gave them to. Left them with. Just a woman I knew.'

'Good,' I said.

'Good?'

'That you were able to do that. Leave them with somebody. Whom you could trust.'

'Well, London's not overrun with those.'

She said nothing more on the subject, however. We were approaching the greater abstraction of The Past. We resolutely steered clear of it – again – as if it were superstition. All they were were hat-boxes containing hats. She wasn't intending them to mean more. Identical cardboard containers, candy-striped and overlaid with the name 'Felaine', consigned to an outer ring of our existence behind the rococo entablature on top of the gilded cream wardrobe.

I whistled through my teeth once, on one of our taxi journeys, at a Bentley Continental which crossed in front of us at traffic lights.

Marina saw the car, but nevertheless asked me why I'd whistled.

'One day . . .' I said.

She shook her head.

'You don't think so?' I asked.

'Not a Bentley like that.'

'No? Why ever not? Can't you see me in one?' I enquired anxiously. 'You never know – '

'It's just the car,' she said. '*That* car. I don't think it would be right.'

'No? Which would be the car – '

'Just not a Bentley.'

I couldn't comprehend her definiteness. I had taken up the subject mostly in jest. She didn't normally mistake my mood. But this time she had. Why should she take a Bentley Continental so seriously?

'A Jag?' I suggested.

She nodded. 'Yes,' she said. 'Yes, that would do very well.'

She sounded uninterested, however. The car and the traffic lights were far behind us now, the moment should have been over and done with. But like perfume, like the tune of a song, it persisted.

FIVE

'Someone was asking me about you,' Trenor said.

I looked up from my work, towards Trenor and then the logs shifting in the grate.

'Well, not about *you* personally. Not at first. She asked if I knew of anybody who might be interested in doing some library work for her.'

'What sort of work?' I asked.

Briefly Trenor was distracted by the wheezing of the ashy logs in the fire.

'She – she sounded very vague. Genealogy. She thought that's what you were doing for me.'

'You were telling her about *this* work?'

It was something I didn't talk about, except to Marina. I felt that Trenor's money ought to be buying him my anonymity; he had never stated to his public that he did all his own research, but hadn't stated either that he did not.

'Not at all,' Trenor said. 'I didn't even know who she was. I've seen her round and about, at parties. I can't remember her name, though.'

'How did she know, then? About my working for you?'

'Can't tell you, old chap. Not a clue. Sorry.'

He didn't seem worried. He must have sized her up, that she was no likely hazard to his reputation.

But I persevered. 'Did you give her an answer?'

'Well, I said I'd tell you. But that you were kept very busy. You *are* too busy, aren't you?'

'I think so. More or less.'

'Of course she could be willing to pay you well. Better than I. She must have the means, although frankly – between ourselves, and God forgive me for saying it, old chap – she didn't quite look the real McCoy. Plate, not silver, yes? EPNS.'

Trenor smiled at his verdict, at how it sounded spoken without a trace of irony. I smiled too. He started to laugh. We both laughed.

'But why me?' I asked him.

'I don't know. She'd seen you somewhere. Leaving a library, or just coming here with your briefcase. You must be the sort she goes for, my poor Charles. She did ask me some leading questions.'

'Like – ?'

'Did you live alone? Were you married? I can't see what that had to do with genealogy.'

'How did you leave it?'

'That I'd mention it to you. And now I have.'

'Yes.'

'But – for more than my purely selfish reasons – I think I'd forget it. She's off my conscience, but if the best she could do was some airy-fairy rigmarole about tracing a coat of arms which she implied had probably never existed anyway – and meanwhile *I*, a mere Yankee, had to remind her what "that funny crest thing" was called – '

There might indeed have turned out to be some money in it. But I accepted Trenor's judgment, quite gladly.

A couple of weeks later he mentioned that he'd seen her again at a drinks party, or she had seen him. Or maybe *not* seen him at all, because to all intents and purposes she had stared right through him. Such a cold empty stare – not even steely, I gathered, but vacant in a supremely indifferent way – as if they had never met and even less deserved to. Trenor shrugged. The gesture meant that he'd wasted enough time thinking about it, she was someone who only merited forgetting.

Until, that is, I found I needed to ask him the same questions later, when the business no longer seemed to me so incidental and peripheral in my life.

About three one afternoon I was halfway to Trenor's when I looked into my briefcase and found I'd left a couple of stories in the flat. I decided I'd have to go back.

When I turned into our street I heard high heels and saw Marina hurrying along the pavement, towards Harley Street. She turned the corner. I ran after her, but without letting myself catch up. I'd forgotten all about Trenor and the stories. When I reached the corner she was fifty yards away, climbing into the back of a taxicab.

Luckily a second cab arrived in Sebastopol Street behind me and I flagged it down. When the driver asked me where to, I nodded to the taxi in front of us, rounding the far corner back towards Portland Place.

She got out in a street of shops and houses on the more genteel northern side of Pimlico, in terrain with the sort of pretensions to call itself South Belgravia.

She paid the driver and started walking. First along one side of the street and then up the other. I sat in the back of the taxi watching her. I caught a glimpse of my own driver studying me in his mirror with a suspicious pulling in of his eyebrows. I dug the money out of my pocket and then chose my moment to make my exit, into the doorway of a pub.

I watched as she crossed the street again, to the point where she'd got out, and started walking again. I went into the pub and found a seat next to a window of green frosted glass, beside a nearly spent coal fire. I heard her heels before she reached the window. I panicked for several moments that she might come in. But she didn't, and walked on. She continued walking, I could tell from the sound of her heels on the flagstones. I got up and went back over to the door. I saw her cross over again at the end of the street and return in the opposite direction.

I had to withdraw. Eventually she stopped, I didn't hear any further stabbings of her heels. I put my face close to a window and peered out, through a quarter-inch rim of clear glass surrounding the green. She was standing with her hands pushed deep into the pockets of her coat, knees slightly bent as if she was feeling cold, with a little-girl-lost look. Her eyes, I could tell, were trained directly across the street, to ground-floor premises a few doors away from the pub. She wouldn't look anywhere else for longer than a couple of seconds. Otherwise her head didn't move, so that her eyes – I supposed – were remaining fixed on that one particular spot.

I could only see what it was later: a fashion boutique, with the name 'Madam Murielle' rendered on a blue panel above in silver cursive script. It was a small shop, crowded with pier-glasses on stands and tapestried screens and a green velvet ottoman. Two small, twinkly glass chandeliers almost grazed the piled coiffures on the heads of customers. In the window a cocktail dress and an evening gown were supported on thin wires in convincingly languid postures: they looked as if they must be occupied by rich, idle ghosts. By that time, when I'd been in the pub for an hour and a quarter and been obliged to call Trenor with an elaborate lie for an excuse, Marina was preparing to leave. She had been waiting for I didn't know what, and had finally had to give up. I was at the door and able to see her consult her watch at a glance – then keep her wrist in the same position while her eyes returned to the plate-glass window and door of the establishment full-square opposite. She shook her head and immediately after that I saw her lips move, making words. She looked behind her, to the entrance of a cobbled lane; a sign on the wall above her head advertised 'Tully's Sandwich Shop'. Her eyes returned to the façade of Madam Murielle's boutique. She read whatever answer was to be found there. The wrist dropped, and her left arm came down by her side. She remained where she was only another twenty seconds or so. She turned away with a last look towards the window – no longer enquiring and carking but, now, resigned – and started to walk away. She pulled up the collar of her coat. It was as if she had shrunk a few inches in that brief interlude between hoping, expecting even, and having a last silent answer given to her across the thoroughfare's mid-afternoon traffic.

When she'd gone I took up her vigil, but watched the shop's façade from the mouth of the passageway where I hoped I should be less obvious. A few customers came and went: modish women between their thirties and fifties with their self-consciousness and haughty demeanours in common. Each of them was greeted in person by the woman I supposed to be Madam Murielle, who extravagantly and in a kind of slow motion threw up her arms on their entrance, in exactly the same manner every time. After a stint I slipped back to the Muscovite for another pint. I stared into the smouldering ashes in the grate. Today *was* cooler than preceding days but not cold, and I wondered – among all the other questions in my head – why Marina should have seemed so.

I downed that second pint. Then delayed my departure with a Johnnie Walker. The fire was banked up with fresh coal, and the very little light that had been left glowing there was smothered. That corner of the room went dark.

I left, and returned along the street in time to catch the last customer leave and Madam Murielle and her assistant embark on their routine for closing the shop for the day. Dust-sheets were thrown over the dresses on their racks and linen blinds were lowered at the window to shield the insipid ghosts from the vulgar gaze. The lights went out one by one: first the wall brackets, then the miniature glass chandeliers. Madam Murielle had changed into more practical wear; she divested herself of her turban and stood before a long mirror to throw a chiffony scarf over her straggling white hair. Her assistant, a neat middle-aged woman with a thin face and French roll of grey hair, buttoned up her own coat, then deferentially fidgeted with the dust-sheets. The pair left the shop together. Madam Murielle double-locked the door. Out on the common street she had a slight limp. Her younger assistant was more clearly striking by natural daylight, but looked uncomfortable in the fussily pleated mauve coat, shifting her shoulders inside the broad yoke; she removed a bus ticket from her pocket, and stood awkwardly while Madam Murielle hailed a taxi and sailed off with a curt 'good night to you'. The assistant glanced over in my direction for several moments, but didn't seem to be aware of me. Her eyes dropped to the kerb ahead of me as she lost herself in thought. She remained motionless while the staff from other shops round about passed. She raised a hand to her hair but did it – I thought – unconsciously, because it was a gesture that she did all day in the presence of their proud, perfunctory and immaculate customers. She seemed to catch herself, and let her arm fall by her side. She pushed the hand into her pocket while the other played with the bus

ticket. She turned and looked over the wide shoulder of her
coat towards the shop. Her final duty of the day had been to
lower the cream blind on the door. The glass surfaces showed
only the reflection of herself. Her head went back and her eyes
must have been reading the name on the board, in script that
belonged to a schoolchild's best ink-exercise.

She walked off with a rather crestfallen air, surely not at all
as Madam Murielle would have wished or required. She was
one of how many thousand such saleswomen in the city: rather
more expensively, but inappropriately, dressed, and walking in
shoes that appeared too tight to be comfortable – or else her
manner of walking was done in unthinking imitation of Madam
Murielle, with her limp that probably owed to the hip. She too
shrank a little, away from the shop, as it fell behind her, as
the distance widened. The panelled mauve coat was top-heavy,
even though the arms – deftly shortened – were the right length.
As shapeless as a bear-skin it was hardly an advertisement for
Madam Murielle's establishment, so I was left puzzling what on
earth could have been the point.

Marina said nothing about having been out. I asked her if she
had been. She looked quickly at me from the little sofa. 'Well,
not really,' she said, converting a shake of her head to a vague
nod. 'Just for a walk. Round the block.'

She asked me how my afternoon had gone in Upper Grosvenor
Street. I told her – I lied – that it had been fine.

'He phoned up,' she said. 'To see if you were back.'

'He rang?'

'Yes. I didn't say who I was, but he called me "Mrs Swale".'

'What about?'

'Just to ask, could he leave a message – if I'd be so kind . . .
He's very polite, isn't he?'

'Oh yes.'

'That he'd see you on Thursday. And could I please let you
know when you got back.'

'"Got back"?'

'Yes. Got back home. Here.'

'Oh.'

She smiled. I stared at the smile. She didn't suspect, I presumed to think: she was only grateful that she could change the subject.

I nodded. She sat smiling in the same harmless, disencumbered way.

'Thursday?' I repeated.

'Yes,' she said. 'Did I pick that up right?'

'Oh . . .'

'It seemed quite simple.'

'Yes.' I nodded for emphasis. 'I'm sure that'll be right.'

She settled back in the sofa. She crossed her legs. She raised a hand to her hair, to the plait she was currently wearing at the back.

I smiled. She smiled. I opened my briefcase. I remembered for the first time since early this afternoon the two stories I'd left for Mayfair without. I was conscious of what Marina called a 'businessy' look sobering my face. We were returning so soon to our equilibrium, and if I was puzzled about some things I was also feeling a surfeit of relief.

Trenor had too much tact to enquire what had happened. On my following Thursday visit, however – when I was very careful to arrive on time – I saw he was studying me with evident interest. I didn't usually elicit his curiosity about my mode of life away from work. To judge from the suppressed smiles he wore that day, he suspected a minor upset behind the scenes, possibly a pulling of wool over conjugal eyes. From his bachelor's stance he could only be a little amused, and consoled, that this was how even a husband of a very few months' standing behaved. *Just what sort of female can you have hitched yourself to, my dear young chap?*

I found a little time to search through her clothes hanging in the wardrobe. The name 'Madam Murielle' had rung a bell with me, and I came across the label sewn into a dress. 'Madam Murielle, Salon Luxe, Samuel Street, Lower Belgravia.' The 'Lower' must have stuck in madam's craw, but not even her most faithful customers would have been convinced by a more extreme geographical inexactitude than that. The afternoon dress, in fuchsia tussore, was one I had never seen Marina wear. It must have been an impulsive purchase, I felt. I pushed it back into rank with the other dresses hanging from the wardrobe's rail, like a row of my wife's protecting sentinels.

After that, of course, I was a little less than certain what happened when I was away from the flat. Doubts, necessarily unspecific, would cross my mind with the stealth of shadows. When I came home I couldn't help looking about me for signs of something – anything – different.

But nothing ever did appear any different. I would find Marina waiting for me when I returned at my accustomed time, when and how I was used to finding her waiting. This was the surface of our normality.

When I was away from the flat, however, the temptation to *know* was too strong for me to resist. Several times I devised a reason to telephone or actually to go back. Once when I called I received no reply; I rang again twice more in that same hour, but there was still no reply. On another occasion when I was supposed to be spending my afternoon at the publisher's, I returned, again on the pretext of something forgotten, and found the flat unoccupied. Untypically her lunch sat on the folding table in the kitchen, half eaten and not cleared away: as if some urgent cause had necessitated her departure and she had suddenly, in a trice, upped and gone.

Silence seemed to have jellified in that room. Then I was conscious of hearing, quite distinctly, the dripping of water in the tank through the wall. When I had stood for several moments at the sitting-room window I heard the mechanism of the carriage-clock on the mantelpiece, a frantic motion of the gilded parts sounding like boxed hysteria inside that onyx case. Crooning pigeons stumbled on the roof tiles above my head. I opened the window and leaned against the fixed lower panel in exactly the same manner that she did. Below me the street, viewed from this almost perpendicular angle, resembled one of those streets of chance encounters which Kertész and Cartier-Bresson had framed with their camera lenses in the Paris of the Surrealists. The scene was as flat as a painting on a wall: a human abstract, but achieved as a composition of quietude in a city of commotion and flux. As ever that summer, while I watched, some heads of thistledown eddied past and it seemed to me miraculous that they should, as if Greater Sebastopol Street weren't what it was but a country lane instead. There were always these same dependable surprises in my day, modest intimations of far greater inexpectations.

Later on, she let me take her to the cinema. Or rather, on the three or four occasions when I suggested we could go out and see a film I'd read or heard about, she was willing that I should pretend to decide for us both.

I presume that having the darkness and its cover persuaded her there would be fewer 'risks' there than elsewhere. We waited until the lights went down and the film had already begun before we entered the auditorium, via the brightly lit but depleted foyer. (Matinées involved daylight trips, but taxis minimised the contact we had to make with the *hoi polloi*.) Once in our seats it took her half an hour or so to relax but eventually she did. She would adjust to the distribution of the audience around us, studying our situation – between upward glances at the screen – by the pastel glow of the fan-shaped lamps inset into the wall and the guiding white lights recessed at the ends of certain rows of seats. She might even unwind so far, comparatively, as to light a cigarette, to wave the match abstractedly in front of her face as she extinguished it, so that I was able to see her features, as enigmatic as Marlene's, as Sylvana's, as Nelly Nyad's or Tedi Thurman's.

I don't know why I should have thought – I had no proof, I mean, to justify my thinking such a thing – that I was attended on my movements between the flat and the library, and the library and Trenor's portion of the house in Upper Grosvenor Street, by the interest of another party.

If eyes were watching me, my flesh didn't creep. But I was alerted to something or other, and I would feel myself tensing. I didn't know whom or what to look for. If I turned round suddenly, there was either nobody there or else a collection of other pedestrians.

I had a presentiment, though. Maybe once a loose stone rattled from under a shoe, or a heel struck a grating, or a hand collided with a railing: or, even more elusively than sound, a shadow moved too quickly across a wall, momentarily a track of sunshine was interrupted. Once certainly I thought I'd caught the smoke of a cheroot when I performed an abrupt U-turn halfway along a cobbled lane I used as a short cut and retraced my steps – but there was no one there for me to see.

Another time I was making my way back to my library carol with a pile of newspapers and magazines when I found a button – the anonymous button of a gent's overcoat – spinning like a counter on the floor where it had fallen. I looked round sharply. The door only seven or eight feet away sighed softly shut and a shape – no clearer to me than a person's presence – was visible behind the glass. By the time I'd dumped my pile and reached the door, the staircase both above and below was silent.

A third time I was walking into a café when I had an instinct to stop, turned round and came out again. A taxi lurched off from the kerb. I stood watching as it smartly picked up speed. I hadn't been able to see who was in the back compartment, all I'd made out was an outstretched arm and a slim hand, a woman's probably, tapping the glass partition.

I continued to go about my business with a sixth sense that movements were coinciding with my own. I was never quick enough or wily enough to satisfy myself. But it also occurred to me that perhaps 'it' couldn't be accounted for by dint of having my senses primed. I was looking to find 'it' for some reason, so find 'it' – whom or what – I very probably would, yet not when I was expecting or hoping to.

A subdued clamour was taking place outside the restaurant as we were preparing to leave. I looked at my watch: at quarter to midnight the group's evening was just about to begin. While champagne bottles were speeded through the hallway beside us, I saw through the front doors the explosion of a photographer's flash-bulb. Faces – a man's and a woman's – were momentarily lit up, their expressions fixed against astonishment. The figures' movements were barely impeded at all as they proceeded across the pavement between limousine and entrance. By the fireplace in the hall Marina was pulling on her gloves as she watched. I felt a thrill to be standing so close to this implied vortex of fame.

I saw how Marina was staring at the activity. She forgot about the buttons on the gloves. Her eyes tightened with concentration. Her face had set like white plaster. I couldn't understand why she was so taken up. She had accused me in the past – pleasantly, though, laughing about it – of paying too much attention to these people who were only courting it. Her implication had been that fame was vulgar. What you should do was turn the other cheek.

Now she was all eyes for whomever it was. But her complexion had a bloodless look, even in the glow from the fire and by the flattering soft pink light of the table lamps. I couldn't make sense of it.

'Who is it?' I whispered in her ear.

She didn't reply. I thought she hadn't heard and nuzzled closer, but she turned away, towards the nearest wall. She inclined her head as if her gloves were her sole preoccupation.

The party meanwhile had drifted past. I couldn't see who exactly was in its midst. The head waiter, so intimidating on our arrival, was reduced to a fawning flunkey. When I turned back, I found Marina had already gone.

I followed her outside. She was standing searching up and down the street for a taxi.

The doorman was in the vestibule attempting to eject the photographer. I caught sight of a taxi and waved it down myself. When I looked round, Marina was standing with her back to me, staring at the goings-on in the foyer. I touched her arm; she twitched, then turned round, raising a hand to her hair as if she was meaning to save it from the wind. She shivered as she walked past me, but smiling stoically on that draughty corner of St James's Street.

'Who was that?' I asked her in the taxi.

'Who was who?'

'The woman in there.'

'The woman?'

'With the man. I thought – ' I nodded back to the doors of the restaurant. ' – you must know her. Know *of* her. Yes?'

'Why?'

'Well – you were looking at her.'

'Was I?'

'I just supposed – '

'Oh, you should never do that, Charles.'

Taxis were our way now. I would have been happy to walk – a mile, or a mile and a half north – but Marina was always more at her ease inside the privacy of the cab than with her arm linked through mine, even when I picked a route for us via the emptiest streets.

She settled into the seat. I felt her arm resting against mine. I put my hand on hers, but she didn't react. I loosened the hold of my hand, but left it folded over hers. Her pulse seemed to be beating especially fast in her wrist.

The next morning our newspapers were delivered as usual: my *Manchester Guardian* and *Telegraph*, and her *Express*. But unusually she was up out of bed first when she heard the letter-box rattle. She tossed my papers on to the bed en route for the kitchen. I heard her making tea but she didn't remember to bring me any. I called through. She came in with the cup and saucer, which was the job I invariably gave myself of a morning. She looked inattentive. She saw from my puzzlement that something was missing. 'God, milk!' I made out it was all a great joke. But she only vaguely smiled.

In the evening, when I'd got back from work, I looked for the *Express* to flick through before supper, as was my habit. She seemed to have forgotten: then she apologised, as if she'd only just brought it to mind, that she'd used the paper to wrap up a chicken carcass.

'Do you mind?'

'It's not important,' I said.

'Sorry.' She breezed past me to the oven, as if it was really quite inconsequential after all.

I could tell by now – most times anyway – when she was ruffled about something, strung up. Her smile had a stretchy, tensile ambivalence. She was clearly muddled on this occasion about what she could permit me to see, and what not.

I didn't want it to matter. I didn't even know why I should have been perplexed myself. Then I remembered what I'd noticed in the morning, standing at the kitchen door in my pyjamas: how intently she was crouched over the newspaper, and how quickly she closed it and folded it when I moved and she realised I was there.

It was simple enough in later days – another four or five months on, when it mattered again – to order the back copies of the *Express* for the approximate period from the stack of the library where I was looking for material for Trenor. I couldn't remember the exact day, but I did find a photograph where the restaurant's name, 'Pompadour', was just visible on an awning above the front doors. The photograph featured a celebrity, to judge from the flash-bulb's glow and the party frolics of those in the background. I didn't recognise the man, and the name further confused me by not signifying a light: the Maharajah of Randagarh. He was small and burly but very dapperly dressed – dressed over-precisely, as if not wholly used to the style – in dinner jacket and cummerbund. By his side, with her hand touching his arm, was an unnamed woman: white Caucasian, perhaps English or American. Her other hand was fingering her necklace, suspended from which – and left unconcealed – was what appeared to be a single diamond, about the size of a walnut. She was maturely attractive, diamond apart, and if not a true beauty she conferred great glamour on the situation. Facially the man was plump and indistinctive, but he was positioned in the centre of the photograph, directly in the aureole of the flash-bulb. I was particularly attentive to the woman's hand, attempting to insinuate some proprietorial hold but not wholly confident as yet about the gesture. The other hand fluttered about her neck,

fidgeting with the pendant chain, but of course it was a ruse –
entirely false modesty – intended not to shield but to advertise
the incontrovertible, one-hundred carat fact of the diamond.

I believed that, with time, Marina would open up to me
completely. She would find her social nerve, and we should
learn to tell each other all our secrets, from the trivial to the
most intimate ones. I had confidence, sitting with her in those
fancy restaurants. One day, and not so long away, we should
be placed in the middle of the room, where the celebrities and
the best-looking customers sat on display. I didn't doubt that it
would happen. I had faith. It was as close to a certainty as any
future anticipation had seemed to me in my life before.

One night, on my birthday, something else happened. Something
instantaneous and, I supposed, slight.

We were leaving the Capricorn Grill, where I'd never taken
her before.

The doorman had flagged down a taxi for us. It was raining,
and he raised his umbrella to lead us out to the cab. When he
turned to us to conduct us forwards, he appeared to recognise
Marina. He tipped his cap with his other hand. 'It's yourself,
madam – ' Her arm, linked through mine, tightened its grip
on me. She didn't speak but looked up under the hood of the
umbrella. The doorman's face went slack with embarrassment;
his mouth sagged, his eyes stared helplessly.

Marina ran forwards, out of the cover of the umbrella. Her
arm held mine, and I went tripping after her, across the shiny
wet pavement. She grabbed my hand and pulled me into the cab
after her.

The doorman had hurried out and was closing the taxi door
behind us. The man's face was still a picture of awkwardness
and discomfort: but whether because he'd been presumptuous
or had mistaken Marina's identity, I couldn't know.

Marina sat back in the seat. She kept her eyes trained straight
ahead as the driver pulled out into the road. She continued to
say nothing, just as she had refused to tell the man if he was

right or wrong. She was wanting the moments to pass. I had my opportunity to ask: I knew that I did. I turned my head to look back. The doorman still stood at the kerb's edge, with the umbrella held over him, watching our departure.

The moments passed. The motion of the taxi compelled *me* also backwards in the seat. The dull streetlamps temporarily dazzled in rain-runs on the windows. The buildings oversaw our solitary progress through the streets like solemn, diligent sentries. London – habitual London that I used to take so much for granted – underwent another of the metamorphoses that had waylaid me every so often since my marriage. Tonight it had dignity, a worn handsomeness, a vast and impenetrable allusiveness. I opened the window a little and looked up over the rooftops, to clusters of stars visible where the puffy blue clouds had parted. All manner of symbols swung on signposts as a breeze blew up to something stronger. Suns, moons, wheatsheafs, lions' heads, unicorns, shells, golden balls, the gilded scales of justice. The city seemed threaded by those primitive folk elements, like masonic emblems. Names on buildings became disembodied from their immediate, literal structures: Griffin Bank, Eagle Assurance, Pearl Assurance, Anchor Trust, Pilgrims' Confidential, White Friars, Mitre Press, Golden Arrow, Camel Cigarettes . . . London was the most elaborate dance of ritual, a fantastical hive of metaphor. In the melodramatic half-darkness the most prominent colours were shades of gold, bronze and silver. A taxi ride through the West End became something akin to a medieval crossing, through a teeming forest of peril and succour. Maybe I had just drunk too much: but not so much that I couldn't hark back in my thoughts, to the doorman standing beneath his umbrella, fulfilling *his* role as some mystical functioning tool in the allegory of our life.

Back home in the flat – our flat which would always be ours whoever was its tenant: claimed by us as our own little theatre – Marina behaved as if nothing at all had happened, other than our having dined in such a superior restaurant. She was restless, but she seemed to be casting about only in a hazy mood of well-being, a nimbus of contentment. Standing at the window in the unlit

sitting-room, with the curtains still held in their stays, she was
positioned with her face turned in the direction of the restaurant,
midway between south and south-west.

Later, with the gas fire turned up and the lamps switched
on, she took out one of her London maps and unfolded it on
top of the half-moon table. With her back turned to me she sat
tracing a pattern – from departure to destination – with her index
finger, then she stopped and used her eyes and memory instead.
Whether or not it was our journey, I didn't know. I didn't ask.
I stood back. I kept to the rear of the room, like a spectre, like
a shadow-man.

In bed asleep she must surely – I told myself – she must
become the vital Marina. Nothing could be falsified about herself
then. She'd be returned to the essence of herself, where she
just *was*.

I would wake quite often in the middle of the night. It was a
very recent habit. Perhaps Marina's keeping the curtains open
accounted for it happening, but she liked to have the room filled
with moonlight and I didn't want to seem so prosaic as to object.
If I'd been alone I might have fretted about the lack of rest for
my brain, especially when I had a deadline looming. But I was
meekly, gladly reconciled to lie awake for however long it was
necessary to me that I should, when I had her beside me to
watch. I angled myself so that I could see her face and the
movement of her body filling with breath and expelling it. She
lay without disturbance, perhaps with one or other of her arms
placed across her breasts or draped over her midriff. I wondered
how remarkably clean and clear a conscience that took. Her face
was calm, but expressionless. I was a little treacherous once or
twice and tried to read in its features a history, but I couldn't:
she carried neither the evidence of travail nor, more unusually,
of origin and class. I understood that this was all part and parcel
of the uniqueness of her, that she shouldn't appear to be this or
that, that she could be anything. She had magnetised me by her
very neutrality, her inscrutability. I had been a man in search of
an enigma. She wished to be with someone who wouldn't need

her to be one version of a woman and only that, who would allow her the silence and the degree of opacity she required. Somehow, by a fluke, we had found one another.

She lay in the moonlight as she had in my room at the Llanberis House Private Hotel. She would be turned away from me and towards it, the source of the light. Her hair and skin were toneless, coloured the same silver-blue sheen. The cotton sheet that defined the shape beneath – breasts, belly, hips, thighs – was a more brilliant, shriller white than any white of my recollection at three or four o'clock in the night or morning. She was lost somewhere between satin and stone. I was always too much in awe to risk waking her, so I would lie quite still, in my watching position, all through my wakeful phase. Somehow I would manage to drift off into unconsciousness with cramp only a blurred sensation, a remote irritation that might have belonged to somebody else. I coasted off on the image of her, her placidity and elusiveness, and in my dreams we re-encountered one another – I emboldened and she deepened in her mystery.

SIX

I could smell her perfume, even though the flat was empty.

I sat down in the kitchen and spread out my proofs on the little folding-table, to work at them until she came back from wherever she'd gone.

The silence round about me seemed particularly dense. I couldn't concentrate. I put down my pen and pushed the papers away from me. The chair legs screeched under me as I stood up.

I walked through to the sitting-room. I sat on the sofa and tapped my fingers on the little padded arm. The silence seemed just as cloying there as in the kitchen.

I sat marvelling at the order and tidiness. Even her maps must have been placed somewhere else, because the surface of the half-moon table was bare.

The silence was vexing, however.

I walked through to the bedroom. Her suitcase was missing from the top of the wardrobe. The matching vanity-case wasn't where she always returned it, next to the dressing-table. Perfume bottles weren't where they always stood, in front of the three triptych mirrors. Unused hangers rattled inside the wardrobe.

I dropped down on to the edge of the bed. I remembered just too late that it was a fault of mine she had managed to cure me of, because – she always said – it did the springs no good. But I stayed put where I was. There and then, of course, she might have walked in through the door. When I lifted my eyes, though, the space in the frame was empty. The corridor outside didn't seem to offer me any hope, it had an abandoned look.

I stared down at my feet in their stocking soles. She wouldn't have approved of a man's shoelessness either, but only done so in the mildest of disapproving ways she had, with a slight shake of her head and her smile kept in careful check.

I put my hands to my head. I tried to think it through.

She had taken her own things with her. Or most of them. So that I knew her going – wherever she had gone – was no accident. She had meant to do what she had done, whatever it was.

I was utterly mystified.

No message. No clues.

The flat *appeared* the same to me, but similar to how it had seemed on the day we'd moved in. Without the material evidence of her, it was as if Marina had never lived here. All I had was the proof of memory in my head. It even occurred to me that . . .

But how could I be entertaining such a thought, that I'd imagined it, our life together? Surely I was imagining *this* instead, and Marina would come back soon, in minutes or hours? There must be a perfectly simple explanation why her belongings had gone missing. Had something happened about the lease? – was she meaning to surprise me by taking out a lease on another flat, and preparing for our evacuation? But she had known how long was still to run on the present one, and the difficulties – the financial penalties – of reneging on the agreement.

I tried to sit down, sit still, just calm myself. I couldn't. I paced the flat. I waited for the telephone to ring.

It didn't ring.

I sat down at last, after half an hour or an hour of walking about, on pins and needles. I slumped into a chair and held my head like a very battered leather punch-ball in my hands.

Twenty-four hours passed.

I heard nothing from her.

Should I have gone to the police?

If there had been nothing missing from the wardrobe, then I might. Concern would have compelled me to. But my concern now included a different sort of bewilderment.

I kept considering my own part in what had happened, the necessity of some blame attaching to myself. I couldn't have reported her being missing to the police without implicating myself – by suggesting to them the areas of intentional ignorance which our marriage had contained. I was afraid, I dare say, of the sight and sound of them picking over the evidence I should have to give them, about the nature of our life together. They would be left to deduce I must have driven her away: or else that she'd had some dark cause of her own why she chose to abandon me, without so much as a word left behind her, only silence as if to punish me more. I should have had to tell those given responsibility for the case how it was that we'd met, how long we'd known one another, why we should have chosen to marry in the way we did. Our life in Greater Sebastopol Street would have had to be laid out before them, to be dissected by them, and no doubt with mounting disbelief.

I came to suspect that, in their shoes, I too should have been incredulous as to how such a state of affairs could be. It didn't seem plausible even to me, in those two or three days of the immediate after-shock when I sometimes lost my confidence about seeing her again, that she was sure – honour-bound – to return to me.

The solution was not to report it; to take no needless risks. *Not in the meantime, at any rate,* I placated my troubled conscience. Mightn't Marina actually be in some danger, and far greater than any I might run up against with the police? But life, I tried to reassure myself, doesn't comply with the dictates of a detective novel, its Gordian intricacies and involutions. Why not give Marina for a little while longer the benefit of my grave agitations and all my doubts?

I only wanted to believe the best of her, the very best.

Marina, Marina!

I'm not sure what I was thinking for those first three days. It's a blank to me. Blind white panic, I dare say, like a snow blizzard. A mental white-out.

Work forgotten, I sat or paced about the flat until dusk, through twilight into night.

The taxis juddering along our street nearly drove me mad with anticipation. I heard our neighbours return, but was afraid of asking them any questions. I remembered to turn on the lights, so that they could function as beacons, but only remembered about eleven o'clock. I prayed that it wasn't too late.

I would stay up all night. I stared at the telephone, waiting for it to ring. My fingers itched for the moment when I'd hear and go rushing over to pick it up.

I don't think I slept. I would watch first light coming up behind the river skyline. London resembled the painted set of a twenties Art Deco melodrama. I was exhausted, I looked like a nocturnal spirit of the twenties myself, with ringed eyes – two circles of kohl – in a long, drawn, pale face.

Where was she? I couldn't focus on answers, because I wasn't able to see her against any backdrop but this one. And Castlebay, of course, although it had become an indistinct memory to me, rarely thought about during the time in which our existence here in the flat had been my preoccupation.

I picked up the green telephone's heavy receiver and dialled the Beaufort Hotel. I dialled Llanberis House. Twice I gave my name, then her maiden name, 'Marina Freeth'. The voices responding to mine sounded distinctly unsure about me, and I realised the fault wasn't theirs.

Four days, five days.

For the first time I properly saw the vulgarity of the flat's appointments. I noted scuff marks on the woodwork I hadn't been aware of before, also a streaky patina of hard usage on the laying surfaces. Marina had declined the services of a maid, and I had been more than willing myself to aim a duster and pilot the juggernaut vacuum cleaner every so often. Marina would give no signs of noticing my oversights, however. The dependable absence of a maid had been the crucial matter to her, and by failing to notice she had forgiven me my lapses of attention along skirting-boards and down the edges and posts of doors. I wondered how much she *had* spotted, and how often she'd had to feign that everything was just fine exactly as it was.

Marina, Marina.

I had an instinct, which overpowered me every time, that she really wouldn't be coming back, that this was only a foretaste of how life was to be for me from now on, a backwater of recollection and remorse.

The hours repeated themselves.

Afternoon. Dusk and twilight. Evening.

The flat always felt chilly, even with the radiators burbling on the walls.

I ate like a sparrow. I thought tea or coffee would excite my imagination too much, but the real irrationality was in looking out the whisky bottle instead. On each evening I must have had four or five toppings-up within a couple of hours, and I am no drinker. The sitting-room started to sway and to tilt away from me. I dropped into a chair, or – perhaps – it came up from behind to grab me about the hips and force me down. Once down, I couldn't get back up, I laid my head back against the cushion. The slippery surface of the striped cream and lime upholstery smelt airless, vacuumed to vacuousness and utterly impersonal. I wanted to disappear into the non-smell, to be consumed by it for ever. I also wished I could be shaken hard, to be released from my torpor, to have myself spirited out of my exhausted and leaden body.

Marina, Marina.

I was beginning to languish dangerously, to luxuriate.

What got me to my feet one evening was the recollection of a song, *that* song. Music to drown myself in. I stumbled about in the dark looking for the record, not thinking to turn on a lamp.

I found the disc and placed it on the turntable, on repeat.

> O will you never let me be,
> O will you never set me free?

I blundered back the way I had come. The armchair

reclaimed me; the singer's voice was my own, he and I sang together.

> The ties that bound us
> Are still around us;
> There's no escape that I can see.

Marina, Marina.
The arm swung back over the record, the point of the stylus found the groove.

> O will you never let me be,
> O will you never set me free?

A whisky dream.

> There's no escape that I can see.

Only that. And in the morning –

> . . . still those little things remain
> That bring me happiness or pain.

The orchestral bridge. My heart was being mercilessly bludgeoned to pulp.

> A cigarette that bears a lipstick's traces . . .

I found the cigarettes in the kitchen bin, under the sink.
Some of them had hardly been smoked. Two or three of them were puffed away to stubs.
Marina, Marina.
There were the lipstick's traces.
I had a picture of her walking through the flat as I'd been used to seeing her. From room to room, holding an ashtray

in one hand. She was dressed, not for another day indoors, but for being seen in public places. 'Night And Day' was on the turntable, but she wasn't listening to it.

> You came, you saw, you conquered me.
> When you did that to me,
> I somehow knew that this had to be.

I breathed in the upholstery's essence of airless nothingness.

> The winds of March that make my heart a dancer –

I raised the glass in a mock toast, to nobody.

> A telephone that rings, but who's to answer?

I examined the room through the refractions of the tumbler's crystal. I spotted through the distortions the shape and colour of the telephone, green like fondant.

> O how the ghost of you clings –

The room was blurred, liquid. I closed my eyes, against memory, against everything.

> The sigh of midnight trains in empty stations,
> Silk stockings thrown aside . . .

Where was she?

A chartreuse sky. Distant thunder. The first heavy drops of rain on the pavements, as big as pennies.

The air so heavy and sticky, it catches in the throat and can't be swallowed.

The thunder roars for miles, overland towards the sea. Forked lightning works silver cracks along the rim of sky, on the horizon. The drops of rain splatter faster at my feet. The coins are fraying at their edges, a wild spree of coppers, not chinking but thudding at such high velocity on to the concrete.

Electric storms in late summer smell of the disturbed earth, of dust and sulphur. They have an apocalyptic glamour. I was in the right and proper mood for them, they could even have been figments of my exercised imagination. They carry a certain danger with them, but I felt I was at a fortuitous remove and risking no worse hazard than a soaking. I was coatless, not having attended to the gathering yellowy-greenness of bruising in the sky beforehand. An enormous septic stain spreading overhead from Essex to Hertfordshire, darkening the streets like dusk, like the day turned out of itself.

The peppermint green telephone would ring sometimes, in the late evening. Only Trenor and the publishers had our number: but he was out on the town, and the office in Bedford Row was empty.

When I picked up the receiver and spoke, no one was at the other end to reply. The line would go quite dead in my ear, and I'd be left listening to that eerie mechanical stutter.

Every time the bell rang the same thing would happen. I'd pick up the receiver and find myself listening to a shuddering silence reverberating down the line at me. Unspecifiable distance ricocheted emptily into my ear.

At night I removed the receiver from its cradle, so my sleep wouldn't be disturbed.

Eventually I slept quite well in that bed like a sleigh, too well, and much better than I could ever have imagined I would after her departure.

In my sleep I'd hear the telephone ringing, but it wasn't really ringing. I'd even get up sometimes and make my way through to the sitting-room to check. The telephone, receiver and body sundered, would resemble in the spectral blue moonlight nothing so much as a confectioner's whimsy of marzipan or nougat.

I kept on my work for Trenor, chiefly because it was the most profitable and because I welcomed the distraction of it.

Every week now I would arrange to meet him, and would present him with a swatch of stories I had elaborated from the original bald source-material. He always found some item among them for his next syndicated column – which was his own main means of income – and there were usually enough in reserve for his radio talks also.

My research on Dorothy Richardson flagged for quite a while, and I proved a bit too inattentive for my superior in the editorial department of the publishing house, who moved me from adults' to larger print children's story-books. The clock-serving impositions of my trade in Bloomsbury weren't quite enough to divert my thoughts from the continuing conundrum of Marina's whereabouts. I had no way of dealing with the incidentals that cropped up there, the panics as well as the tedious obligations – and I can't even remember if I did deal with them.

I still – obdurately – clung to the hope, the sanguine hope, that I'd hear footsteps on the stair, a tap on the door – and there she would be, suitcase in one hand and vanity-case in the other, smiling sadly but glad in her disturbed way to have the sight of me again.

I took those clothes she'd left behind out of the wardrobe and, one by one, draped them on top of the coverlet on the bed. Then I laid down beside them, each of them in turn. I caressed them as I would have done – as I had done so many times – her own body. I discovered by holding them against my face that I could smell her in the fabric: her skin with its after-traces of perfume and powder, her hair aromatic with herbal shampoo. I seduced the garments as a lover, I *made* love to them just as if it had been to herself.

I waited for the heat of summer to return, but it was already too late. Weeks had gone by since the last heatwave, and we were well on our way to another season. I should have realised, but I was – for that rime of time I'd fallen into – an unreasoning man.

I returned one afternoon to find a record playing on the turntable, on repeat. 'Night And Day.'
So she was back!
I yelled for joy.
I called out. I called her name, several times.
I stopped. Listened.
But there was no sound of her.
'Marina! Marina!'
I went to look. She wasn't in the flat. It occurred to me she might, uncharacteristically, be playing a prank. I peered into the broom cupboard in the kitchen. I returned to the bedroom and opened the door of the wardrobe.
The rail was almost bare of clothes, as before. The hangers rattled like crazy percussion when I touched them.
I went through the flat again. I'd forgotten about the record on the turntable, but it was still playing.

> Only you 'neath the moon, or under the sun.

I ran to the windows, opened them, and looked out.

> Whether near to me or far,
> It's no matter, darling, where you are,
> I think of you . . .

I searched again for a note of explanation, but there wasn't one.

> Day and night.
> Night and day.

Our neighbours beneath were out. I asked at the lawyer's

on the ground floor, but the receptionist showed such sniffy unconcern that I immediately turned on my heels and fled.

I ran outside, looking up and down the street. I sprinted as far as the taxi rank at the BBC and asked there, then returned.

I reached the flat out of breath, and no wiser.

The record was still playing.

> Why is it so,
> That this longing for you follows wherever I go?

Superstitiously I didn't take it off – as if the sound of it might lure her home, as if she had only just stepped outside and would be back before the song finally ended.

> In the roaring traffic's boom,
> The silence of my lonely room –

I paced backwards and forwards.

> I think of you day and night,
> Night and day.

I stared at the green telephone.

There was no one I could call, no one at all. We had lived so entirely alone, with only one another. Or at least I had presumed – for most of the time – that we were living with and for each other.

> Only you 'neath the moon . . .

I stopped shaving and the semblance of a beard grew in. I was never expecting to see whom I did see when I glanced into a mirror. I had always been conventional-looking: I could have passed as an accountant or a bank official, say, with hair cut short and with my clean and tidy cuffs and polished shoes. That was how I'd been brought up, to conform – and I had complied, simply because I'd felt there were better things my mind could be concentrating on than how I appeared to other people.

Now, unshaven, and in an unironed shirt and stockinged feet, I was halfway to being a stranger to myself, in this flat of which I was a tenant and about whose owner I knew no more than the name on an envelope. How Marina had seen me in Castlebay was the image of the man she was familiar with, the *only* image she was acquainted with, and I told myself that by changing my appearance I was betraying it, and her. Maybe I felt that I had to now.

Finally I went to the letting agency and arranged a further six weeks' extension of the lease. I thought it must be the necessary leeway anyway, allowing Marina the time she needed to return to me.

That was how I was feeling on one of my better days, when I could envisage that she would – she must – come back to me at last. I should ask her no questions that might cause her distress to answer.

I continued to wait. For a brief interlude of days the weather picked up and we were back in summer: but only, of course, in an imitation of it. I opened the windows wide, filling the rooms with warm air and releasing music – in my neighbours' absence – whatever I thought might call her home to me.

I returned to the flat one evening and knew for certain, even in the silence, that she had been there.

I knew by the little currents of perfume I caught at certain points. Her presence was drifting through the rooms.

She couldn't have left long before I arrived: less than half an hour, no more than minutes maybe.

After the shock of the discovery, it occurred to me that the proof of perfume was here by no simple accident. She had anticipated that I should notice. But that didn't tell me why she should have come back, after this unexplained interlude of weeks.

I ran to close the window I had opened on coming in. I encountered two separate eddies of the perfume. I didn't want to lose any of it sooner than I had to.

For the rest of that evening I thought I could catch traces of it. By the morning, though, they had gone. I wasn't surprised, because she wouldn't have worn the type of fragrance that lingers overnight. I hadn't been able at the time to distinguish between the contents of the three or four bottles and phials that she would set out on the dressing-table. I only knew now that this was one of them, and that she had trusted that I should remember.

I sat for ages by the green telephone, tracing and retracing finger lines in the dust gathered in the cradle and around the rim of the wheel. A ridiculous contraption. It was a mechanism made for a stage play, to furnish fate in a tart's boudoir in a French farce, the instrument by which lives and destinies become endlessly crossed.

It was at this same juncture that I noticed the trees had begun to turn.

I watched the progress of autumn from one day to the next. I properly observed it, I mean, perhaps for the first time in my life.

Slowly all the trees turned to flame, to elegant conflagrations.

Sparks fell and the leaves spluttered out in days on the greasy pavements.

The detritus finally caught the pestilential dampness of London in October and amassed in drifts to rust under railings, on the iron grids of drains by the kerbside.

The extension of the lease came to an end.

I had to decide what to do. I had remained so that Marina would know where to find me. But she hadn't returned, not for more than moments, not to take up her old life again. I sensed, in that season of runnings down, that a proper return was unlikely now. If we were to find one another, it wouldn't be here. Our new existence would have to be different, containing rather more in the way of explanation than we had allowed one another previously. But paradoxically Sebastopol Street would have to become history, ancient history, and its memories a kind of archaeology.

In the end, at the last possible minute, I gave up the lease. I packed my things, and with them the little that Marina had left behind to tantalise me with.

My possessions amounted to nothing much. A couple of suitcases. My briefcase. A mackintosh which doubled – tripled – as winter overcoat and dressing-gown. The grey felt hat Marina had bought me. An umbrella with a good malacca handle I was left with when my own inferior one was taken by mistake from the cloakroom in La Fourchette.

This was the sum of my life, more or less, in visible terms.

Meanwhile the stage-set was left awaiting its next act, some new characters, recognisable emotions doubtless to be given a new twist.

When I tried to bring Marina to mind away from Sebastopol Street, her face persistently eluded me. It wasn't because I couldn't remember the details, but because I couldn't make the face do – by means of its expressions – what I wanted it to. Now it was always too fixed: charmingly fixed, with that seductive smile riding a little higher on the left-hand side, yet ultimately as predictable and undiscoverable as a mask.

I found myself in endless service to these thoughts. I was as brazed to the memory of my Marina as I felt any man ever was to his wife. I was coupled to her as incontestably as any trailing shadow must be to its principal.

Mask and Shadow.

The leaves still fell. In Greenwich, where I temporarily settled, I had to pick my way carefully along pavements slippery with the mush of them. I traversed the streets on those dark foggy afternoons when I had to be out, on business for Trenor or the publishers. I felt very disorientated by my surroundings, and had to work hard at keeping my balance. By the fitful yellow light of the primitive electric lamp standards I guided myself along those unfamiliar conduits, holding on to area railings and pitching for the lampposts to prevent myself from slipping and sliding. Others around me, more used to the locale and its little treacheries, slithered even so. It was the prospect of finding Marina again that kept me, for the most part, upright and buoyant. I should have to *do* something, I knew – actively apply myself in the search for her, rather than reckon on accident and fortune: I couldn't justify this prevarication, this putting off, any longer.

SEVEN

The curtains of grey velvet parted and Madam Murielle advanced from the back of the shop. She was a frigate in full, imperious sail. As she bore down upon me, suspicion swelled in her.

She told me, without deigning to enquire why I should be interested, that Miss Smith – to whom she supposed I was referring – had not been the fixed and steady sort of employee.

'Not a stayer.'

I asked if she had left any address where she could be contacted.

Madam Murielle straightened the pink satin turban that concealed all her hair and gave such a severe set to her face.

'If she did, I don't have it now.'

'Do you think you might be able to remember?'

Madam Murielle didn't reply, which I was left to deduce *was* her answer, that she had much more worthwhile employment for her thinking faculties than to crowd them with trivia of that nature.

'Did she say why – '

'She left quite of her own choosing. Not of mine. At a week's notice.'

She stared at me with sternly mustered pride.

' – was there any reason? Something personal?'

'I knew – I *know* – nothing about her.'

'Were you aware,' I asked, 'of any young woman watching her? Watching her in this vicinity?'

Her eyes swept past me to the window, to the view of the opposite side of the street. Her eyelids, hooded and without lashes, closed for emphasis.

'I know of no young *woman*,' she said. The stress fell on the noun. 'In this vicinity or not.'

'Or anybody?' I hazarded. 'Who might have been watching her?'

Her eyes glided over some of the shiny reflecting surfaces in the room – a cheval glass, the glass top of a little coffee table, the glassed framed photographs of Sunny Harnett and Suzy Parker hung on a wall, a slithery green satin dress suspended on its hanger from a wardrobe door.

'Women without husbands,' she said, 'attract the wrong sort of attention.'

I let my puzzlement show on my face.

'Once or twice,' Madam Murielle said, 'I believe she may have had a rendezvous.'

'Hereabouts?' I asked.

'Any woman who gives custom to the "Muscovite and Ten Tribes" is inviting the wrong sort of company in my eyes.'

She didn't mistake 'woman' for 'lady'. She wasn't looking for the impossible in her aides – a *vendeuse* would always be a woman and no better.

I could elicit no further information from her than that. She turned for the door, and I was dismissed with a brisk but immensely dignified Queen Mary-ish nod of the head. Her neck and chin settled back into their customary folds. With the door shut, she pulled down the blind, even though it was the middle of the afternoon. In the window two ghostly, invisible mannequins invested their very material dresses with consummate elegance, performing life for all it was worth to them as a round-the-clock soirée.

After I'd picked my way through the back copies of the *Daily Express* in the library, I showed Trenor the photograph of the Maharajah of Randagarh and party. He could put a name to the man without needing to put on his spectacles for the small print. The tip of his forefinger hovered over the female figure beside him.

'Do you know who she is?' I asked him.

'There's something vaguely – I can't quite – '

'Do you know anything about him?'

'Oh, the Maharajah's a man of mystery. And vulgarity too, of course.'

His finger prodded at the photograph.

'It's a diamond?' I said.

'The Star of the Desert. It's an heirloom. There aren't so many of those in the family, but the diamond is the finest. Someone told me she'd seen the couple and it was being worn in London.'

I nodded at the information. It didn't signify much to me, however. Marina must have read something about the stone and been attracted by the romantic legend. In our post-colonial era it was like a reverse fairy tale, a turnabout of the British wooing of India. The operation had been anything but a wooing in fact, and I wondered how far the ironies of the Maharajah's situation extended as he intrigued and excited the *beau monde* and newspaper photographers alike.

'The Star of the Desert?' I repeated.

But Trenor had found something else further down the page which had caught his eye. He slipped his spectacles on to his nose. He peered closer. His lips moved, and he silently recited names he was quite familiar with, gathering them into himself as if they were the tenets of his faith.

I found Tommy still behind the Beaufort's cocktail bar.

Why shouldn't he have been there? I was surprised, none the less. It felt to me than I had been away from the hotel for years, not for the length of one season.

Tommy with his sandy boyish quiff was still in place. My beard confused him for a moment or two – but then he greeted me as if it had only been yesterday that we'd last spoken.

He asked after Marina, of course, my wife.

I told him that she had stayed behind in London. He accepted my explanation, and I found myself surprised again that he did.

He remembered my favourite poison, as he called it – a

whisky sour. He remembered that Marina's had been a Blue Lady – blue curaçao, dry gin, fresh lemon juice, and a dash of white of egg – and inevitably I was saddened at the mention of it. But I also didn't want to dissuade him, so I tried to smile.

A little later, as we talked, he told me he had a souvenir of Marina in his possession. He reached under the counter. From a shelf beneath he produced a paperback book; the spine cracked as he opened it. He smoothed what I supposed to be a bookmark. It was in fact – I saw when he turned it over – a photograph. He slid it across the polished wood towards me, rotating it with his fingers so that the face was quite visible to me.

Marina. They were *her* eyes looking up into mine. Marina's eyes – taken by surprise, and furtive. Her mouth was faking a smile, a game but alarmed smile.

'It's a nice smile,' Tommy said, 'isn't it?'

He was being quite sincere, I could tell.

'I had my camera with me. I just took it. There and then.'

My wife's smile became more uncertain the longer I looked at it. Troubled. Melancholic maybe.

I felt so much pity for her then, while I stood leaning against the padded counter-edge of the bar.

'When was it?' I asked. 'When was it that you took it, I mean?'

'Just before the wedding. In the morning. She came in to look around. To check over the details, I suppose.'

I nodded my head. I stared at the face, at her neck, at the line of her shoulders. I tried to remember what I could have been doing at the time, while my bride-to-be had gone downstairs to the cocktail lounge to cast an eye over the preparations.

What preparations anyway?

'Could I – ' I cleared my throat. ' – would I be able to get a copy of this made, do you think?'

'Oh yes, sir. I've got the negative. I'd give you this one but – '

I shook my head.

'You're sure?' he asked.

'Yes, yes.'

'I like to have the memento. But I'll get another one made
for you.'

'I'll pay you for it,' I said.

'That's okay – '

I took out my wallet.

'No. Really, sir,' he said.

Maybe, I thought, he was afraid the second image wouldn't
be so clear as the first?

'But you've got others?' he asked.

I could tell from the tone of his voice that he wouldn't have
presumed otherwise, that it must be quite the most natural
thing that I should have a plentiful supply of photographs of
my young wife.

I shook my head.

Tommy too, I realised, belonged to that earlier and more
innocent translation of events. I preferred to keep him there,
in that happier version, where all we were was a couple of
newly-weds with Tommy a glad witness.

He wasn't making any attempt to disguise his admiration of
Marina, his fond regard for the image in front of us both.

I lightly fingered the edges of the photograph, as if to confirm
such a seemingly literal fact. I thought when I glanced up that
Tommy was eyeing my actions a little fearfully.

I smiled: faked a small smile, as Marina had done.

I considered her face again. I stroked its outline, with my
fingertips in contact with the shiny paper. Her eyes were wider,
perhaps exaggerated by her sudden concern. Her cheekbones
were more prominent than I could actually recall, and her skin
paler. Her nose still had that sexy tilt, but – wasn't her face
just a little sharper after all?

Tommy sent me the copy of the photograph he'd promised.
He sent me two in fact, as if he had a full sense of its
importance to me.

Marina was now more present to me in my new surroundings
than she had been previously. Her pose and expression –
seeming tightly sprung, forcing herself into a smile – had felt

unfamiliar to me when I'd first happened to see them, offered to me on top of the bar counter. But as I lived with them, I could believe more easily that they were an equally true manifestation of the woman with whom I'd spent those four and a half months. It was just that the circumstances – Tommy chancing to come upon her on the morning of her wedding day – had caused her to show a somewhat more extreme sort of anxiety: an exaggeration of that watchfulness, the willingness to please, which I had recognised for myself from the evidence of her behaviour in Sebastopol Street. At times I'd thought she seemed not at all sure where she was, and why: like a woman first waking from a long, deep sleep, who's trying to find her bearings in a room she can't for the life of her bring to mind, remember from where . . .

With no one to watch me, I was free to turn the photographs to the light, to slant them this way and that in an effort to read and decipher them, to maybe find something new to aid my understanding. But everything remained on that flat and level plane. Nothing was prepared to surrender itself, of the veiled life behind her, the causes and explanations which I supposed must be there, just out of the camera's viewing range.

Two of the head waiters in London to whom I showed Tommy's photograph denied acquaintanceship – they both told me 'no' – but with such awkward hesitation in each case that I was left doubting them. I offered them both another opportunity for recognition, but they repeated the same cautious 'no' and accompanying headshake they had given me the first time.

I was dissatisfied and disheartened. I had an instinct that they'd been untruthful. Of course they could have been con-fused, but I felt that in that case they might have risked a guess at her identity. They were being very intentionally guarded.

That gave me still more to think about.

At L'Aquitaine in Clifford Street I had a little more luck.

The *maître d'* hesitated, but this time for a different reason, to ensure that he really was looking at one certain face. He turned the photograph towards the daylight from the window. We were sitting in the becalmed quiet of an afternoon restaurant, at a table cleared of everything except its undercloth.

'Oh yes,' he said. 'I know who this is.'

It was a partial truth, like so much else that I was to discover about Marina. The man wasn't acquainted with her name, nor her history. But he *was* familiar with her face, he confided. Quite familiar – he could be in no doubt.

She had come in several times, in the company of one of their regular diners. They had sat, not at the gentleman's usual table but – because he requested so – at another with a more discreet location. Normally he would be entertaining business colleagues, but clearly his companion was not one of those.

'You know that?' I asked.

'She was a woman, sir. And dressed just like – like a mannequin.'

All the clothes she'd brought back to London from Castlebay in the hired Daimler Conquest had had an 'informed' and original look about them. For our outings she would be wearing the season's new clothes, but these must have been bought a season, or two seasons, in advance. She wore them to eat in, on the nights when we went out, but otherwise they were simply for our little flat, something which at the time had struck me as a waste – for her – and in another sense as a luxurious, indulgent extravagance for my eyes. She didn't need to use any of my money to buy the additional clothes she did, although I offered and would very gladly have done so, even if it had stretched me to the very limit.

I nodded at the man's use of the term 'mannequin'. I could identify a resemblance from the word. The possibilities of error and confusion had been lessened.

The *maître d'* stood up. I got to my feet more slowly.

He held the photograph respectfully, as if for another reason than that it was someone else's property. Sightings were resurrected in his memory, connections made. I found he was staring at me, and the expression on his face was – ever polite, but – sceptical.

He returned to his post by the doors. I followed him. I cleared my throat, casting around without confidence for an explanation which might convince him, reassure him.

All I could think to tell him at last was that I had been instructed to pass on a message to this person. I asked if he could give me the name of her male companion.

The response was an automatic clamming up: as I might have expected from someone who provided for the needs of favoured regular customers with self-styled 'discretion'. He stood at his lectern studying the photograph, and myself, alternately, for several long moments. He placed the photograph between us, on top of the closed Reservations Book. I felt that, in a manner he wasn't able to specify, he was seriously sympathising with me. His eyes hinted at an experience of unexpiated silence in his own past life.

He lowered his eyes.

'Eglantine,' he said quietly. 'Mr Eglantine.'

He collected his menus together and walked smartly away.

The doorman at the Capricorn Grill shook his head when I showed him the photographs. He told me, 'Definitely not. Definitely not,' so I knew that he must be concealing something. I gave him an opportunity to consider again. He started to fuss with his gloves, then his umbrella. 'I'm not able to help you, guv'nor. I'm sorry.' His eyes trailed from the menus in their outside wall-mounts, to the doors of stippled glass, to the oval room of empty tables and vacant chairs beyond.

In the street – two streets away from Ryder Street, to be precise – he wasn't the same man. In civvies he lost three or four inches and that theatrical air of authority. He walked into the north wind with his hands pushed deep into the pockets of a thin, flapping raincoat.

'Maybe,' he told me at last, when I'd finally persuaded him to stop. 'Maybe.'

'When? When was the last time? Before she came with me?'

'Not so long ago. A few months?'

'No.'

'Nine months, then. A year even.'

'It *was* her,' I said, without phrasing the remark as a question.

'If you say so, guv'nor.'

'How often?'

'Every six weeks maybe.'

'Who did she come with?'

'Whoever brought her.'

'A man?'

'Different men. Look, sir, I don't think I should be – '

'Are you so tactful about *all* your customers?'

'There's some people who prefer you not to notice them.'

'She didn't want you to notice her?'

'Oh, *she* didn't mind. Never used to, any road. I mean, one or two of the men.'

'Why not?'

'Some of them had wives, of course.'

He looked askance at me and at my ignorance.

'They would bring their wives sometimes instead?'

'Maybe. Or they'd be in parties, with their friends. I might get a special tip, so that I wouldn't remember someone had been in just a couple of nights before.'

'Can you say how – '

'No. No, sir, I can't tell you any more.'

'You recognised her when she came? With me?'

'Of course. She'd usually say, "Hello, George – "'

'It *was* her?'

'Oh, yes. It was her all right. But can I ask, sir, what it might be to – '

I interrupted him.

'I was married to her.'

He turned, and while I kept my eyes averted I felt him staring at me. Then he looked away, as if this matter also shouldn't be confronted straight on.

'Does the name Eglantine mean anything to you?' I asked.

He didn't reply. I made a deduction from his wheezy silence as we continued walking, as he tried to walk faster to gain a step or two on me.

'A Mr Eglantine?' I asked again. 'Or a *Mrs* Eglantine?'

He remained silent, but his pace very definitely quickened. I had to skip-step to keep up.

'Mr Eglantine,' I said, 'and my wife? Did you ever see – '

At a certain point I realised it was useless. I stopped, and stood watching as the figure receded at the rate of knots. It was after midnight, and the street was empty. I listened to the scurrying pads of his shoes on the pavement grow fainter, until the sounds were indistinguishable from the spiralling of the wind in the coils of my ear.

Dorothy Richardson died, with still only three volumes of *Pilgrimage* published. My work on her had been suffering anyway. I stopped, temporarily. She'd waited seven years for me all told: piqued more than saddened by her death (it was a little too much like betrayal) I conceitedly decided that her spirit, with more immediate considerations of the afterlife to deal with meantime, could well wait a little while longer.

I returned to Cromwell Road and Chesters Avenue.

Marina didn't reappear. On my third visit, however, I saw the woman from the basement flat. She was so recognisable from her bohemian colours that I presumed I must have been wrong after all in my conjecture that some connection existed between her and my wife. My aberrant bow tie apart, Marina was innately subtle in her dress sense: she underplayed at life while, clearly, this young woman with the beaded shawls and copper bangles and lime woollen stockings and flapping sandals did not.

I followed her as she retraced the route Marina had taken that day, but in the opposite direction. She was no older than I or Marina, and proceeded briskly in her prematurely ageing pretend-gypsy garb.

I tailed her for five or six blocks, further up into Kensington. She turned off, into a road of superior white villas leading to a quiet tree-fringed square. She turned off this road after a couple of hundred yards, walking on to cobbles.

I continued to follow her. A gulch of mews lane stretched ahead. Her destination was a high, narrow detached house halfway along its length. The architecture distinguished the property from its neighbours – it was in Dutch style, of red brick, with tall atelier windows. The building was separated from the roadway by a paved yard stocked with tea-roses, and by seven-foot railings and two scaled-down but extravagantly ornamental gates, like an excluding rood screen. I was put in mind of a doll's house: the dimensions didn't quite seem to fit with the 'reality' which was to be found just round the corner, in Fitzsimmons Road and Monmouth Square. Above us, white clouds scudded across a scoured and boundless sky of the sort they have in Dutch Zeeland.

The woman unlocked the padlock on its chain and one of the gates screeched open as she leaned her weight against it. She sidled through and closed the gate behind her, without locking it. She stopped to examine the heads of some roses, then clattered her way in sandals across the flagstones to the white front door. She peered through the small glass panes first before selecting another key from the ring and fitting it into a lock. After that she took another key and pushed it into a second lock.

I watched from the lane as, one after another, the rooms were briefly lit. It was still daylight, but she illuminated them none the less. She went round the rooms in turn, switching on a glass chandelier in one of the downstairs public rooms, then a standard lamp in another on the opposite side of the hall, then shaded wall-brackets in the two upstairs rooms, and then a fringed centre-shade in the little room up in the stepped front gable of the house. Back downstairs in the hall she turned on a table lamp: a great wide-bellied Chinese base beneath a square pagoda-winged shade, whose size must have determined its location.

So far as I could tell, the decor was classical, patrician. Japanese lacquer screens. Ornamental mirrors. Tall Adam fireplaces, whether genuine or not. Water-colour views, a large oil conversation-piece. Pale vases.

It was like a much grander house reduced to a miniature, one room wide, except at the back behind the hall where – I guessed

– a kitchen was attached. Over the white-panelled drawing-room extended one of the bedrooms, with a long windowed wardrobe and a sheeny fabric canopy draped above the bed. Over the dining-room was a room equipped as a study, but the books on the dark wood shelves had a synthetically uniform appearance; I noticed a free-standing safe, the kind where the handle is a black clenched fist of iron fingers.

Something occupied the woman in the back quarters, because she was lost to my view for a time.

I looked about me meanwhile.

They were an eccentric collection of houses round about. Some attempted to disregard the lock-ups directly beneath and aimed loftily at Georgian or even Tudor grandeur. There was a little thirties land-yacht, shark-like, all aerodynamic white lines and streamlined wrap-around glass. Two along was a gingerbread house, straight out of Humperdinck. Opposite that, in a garden behind blue wooden palings a Union Jack cracked on a flagpole. A sprawling Lagonda occupied the space across two garages' doors. A gas-lamp disappeared into a profusion of honeysuckle absconding over a wall from a hidden garden.

The sound of a lock biting shut alerted me, and I was able to make myself scarce just in time, before the woman could turn round and see me.

She didn't look to left or right as she crossed the courtyard to the gate, then stepped out on to the roadway. She locked the padlock and rearranged the chain. She walked off and didn't glance sideways, let alone back. It wasn't the first time she'd made the journey here and back, I was quite sure of that. She picked up her pace and went hurrying on her way. She might well have suspected that she was under observation from one particular direction: her head didn't deviate from the straight and narrow lane ahead.

I stepped back, into the shadows of afternoon tangled into evening.

I picked a day to return to Chesters Avenue.

I heard piano music from street level, so didn't have to

work out which basement area was the one I was looking for.

But when I knocked on the door and footsteps sounded from
inside the flat, the piano-playing continued. The door was opened
to me: a woman with her body shielded stood behind it, and
I looked straight into the small living-room. Against a wall I
noticed a record-player with its lid raised.

The woman hesitated for several moments after I'd explained
why I'd come – her hand had tightened on the ball of the handle
at the mention of Marina's name. Then she seemed to overcome
that initial surprise and indecision. She stepped back to let me
enter, and apologised to me as she turned to view the untidiness
of the room.

The music continued to trill from the record-player. Chopin,
surely: an Étude? Against another wall stood an upright piano.
Sheet music, dog-eared and annotated with scribbles and
question and exclamation marks, was scattered about the laying
surfaces of the room. When I looked at the woman again, her
eyes were moving off me. She lifted her shoulders and dropped
them, offering a little smile over her bosom at the matting on
the floor.

She was 'artistic' in the way films encouraged us to believe
was the obligatory manner. Her jet black hair was plaited into
a bun and secured at the back with combs, contrivances of
outsized cocktail sticks impaling patches of coloured suede.
She wore a multicoloured cartwheel dirndl skirt and a faded
lace blouse. Several copper bracelets jangled on either wrist.

The needle was dragging on the record. The flow of music
had stopped. She didn't realise for another few seconds. When
she did she jumped and darted across to the record-player to
lift the arm and return it to its bracket.

As well as the record-player on its splayed legs the room
was furnished with two modern mustard-coloured armchairs,
an ugly Edwardian sideboard, a lilac porcelain jardinière of the
same vintage, a souvenir-shop tin bust of Mozart placed on a
low three-legged log table à la Snow White, a cracked oval
mirror propped against a wall.

Above us, through the iron bars at the window, life moved

– intermittently, and slowly when it did – up on the street. A man's trousered legs sauntered past: then a stout pair of woman's, lagged in wrinkled stockings: then a dog went sniffing along the pavement's edge. Greenery grew in the stonework of the well – an accidental garden, of the more presentable variety of weed.

I introduced myself as a friend of Marina's. Again she seemed hesitant. I produced one of the photographs from my pocket. She took it, and almost immediately she forgot about her apprehensiveness. As she examined the image her mouth formed silent words she wanted to speak – words, and so many of them.

We sat down, at the one orange bar of the electric fire, on those two armchairs with their rough piqué upholstery and slippery crocheted arm-rests. She glanced away when my elbow slid off, on to my leg. Then she leaned forward, leaned back, crossed her legs in their rust woollen stockings, exercised the uppermost ankle.

A hunch, wild inspiration, had brought me here. But a door had been opened to me. Suddenly I found I was catching my breath. With Marina, just where to begin?

She told me that she would go to houses, as a pair of hired hands, and play during soirées. Chopin, Liszt, Brahms. The sort of socialites who employed her rarely selected the programmes of music, but maybe their guests presumed that they did. No one became any the wiser, however, because she was paid to play and not to engage in idle party chatter.

I said something glib about the talent it must take.

'Why?' she asked me.

'Because you're in demand.'

'Oh, it's all quite mechanical really – '

'Do you give public concerts?'

'If I did,' she said, through a candid smile, 'would I bother with these awful parties?'

'I don't know. An artist's life – '

'Oh God, I'm not one of those. I play for my supper, that's all. I know my capacities. It's a sad discovery, but at least I made it. I made it early, so it saved me the disappointment later on.'

She stretched back her rounded shoulders.

'I've got the measure of Rosalind Wilks all right.'

Her forearms protruded stiffly by their coppery wrists over the arms of the chair. Her smile was rueful.

'But you didn't want to hear about me,' she said. 'You want me to tell you about Marina.'

'If you can,' I replied. I let my gratitude show. 'If there's anything you're able – '

They had first encountered one another at one of those same soirées. At some point in the proceedings a colluding smile was exchanged between the two of them. Momentarily my informant had paused in her playing – the piece, she remembered, was a Schubert Impromptu – but she had prevented herself from stumbling. She had recognised that the woman's smile saw right through the situation, as if everyone's socially aspirant intentions were transparently clear to *her*. All of them the same, just a crowd of social parvenus really –

The two women's paths had continued to cross. Sometimes Marina only had time to smile, at other times they had leisure to speak together. They'd sat on staircases talking, or found unwatched corners of gardens where they could smoke and run down the evening and the company.

To Miss Wilks it was only an occasional friendship. She hadn't foreseen the gesture of trust which Marina would finally return her.

'I kept an eye on the place when she wasn't there.'

' "The place"?'

I already conceived what her reply would be before she gave it.

'Her house.'

I found I wasn't surprised, but I didn't know why. I wanted to be particular, exact.

' "Her house"?' I repeated.

'Yes. In Monmouth Mews.'

'The Dutch house?'

'You know it?' she asked me.

'I've *seen* it, the outside, that's all – '

'The one with the rose garden.'

'You kept it, you said? You don't now?'

'Until this month.'

'How often was that?' I asked.

'Not very often. When she went away. It wasn't an imposition. She paid me something. A minding.'

'Did she – ' I paused. ' – did she say why she wasn't living in it? The last time?'

'No. No, she didn't tell me, so I knew I wasn't supposed to ask.'

'What did you think?'

'That there might be a man involved in it somewhere or other.'

'A man?'

'She knew so many men. That was her – business.'

' "Business"?' My voice was unsteady.

'I never really got to know. She did try to explain. About geishas. Tea-hostesses. How they used to dance, make conversation. Just be sociable. Well, mostly that – '

'Did you know she was married?'

'When? Once upon a time? Oh, that sort of marriage doesn't count.'

'No. At the beginning of the summer.'

'What?'

'To me.'

She stared.

'You mean you were both married? To each – '

'Yes.'

'I – ' She laughed timidly. 'Well, well, well.'

'I'm not what you were expecting?'

'I – '

'Did you think she *wouldn't* marry?'

'She never mentioned marriage.'

'Did she have many offers?'

'I didn't hear about them, if there were. She was very – very *popular*, of course.'

'What did she mean, "geisha"?'

The woman lifted and dropped her shoulders.

'That was what she told me.'

'Was it true?' I asked.

She moistened her lips with her tongue, delaying for a second or two.

'She didn't lie. It was true – as far as it went. Sometimes she was a geisha. An English geisha.'

I closed my eyes for a couple of moments. I concentrated on taking even breaths.

'Before you married – did you know her here – in London?'

I shook my head.

'Not at all. We met down in Castlebay.'

'Are you old friends?'

'No.'

'It's amazing.'

'Yes,' I said. 'Yes, I think it probably is.'

My attitude – as the news – had her flummoxed.

'Well, well, well,' she repeated.

'But now she's gone,' I said.

'I've heard nothing, though.'

'When did you last see her?'

'She dropped by – oh, ten or eleven days ago. She didn't tell me what she was going to do with the house. Or where she'd been all that time. She just received the keys back from me and thanked me. She gave me a little ivory figurine – it's Japanese, I think – for my efforts.'

From inside her lace blouse she extricated a leather twist. Hanging from it was an ivory netsuke.

'She told me some name or other. I should have got her to write it down for me.'

The ivory carried a very fine carving in miniature of a ferocious face. Whether human or animal or mythical creature, I should have had to peer much closer to tell.

'Funny little fellow, isn't he?'

'There are serious collectors for these,' I said.

'I'd never sell it.'

'No. No, of course not.'

She put it away again, considerately ignoring my tactlessness.

'We had a drink,' she continued. 'A chat. A laugh about this and that. Had a high time, pretty much.'

'Did she say where she was going?'

'Not a word. She didn't actually say she wouldn't be using the house. But I guessed.'

'How?'

'Everything she mentioned about London "was". "Was", "were", "had been". Like that. Always the past tense.'

'So,' I said, thinking aloud, 'she really *has* gone?'

'She'll be back, won't she?'

'Can you be certain?' I asked.

'No. But – ' She smiled.

'Has she always kept in touch before?'

'Until this time, yes.'

'I see.'

'But why shouldn't she be coming back?' she asked.

'Do you know why she left her house in the first place? The first time it happened – ?'

My informant shook her head. She turned all the bracelets and bangles on her arms, thinking her own thoughts.

'I've always known where to get hold of her before,' she said.

'You don't have an address?'

'No. Sorry.'

'Can you guess?'

'It *must* clear itself up,' she said.

'You really have no suspicions?'

'Why should I not tell you? I'm as much in the dark as you. And I've known her for such – '

She paused.

' – for much longer than me,' I said. 'Of course you have. You've as good a right as I do to know.'

'I'm very sorry,' she told me. 'Truly.'

I nodded. I understood that she was speaking her mind to me. I was ready, for Marina's sake as much as my own, to take her wholly on trust.

EIGHT

Over time I found voices to speak. Nobody whom I tracked down to ask denied me. They were quite prepared, even happy, to describe that time to me. I let them talk, and in my mind's eye I acquainted myself with the interior of that three-quarters-sized Dutch house in the mews lane. I mentally filled with party light rooms which I knew languished now in the darkness of winter afternoons, abandoned to a mystery too enticing (couldn't Marina guess?) for me to resist.

'She must have seen me once, and I must have made an impression on her.

'Grey jacket, dark pinstriped trousers. Just like I was a legal gent. Grey cotton gloves, so I could have been a dealer in diamonds. A forensic scientist, even.

'What I was was something between a butler and a steward. I admitted the guests when she had company. Then I'd wait upon them. Me and the maid from the same agency. The housekeeper, Miss McKenzie, she directed operations from the kitchen.

'After a few sessions I got quite adept. I think some of them presumed I was a permanent fixture. But I was only for evenings when she "received". Starchy affairs, but then she was planning to be a – what-d'ye-call-'em – a socialite.

'The guests, I don't think they knew too much about her. I saw glances. Between Miss Freeth and some of her men guests. Exchanges, like. And some of *them* would be watching each other. Over the rims of their whisky glasses, through that blue fug of cigars. Everyone else just kept moving around. Miss Freeth, she *glided* about. At the centre, sort of thing.

The women kept looking at her, but sideways on, pretending not to, so she wouldn't be able to catch them at it.'

Both public rooms on the ground floor were used on those occasions. Larger houses engaged the first floor on party evenings, but Miss Freeth's wasn't in that league, architecturally speaking, even if a good number of the company were of the first-floor sort.

Miss Freeth had been very ingenious in organising space. All the mirrors and the small-paned glass doors gave an impression of more space than there actually was. The flower arrangements also lent the rooms a feel of outdoors, especially before the cigars were lit. She hadn't crowded the rooms with furniture: by using Japanese artefacts for decoration, and choosing light colours for the walls – silk papers, with cornicing picked out in white and primrose yellow – she conferred on the rooms an orientally spare but spacious, unfussy look. When the rooms were empty of people they recovered an atmosphere of calm and restraint and, yes, of serenity. That was her gift, to have altered the interior dimensions of a house which in other hands would all too probably have seemed cluttered and poky and a social liability.

'Not having much space was a challenge. When I was doing the serving with Mr Ormiston, we had to watch our step. Be very careful with the glasses and crockery, I mean.

'We worked out a system. In those days we were both skinny enough, we could pass one another, back to back. Between the guests.

'Very polite and pleasant evenings. I haven't much more than that to say about them. They were my job of work. Miss Freeth was a regular customer. Client, rather, as we had to call them. Of the agency, I mean. She wouldn't have kept us on if she hadn't been reasonably satisfied with us.

'She was always so elegantly turned out, and that pretty. People floated about her. She held them somehow. It was some influence she must've had. When she spoke to you –

to me, even – she gave you all her concentration. That's what it seemed like. But she was a proper hostess too, and had an eye for everything.

'There was never a shortage of guests. As many as she could fit into those narrow rooms. *Comfortably* fit in. They weren't so haw-haw – as I called them – not like some of the types we saw on our agency work. A few did have titles, but mainly they were professionals. A few in the law, a few medical. And some businessmen too, of course. But not an arty crowd anyway. Quite a lot were upper middle class, I'd say. Or middle middle class, with designs for themselves. You know? I never could decide about Miss Freeth, about her origins. She had old manners, but new jewellery. Her dresses were finer quality than anyone else's. So I suppose she must've thought about them more. More than English women are in the way of doing. You know?'

'I used to go to the house for fittings.

'An exquisite house it was too. A lady's house. Cut flowers, and little perfumed pomanders and dishes of petals. Creamy soaps and soft fluffy towels.

'Only a woman would have had the *touch* for it. She knew the physical pleasure of these things for herself, and she offered the same to her guests.

'I went along two or three dozen times. My time in the house was taken up, but Miss Freeth always thought to make me comfortable. That was her way, and I appreciated her consideration. So many of my customers have lacked that talent – to put me at my ease.

'The study was set aside for me. I was able to spread out there, on the floor, with papers and fabric. There was always a fire lit, unless in summer. Miss Freeth would chat to me when I was fitting. Just as easily as if we had known one another for many years. About the fashions, about household matters. About how the weather changes your mood, things a woman – not a man – notices, on her skin first. Sometimes we listened to music on the gramophone. I would sing along if she invited me to. She had to invite me, though: I should never have thought to take advantage of her kindness to me, not for a moment.

'She also asked me to check the dresses when they came back from the dry-cleaners. She didn't make wrong choices with her purchases. The shop clothes. Most of them were in frequent use, I think. My own too, although they were more specialised. Gowns, cocktail dresses. One with some antique black lace. A couple of afternoon suits. And some lightweight things, for a cruise. I didn't enquire where she went in them all. I didn't have many clues. She was careful, she treated that part of her life just how a man would have done his job. I used to look in the magazines. If I spotted her in a photograph, though, usually the caption failed to mention her. Very strange, that, I never did understand why.'

'I worked for the Selwood Superior Car Hire and Chauffeuring Services.

'I was Miss Freeth's driver, when she needed one.

'She trusted me. I knew her ways.

'She appreciated punctuality, for one thing. And a decent turn of speed. The Daimlers – the One-O-Fours – they've got three and a half litres. She wasn't one for a royal progress, Miss Freeth, not like some.

'It cost her in the long run. Almost as much as the expense of a car of her own. She would have had to keep a driver too. Domestics expect their regular evenings off. Sometimes she'd just want to go out, though, on an impulse. Which was where I came in.

'The office would take me off another job and put me on to hers. They seemed to think she was a model customer, never mind no booking up. To them she was a good payer, right on the nail.

'She was very orderly and collected like that. Even if she didn't like to plan days and weeks ahead, how most of our customers do. I was amazed, because she once told me she didn't keep a diary. For engagements.

' "But you're out and about so much," I said to her.

' "I keep it all in my head."

' "Have you ever forgotten anything, madam, might I enquire?"

' "Too little for it to matter. You train yourself to remember."

'Her exact words.

'Mostly I took her up into town. She'd have me for an evening, and I'd come back for her when she had asked me to.

'She was always ready. At the time she'd stipulated. I had to be extra-punctual.

'Sometimes she went into the country. Then she'd hire me for twenty-four or forty-eight hours. I'd be put up in a pub or a boarding-house overnight. She took care that I should be comfortable. She'd have attended to the arrangements herself beforehand. She had a lot of consideration and thoughtfulness, for a woman in her position.

'I say that, about her position, but I still don't know quite what that was. She wasn't married, we were pretty sure of that. Or widowed. Or divorced either. She called herself *Miss* Freeth, and she didn't wear a wedding ring.

'She had lots of male companions. A full complement. They varied, though. Some older, some younger. Some familiar, some formal. They weren't all of them natural-born gentlemen.

'When she was in the car with them I had the feeling she kept one eye on the driving mirror on the windscreen to see how much I was attending to the road and how much to my passengers. She wasn't uncomfortable, not so far as I could tell, but she took care about appearances. Great care.

'Occasionally she might have her hand held. Or she let it happen. But talking away all the while. And looking out the window into the dark streets.

'I think she chose the Daimlers because they were so dignified. They're ceremonial cars. In one of those she could pretend she was above all the silly hand-holding.

'I don't know what took place afterwards. When I'd dropped them off at her house, I mean, when I took my leave.

'Her voice was quite low, soft. In a way that made you

concentrate all the harder on what she was saying. She had a lovely laugh. Light, buoyant.

'I don't know why everything just ended. I never saw her or heard of her again. In a business capacity, that is. Not ever, during all the years that I had left to me as a driver. It *is* a small world, I feel as though I ought to have done. She seemed to be so well acquainted with London. I couldn't imagine her settling anywhere else *except* London.

'Only once, there was something. Four or five months after the office found out she wasn't at home. And when we knew she hadn't taken up with any other chauffeuring firm. I thought I did spot her once. I thought I saw her walking alone on one of the quiet streets up near the BBC, Langham Place – Portland Place way.

'Very nippy on her feet, she was. If it *was* her. This woman was wearing a scarf on her head and sunglasses for a grey day. And looking down at the pavement all the time. And since she'd been in my thoughts just a day or two before, Miss Freeth, maybe it was only wishful thinking. What d'you think?'

'Once Mr Ormiston asks me – only because he's got a couple of pints inside him, and because maids like me are supposed to be fair game – has it ever occurred to me Miss Freeth might be queer?

'*I* think he means "odd". I start to say something.

'"No, girl, a rum sort," he tells me.

'I *still* think he means "odd". He shakes his head.

'"I mean," he says, "aberrationist. A deviant."

'My mouth drops open.

'"A lesbian, you nincompoop!" he says.

'I just stare at him. I'm sort of cottoning on, though.

'He finally comes straight out with it.

'"Does she fancy women?"

'I just keep on staring, and then he's breaking out in a laugh. And I shake my head.

'"Has she ever tried anything out on you?" he asks me.

'I stop shaking my head. With the shock of it. He knows

I mean "no". If Miss Freeth – if she had come on to me –
she wouldn't have got very far. I would have been too stupid
about it.

  'But after that I paid the woman special attention. I wasn't
so clever that she didn't notice. I couldn't glance away quickly
enough. For a while the house seemed to be all eyes. That was
how everyone made contact, I realised. And the eyes confessed
it all, even though the mouths might be saying something quite
different.

  'I had no reason to be suspicious, though, I could tell that. The
objects I found about the house, where they'd fallen, they were
all men's belongings. A handkerchief, a pen, keys, even a wallet.
There was only one woman's perfume. My nose told me that.
Her perfume. And of course that after-smell men leave behind
them. Rather sweaty, a bit tobacco-y, flannelly. The odour of
their work, and a long day, and their excitement.'

I had to search the dress-shops of London before I found Madam
Murielle's *assistante*, and in the end it wasn't in one of those that
I found her, but in the couture department of a large store in
Kensington High Street.

  When I announced myself and mentioned Madam Murielle,
she denied that she was who she was. I assured her that my
business had nothing whatsoever to do with Madam Murielle
and at that she relented, she hesitated between one hurried
untruth and the next, and duly into the breach I rushed.

She was thinner, sharper, more angular than her daughter.
Her complexion was drained of colour. The greeny blue had
been almost washed out of her eyes. Her fair hair had been
half-heartedly tinted with henna. Several of her fingernails,
varnished pink, had chipped or split.

  She wore an engagement ring with a single dim diamond,
but no wedding ring.

  She spoke quietly. It was a pleasant and seductive voice,
not unlike Marina's. Although what she had to say pained her
– about having had to start a new life at nearly forty years old,

and losing the old – the timbre was gentle, rounded, that of an intelligent and unhysterical woman.

The traces of a country accent still remained.

She expressed no indignation that I should have tracked her down. She didn't eye me as if I were a hostile fate.

'You guessed?' she asked.

'Yes.'

She nodded. 'You must have done.'

'Why? Why "must have"?'

'She would never have told anyone about me. I know that.'

She let me take her to the little Polish restaurant I suggested. She seemed reconciled, in a slightly despondent but at the same time quite reasonable and sociable way.

She didn't hold back. She explained her circumstances with seeming gratitude for the opportunity.

'I used to be fairly good with my hands. I was a neat sewer, although I do say so myself. When I came to London I found work with a dressmaker, out near the Elephant and Castle. Piece-work, then a table job on the premises. One of our customers was in business, and it was she who put it to me, I ought to try shop employment. I went to interviews, and ended up at Madam Murielle's. It was easier work certainly. I expect she would have liked me to do something with my needle too, but she couldn't keep staff – and I stayed, so that was my value to her. Other women could take up hems and trim waists, but not so many would be willing to put up with her airs.'

She looked down at the ungiving folds of her voluminous mauve overcoat. She may have felt guilty to be speaking as she was. Or she may simply have grown a little weary of thinking about her time at Madam Murielle's, now that she had found a new position in the department store.

I went on to explain with some embarrassment who I was: married, I informed her, married to her daughter.

'Oh,' she said. She screwed up her eyes. 'Oh. I see.'

'Your son-in-law,' I said, laughing croakily.

'Of course.' More colour faded from her eyes. 'Yes.'

'You didn't know?'

'We haven't met often. It's not like normal mothers and daughters. I wasn't – I wasn't that sort of mother . . .'

I told her, in the principal and undisguisable details, why I was here. She looked politely interested by my account, but she didn't offer me any sympathy or concern in words. I even sensed that it was a solace of sorts: the situation wasn't as it might have appeared, she wasn't allowing herself to be taken out – picked up – by a pushy type young enough to be her son. I was only her son-in-law after all.

When I'd delivered a résumé of what I knew myself about our marriage, she nodded her head, seriously but not gravely.

I diverted the subject to her past, without elucidating how exactly I had found my way to her. She nodded her head again, perceiving the impulse that made me enquire, as a man deserted by a wife who had preserved the full enigma of herself. Maybe she saw too how my ignorance was starting to turn me, further, into an enigma to myself.

From what she went on to tell me, I devised a picture in my mind. From what I was to learn subsequently from those who had known Marina in any respect, I was able to flesh out the story. It took me many years to locate the facts, and those conspired with my imagination to produce . . . what? The result will read like fiction, because even though working from the evidence of others I have been obliged to *envisage* what her life was (very probably) like. I have wanted so much to understand her. All along I have only meant to be fair to Marina, to come as close as I can to how I believe she must have lived. In part what follows is – necessarily – an invention, but it is also as true to those facts which I subsequently uncovered as I have been able to make it.

Mrs Frith had lived with her husband and their daughter in a small backwoods town in Suffolk.

'Sometimes I thought it might be a little town. At other times it seemed just like a village. A straggling, overgrown village.'

Mr Frith owned a garage, the only garage in Saxbury. Home was above the shop, so to speak, looking down on to the yard in one direction and over a hodge-podge of rooftops in the other.

She kept house. Three times a day she would make a pot of strong tea for her husband and the two lads out in the workshop. Sometimes she would be dragooned into lending a hand at church bazaars and the WI, only on account of her being fit and able to add up in her head, not because she had religious leanings or even a spirit of community. War help had been an obligation, of course, but everybody had been called upon – collecting paper salvage, boiling bones, bringing in the crops.

She used to walk their cocker spaniel, but Pip was run over in the yard one day and had to be put down, and walks after that seemed a bit pointless. Going to the shops and back was walking enough, although her husband liked them both to get some air on a Sunday afternoon, along with half the population of the place. She complied – she *had* complied – because, really, she hadn't thought to do anything else.

Her whole trouble was, in Saxbury she hadn't thought about anything very much at all, not in years.

'The cars coming and going.'

Marina's mother sat remembering from the little Polish restaurant where we ate.

'People were always on the move. Sometimes they were strangers, passing through, in ordinary cars. But the amount of dust on them told you the distance they'd come. In those days –' She paused. ' – in those days I thought that the distance was a virtue in itself. Travelling must be an adventure. The opposite of everything my own life seemed to be. I'd look out for the smart Charlemont crowd from London descending on us again. Then making off whenever they'd grown a bit tired of their big house. I thought it must be wonderful to be able to wrap your tiredness up into a parcel like that. Nothing, no place, would have to become too familiar to you. Whereas – ' She paused again. ' – my existence was the very – what's the word? – '

'For "opposite"?' I offered. ' "Antithesis"?'

'Yes. Yes, that. I felt too – I felt I was growing roots in that spot, through the concrete of the garage forecourt. It was such a dull little town. The road, it just carried other people through and past and away from us. There were days when it seemed I couldn't move. It sounds stupid. And in my head too, I couldn't think to do anything else – '

She fell silent.

'You had your husband, though,' I countered at last. 'And your daughter. Marina.'

She lifted her bleached bluey green eyes from the table and looked puzzled at what I'd just said.

'Marina?'

'Yes.'

'No, Mary Ann,' she said. 'My daughter was Mary Ann.'

We stared at one another.

'We christened her Mary Ann – '

'It's quite near,' I said.

'But it's different. From the name we gave her – '

I nodded.

' – from how I thought of her then,' she said.

'Did you know anyone called – ?'

She shook her head. It was an unnecessary question. It was enough that the name should have existed, for the girl to have been attracted and become intrigued by it. It had evoked whatever her own name – as she'd heard it used countless thousands of times – did not. A duchess and royal princess bore it. It was suggestive, by its derivation, of the sea: it conjured up the colour aquamarine . . .

The woman sat shaking her head slowly and sadly. When I went on to ask her other questions, about the town and her life there, she replied, not unwillingly, but in the same distracted, undemonstratively disconsolate way. Now she was only reciting to me her prehistory, and it was as disconnected from her present existence as the paper life of a woman in a library novel would have been.

NINE

I had a feeling – no, something much stronger: a conviction, surely – that Marina had wanted me to discover.

She knew, for instance, that I was – so to speak – glancing over her shoulder whenever she consulted her maps on our little half-moon dining-room table. I was being given these moments to remember, to mull over, to determine the relevance of.

I was to be her memorial-maker, a sort of conscience. It was as if she was living already with the full anticipation of her disappearance. I would be the amanuensis of her life, and if I didn't wholly understand and was tempted into some fictional touching-up, my own quiet myth-making exercise, then that was the risk she took with me.

In the pocket of Suffolk where she grew up I've found enough people who remember, or think they remember, or have powers of deduction, or the experience of place and time – that place, at that time – to offer me the material from which I can reconstruct a version of the young Marina who complements, but in surprising and contradictory ways, the one I encountered in her later life.

These are the voices, but they don't always speak with great assurance. There are gaps and silences where witnesses so-called cannot quite trust their faculties to be accurate, and all that is possible then is my sympathetic guesswork.

The constructions are mine, worked through these local recollections and through my own imagination, but I believe Marina must already have accepted the premisses. With what is available to me I have done what I think she would have understood I wanted to do for her: not to spare her (or myself, for that matter), but to forward some systematic account of how it happened – or might have happened – that she became the woman I married and tried and largely failed to know.

She was caught between history and personal interpretation, her own of events and others' of her. She was stranded between her hypothetical freedom to make an existence for herself and the ministering commands of fate regarding how that same life had to be lived.

As a child Mary Ann was never to be certain where the grounds of the estate extended to, where Saxbury ended and Charlemont began. It was a much simpler matter with the house itself, because a high wall skirted the parkland on the road side and, behind, several thick breaks of hedge functioned virtually as a wall to protect the property from intruders and prying eyes.

It wasn't quite a solid wall, however. Cracks could be found in those nether defences. Hands could prise back the branches of beech and conifer if arms reached in far enough, to catch a glimpse of the reverse activities of the Georgian house. At the rear were the kitchen, dairy, cold pantry, laundry, and stables. The staff weren't local but transported from London; they didn't mix in the small town, so they too were considered a valid sight – maids beating rugs or polishing silver and copper, the cook like all cooks that ever were sunning herself in her wheelback chair, the definitive butler smoking his master's (in this case, mistress's) Egyptian cigarettes, the renownedly handsome blond second gardener (another portable household accessory) prettily upended over his pots. The garage housed a maroon sports convertible and a long, graceful, dove grey saloon and any visitors' cars there might be. The stables were still stables and in use, because Miss Courtney had a passion for riding: she kept a selection of mounts for herself and her guests, and the sounds of whinnying and cobble-clopping could be heard from the unofficial footpath beaten by the curious along the edge of the cornfields, on the other side of the beech, yew and conifer palisades. Here and there holly grew, to catch the unwary or over-inquisitive: infuriatingly positioned, by accident of nature or by careful instruction, at just those points where otherwise you might have had the upstairs bedroom windows in your line of vision.

The gates on the east side – unlike the ornamental bronzed iron ones on the south, on the road side – were of stout wood. On the few occasions that it happened, they opened on to a lane which gave access to feeding and arable land farmed by the lessees. There it was, across the fields, that Lydia Courtney and her London company rode, keeping in trim for those less frequent outings when they dressed in scarlet and mustard and set off – hooves clattering on the tarmacadam surface of the Saxbury Road – to collect at a meet. They rode to their own hounds, a dozen beagles which barked and bayed from their kennels on one of the Charlemont farms.

Before the war – and even during it, when the rest of the country was on rations – Miss Courtney lived just like an aristocrat. She was said to move only with smart and fashionable people – invariably the freshest names – in her inner circle of social high-fliers in London, which seemed to constitute her native terrain. She lived rather better than an aristocrat indeed, since her hunting outfits were fitted for her, and her boots always had the shine of newness about them, and because her cars – one the maroon roadster, the other the long dove grey saloon – were always the year's current models. All her bills were paid to the provisioners directly on request; there was to be no shortage of food or petrol coupons where Charlemont was concerned.

In the locale she was everywhere known – known *of*, that is – but at the same time she remained the subject of conjecture by almost everyone. She had, literally, spoken to no more than a handful of people within a radius of two miles, excepting her fellow huntsmen, who demographically were a rule unto themselves. No staff gossip was available for the common consumption. The cars came and went, and they slowed or stopped for nobody. Two gardeners from Saxbury attended to their business in her absence, but they discovered little to tell, with the factor's auger eyes forever on the look-out. Returned to London, the mentions and photographs that appeared in magazines and newspapers over the years only made her seem remoter still: the omission of her name in a caption was simply keener fuel – to labour a metaphor – to feed the rampant flames of impertinent enquiry.

There were ways into the garden of Charlemont (which, in the days before Miss Courtney, had had another name, Ridgewood House), practical rumours that spread among the children at Saint Botolph's Church of England School.

You had to be sound of limb and nimble, able to compact yourself into a smaller version of yourself, to ease forward through the entry places known only to those and such as those. It was proof of courage to have made the crossing through close beech and bramble (holly for the most daredevil), and to return to tell the tale.

Inside the defences was where the true danger began, but nobody chose to claim that they had been spotted. The difficulty was in not making yourself visible after surviving the tunnel in, when you were in the grip of relief, elation even, but also gut-knotting fear.

The day Mary Ann did it, she took the advice of her predecessors and rolled forward like a hedgehog, like the human cannonball. She found that there was already a groove worn into the earth. The ground sloped, which she wasn't expecting, and that would have been enough to give her the momentum she needed without having to hurl herself forward as she did. As the garden loomed, a sward of running green, she found herself grabbing at branches to slow herself, so she wouldn't be propelled across the path on to the lawn. In the event she ended up – in a little scatter of leaves – on the path, which was a cinder-track, and a torture to land on. She grazed both legs, and didn't immediately notice that she'd cut her knee.

Firstly she had to get to her feet and hobble off, back into the shade of the hedge. Her legs hurt, and it was only after another half-minute or so of trembling against the crackling wall of beech hedge that she was able to unlock her neck and look down and see the thin, squiggly trail of blood. She blinked at it, then at a sharp angle of white sunlight on the ground only three yards in front of her. She blinked hard until brilliant colourless spots were dropping in front of her eyes, slowing to transparent tadpole flares, until her head behind her eyes started to fill with a blazing emptiness. Sickness churning in her stomach suddenly started to rise, it rushed up through her chest into her throat and she opened her mouth to let it out and to breathe in air. The sickness stuck in her throat, though, and all that spurted into her mouth was a vile bitter taste, smeared over the back of her tongue.

As she sat there, slumped against the base of the hedge and with the twigs scratching her back like nails, the sound of laughter – adult laughter – trickled from somewhere. It seeped into the white and greenness of the afternoon. Women's giggles and men's guffaws. The sounds approached. Mary Ann panicked. She tried turning round, but couldn't find the entrance. She pulled at the lowest branches of the hedge but nothing gave. She tore at the solidity of hedge and it clawed back at her. Frantically she looked to either side of her. Tears filled her eyes. She heard scrabbling behind the hedge; the commotion grew fainter and she realised that her friends whom she'd left there were running off and abandoning her.

Very woozily she was aware of footsteps, and of forms advancing her way. Men's tweeds, an airman's blue uniform, long trouser legs: women in swishing skirts or the closer cut of suits, wearing stockings and heels.

The red cinders crunched.

She stared up.

'So . . . What have we here?' a man's slow voice asked. Another man chuckled, and a woman behind him trilled *sotto voce*.

Six or seven pairs of eyes met Mary Ann's. Nobody else spoke. Everyone seemed to be waiting for something to happen. In the silence Mary Ann realised she was sitting and they were not. Inelegantly, with the blood inside her head singing in her ears, she got to her feet. A hand helped her when she was halfway up. She lifted her eyes, to the face of the man who had spoken, who was now smiling at her quite gently. Beside him, at the centre of the group, stood Miss Courtney.

Mary Ann was never to forget that first impression, and she would often consider the paradoxes of what she had seen. Close to, Miss Courtney was as arresting as the rumour of her appearance made her seem in their imaginations, a presence of imposing grandeur rather than beauty. Her face had the contours of a young woman's, with the suggestion of charm and naïvety, but somehow the same face, its effect, had been frosted. There was a certain glaze – of time and experience – superimposed on top of the original face, just as conspicuous as the heavy dusting of powder and the colour applied to the cheeks and the faint blue lining etched around the eyes.

The details all registered with the child, but not the implications. She had the span and scope to look and study, because this Charlemont version of time seemed hugely elastic and boneless. The lady's charm was temporarily switched off, the features of the face were set in a plaster mask. The mouth which smiled in the magazine photographs so often studied by her mother formed an expressionless straight line. A little tic started up in her cheek, beneath one eye.

Mary Ann watched, fascinated and afraid.

'Your fame is spreading, Lydia.' A man, the airman in uniform, was speaking. 'Now, you see, you have gatecrashers.'

'Hedge-crashers,' a woman's voice said. 'Toby told me he thought it must be foxes – '

'Have you seen any foxes on your travels, young lady?' another man asked her. 'Can you bring us any news of them?'

'I thought,' the woman's voice continued, 'I heard them last night from my window – '

'They bark.'

'This was crying, Torquil.'

'A deer?' a man's voice suggested from behind.

'No. Foxes wail like that. It's very mournful.'

Mary Ann looked from face to face to face. Her eyes were carried back to the silent Miss Courtney, because she was the most handsome and prepossessing person there, as well as the woman she must be answerable to.

Another man chimed in that it was easier to sleep in the city, even during a war. A woman's voice asked, good-humouredly, if he meant to decline any future invitations to Suffolk. The man replied, with equal good humour, that he was teaching himself Portuguese on the nights when he couldn't sleep, and Charlemont was terribly good for his irregular verbs. That led to a brief discussion of the advantages or shortcomings of Lisbon.

Miss Courtney wasn't saying anything, and Mary Ann now tried to keep her eyes from looking at her, sensing some danger. There was more chatter about what each of them could make their study in the night if and when they couldn't sleep. The talk ended with the man who was teaching himself Portuguese asking if they'd given up on 'Still The Night' round about here at Christmas time.

'Oh, Christmas is for cities,' Miss Courtney said.

'Any city in particular?'

'Anywhere with supper places that stay open. Party places.'

'Not yule logs and plum pudding?'

'I wassail,' Miss Courtney said in a light tone of voice and chiselled accent, 'in my own fashion.'

'Weren't you in St Moritz last year?'

'That's not a city, Lydia,' a woman interjected.

'I cheated. I admit.'

'Yule logs anyway, lots of snow – '

'Mercifully not *lots* of it. I needed galoshes, that was all.'

'Did you have a Christmas tree?'

'Not in the suite, Anthony. There might have been some about, I suppose. I forget.'

'Those damned needles that drop off – '

'But this year,' Miss Courtney said, 'Teddy can invite us all to Lisbon. If this bally war's done with by then.'

'Sintra, Lydia. It's awfully smart, you know. But *not* a city.'

The chit-chat petered out. Mary Ann had a feeling that it was helping to cover over the embarrassment of a situation that she had caused to come about by her own foolishness. It was all done jokily enough. The face of the man who had spoken to her first creased into kindly smiles. Some of the others' smiles were a little less confident, but the people themselves seemed to be in a party frame of mind.

Only Miss Courtney's smile was more frugal. Mary Ann guessed that she was irritated, notwithstanding the levity of the conversation.

But then, quite unheralded, the situation took a different tack entirely, to a conclusion Mary Ann couldn't have anticipated. She wasn't foreseeing anything in particular, only a trespasser's fate, whatever that might be. But, not credibly at all, the company moved off: not without backward looks, but those were forgiving enough. Afterwards, when she was back home and swaddled with her guilt, she couldn't recall if Miss Courtney had glanced back at her or not. No one even enquired what her name was, she fell behind them with the inconsequence of something glimpsed from a speeding car. The rejection was joy to her. Her limbs unfroze in the full, brazen heat of the sun directly overhead. She got back her breath. She found her balance again, she steadied herself, was able to look around her in the silence with the voices gone.

She left by the side gates. She walked all around the lawn to reach them. Nobody appeared, she wasn't stopped. No voice called across to her. She approached the gates as if she were wholly legitimate and entitled. A serious doubt occurred to her as she drew closer. But when she reached out her hand, she found that there was nothing to hold her and bar her departure. The gate swung open on its hinges, and she couldn't quite believe that it was offering her no resistance, as if it were constructed of modelmaker's balsawood and not the genuine thing, of solid English forest oak. She passed through and she was always to see herself in reconstructed time at a moment that might have been perfect, cutting a swathe between all the obstacles and imponderables of her life, as if they could never harm or deny her again.

Miss Courtney continued to appear in informal group photographs in society magazines.

Mary Ann found another magazine under her mother's

frilly covered chair in the living-room. (Her father still joked about her purchases, but a little more indulgently now than before.)

Of its own accord the magazine opened at the page. Photographs occupied a little less space these days (the saving of ink was presumably judged patriotic), but the face and the poise – both reduced – were instantly recognisable, even in far-off London, even at a charity ball.

The curious feature was that although Miss Courtney was positioned as far forward as the others in that group of women and was easily the most glamorous of them, the caption – in the dwarf typeface of wartime – failed to name her.

Mary Ann paired off the names with the faces, but there was one face too many. She thought the name's omission so unfair.

She returned the magazine beneath the skirt of the chair's cover, as if it were illicit contraband. It remained in furtive circulation for the next few days, Mary Ann noticed, either stashed in rumpled fashion under the chair or rolled up and secreted between the cushion on the seat and the padded arm. The next time she picked it up to look again at the photograph, a couple of days later, the magazine fell open with the sound of its binding ripping. The glossy page – a luxury for wartime – carried the prints of her mother's fingers, where she had been smoothing the surface flat. The paper was duller from the contact. Nothing had been said in front of her, or that she had been able to overhear, about Miss Courtney's inclusion in the photograph. She had watched her mother for some little betrayal of her curiosity in the woman, but could detect no difference in her behaviour from her usual. She made up her face with the same care, and was scrupulous as ever that her clothes were clean and neat.

Mary Ann felt that they themselves must be the most mundane and unexceptional people in the world. She couldn't be sure how a person like Miss Courtney connected to this utterly ordinary element of their lives at all.

In the evenings, when supper had been cleared away, Mary Ann would seat herself on one side of the dining-table with her homework while her mother seated herself on the other.

Her prevailing memory of their evenings was to be of her father with the oil cleaned from his hands reading his newspaper if there were no Defence duties and smoking his pipe, herself not very conscientiously working at her books, and her mother engaged in her dressmaking. She would hear the bowl of the pipe being knocked against the grate, her own fountain-pen scraping across the paper, and her mother holding and exhaling her breath as the big sharp cutting-scissors strode up-line and down on a length of the fresh material she had a knack of tracking down in those times of making do. A little later there was to be a sewing machine, an old third-hand trestle Singer, which her father bought to try – belatedly – to make some amends, since he'd realised how important it was for everybody's sake to satisfy his wife's silent pent-up wants and yens. The machine occupied her for hours, and she would sit up with it after the others had gone to bed. Mary Ann would get up sometimes and tiptoe downstairs and ease the door open to watch through the crack as her mother's foot and hands worked in a frenetic trance of activity: her head would be hunched forward, directly under the light, and her face – rapt – would be only inches from the stabbing needle. In just a few weeks she was able to turn the material as quickly as if she'd been doing it for years – with such intensity of purpose indeed that her life might have been depending on it.

From the time when she pushed her daughter about Saxbury in her pram Mrs Frith was always smartly turned out. She was maybe a little too much so for the town, where smartness was considered the privilege of the Charlemont set. Too methodical attention to one's appearance – even though there was no vanity in Mary Ann's mother's behaviour, only an extreme carefulness about maintaining her own standards of presentation – was supposed to indicate a mind that couldn't put all its thoughts towards industry and duty.

In Saxbury's preoccupation with the fulfilment of obligation, Mary Ann came to realise that there was, incorporated into it, a highly developed philosophy of selfishness. It was based on a perverse pleasure, a masochistic *frisson*, in self-abasement. Her mother however had exhibited none of those airs of self-congratulation which their neighbours did.

Applying herself to her dressmaking, the woman continued to live beyond the system. With the purchase of the Singer machine the process of ostracisation was speeded up. The dearth of paper patterns for men's clothes saved Mary Ann's father from the fate that befell his wife, but – more important to the general thinking of the place – he was the sixth generation of the Friths, so that the business of his marriage (in purely historical terms, sixteen or seventeen years assessed against three hundred and fifty) was all but irrelevant. Yet by her making dresses for their daughter also, the strain was to be inherited by another generation.

By the time Marina could afford to buy dresses that her mother had had no opportunity to, when she had long since realised that she hadn't acquired her mother's talents as a seamstress, she was moving in a very different milieu. Yet here too there were disciplines and hierarchies. She would never be able to get away from them, wherever she went in this England. She had more of the chameleon in her character because she was also the child of her father, the obliging garageman, so that she was equipped to disguise herself – her history and intentions – really by intuition. It took a long while to pass muster, though, partly because she hadn't complete knowledge and confidence to, and partly because the people she mixed with didn't wish her to either. So long as she could acquit herself as required in a public place, in a restaurant or a hotel bar, she could be whatever and however she decided in private, that was *her* privilege and the special attractiveness about her which men, interested parties, were quite willing in the fullness of time to pay good money to enjoy for themselves, behind closed doors.

Her mother ought to have known better about that ianthine coat I saw her in, supplied out of the previous season's reductions at Madam Murielle's. But she had not been in a position, so lowly as it was, to contest the point with her employer, who persisted with a notion of how expensively if not appropriately dressed her assistants ought to be. Mrs Frith – 'Miss Smith', as she called herself – toed the line, in that voluminous and over-pleated coat, in order not to lose her job. She needed money to survive if she was to be an independent woman: and hardly that, as she came to discover. Nobody was her own self, not even Madam Murielle who said one thing to her customers and quite another behind their backs, in the stuffy back room where employer and employee retired for their chipped cups of Lipton's tea. It was a fallacious condition. Only Miss Courtney, with the splendour of Charlemont to her name, had come close to the ideal: she, because Mrs Frith like her daughter and the rest of Saxbury needed to believe it, had been uniquely and unassailably placed in a paramount class of her own.

Mrs Frith was there in the house one day, and the next she was not.

It was as simple and as complex a matter as that.

A note was left, but it contained no more than instructions to her husband as to where which foodstuffs were kept, when to turn the mattress, how often the nets needed washing. No forwarding address was supplied.

She had taken a suitcase with her, so her going was clearly no accident. She had packed only personal things – clothes, shoes, some bits and pieces of 'jewellery' (as Mary Ann's father naïvely insisted on calling them when the police enquired), odds and ends of cosmetics. Nothing else was found to be missing – no photographs, no small mementoes of her husband and daughter.

In vulgar parlance she had cleared out, but without histrionics, as quietly and as tidily as she had always done everything about the house. Mary Ann tried to remember if she had actually witnessed the preparations herself, but failing to understand their significance. 'Not really,' she told her father when he asked, and that was properly overstating, because she couldn't recall anything particular happening on the day before which hadn't happened in the house hundreds of times previously. Her mother had never gone in for showing her feelings much, nor for letting others see from the expression on her face what she was thinking. The reserve and self-containment hinted at depths, but custom stales and you accept a state of affairs – even at thirteen years old – without wanting to define it or question it.

The police, although rushed off their feet, paid a couple of visits to the house. They read the letter, which dutifully covered both sides of the page according to Board of Trade directives. They examined the personal belongings left behind and compiled an inventory of those taken. They were very practised and matter-of-fact and kept the lid tightly closed on a stressful situation.

Nobody buckled or broke under the strain, however, least of all Mary Ann's father: although she felt that somebody ought to have done. As the days passed, the less likely that option became. With dry eyes Mary Ann studied the comings and goings to and from their house, and she quite factually observed those evasions that occupied passers-by when she had to walk to and from the bus stop at the beginning and end of every school-day. She scrutinised their apparent failure to scrutinise *her*, and wondered how much was furtiveness and how much was natural, accidental oversight.

That turned into the real conundrum for her in those hot and windless dog-days of a boon autumn.

At first her mother's disappearance was as much a shame to her as a mystery.

She understood what was being said about them in the town. She blamed her mother for leaving them in the lurch, and for spiking her with question marks like a pomander. She was conscious of eyes in the street following her once she'd walked past, and of the mouths quivering to begin speaking about her and her father and the selfishness of that woman when others were on munitions lines because good men were laying down their lives. The garage was kept as busy as it ever had been, but those who used it had attention for more than their vehicles and the Defence gossip.

The house seemed emptier – of course – but it also seemed to waver in its dimensions, to expand and shrink depending on her turn of mind. Sometimes she could be miles from her father when she kept upstairs. At other times she felt like Alice after she'd drunk the potion, head scraping on the ceiling and elbows bending the walls out. Her father had an infuriating habit of trying to fill all the silences, humming through them or coughing over them, rustling the pages of his newspaper. It was claustrophobia and an intensity of distance at one and the same time.

For a while she felt bitterness for the person she could believe had been the cause of their dreadful quandary. She put her photographs of her mother at the bottom of the drawer of knickers and vests in the chest in her bedroom, and attempted to forget all about them.

She seemed to be living herself in a new cold country. She didn't attend to her homework, her marks slipped, she didn't care very much. Her father took a different attitude, but she knew that he had to anyway, because adults were required to behave in certain ways. The exception was – had been – her mother. Saxbury talk made out that she'd been loopy, and maybe she had. Mary Ann still didn't have it in her to see that as hero-ism. She tried, but she couldn't. That left her feeling saddened and dispirited about herself, because she could do no better.

Afterwards she came to realise that her mother would have been ashamed of her for taking the town's side, and supposing only what was expected of her. She exhumed the photographs from beneath the pile of linen and placed them about her bedroom when her father wasn't there to see. The room would return, for a while, to something like its original proportions. The photographs calmed her. The room was also a refuge for her mother. One day she found herself crying for her, hot and peppery tears.

She started to feel a different, more complicated sort of shame. It grew and unravelled in all that time she found she now had to herself, sitting in the house – which sounded more silent the more her father struggled to disguise the fact – and watching the dullness of life in the town through the streaky windows. It was the view she had known all her life, but now without the advantage of her mother's netting, which had torn and shredded in the wash. As she stared out, Mary Ann felt her heart contracting in her chest, hardening to a shrivelled little apple at the sight of it. When she looked closely she noticed how much dust there was on the sills as on the roads, how weeds threatened wherever they might get a footing, be it along the edges of the pavement or high up on drain-pipes and roof tiles. Vegetation was seeding in the crannies where mortar had crumbled between bricks. Tedium was complicitous in the process of decay, because people's common inertia seemed to render them helpless to do anything about it. Saxbury was mouldering on all sides of her, it was eroding right in front of her eyes.

Mrs Frith never returned, so far as anyone was aware.

A small Christmas card, on murky vegetal-looking paper, arrived at the house that first year; it was signed by her 'Affectionately', but included no message. After that her husband and daughter didn't hear from her again.

She started to slip from Saxbury's memory as an individual, and failed to become a myth like Miss Courtney. Mary Ann was aware that this was so, but she didn't know whether she should be more thankful or insulted. Her mother was disappearing from them like a song, like smoke in rain. It was so easily and so callously accepted. Other people failed to distinguish between disappearance and death. She wanted to reverse what was happening and to ensure that her mother was *not* forgotten, even in her own home. She wanted to devise some memorial to her which would be unavoidable, which no one would be able to put out of mind.

There was something wrong with the Daimler, purportedly, although Mary Ann's father couldn't detect just what it was.

Miss Courtney herself got out to watch as he poked and prodded underneath the bonnet. The car was regularly looked over and serviced, both here and in London, so was kept in the very best nick. Even Mary Ann knew that, from having seen the priority attention it received whenever it was driven in and having heard the respectful exchanges between the chauffeur and her father. But Miss Courtney in person, without the chauffeur to offer an explanation, was insisting something was wrong. Mary Ann's punctilious father was keen to discover, and he tapped and wrist-twisted away.

'I shall wait inside for a few moments, shall I?' Miss Courtney asked him.

He was full of embarrassment as he looked into the office.

'Please go through into the liv- . . . the sitting-room,' he said.

'Oh no, Mr Frith, I can't trouble – '

'Please,' he entreated. 'Please do.'

So while Mary Ann watched from her bedroom window above the yard, Miss Courtney was shown into the house by her father. He was still wearing his overalls, which was something her mother had always steadfastly refused to have him do indoors. But Miss Courtney was an exceptional circumstance, and Mary Ann started to feel flustered herself about the state of tidiness in the rooms.

Her father called up to her, and she was obliged to go downstairs, after brushing furiously at her hair. She was in her house clothes: the cardigan had thin elbows, and her shoes were scuffed. But Miss Courtney gave a very convincing performance of failing to notice. She was seated in her mother's chair, perched on the edge of the cushion, looking as much the expensive châtelaine as ever. She smiled in the inattentive way she did whenever she was to be seen in Saxbury. It was a smile for strangers, but Mary Ann remembered it from that afternoon three years before when she'd tumbled through the hedge into Charlemont's garden, a smile also for her London friends: a workaday version of the cautious reflex-smile she aimed at magazine photographers.

Her father asked her to infuse some tea right away for their guest. Miss Courtney demurred, but Mary Ann's father nodded his head violently.

'The orange pekoe tea, angel, remember. In the good cups.'

' "Angel"?' Miss Courtney repeated.

Mary Ann saw her father blush. She felt clumsy herself, hot and sticky-wet under her arms. She retreated to the doorway and reached out her hand behind her for the brass knob.

In the kitchen she made tea in a muddle of spilt leaves and slop from the spout. She brought through the loaded tray. Her father had gone. After she'd poured, with a trembling hand, and handed across the cup and saucer not at all steadily, their guest motioned her to sit down.

'Thank you so much,' Miss Courtney said, as if she was receiving the hospitality of a very grand house.

Mary Ann seated herself on the sofa, in her worn bottle-green cardigan and the pale blue dress of sprig roses her mother had run up for her. She pulled the slack cardigan about her hips and tried to conceal one shoe behind the other, as if that way she might reduce her shame. She was mortified with embarrassment, not for her own or her father's sake but for her mother's.

Miss Courtney's eyes were fixed on her face, however, and might have been quite oblivious to what she was wearing. She was looking at her very carefully, over the vague smile, as if she was recognising someone other than happened to be there in the room with her. Of course their few family friends would remind Mary Ann and her father of the physical similarity to her lost mother, but she had always thought they were doing it to be just a little charitable. Now she wasn't so sure about that. Maybe all along they'd been afraid of the same madness revealing itself in her?

Mary Ann gazed in astonishment as Miss Courtney stood up and crossed to the door into the back corridor, closed it, and returned to her chair. She started to speak, quite quickly, in the sort of cut-glass accent women on the wireless used but with a very slight American twang mixed in with it. First of all she mentioned the afternoon of her rolling under the beech hedge into Charlemont's garden. Mary Ann caught her breath. Was the solicitude in her voice a trap? But Miss Courtney smiled again, attempted a little laugh, and waved her hand as if the entire incident had been a comic inconsequence.

Mary Ann turned to the window, scarcely recognising the view of the dusty High Street and all its accumulated tedium. A purply green cloud was trailing across a pink sky. A car backfired somewhere. A lone dog barked. She thought she could hear a knocking and testing sound from the direction of the garage workshop sideways-on to where they were sitting.

She looked back at Miss Courtney, who was watching her as if bemused by her apparent casualness. But that wasn't how it was at all, Mary Ann knew, not with her insides heaving as they were.

In her confusion she forgot the tone of concern and confidentiality she'd thought she heard, and failed to remember the little laugh. Had Miss Courtney come, three years later, to extract some punishment, some revenge, for her trespass into Charlemont that day?

'How . . .' Miss Courtney replaced the cup and saucer on the rickety poker-work table with the three bamboo legs, and set it rocking. '. . . how would you like to help me, Mary Ann?'

The girl was too nervous even to repeat the words.

'Would you like to do that?'

Fearfully Mary Ann inclined her head, not having a clue what the question meant.

'Would you like to run messages for me?'

The girl stared at her. She knew there was a household of servants at Charlemont. Enough of them surely to do all the fetching and carrying that could be necessary.

'Private messages. Just when I need you to take them for me.'

'But – ' It was all she could think to say. ' – but I have to go to school.'

Miss Courtney laughed: not in the polite party manner of her friends in the garden, but as if the answer assured her and she couldn't help herself laughing.

She took a few moments to compose herself. The words she

spoke next might have been worked upon beforehand, Mary
Ann was to conclude in the hindsight of future weeks.

'This would be very occasionally. I should drop the note in
here, you see. Garfitt will come in for petrol, and hand it to
you. You'll know when. At some regular time. We have our
own pump, you see, so this would be special.'

'What, though,' it occurred to Mary Ann to ask her, 'what
if I'm not here?'

'Then – ' Miss Courtney hesitated, but only momentarily.
' – then I shall have Garfitt give it – '

' – to my father?' Mary Ann couldn't prevent herself
interrupting. She immediately reddened at her rudeness.

'No. No, to Bob.' Miss Courtney spoke as if the rudeness
had gone quite unnoticed by her. 'That's what the boy's called,
isn't he?'

'The boy?' Mary Ann repeated stupidly.

'In the workshop. The tall lad. He's Bob?'

Mary Ann nodded.

'A very *private* message. I must warn you.' Miss Courtney
leaned forward in the chair that had been Mary Ann's mother's.
'No one must know about it.' She was intent on conveying the
full seriousness of what she had to say. 'I shall tell you the
recipient's name, and his address, but I shan't ever write them
out.' Mary Ann nodded, less confidently. 'And you must never
– *never* – breathe a word to anyone of this. Our arrangement.
Now – do you agree?'

'Yes.' A voice inside Mary Ann took command and spoke for
her. 'Yes,' it repeated, and the girl was doubly surprised.

Miss Courtney seemed relieved. She reached out for her
handbag. She opened it, took out her wallet and from inside
removed a note. She had second thoughts, and took out another.
She leaned across and pushed the two five pound notes into the
girl's hand. Mary Ann stared at them. It was more money that
she'd ever held in her hand in her life before. When she looked
up Miss Courtney was watching her. She seemed anxious. She
opened her wallet again. 'No,' Mary Ann said, understanding
only that there was a misunderstanding. 'No, please.'

The clasp on the handbag was snapped shut. It bit like two

gold teeth. Pirate's teeth. They belonged to this fantastical situation, Mary Ann felt. The notes crinkled in her hand as she folded her fingers over them. She was rich, like a captain of brigands herself.

When Miss Courtney had gone, she went upstairs and watched from her bedroom window while, down in the yard, Miss Courtney received her father's verdict on what might be wrong with the car. He was standing scratching his head, as if for once he was stumped to know. Miss Courtney waved her hand, meaning the matter mightn't be so important after all. She got back into the grey car, in her elegant manner. Mary Ann saw that when her father had his back turned and was directing her out of the yard, Miss Courtney's smile noticeably shrank. The woman looked more severe than at any point since she'd first driven in.

Mary Ann watched as she expertly reversed the car. She saw her raise her head and level her eyes on a diagonal at the height of the bedroom window. Mary Ann stepped back, but just too late and not far enough back to hide herself. The smile reappeared, it lifted a little on one side. The engine revved, and the driver looked down at her feet, as if she'd slipped her hold of the clutch pedal. She stepped on the accelerator again, this time more purposefully.

It was important for her – for a woman in those days of men drivers, and as the figure she was to awestruck schoolgirls like this one confronted with a man's world – to be seen in charge, of the Daimler every bit as much as her own destiny.

The letter's recipient had rented a lodge on an estate three miles south of Saxbury. The cottage, in story-book woodman's style, was the secondary lodge at the rear of the policies. The most obvious route into Saxbury was by the Harlden Road, but Mary Ann was familiar with an alternative route, a cart-track fringed by trees on one side and by more cornfields on the other. It was this back way that she took on her bicycle, knowing she ran fewer risks of meeting anyone. It was harder to cycle the distance, even though it wasn't so far as by the main road. Sometimes the bicycle wobbled and her arms would begin to ache trying to keep tight hold of the handlebars. Stones skittered and slithered under the wheels; ahead, rabbits turned white tail at the sound of her; she accidentally set off commotions high in the trees.

The name that might have appeared on the thick creamy envelope but purposely didn't was 'Leonard Askwith-Jones', spelt out for her just so by Miss Courtney as if there must be no possibility of confusion about it. He told Mary Ann he was a painter, from London. He had a wife, he also told her, but intending – she understood – to warn her. Another time he informed her he'd been a war artist, but was recovering from an operation on land-mine shrapnel in his leg.

Conveniently he mostly worked out in the fields by daylight, which meant that she didn't have to go to the lodge itself; but it did give her the additional responsibility of finding where he was. Fortunately he chose quite prominent locations to set up his easel, and she only had to keep an eye open for the blue of the large umbrella he always worked under, seated on a canvas stool and with a walking stick at his feet.

She didn't know what to make of his canvases, least of all when he invited her to look and make any comment she felt like making. She sensed that he wasn't very used to landscapes, just as she wasn't used to the modern methods of art or of judging them. He told her he might be better off painting what people expected to see, and she smiled at the remark, for want of knowing how else to respond.

He received her letters with downplayed eagerness, tucking them to read later in the inside pocket of his long linen jacket. He was a tall, lean, angular, rather harassed-looking young man with rapidly thinning hair. He had a very straight neck, and beautiful hands, and tended to peer through his round gold-rimmed spectacles. Mary Ann had spied on the lodge unbeknown to him, and had already observed his wife several times. She was almost his physical opposite, small and stocky and wide-hipped, with thick unruly curly black hair. She had heard her too, calling for her husband from the little kitchen garden: a voice to shout across gymkhana grounds or send booming between racing yachts, a lazy and chewy boarding-school-manufactured accent spare with vowels and diphthongs. An unbridled delivery would send the garden birds soaring full pelt for the cover of the trees.

In the evenings they kept their curtains open and Mary Ann saw their activities. On one occasion the woman initiated a boisterous game of tig, having her husband try to touch her with the tip of his walking stick. Another time she started to yell at him because she couldn't find something in the kitchen. On the third evening when Mary Ann again buried her bicycle in the bushes she saw the woman upstairs, alone in the house, combing out her hair at a mirror and turning to it side-on, this way and the other, to get a stranger's view of herself.

There were never any replies to carry back. Mary Ann was told by the man that they wouldn't be necessary.

He didn't once forget to thank her as he pushed the de luxe quality envelope and its contents into his inside pocket. He would immediately pick up his brush again and stab it into the colours on his palette. Sometimes she caught him looking at her, studying her for evidence of knowingness, but he could somehow suggest with his manner – holding the brush in his paint-stained hand – that he was only giving her the briefest going-over for artistic purposes.

She rather liked the implication, the subterfuge, even though she could guess quite well that that wasn't really the way of it at all.

It had never occurred to her that an artist could find something to paint round about here. The country was so flat, and so without drama. Just alder and birch trees, reminiscent of Russia, but the most English of cornfields.

Maybe the man was realising the truth of the situation. Maybe he also came to realise something about his own abilities, because a little later he appeared more withdrawn, even edgy in the way of his wife. He leaned on his walking stick and stared at the canvases and there was just the making of a scowl on his face. Mary Ann didn't like to look too closely, in case she should happen to find herself included in that disapproval.

He seemed less sure of what he was doing – with the canvases, and in this place – than he had been at the outset. He even considered the letters with more caution than he had, with an expression of unease and some foreboding. He received them from her more solemnly, and once she even noticed that his hand was shaking as she delivered yet another missive – a weightier piece of correspondence sealed inside the envelope, doubtless only one side to a page – hard on the heels of yesterday's.

The landscapes on the easels had become swirlier, more troubled, as if their remote corner of Suffolk was now a strain on inspiration. Had it started to bore him, like his routine here? Mary Ann felt that only Miss Courtney and her bird-of-passage friends were immune to the tedium of their locale; while she as a native knew all about Saxbury's consuming ordinariness. She tried to alert him to how sympathetic she was, by lightly sighing or stubbing the toe of a shoe into the flints at her feet.

Mary Ann also enjoyed the secrecy of those summer days.

The friends – the handful of proper friends – she had at the girls' grammar school lived as far from Elixton on the other side as Saxbury was on this. She had little company here, among her local contemporaries who thought a garageman and his wife had had ideas above their station, wanting her to be educated in a class of clever-clogs and aldermen's daughters.

She wasn't afraid to make her way along lonely rights-of-way and home again in the afternoons. Her after-dusk excursions were nothing to her either, on evenings when her father was out at his Defence drill, which had replaced the Masonic and Rotarian meetings of peacetime. She felt strangely elated with her fearlessness, not supposing that she should meet any Nazi in gamekeeper's guise to ask her directions in a fractured, guttural version of English. She possessed the place, colonising it – maybe as a final spell against misapprehension – with the animations she had believed in as a child: a tree with a trunk formed like a face, a brook burbling with a distinct chuckle between certain stones in its flow, a wooden bridge with rattling planks like a skeleton's jigging vertebrae. She also reverted to more tranquil, consoling memories – of

Sunday walks with her father and, more importantly, with her mother.

So, it was quite easy for her to give herself to the mission. At the same time she took pleasure in doing what she did behind Saxbury's stolid, heavy-set backs. That inevitably meant more than the Charlemont connection, because her only method of communication was the one Miss Courtney had stipulated on the fateful day when she'd called and taken tea, with her programme already well drafted in her mind.

The enveloping tedium lifted for those weeks. The weather held fair, as if propitiously. A rumour went about that among a succession of guests at Charlemont was the man reckoned to be Miss Courtney's keenest admirer and in all probability her future husband. Sometimes when Mary Ann cycled along the track to the lodge, she was following the wooded edge of a steppe, under a Baltic or Ukrainian or Siberian sky even more barrel-vaulted than their own, inhaling a tangier compote for her nostrils, of Rossiyskayan pine and fir and spruce. Her mind filled with a wider vision of the world. When the man emerged from under his blue umbrella at her approach, smiling a greeting to her, she recognised someone like herself trapped by circumstance: but, like her, he was capable of these same wild flashes of optimism.

Their going was quite sudden, like a flight by night. One day they were there, and the next not.

This had happened to her before.

She knew they were leaving when she saw the couple drive into the garage forecourt and ask her father to have the petrol tank filled. The easel had been roped to the lid of the boot, a suitcase secured with straps to the roof, and the man's wife was consulting a map and talking loudly enough through the open car window for Mary Ann to be able to hear her voice from upstairs in her bedroom. When the coupon book had been attended to and the car moved off, the rear axle was sagging and the chassis behind the back wheels very nearly scraped on the concrete.

She found the lodge in darkness as twilight fell. All the

windows were closed. The cycle track back had never seemed less Russian, less capable of being imagined as somewhere else.

She realised with the man gone how little she had really understood: about the particulars, of course, but also about his actual cast of mind. She had convinced herself that they might actually have certain character traits in common, because they were each exiles, strangers in this same strange land.

She was aware of the silence at home as she hadn't been since the days that followed her mother's disappearance. She also heard the lack of silence. The clock in the case on the wall. The cold tap in the kitchen scullery. Scurrying and scratching behind the skirting-boards. Every now and then a slow, dry sifting sound inside the walls, only inches away from her but invisible. The blood drumming against the sides of her head.

Another letter was left, but addressed to Mary Ann herself. Inside, above the signature 'Lydia Courtney', was a scribbled request – on one shameless side of the page – that she should 'present' herself please at Charlemont. The writer specified a certain time on a specific day. If – added as a qualification, or an afterthought – if it was quite suitable to her to do so. (Or was the tone, just possibly, acerbic? Suitability may have had nothing to do with it, Mary Ann thought. The letter might be couched in *politesse* while all the time the intention was to worry her with a concealed barb – an undeclared reference to her previous visit, her uninvited entry to the west garden by way of the beech hedge.)

But when Mary Ann did present herself, with knotted stomach, in the colonnaded front hall of the house and Miss Courtney was summoned, she found she was being treated with a great show of civility. (So demonstrative because it was, after all, only a ruse?) Miss Courtney conducted her from the marble hall with, first, a sweet and cryptic smile and then with a concise unravelling of the house's history. She led her into her little sitting-room, as she called it. To Mary Ann the woman employed a quite different vocabulary from the one she and her own sort spoke. The room was neither so little nor so informally furnished that she could imagine anyone quite being at rest 'sitting' there.

The décor was a rich heady mixture of chintzy English and Japanese exotica. Swathes of luxurious fabric – floral patterns for the loose covers and drapes with pelmets – but also the most exquisitely restrained oriental taste: a folding red lacquer screen decorated with ethereally fragile flowers in gold leaf, a tall yellow vase of white chrysanthemums, delicately patterned spread fans mounted on the walls. The carpets were Chinese, Miss Courtney explained when she saw the girl looking down in trepidation at her feet, Chinese not Japanese: bought for her in Shanghai and Canton.

'Have you,' Mary Ann asked, mouth drying, 'been to Japan?'

'I could tell you "yes", of course. People do ask. But I doubt if anyone could ever be certain.'

Miss Courtney smiled languidly, seeing that her guest was having difficulty with the reply.

'I lived in Paris for a while,' she said, in a slightly Americanised delivery. 'For a couple of years. But it was a long time ago.'

'When you were a child?' Mary Ann ventured to ask.

'Oh no. I was older. Old enough to think I knew my own mind.'

'Did – did you?' Mary Ann asked.

'Did I?' the woman repeated.

'Know? How you said you – '

'Oh that. Know my own mind? I – no, I don't expect so. That's pretty much an illusion, I should say. At any age.'

Miss Courtney smiled and Mary Ann wished she knew where she was with her. When she seemed to be speaking lightly, the woman's expression grew more serious. When she was speaking seriously about something, her movements were fluttery and throwaway and her eyes had a glint of ridicule in them.

In the silence Mary Ann looked away. About the room, she noticed, were distributed wide shallow bowls of dried aromatic petals and leaves. Where she had been invited to sit, she was midway between two sources of the lush but faintly bitter, nippyish scent that smelt of no garden she could imagine.

Afterwards tea – real tea – was served to them, and they drank it formally. They drank not in the Japanese fashion, but in sips from fine cups with handles.

'Is geography one of your subjects? At school?'

'Yes. Yes, it is.'

They both nodded.

'Have you been there?' Miss Courtney asked.

'To – to Japan?'

'To Paris.'

'Oh *no*,' Mary Ann said.

'Wouldn't you like to go? If you save up hard, then you might be able to.'

Mary Ann wondered at the remark, if Miss Courtney was a woman who knew the advantages of hard saving. She had always supposed she must be automatically rich.

'One day maybe, Mary Ann.'

'Yes?'

'I had a Japanese friend. A friend of a friend. In Paris. She told me about her life there. Her quite extraordinary life.'

Mary Ann was silent, not knowing if any fuller explanation might follow. But the matter of Paris – and Japan – was left where it was, more secure in its past. A tiny sigh rolled over the back of it and that was all. The smile on Miss Courtney's face that replaced her sigh was proud and stoical.

It was to prove a most curious afternoon altogether. Miss Courtney didn't seem to be angry, let alone irritated, by what had happened concerning the unspoken-of Leonard Askwith-Jones. She didn't even seem sad. In Marina's adult recollection, her attitude was that of resignation. Perhaps there was relief mixed in with it too, that a train of events which could be taken no sensible stage further had reached its conclusion. Matters, such *affaires*, could too easily get out of hand.

'Should you like a keepsake?' Mary Ann heard Miss Courtney suddenly ask.

She wondered if she could have heard properly. Had the question been directed to *her*?

'Of course you are too polite to say so. Please – ' Miss Courtney rose from her chair. ' – come with me.'

The girl stood up, and followed the woman from the room. They crossed the broad hallway to the staircase, to the first flight of shallow steps. There were three such flights to the first-floor landing with its pillars. From high overhead daylight cascaded down, but subtly radiated into various conflating shades of the prism by panes of stained glass in the skylight.

Miss Courtney opened a door and led the way into the first of two rooms, the anteroom of a bedroom. An older woman was seated at a table by the window. She wore pince-nez and a pink pleated satin turban, and held herself grandly as she plied her needle. She must have thought a maid had entered because when she deigned to turn round her face was immediately put out of countenance. Her mouth, in shocked silence, articulated an alphabet 'O'.

'Miss – Miss Courtney – '

The woman's cheeks flushed, as if the colour had run from her turban.

'Please don't let us disturb you, Madam Murielle. I only mean to find something in the tallboy.'

She stopped by the table.

'What beautiful work, Madam Murielle.'

'Well, it's such fine silk, Miss Courtney.'

'Do you remember that length of green last year? The jade?'

'Indeed, Miss Courtney. I've never seen shades like these foulards.'

'It was you who suggested I might try this – '

'Ivory, Miss Courtney. So refined. And you have the complexion for it, the skin tones.'

Miss Courtney smiled, and was thoughtful for a few moments while the woman resumed her sewing.

'You have given me an idea, madame.'

'I have, Miss Courtney?'

'One moment, Mary Ann – '

Mary Ann stood still and waited while Miss Courtney passed through the second doorway and disappeared, into the bedroom

beyond. After a few moments she switched her eyes and
watched the speed with which Madam Murielle was turning
her needle, like someone bewitched.

Hadn't this happened to her before . . .?

The sounds of the woman's breath lapped about the room.
Mary Ann felt she had been granted entry to – to a succession
of magical sea caves. The light was greenish, filtered through
the trees outside and tempered by the folds of green velvet
hanging at the windows. Mirrors placed here and there, by
no haphazard arrangement, bandied the light about, into secret
distances. The patterned oriental carpet had a bluey silverish
sheen. A blue glass chandelier shimmered with crystals, like
the salt quartz stalactites of a grotto. The dark walls were
veined on the heights of embossed plush like skerry rock. A
log split in the grate of the fireplace and sparks rose into the
lightlessness of chimney like tiny darting scarlet fish, in a rush
of subterranean wind . . .

She refocused her eyes in time to see Miss Courtney
returning, pulling the door of the bedroom quietly shut behind
her. The woman walked towards her, holding something in her
hand – a very small object, nestling in cotton wool.

Her gift for her was a miniature ivory carving, a 'netsuke'
as she called it, a toggle fastening for a kimono. The oval
was carved as a face: a dragon's or a lion's face, with
wide eyes and with a mouth gaping open to form a deep
grooved aperture where conceivably the head of a pin might
have fitted. Mary Ann was more fascinated by the thing's
strangeness than she was attracted by its appearance. Miss
Courtney told her that the piece had been a gift to a lady
friend of hers from a Japanese noblewoman she had got to
know – and work for – in Paris. 'Didn't I mention that?'
It was regarded as a fine example, given to the Japanese
woman by an elderly woman in Kyoto whom she in her turn
had known.

Mary Ann stood fingering the netsuke. Minuscule teeth were
serrated about the edges of the mouth, just inside the lips. The
sides of the head were carved with the sweeping contours of a
mane. Eyebrows, of superhuman amplitude and ferocity, met in

the space between the eyes, on the low bridge over the broad
flat nose.

'Please take it as a token,' Miss Courtney said. 'As a
memento. It seems nothing much to you at the moment, I
dare say. I quite understand – '

Mary Ann glanced over towards the window and saw Madam
Murielle watching her with the most intense interest, needle
motionless between her fingers. She dropped her eyes again
to the streamlined oval of ivory she held in the palm of her
hand. The face was almost human for a moment or two, before
it resumed its animal character. The expression might have
been of vast ineffable boredom, a self-devouring yawn, or else
one of fervent fury, or maybe of something worse – ill intent
and malice.

She was intrigued, and she was flattered, and she was a
little afraid. The object's lineage was quite daunting. When
Miss Courtney placed her hand on her shoulder, she jumped.
Behind the squeak of the woman's smile she heard the lapping
sounds of Madam Murielle's breath, washing softly against the
shadowy walls, like hidden reefs. The pressure of the hand
remained, both gentle and at the same time persuasive as it
compelled her to turn, back to the door through which they
had entered.

Miss Courtney had a condoling spirit, Mary Ann believed,
she had sympathy, and it was exactly that quality which her
own life since her mother's vanishing had lacked.

How curious, then, and how disappointing it was to prove to
her, that she should never have contact with Miss Courtney
at Charlemont again.

She did continue to come about the town, but infrequently now
that her visits to her property were markedly more seldom than
of yore. In future years the house would have its shutters drawn
for, in toto, nine or ten months of the twelve. Children weren't
so tempted to go rolling under the hedges into the garden since
the chances of discovery were less.

Naturally, in the period following the Askwith-Joneses'
departure, no further messages were left at the garage. In that

lenghtening after-time no more artists appeared in the locale, either bearing easels or passions to be assuaged. A new rumour concerning Miss Courtney did the rounds, to the effect that one of her friends – the famous male companion/confidant – was disapproving of a number of her other friends. Another rumour claimed that she had taken out a mortgage on Charlemont to finance another purchase, and that she was dependent in her dealings on the very friend who was apparently so insistent that she should expend the time she would have given to her 'set' on himself instead.

Since she didn't reappear, or did so so very rarely, the general presumption in Saxbury was that she had swallowed her pride and done the decent and (because not, by any report, 'wifely') the 'womanly' thing.

The silence of the long afternoons.

A tap dripping into the deep stone sink in the kitchen. The movements of the clock: sometimes sober and funereal, at other times fraught and racing to hysteria. Scratchings behind the skirting-boards. The straining of the timber joists as the temperature changed throughout the day, like joints cracking, a ceaseless readjustment. Twitching sounds upstairs, maybe scurrying and scrambling. The fretting of a certain branch on the scullery window. Coals falling in the grate, sparks hissing. The sifting of dust, the crumbling of masonry perhaps, behind the walls.

Mary Ann knew the geography of every wall in the house: how the paper lay, smooth or wrinkled or cracked, and the intrigues – the ins and outs – of every paper's pattern. Sprigs, latticed trellis-work, urns, domes and cupolas, palms and minarets, moons and stars. She could close her eyes and be transported, from room to room through the arabesques of repeated motifs into the plane of objects depicted on that flat paper world.

But eventually it held and trapped her just as the other world did when her eyes remained open and she made her way leadenly through the house. The furniture shocked her with its dead weight, its immovability: subservience which had become the opposite – domination. The thinginess of things, all the artefacts in their lives, appalled her. So often she felt the air stuffy, cramming itself into her nostrils and mouth and down her throat. Or if not, the air – contrarily – thinned and thinned until she was having to open her mouth to gulp at it, to keep herself breathing, a terrifying lack of something vital to her life.

When she panicked she had to lie down – on her bed, or on her parents' bed, or on a floor, anywhere. But then the ceiling would seem to come lower the longer she kept her eyes fixed on it, the walls felt nearer as she stiffened her arms and reached out in readiness to push them back with the primed tips of her fingers. So she would have to get up, have to keep moving, not sit down but not let her concentration lapse either as she paced about, from room to room, room to room, just in case.

Those were her worst days. The rest were merely unendingly wearisome. The hours dragged, like the scimitar of fogged brass in the case clock on the living-room wall. Tedium was the foe – the very same foe – and she found it at every turn, too dreary to become any friendlier with, so excruciatingly, ruddy bally damned bloody predictable. She longed, she ached, for surprise, for whatever might be different. As it was, nothing changed. As it was, had been, and always would be, for ever and evermore. So help us, Jesus Christ Almighty. Amen.

The hereness of everything, and yet if she allowed her eyes to close . . . The things became less sure, less oppressive. There were moments in the day, of stupendous and grandiloquent perceptiveness, when she saw the hereness and thinginess as provided for no lesser cause than to *be* her surroundings. Then, she was almost ready to accept them, to take them upon herself, to believe that a superior harmony applied to the separate dullnesses of her existence – the familiarity of items of furniture bought in salerooms from the circumstances of other people's lives, the drips of the tap into the stone sink, the smell of food that lingered in the curtains, the infestation of moss on the outer north-facing windowsills, the diagonals of rose sprigs extending from her dress up and across her bedroom wall into presumed infinity. She imagined then that all had been devised so just for her benefit, that there was a purpose to it, that she could un-wish it if and when she wanted to and re-create her life in another place, for a future of novel manufacture. They were there expressly to serve her, and the whole world existed as she perceived it far behind her eyes, in her mind. Even the flying sparks in the grate defied gravity and soared skywards.

But she would lose that selfish clarity of insight. It would shrink from her and fade away; the atmosphere of tedium soaked it all up again. It was quite useless to try to fetch it back, it was gone. Things reverted to the fullness, the massiveness of their solidity. Firstly indifferent, then – gradually – defined by their hostility towards her. Again she was a trespasser into enemy territory. The air was either thick with conspiracy or thin enough to kill her, to collapse her lungs perhaps but failing to leave a single mark on the outside of her person. Exteriority meant all.

Everything physically was defiant and incontrovertible. Ruthlessly three-dimensional, here was the terror of dreams granted literal form.

But the fire grew cold for lack of attention and the cinders paled and gave no more light.

She – Marina, my wife as she was shortly to become – was walking up Sloane Street, at speed, as she had a tendency to walk now. She kept to the side further from the traffic and closer to the shops, but not *so* close that a figure emerging from a doorway could possibly have reached out a hand and laid hold of her. She was permanently in suspense, in a state of alarm, but chiefly for signs of human danger: hazards, that is to say, emanating from people.

Which was why, that day in the spring of 1957, she was to be so astonished, ambushed – indirectly – not by a person but by an object, an *objet*.

She was watching the reflections of passers-by in the plate-glass windows, and making crab-like progress. Then her eye was caught, through the reflections. She slowed at once. She stopped in her tracks.

A gallery window. Two paintings rested on stands. That on the left was as familiar to her as her life, although she had never set eyes on it before.

She stared at the signature. *L. A.-J.*

She was immediately horrified.

A view of trees, a corn yellow foreground. An easel. A blue sun umbrella. The artist himself was missing, but standing just beyond the easel and umbrella was the figure of a girl. While her face was shaded by the umbrella, her youth and curiosity were both rendered quite clearly. One shoe kicked up dust from the flint track. Behind the girl, among the brushstrokes of vegetation, a bicycle was just detectable, placed there by deft, economical suggestion.

The whole painting was effected in a simpler and more accessible style than she remembered from his canvases on the easel. Now she could tell the elements apart, which she hadn't been able to do then. Everything in the foreground was clear and apparently defined. There was nothing there for the public to fear.

But she wasn't the public, not in this case. Even as she tried to look at the picture objectively, critically, she was terrified.

She couldn't move for a long time. She knew as she stood there, as transfixed as the girl in the frame, that she was making herself so much more vulnerable than she ought to be. It was the coincidence as much as the painting itself which kept her rooted to the spot with disbelief. She had the evidence of the thing, and its happening to be here at this moment, so – she also knew – she had no grounds not to believe.

She smiled into the back of her hand. She felt like an atheist caught out by a miracle. She shook her head, and saw herself – while someone moved behind the window glass, perhaps disturbed by her posture – being of all times and all places. It was as if the world, after all, was pre-coded for us in advance. Our experience, our destiny, is written out for us even before we're born, and all we do is live out our own story, obeying its rhythms and rhymes.

A car backfiring restored her to her senses. She jumped
with the shock of it. She looked back over her shoulder. A
different sort of hostility, the kind she'd been living with for
weeks, paraded these streets. Slowly she turned back to the
window, to the painting secure behind the thick glass, resting
on its stand.

The girl in the picture seemed to be waiting on the threshold
of something, didn't she? Watching the girl watching, she could
see now other reasons for the painting's happening to interrupt
her life at this juncture at which it had. The little canvas inside the
large canvas was – she only noticed at this instant – blank. The
girl, like herself, was anxious to view what might appear.

View what?

A prospect of trees? A cornfield? Or the figure of herself?
– just watching, herself and herself and herself ad infinitum?

Thirteen years later the woman stood asking herself, could
she shift into a different story, might she redirect herself now
into another fiction altogether?

TEN

I found Marina's father living in a small modern bungalow, the last in a cul-de-sac of identical small modern bungalows tacked on behind Saxbury. The name End O'Lane Cottage was slanted in wrought-iron script across the front latch gate into the garden. In the red sandy soil hydrangeas grew in abundance, top-heavy with sagging heads now faded. On two sides of the house were beet fields, on a third a cornfield. Just visible was what might have been a bridle-path or cycle track.

Mr Frith was his own master these days, with only himself and not customers to think about. The furnishings in the house weren't what I was expecting: voluptuous flower prints on the curtain and chair fabrics, a reproduction Georgian dining-suite in the alcove, by a window a small reproduction knee-hole desk on which he was constructing an Airfix kit of a Wellington bomber. The kit apart, and except also for a glimpse I had through the kitchen doorway of spanners and screwdrivers sticking up out of a unit drawer, the house was kept impractically spick and span. But I guessed the man's natural condition was not tidiness, and that domestic help – like the furnishings – had been wished upon him by someone else.

He acknowledged as much in his first remark to me.

'I suppose this must be about my daughter?'

I couldn't deny it.

'She told me not to talk about her after last time.'

' "Last time"?'

In the spring, he explained, a smiling and uninvited guest had come calling. In a waxed two-tone Sunbeam. A Mark III saloon. Not many such appeared in this back end of Saxbury, let alone stopped. He'd been immediately interested, of course, and so his tongue was loosened up for him.

'And – might I enquire – ' My question seemed to be inviting itself. ' – who was he?'

Mr Frith shrugged.

I took another tack.

'Why shouldn't you have spoken to him, though?'

'I thought he must have lost his way or something like that – wanted directions.'

'But that wasn't why he stopped?'

'Mary Ann told me no.'

'Who was he? Do you know?'

'*She* knew. She guessed. I didn't ask. She doesn't tell me much about what happens. In London. But anyhow, I shouldn't have spoken to him – '

He gave me a once-over. He didn't know what to make of me, quite obviously. But he wasn't a suspicious man by nature. He was lonely probably, and wanted to talk.

'Do you know Mary Ann?'

'Yes,' I replied. 'Yes, a bit. But I'm a friend.'

'That's all right, then.'

I had told him as much as he needed to hear.

'I've been trying to find her, you see,' I said.

'You too?'

'What?'

'Like the man was?'

'We – we shared a flat for a short while.'

Her father expressed no surprise.

'She's been away,' he said.

'Yes.'

'I thought, maybe I'd have got a postcard from her. But . . .'

It was she, I learned, who had arranged everything at End O'Lane Cottage. Except, I presumed, the name: but she had been agreeable to that, too, in as much as she recognised that it gave her father satisfaction. She wished for his contentment, or the notion of it. He was her link to a past she didn't mean to sever herself from completely. Even her present name was only a rejigging of the old one.

There were no photographs that I could see, nor any other explicit mementoes of the past. It felt more of a house than a home, as the song goes. The décor had unmistakably been concocted at a distance. My host was on his best behaviour, probably because the domestic help was morally responsible to the woman who paid her wages. The sofa had a firmness in the seat and a pile to the fabric which suggested that it was rarely sat upon. An arrangement of dried flowers on the teak sideboard exuded an occasional sour whiff, like neglected perspiration.

He moved like a man encumbered, with drooping shoulders. About the garage he had walked tall, I was to discover, but less so after his wife's disappearance; he would only aspire to his full original uprightness when a fancy car from Charlemont drove on to the forecourt, causing the cable-bell to somehow ring with a shriller authority than its usual.

From a drawer he produced a business card. I thought it was his own. But the name was 'Bullivant', and the address – bracketed 'Agency' – was one in London, 'Caldicott Court By The Strand'.

I turned the card over. Another name had been scribbled in ink on the back. 'Miss Hay.'

'He gave me the card. The man, my visitor. He said if I had any news to pass on to him, could I tell that young woman. She'd make sure he got to hear about it.' I memorised the address and the printed name and handed back the card. I knew where I must call next.

'You must mean Hotten. *I'm* Bullivant.'

The man spoke as if there could be no doubt, not from the brief physical description I'd been given by Marina's father. We were sitting in his office, four floors up on a dim yard off the Strand. The 'Chandos Agency of Investigation' consisted of two small rooms and several scraped and buckled metal filing-cabinets. As I arrived, a secretary was valiantly flicking a cloth at the dust and soot on some of the higher surfaces. She stopped when I reported for my appointment. Once I was admitted to talk to Mr Bullivant she started again in the vicinity of the office door, which had been left a little ajar.

'There was a parting of the ways,' the man properly called Bullivant was telling me. 'Not entirely amicable, but business is business, isn't it?'

He looked over at me. A radiator groaned. I nodded.

'It was a case of keeping this business *in* business or letting him take his wages and then go swanning off on his moonlighting jobs.'

Mr Bullivant sat back in his revolving chair. It slanted badly to starboard, and one of the castors screeched every time he repositioned his weight on the seat.

'"Moonlighting"?' I prompted him.

'For some of our less savoury visitors. Those who've wanted me to take them on as clients. I'd say no. Then I would find out that he'd got in touch with them behind my back. That he'd taken on the work himself.'

'What sort of work?' I asked.

'The sort you'd expect from people with grudges. Probably a lot of the types I do take on have them too. But I don't give my time to folk who wear them on their sleeves. So to speak. People who just want their revenge, I don't deal with.'

I nodded sympathetically.

He asked me what my interest was. I disclosed to him just as much as I knew. He told me, he was sorry but he couldn't help me there. I mentioned the use of his name, and the agency's. I watched the man's face redden with anger. He asked me if I was certain. I assured him that I was.

'If he went down into the wilds of Suffolk, it must've been worth his while. When was this?'

I explained. The man got to his feet and crossed to one of the filing-cabinets. He sifted through a sheaf of papers inside a folder. But in the end he learned nothing, and apologised that he couldn't be of any help to me in this regard.

That effectively was the end of our conversation. I took my leave, surprising the girl in the other room who was hovering with yellow duster in hand just outside the door. Her employer noticed and nodded to her to return to her desk. He looked behind him, into his room, then closed the door before accompanying me across the general office and out on to the landing. Beneath us the curving stone staircase and wrought-iron balustrade receded down five floors like the coil of a spring, like the tunnel of an ear.

I shook the man's hand. As I turned to leave, I noticed the secretary's arm and shoulder visible behind the thick corrugated glass panel of the door. I remembered afterwards – the picture remained – and I was already in two minds myself when the telephone rang in my Greenwich flat a couple of days later and I found it was she who was talking to me. She hurried through the clumsy formal introductions. 'My name is Hay – Miss Hay – Grace Hay – ' When I'd left my coat on the stand, she said, she'd been so bold as to look in my pockets for some proof of who I might be and had found an unsealed envelope and, inside it, a note with an address and telephone number I'd written. (A scribbled communication with Trenor, I realised.) I thought at first she meant she'd been carrying out her employer's bidding: but in fact she'd done so for her own purposes.

We met one evening, as she requested, in a tea-shop on Theobald's Road, behind its windows dripping with condensation.

The girl was in her twenties, skinny, pale and freckled, with a sharp bony chin and large heavy eyes.

We ordered tea, and it was brought. Hot strong urn brew, as brown as coffee, slopping into the saucers.

She explained unashamedly that she'd overheard the conversation in the office. She realised I was keen to know certain things. But so was she.

'I have to find Reg, you see.'

'Reg – ?'

'Reg Hotten.'

'Doesn't Mr Bullivant know? Where he is?'

'They had a real to-do, whatever he wanted you to think. They've both got quite a temper on them. But I don't know where he's gone. He may not even be in London.'

'It's important to you? To find out?'

'We had this . . .'

She paused tellingly, with the narrow points of her elbows

on the table and the cup cradled in her hands. It was difficult
for her to paraphrase the relationship between them, with its
obsessive impulses and tensions.

I nodded my head.

'It's Reg's wife, you see. She leads him such a dance. She
demands so much. I don't know how he's put up with it for
so long. But – but he has.'

She stopped. She replaced the cup in the damp saucer. She
crossed her hands on the table top. Small neat semi-transparent
hands with their network of blue veins alarmingly visible. She
placed one on top of the other in a bid to keep them steady. Her
gamine eyes, Judy Garland eyes, darted about the room.

She had understood about the money, she told me. Why
he'd had to go behind Bullivant's back, because of his wife's
airs and graces and her way with money. To a girl who
could believe herself so much in love, I imagined, it was all
perfectly logical.

'Before Reg left – left London, I mean, before we lost
touch – he'd been to see a woman. On one of his cases. A
Mrs Eglantine – '

I started at the name. I repeated it.

' "Eglantine"?'

'She called herself something else at first. They usually do.
But I found out what her real name was.'

'What kind of case was it?' I enquired.

'Adultery.' She shifted in her chair. 'Supposed, at any rate.
She'd come to the office.'

'Bullivant didn't take her on?'

'He goes by his instincts. He's correct most of the time.
Adulterers – ' She shifted again. ' – they're usually easy
pickings. But something must've persuaded Mr Bullivant, that
he shouldn't get involved this time.'

'And was he right?'

'I don't know.' She shrugged. 'Perhaps. But Reg isn't here
to ask.'

'He took the case on?'

'I know he was going to, yes.'

Mrs Eglantine was described to me, in quite some detail. A

woman in her late forties. Mink coat to her ankles, the sort of coat Reg's wife could only dream about. The finest kid gondola shoes. Plain features, starting to sour. Expensive perfume. Rouge, plenty of concealing powder. Manicured hands, and thin but strong fingers, probably better than a wrench at wresting the tops off bottles and jars. A thick gold band, and an engagement ring of diamonds and emeralds, worn next to a spindly unconvincing ring of imitation gems.

'The cheap ring puzzled me,' the girl explained. 'Eventually I cottoned on. That it must've been her original engagement ring. When he could afford to, her husband bought her the other – and a new wedding band – to replace what she had. But she'd kept it for sentimental reasons. As if she was defying people. You know, daring them to say something, make a joke of it. I got the feeling, though, you don't try to cross *her*. Not Mrs Eglantine.'

It seemed as if fate was drawing me to this name, or rather to this person, a figure very slowly acquiring shape if not – as yet – any definite purpose in Marina's story and mine.

'Do you know,' I asked, 'what she told Bullivant?'

'Her husband was deceiving her, she said. With a woman. She was sure so. But she didn't know the details.'

'She wanted – what? – '

'To get evidence.'

'To take to a lawyer?'

'Oh no. To confront her husband with it, I expect.'

'But not to make a case with it? A legal case?'

'Well, I can't imagine she wanted to *lose* him. Do you?'

She stared at me, very seriously and intently. No alternative reading was possible, the look implied.

'She wasn't going to give him up.'

'No?'

'I'm quite certain of it,' she said.

'And your – your friend Mr Hotten – '

'Whatever she needed him to do – I suppose she asked him – '

'And he agreed?'

'They're easy money. As I said. The best. I see the books and the figures – '

For a few moments I wondered if she was spinning me a yarn, leading me up a long and meandering garden path. But the intentness didn't leave her face. Her mouth didn't once threaten to break into a smile.

'Do you know where she lives?' I asked. 'Mrs Eglantine?'

'I didn't discover that. Her vowels, they still had something of the East End about them. She'll fight like a vixen not to give up her new life, I can tell you that.'

'Why – ' I pushed my cup and saucer aside. ' – I don't quite see why you've told me all these things.'

'You can't?'

I shook my head.

'I didn't think you would have come to the office if you hadn't been quite serious about whatever it is. You told Mr Bullivant about the man you'd gone to see, your wife's father – and the man *he* told you about.'

'Maybe mine is another adultery tale too?' I said.

'*You* don't believe that, though?'

I stuck my elbows up on the table and clasped my hands to my cheeks.

'My wife has disappeared,' I said. 'Your friend knows something. Why should he have gone looking for my wife's father in the back of beyond? I have to find her.'

'Of course you must.' She touched one of my elbows with her child's hand. 'I understand that.'

I looked past her, into the hot room where love – or lust – did its furtive, zealous work among the pairs of customers. How confidently and imaginatively Marina might have hypothesised about them, as she used to do in Castlebay.

Life outside disappeared behind the misted windows. The tea urn spluttered and hissed, and heads bent closer.

I remembered a paragraph I'd read in the *Telegraph* or *News Chronicle*. I remembered against all the odds. Yet it was my memory – for the printed word – which had commended me

to Trenor, and it was that which had made me a better editor
than some, able to carry the whole of a novel in my head for
an intense period of concentration on a manuscript.

It was the mention of the two-toned Sunbeam Mark III. I'd
noticed a newspaper photograph of one upturned in a ditch and
suggested to my current novelist that it would help to make the
anti-hero's car in his bleak new book somehow more distinctive
on the page.

I dug out the newspapers in the British Library and worked
my way back through the daily editions from the early summer.
It took me two entire afternoons, but I finally found the
photograph. The story referred to a road accident which
had occurred in West Sussex a few days before I gave
up on London, six or seven weeks after leaving Joan, and
before I moved down to Castlebay for a change of scene.
The photograph showed the Sunbeam lying on its roof. I saw
again the resemblance that had caught my eye the first time,
to some felled animal with its wheels helplessly airborne. The
accident had taken place on a stretch of road between two
towns thirty or forty miles along the coast from Castlebay.
The driver had been taken to hospital. His physical condition
was reported as 'satisfactory'. What had probably also taken
seed in my imagination at the time was the mention of his being
found to be amnesiac.

I deduced which hospital.

From the records I learned that the patient had remained
in care for ten weeks. His memory had returned, but fitfully.
The official diagnosis contained a number of question-marks.
Perhaps the patient hadn't wanted to remember everything.

He had given his name as Cyril Bullivant, with a business
address in the Strand. Described as between thirty-five and
forty years of age in the file, I recognised the wily presence
in the bed as Reginald Hotten's.

I thought of telephoning Miss Hay, but I wasn't sure what
I could tell her. If he *had* lost his memory, presumably he had
recovered it, or recovered it selectively.

*

After enquiring from one to another, I found the garage where the Sunbeam had been transported to after the accident. The owner could still bring the matter quite clearly to mind. He'd discovered that the steering traction system had been severed at one point and re-soldered in very makeshift fashion. The repair would have fooled nobody. But the severing had been cleanly done, as if by no accident. He told me it wouldn't have taken a genius to realise that anybody driving the car was heading straight for trouble. There were easier ways of ensuring that a car would go spinning out of control, but with failed steering on these coast roads, the result was guaranteed to be spectacular.

Undoubtedly my next step – an act of chivalry if nothing else – should have been to let Grace Hay know. My course of action was surely quite clear.

I didn't get in touch with her, however. My initial hesitation glaciated into something else. I tried persuading myself that I should only be confusing the issue, alarming her when it might be unnecessary, raising false hopes. But in truth I was afraid of confronting her, and of seeing a reaction, and of having to respond myself to her anxiety, her trembling mouth, tears. With Marina there had been no tears, not once: in that respect she had been quite unlike any woman I'd ever known. I didn't think that at this juncture I could face emotion again. Life was easier, mess-free, without ostentatious and vulgar sentiment, when everything could be contained inside a person and asserted itself only as rote and ritual, as the observances of devotion and (sometimes) of sacrifice.

Tommy greeted me like a long-lost friend. He presented me with a whisky sour, even though the bar was closed.

'On the house, sir.'

He asked me if my wife was with me this time. I told him, no.

'Does she approve of the beard, sir?'

I tried to be as convincing as I could in my replies to his

enquiries. He talked nostalgically of the wedding. I smiled to hear him again, but rather sadly.

More than ever Tommy reminded me of a young American, with his fresh crew-cut and good, lightly tanned skin and sportsman's stockiness. As he spoke, I was wondering if he had felt any romantic stirrings in himself for Marina at the time.

I walked about the town afterwards. There were already Christmas displays in some of the shop windows. The sight of coloured light-bulbs strung across Gane Street on drooping wires filled me with despondency.

Back at the Beaufort I had two courses for dinner in the dining-room, which was virtually deserted. Then I returned, inevitably, to the cocktail bar and to Tommy.

At first I sat by the fire, but I grew tired of the restive, fizzing logs. I moved to the counter, and hoisted myself up on to a stool.

Perched up high, I drank too much. By my third whisky – single, and 'straight, no chaser' as one of Trenor's countrymen might have expressed it – caution momentarily lapsed. Tommy was too much of a professional to miss the hint of a revelation. He came back to the matter later. I asked for another whisky. He was reluctant, but my voice must have been full of pleading.

'I won't disgrace you,' I told him. 'Won't fall off my stool. I promise you.'

In the course of the fourth whisky it came out, Marina's leaving me so mysteriously. I knew as I was speaking, trying to scoop up the words and then set them in order like threaded beads, that I might come to regret my candour. But Tommy, I was quite aware, was discreet.

He too opened up to me, by a sympathetic instinct. He too made himself vulnerable. He unfastened his wallet and showed me a photograph. Another photograph. It was a head and shoulders shot of a young man of about his own age. Short hair but dark, a good lightly tanned skin, a neat moustache, sportsman's build. A smile broke on Tommy's face, he couldn't help himself. He lowered his head, but beaming with pride.

A brother? I was wondering. Or just a friend? Then it dawned on me. I watched how tenderly he took a last look at the photograph before folding his wallet and returning it beneath the counter.

'Colin works in a hotel in Mildencombe. He's a barman. I learned some of the tricks of the trade from him. He comes here when he can, or I go over there.'

I nodded.

'That's where I saw your wife first, you see.'

'Where?'

'In Mildencombe.'

'You saw Marina?'

'At the Imperial.'

'When, Tommy?'

'A couple of weeks before she came here. Or ten days maybe. But it was definitely her.'

'Oh.'

It didn't immediately occur to me how significant this incident must be to our story.

'She didn't recognise me, when she came on to Castlebay. But I'd been in the bar – at the Imperial – keeping out of the way, so the other staff wouldn't – well, you know – put two and two together. About me and . . .'

I nodded.

'At the Imperial she'd had other things to think about, I guess.'

'What things were those?' I asked.

An intuition had me straighten up on my stool.

Tommy hesitated. He was well intentioned. I wasn't too tipsy not to realise that. I appreciated that he had an honest face, a temperament without edge.

'I don't know who the man was. Someone she wasn't expecting to see. I don't think she knew him. He started talking to her, but Colin told me it wasn't an accident, he'd been in before as if he was looking for her. She was sitting on one of the bar stools and he joined her. He said a name to her – something like "Ellington", "Elgington" – and she went sort of rigid.'

'Eglantine?'

'It might have been, sir. Yes, something like that.'

'Go on, Tommy.'

'She asked him how he knew about her and he didn't say very much. Then she asked him if he had something to do with Mrs – '

'Eglantine?'

'Yes.'

'What did he say to her?'

'Colin got called away for a few moments. I wasn't looking very carefully, but she shook her head and then she laughed. In a stagey way. Whatever it was wasn't amusing to her, she wanted him to know, but she was treating it as a joke. Then when Colin got back he heard her telling him, "I don't believe you." She asked him why he was letting her know these things. Then something about, why should anyone want to harm her? Really harm her? Then the man saw Colin was close by, and he nodded that they should move to a table. She hung back, but I suppose she wanted to know more, so she went with him.'

'Did your friend hear anything else?'

'No. I picked up just a little myself, but I didn't know what it meant.'

'What did you hear, Tommy?'

'She asked him, what if this woman found out that he'd told her? He said he hoped she wouldn't. Because she wasn't a woman to get on the wrong side of. But this wasn't the kind of job he wanted to get himself involved with. He'd been stupid to take it on. He understood that now.'

'And – ?'

'He looked round the bar and I don't know if he suddenly didn't trust any of us, but he took her arm – gently, though – and got to his feet. So did she, and then they left. Went outside.'

'Did you see them again?'

'No. Not the pair of them.'

'Did your friend?'

'No, he didn't.'

'That's as much as you know?'

'Yes.'

'Did she return to the bar?'

'Once. The next day, Colin said. She was by herself. She seemed jumpier than she'd been before. Coal sparked in the fire behind her and she shot up out of her stool. She wasn't very talkative with Colin. Just to say that she thought it was time for her to be moving on.'

'Moving on to where?'

Tommy tapped the polished wooden counter of the bar.

'To here, I suppose, eventually. After wherever she went between there and here.'

'You recognised her again?'

'Oh yes. At once, as soon as she walked in. But she didn't realise I'd seen *her* before.'

'You didn't say?'

Tommy shook his head. His visits to his friend at the Imperial were not a fact to acknowledge to every stranger.

By implication then I wasn't a stranger to him. He was telling me something he wanted to disclose to me, because he felt it might be of some assistance in the circumstances. All the time he'd been there, behind the bar, as witness to our high-speed courtship, he'd had his prior observations at the back of his mind. He had let himself be swept along in this business of romance because – perhaps – he had seen the common need demonstrated by the example of ourselves, Marina and me, to belong especially to somebody.

The whisky had turned me sentimental. I placed my hand on Tommy's arm, on his wrist. I shook my head, just like an actor in a film, really because I couldn't think of anything else to do. I wanted then to believe the best, the very ultimate best of everyone: of everyone involved, by contrivance or by accident, in this labyrinthine story of ourselves.

Back in my bedroom upstairs – the expense of accommodation didn't matter to me now: I'd sell some of my books if I had to, to cover it – I tried to piece things together.

Marina. The unidentified man who spoke to her at the Imperial. The upturned Sunbeam with its steering system wrenched asunder. Mrs Eglantine. The Chandos Agency. Amnesia. Marina's father, End O'Lane Cottage. The tea-room on Theobald's Road, the condensation-soaked window. Love and lust. Grace Hay. Tommy. Tommy and Colin.

They spun around in my head. Words repeated themselves in my ears.

Why are you telling me these things? Why should anyone want to harm me? Really harm me? But she's not a woman to get on the wrong side of. The sort of job not to get involved with.

When I got to sleep at last, my dreams were waiting to shanghai me.

A faceless man sitting in the cocktail bar of the Imperial Hotel. Colin's moustache. A woman's perfume. Coals crumbling and sparking in the fire. Lipstick on a cigarette. Then myself driving the two-tone Sunbeam along the coast road, the switchback. The steering system going dead between my hands. Flailing at the wheel. The car careening across the road and roaring for the darkness of trees.

I woke in a streaming sweat, my head flew straight up off the pillow. I stared into the darkness of the bedroom. Slowly, while I recovered my breath, objects shaped themselves out of the black. Moonlight from the sea seeped around the edges of the curtains.

She was *some*where, Marina. I knew it, I knew positively in the silence of the night. She hadn't vanished off the surface of the world. There was a point upon it where she was to be found. Find it and her I would.

On Sundays – as Bullivant has helped me to discover – the Eglantines are patrons of the Caroche. They have lunch there every Sunday, seated at the same table, in that fetching room decorated with Topolski illustrations of the famous etched on to glass.

The crowd is fashionable and expensive, people who hold to the tradition of the occasion – Sunday lunch – but who have reasons for not eating at home. They acknowledge a domestic rite, they give it sanctity, but publicly, away from the physical confinement and mental claustrophobia of their own homes.

They may well be of an age in fact, the Eglantines, but she appears older than her husband. Maybe her manner is responsible in part – her motherly fussing as she gets everything right on the table, the hard looks she turns on whoever impinges upon them, a bitter little twist to her mouth which she sometimes remembers to conceal from him behind her napkin, the tenseness she tries to rub from her bony shoulders when he is looking the other way. She patently isn't at her ease, although she goes through all the social motions.

The years have treated her husband sympathetically by comparison. Her hair is an unlikely, too even tawny shade while his is black flecked with grey, a natural effect that's commonly held to be 'interesting' and 'distinguished' in a man. His face is fuller than hers – she seems quite gaunt at certain moments – but fuller in a hearty, boyish, extrovert way. He has a slightly ruddy look, yet it's a healthy complexion, the sort a Saturday rugger-player might have grown into. She is much more pallid alongside, with too little spare skin to take a good colour. When he relaxes, his smile has charm. Whenever *she* makes an effort to appear relaxed, her smiles are fraught and unconvincing. She seems primed against anything that will disrupt the contrivance of outer harmony. He may well be a straightforward hail-fellow chap, but from where I sit I'm left with the suspicion that he has obliged himself to come here with her. His compensation is the general company, which he lets his eyes survey every time he lifts his glass to his lips and whenever movements past their table provide an excuse for his distraction.

Once a plate falls from the table: her arm shoots out as if on a spring, and she catches it in her hand. Another time he tries to undo the top of a salt cellar; he can't, though, or isn't attending properly – she takes it from him and, with the strain of the effort pulling in her neck, she unscrews the top from the bottom with her thin, strong fingers. She has knobbly but powerful wrists: everything she does with her hands is exactly controlled. Her shoulders flex, sinews jerk in her forearms. A great force seems compressed inside her. She is coiled like – like a mother lion, I decide lamely: although I surmise that she is no mother herself, giving every indication of having a morbidly selfish closed-circuit mentality.

Nothing eludes her. The food and drink are the least of it. She is watching how the room is watching *them*. She intercepts every pair of straying eyes. She tries to, as it were, ring the pair of them in barbed-wire. But she can't be in command for every second, with a view on every angle. Briefly I enter her orbit of attention but I am a man and it's women on whom she fastens that gimlet gaze. Any of the younger women, younger than she, gives her temporary cause for concern. Sometimes older acquaintances pause and speak *en passant*. Her face is only a mask of conversance, however, the minimum which is required for appearance's sake. Alone together again, her features acquire a terrible fixity and inflexibility now and then, when she sits back in her chair with such affected ease and she studies the effect on her husband of a current of movement here or there in the room. The atmosphere of well-heeled and dressed-up domesticity – married couples and families – intensifies her grave disquiet. I can believe that she hates it, but that she puts herself through the ordeal of this observance to confirm that they can creditably pass themselves off.

I didn't give an account of my exploits and discoveries to Trenor. He would have told me, too much light and *certainly* too much shade, my dear young chap.

A viper like Mrs Eglantine would have been well beyond the pale. He wasn't a man for heroines and villainesses. Such sloe-eyed manipulators belonged to trashy pulp novels, to silent movies with story-board titles, to vampland. He would have shaken his head, laughed in his benevolent way, but on this occasion wouldn't have been curious to know more. 'Next one, dear chap, next one!' (He only ever travelled on a bus to hear a remark of the clippies that particularly delighted him. 'Move along now, please.

Move along, if you will' – and I always mentally applied the words whenever a story idea was despatched to the pile of cast-offs.)

I was learning the knack of anticipatory censoring for him if not for my much less clear-sighted self.

Eglantine's retail business dealt in high-quality electronic goods, mostly hi-fis. He owned a number of shops in west and north London. On the profits he drove a Bentley Continental and ate out in restaurants three or four evenings in a week. He entertained others in his line of trade – senior company representatives, and occasionally owners of shops he had an eye on with a view to purchasing. The restaurants he patronised with his custom appealed to those who believed themselves in the van of things, metaphorically rubbing shoulders with fellow smart dressers and quick-thinking entrepreneurial types on the rise and rise.

I asked Trenor again about the woman who'd once made enquiries about me.

'Which woman was that?'

'Who knew I worked in libraries. Who invented the story about a family tree.'

He removed his spectacles and closed his eyes for a few moments to remember.

'I'd forgotten,' he said. 'But, come to think of it, I don't think I've ever seen her again. Are you disappointed?'

'No.'

'*She* must've forgotten too.'

I didn't reply.

'You're not in the market for work, Charles?'

'No,' I said. 'No, I'm not.'

'I don't have rivals for your services, do I?'

'Not' – I smiled. ' – not that I'm aware.'

'Good. A woman like that – '

'You remember what she looked like?'

'A virago, a harridan. Mean mouth. Her hair – sort of gingery
– *not* what she was born with, I tell you that.'

In the restaurant Mrs Eglantine had been wearing a little
pill-box hat, with a veil pulled back, but I had remarked the
hair: brassy-coloured, a lighter hue of copper.

'Handshake,' Trenor said, 'like I don't know what.'

'Like – a fish?'

'A shark is an elasmobranch, I do believe.'

'A *strong* handshake?'

'Like fury, my dear young chap.'

He laughed as he replaced his glasses on his nose.

'To work, *mon ami*, to work. Before I lose you for ever to this
temptress – this filcher of young men and their ambition – '

I had Tommy's photograph of our wedding day, and I took that
with me when I called in at the larger hotels within easy reach
from the coastal road, on the stretch between Mildencombe
and Castlebay.

I drew a blank at the first three. At the fourth, the
Monopole-Metropole in Welbornhaven, the tables were turned
on me, in a manner of speaking. The woman at the bar had been
pinning up Christmas tinsel when I enquired. She stopped her
work and considered the only piece of evidence I could offer
her. She raised her eyes from the photograph to myself. She
smiled with a recognition that meant nothing to me.

'But you came here months ago. Didn't you? April, May
time?'

I stared at her.

'I remember.'

'You do?' I said.

'With your photograph.'

'A photograph?' I repeated.

'Yes.' She laughed at my literalness. 'Yes, of course.'

I turned the photograph round on the bar counter.

'Are these flowers for a bride?' she asked, pointing.

I nodded.

'It wasn't a wedding photograph, though,' she said. 'Was

it? Last time. I don't remember a wedding. I'm sure it wasn't that.'

'Me? You remember me?'

'Well, it must've been.' She laughed again. 'I remember the face in the photograph. You asked me, did we get so many beauties in Welbornhaven that I could confuse her?'

'I did?'

'And you told me to take a good look.'

For a few moments I actually thought she could be making it all up. But then I saw the puzzlement in her eyes.

'It was *me*?' I said.

'Wasn't it? I could've sworn . . .'

She looked several times between the face in the photograph and my own.

'. . . when you walked in.'

'No,' I said.

'You had your beard – '

'No.'

'Are you sure?'

'Positive.'

'But it *is* the woman in the photograph. The same woman. Holding the sunglasses. That's easier to remember.' She laughed again: an embarrassed, distracting giggle. 'I kept my eyes open after that, you see. For a while. Until I forgot to.'

'Why were you supposed to be looking?'

'Because he had news for her, the man. Important news. I asked him, was it a windfall? He hesitated, I remember. Then he said, possibly. I was thinking, well, it either is or it isn't. But I couldn't know really, anything about it. Could I?'

She was going to touch the white border of the photograph with her fingers. She stretched them out, but then withdrew them at the last moment.

'A bearded gent. You're *sure* it wasn't you?' she asked, sounding more anxious again.

'I'm quite sure,' I said.

'Ah.'

'Can you tell me what he looked like, this man? Apart from the beard.'

'Well – not so very different from yourself. Your height, build.'

'Age?'

'I don't know. Thirty odds. Thirty-five.'

I ignored the implications of her answer.

'Hair?' I asked.

She looked at my own. She nodded vaguely.

I nodded also. Her haziness was understandable. From the other side of the bar I must have seemed a common enough type. Five foot ten, medium build, my proper body weight, receding brown hair, no identifying features. A full beard. The essence of blandness, in other words. I stood wondering what on earth could have been my attraction for Marina: if not in fact my very ordinariness, my being so average. Some commendation of myself that was.

'Did you think,' I asked, 'there was – well, anything odd about it? His behaviour?'

'But *you*'re asking me too,' she said.

'Yes.' I nodded. 'Yes, that's very true.'

'It seemed natural enough. That he should want to find her, I mean. He said she was in the area. I tried to be helpful, to seem that I was. I told him "no" politely. He wasn't surprised.'

'That you couldn't? Help him?'

'Oh, but I *could* have done. That's just the thing.'

I stared back at her.

'Oh yes,' she said. 'I knew that I'd seen her. I couldn't have mistaken her.'

'You told him that?'

'Oh no.'

'Why not? Why didn't you tell him?'

'Because I'd seen the woman was afraid. At first I thought she was just preoccupied. But it was more than that. Feminine intuition, let's say. The relief when she saw it was a woman behind the bar. Keeping out of the way of the other customers. Drinking neat gin to keep her spirits up. Something about the way she sat, hunched and twisted round on the chair. How she would look up every time the door opened – '

'That's why – why you didn't tell the man? That you'd seen her? Because you were sorry for her?'

'I suppose so, yes. And – I have to say – something made me distrust him. His smiles. Foxy smiles. And those dog's teeth.'

'But,' I said, 'now you're telling *me*?'

'*You* don't smile like him. You don't have dog's teeth either – '

'You can be sure? About him and about me?'

'I think so,' she said. Her expression was attentive and serious.

'You confused us, though,' I persisted. 'A few moments ago.'

'The photograph confused me. Because you too were asking me about a photograph. That hadn't happened to me before. If it happens twice, and about the same face – '

I nodded.

'And this,' I asked her, 'is the woman you served? The woman in the man's photograph too? Both of them?'

'The same woman, yes.' She bent forward and looked hard at the photograph. 'She asked if I knew how to mix a Blue Something-or-Other.'

'Lady,' I said. 'Blue Lady.'

'But I didn't have all I needed. Some liqueur. Made with bitter oranges, was it?'

'Curaçao?'

'Yes. Yes, that's what it sounded like.'

I cleared my throat.

'You see,' I said, 'we were married.'

'Yes?' She lifted her head, examined my face. 'But – but why are you asking me? If this is your wife. Is . . .?'

A silence encircled us.

'My wife has gone missing,' I said.

'Oh. I'm very sorry – '

'Well . . .' I gave her an awkward smile. 'It was after you saw her that we married.'

'Really?'

'We married suddenly.'

'A whirlwind affair?'

'Yes.'

'How romantic!'

'In Castlebay.'

'Castlebay?'

'Yes.'

'She was asking me what it was like.'

'She did?'

'I guessed that was going to be her next port of call. After here, after Welbornhaven – '

I took the photograph back. I replaced it in my wallet. With a fingertip the woman traced an oblong on the counter top where the photograph had lain between us.

'You saw her,' I said, 'very shortly before we met.'

'You must have taken her mind off her problems. Whatever they were.'

'I don't know,' I said, '*what* they were.'

'You don't?'

'She kept them from me.'

'She didn't want to burden you,' the woman said.

'Maybe – ' I debated whether or not to say the words. 'Maybe – she didn't think she could quite trust me enough – '

The woman shook her head, either in disbelief or commiseration.

'You didn't see the man again?' I asked.

'No. But I told the woman the next time she came in. What he'd been asking me. That was her last time in here.'

'What did she say?'

'She didn't speak about it much. Apart from going over one or two of the things I'd told her. But since she didn't come back after that, I don't know if I *should* have told her or not.'

'What happened? That last time?'

'She had another gin. She opened up a road map. She seemed to be making up her mind about something, working it out in her

head. I could tell by the way she got to her feet when she'd
finished her drink. Quite positively. How she smiled over at
me. Bright, sure. Recovered. Not how she'd been the day
before.'

'So – it was all right that you told her?'

'I didn't see her again. I can't know one way or the other.
I just had to hope so. That's all.'

The solicitude in the woman's words stayed with me for
the next few days. It was a comfort, until I started to lose
faith a little in the efficacy of that hope. What secrets had
Marina been guarding, and why couldn't she bring herself to
share them with me? Had I proved to be so little capable in
her eyes?

I asked my next questions at the hospital where they'd taken
Hotten after his accident.

Had the patient who called himself Bullivant been clean-
shaven or bearded when they found him?

Clean-shaven, a nurse recalled. A doctor who'd taken an
interest in the amnesiac's case confirmed as much.

'He was quite particular about his appearance and his
hygiene.'

'Could he have shaved it off just before?'

'In my own experience,' the doctor said, 'it takes the skin
some days to recover. He had quite a deep tan on his face.
All over his face and neck – '

So the other man who'd been enquiring about Marina, in the
lounge bar of the Monopole-Metropole, hadn't been Hotten.
Hotten must have been warning her about someone. About a
man she had to be very careful not to encounter if she valued her
safety. The prospect had driven her to no-nonsense neat gins,
even though in the few months of our life together I had never
seen her drink alcohol straight as it pours from the bottle.

It came into my mind one Sunday afternoon when I was walking
down by the Thames for a bit of exercise. I don't know why I

should have remembered what I'd forgotten for so long, since the days when I'd first made Marina's acquaintance in Castlebay. But why else should Trenor have called me 'Charles Swale the Memory Man'?

Perhaps a gull squawked, or came swooping low. What had been one sound among many, or a flash of movement in the corner of my eye, distended in my mind until I was sitting again in the cocktail bar of the Beaufort Hotel. It might have been one day or two before I noticed Marina for the first time: or it might have been the very day itself.

I checked through my files at home, until I found it. The news story, which had appeared in one of the West Sussex papers, dealt with the subject of seagulls. Several had dropped like stones out of the sky one weekday afternoon, into a number of gardens at the west end of Morpington by Sea, the town next to Welbornhaven. (I'd sat picturing the apocalyptic scene to myself, wondering idly about its suitability for Trenor, maybe just as a detail within another story. A harmless blue sky, the plummeting birds, a little flurry of white feathers like spiralling snow in a hot summer.)

The tone of the article steadied . . . Small puncturing holes had been detected in the flesh of the birds. In each case reported to the police, forensic investigators confirmed that bullets were the cause of death. Although no evidence to this effect had so far been received from the public, it was assumed that pot-shots had been taken by a person or persons unknown.

All the bullets matched. They had been fired not from a long-barrelled shotgun, a rifle, but by a revolver. Someone in the west quarter of the town must surely have heard the gun going off, although since the incident happened in the middle of an afternoon police accepted that residents might have assumed any noise was owing to a car backfiring on the cliff road. The police admitted that the person or persons who had undertaken the live target practice might well be out of the area by now. They were asking locals to recall if they'd had dealings with any strangers to the town who might conceivably have committed or conspired in the deed.

One woman recipient of a dead gull was quoted, to the effect that it had missed her baby in his pram by no more than a yard. Another spoke of the heartlessness of the perpetrator, to have taken pleasure in the slaughter of God's innocent creatures. A third person, a retired army major, had done a double-take when he saw white feathers floating out of his drawing-room fireplace. More dramatically, a fourth, a housewife, claimed that a white candlewick bedspread airing on her washing line had shown a bloody trail, like a stigma, in the shape of the curling stave of a question-mark.

Perhaps the dead gulls were intended to bluff her. Or perhaps they were genuinely, seriously, the objects of target-practice, and somewhere in the vicinity of Morpington by Sea was a man trying to perfect his aim.

Whichever, Marina must have been frightened. She couldn't afford to take any risks. Mrs Eglantine was an unknown quantity, a woman not to be crossed: she might be crazed with jealousy and she was paying the wages of a man with a gun and offering proof of a sure eye and steady hand.

In Castlebay Marina timed her steps to coincide exactly with mine. As we walked (I, ever the eager gent, on the outer kerb-side of the pavement) she countered bluff with bluff. We moved as one.

After a week or ten days maybe a fancy took hold of her, as it did me, to see what it might be like to live as others lived. She would have to become someone else in the process, or alternatively she would need to subtract much of what had made her the person she'd been. She may have been wearied, bored, grown temporarily indifferent, so that it seemed to her as plausible a next step as any other. I was as ignorant as she was, and just as directionless in that interim. It was only marriage that we eventually found ourselves contemplating, no more than that. She had the example of her parents to warn her off, but she may have imagined that she could somehow reconstruct *their* experience, by cancelling out its failure with the demonstrable success of ours.

ELEVEN

The trail went cold for a while, and I had to get on with my life as best I could.

Then in the springtime of 1958 Rosalind Wilks wrote to me from Chesters Avenue, asking if I had been over to Monmouth Square Mews of late. If not, I wouldn't have seen the 'To Let' sign nailed to the post in the garden. She'd gone out of curiosity to the agents, and of course they hadn't believed for a minute that she was an intending client. Never mind, she *had* learned this, that the house had been rented all along. She had only ever supposed, since she hadn't been informed to the contrary, that the house was Marina's own. She had made an additional enquiry or two and been told, while the man sat fidgeting at his desk with impatience, that the occupant had decided not to renew the lease. 'Do you know why *he* . . .' she had probed. But the man, although pen-rattling and paper-rustling, had been alert enough not to fall for that. 'It was held on a long lease,' he told her, repeating himself. 'The occupant has decided not to renew it.'

That was all he'd had to say on the matter, but she thought that I might be interested. Could I make anything of it?

It gave Marina's life in the mews lane a temporary, less settled air in retrospect, which I was grateful for. Did that mean she'd been less dedicated to her style of life there than I had naturally assumed?

I doubt that it did. It meant only that she had been a free agent. She didn't need to be dependent on individuals, nor would she fall into the mortgage snare which took the collective legs from under the bourgeoisie. Her glamorous, *recherché* mode of existence was a masquerade but no accident, since it required

vision and a particular aesthetic good taste. She knew that
you could appear to be such-and-such, on the surface, while
she understood just as well that it's the compulsions of the
submerged inner life which truly define us. The refined top
surface was a necessary article of faith for those county
aristocrats and *arriviste* businessmen alike, with their overload
of frustrations and repressions.

So why hadn't I hit on the circumstances earlier, when I'd
stood outside on the cobbles observing the red brick Dutch
house? Everything I saw had been just too, too correct. I ought
to have been capable of reading the evidence, like hieroglyphics.
At the time, though, I had lacked a developed instinct for irony
– unlike Marina, who'd had no trouble viewing a situation in its
three dimensions. She could detach herself *from* herself and
walk a circle, of the woman called Marina, of the husband
she had married, of the circumference of our bijou flat, of the
walls of the bespoke residence like a doll's house in Monmouth
Square Mews.

In 1965 I received a letter from Italy, from Trenor in Forte
dei Marmi. Again he recited a litany of names, of those
acquaintances with whom he'd been spending time – *some*
time (I guessed) but never too much lest he outstay the
welcome offered him as an outsider.

In the course of his rambling report – and properly *à propos*,
since he was more involved in recounting his own circumstances
– he mentioned that the branch of Van Cleef & Arpels in the
French resort he'd visited before travelling to San Remo – to
stay with the Seldens, who were entertaining the Gruenbergs,
friends of the Cabots – had been instructed to sell a diamond
they were referring to as 'The Star of the Desert'. Mrs Hugo
Buckholz had told him and, as good as her word, taken him
to see. The vendor was anonymous, details of the diamond's
history were intentionally being kept to a minimum, but he had
good reason to believe – from the Buckholzes' source, who was
involved in the sale – that care was being taken not to offend the
sensibilities of certain individuals in an Indian dynastic family.
They might be expected to take umbrage at the business should

– should (the conditional had been stressed) – their attention be drawn to it.

That was as much as my correspondent told me. The implications didn't strike me at once. A week passed before I took to considering those seriously. The diamond. The daytime glow of the photographer's flash-bulb. Marina's secretive interest in the newspaper report, her telling me she had discarded it. Her behaviour in the crowded vestibule of the Pompadour, the intensity of her concentration, the sudden draining of blood from her face. Her turning from me to the wall. Her disappearing without a word out on to the street. Our standing together on the cold, draughty corner waiting for a taxi.

I really had nothing to go on. I didn't know what to do. Marina was a stranger, but the ghost of her clung, in spite of my cautious instincts. I found myself confronting my guilt at my own ineffectualness, and having nothing in prospect but a dead-end, an echoing stone wall of blame.

And anyway I needed a change for my work's sake, I kept assuring myself over the rattling of the train's wheels as we left Paris behind for the Midi and the South. I needed a change of scene for the sake of those poor sods I now edited, for the sake of hapless Dorothy Richardson whose critical (but not crucial) reputation I arrogantly kept simmering on the metaphorical back burner of history.

It was everything that those English resorts ought to have been. There were physical resemblances, but in France the waving palms and shuttered white façades seemed to be the English versions in their complete and fulfilled form. The air was balmy, the sea warm, the avenues smelt tangy and sweet, of pine and bougainvillaea. The Hotels Hermitage and Excelsior bore legends of Farouk, Dietrich, the Windsors, Chanel, Sinatra, Onassis. The peerless, biscuit-coloured casino on its headland fluttered its petticoat of scarlet awnings and marquees; beneath, fishing smacks bobbed in the harbour of the Old Town, sheltered by the long crooked arm of sea wall.

I also had a strong sensation that the town had been here waiting for me, for us, waiting for something to happen. It felt to me a fated coincidence: an ordained collision of destinies was afoot. From a stage set Marina and I had advanced to a film set. It seemed wholly convincing to me, more than life indeed. I was familiar with just such a town from hundreds and thousands of photographs I'd seen, from Claude Lelouch and Jacques Demy films, from music and from my dreams.

I frequented the two big hotels, lured there by the fame and glamour they'd accumulated over decades. Unlike most hacks I had never been very impressed by the rich. It was something else about the ambience, of which splendour and wealth were important contributory elements, which was attractive to me. Was it the ceremonial, almost sacramental atmosphere? – or alternatively, an air of decadence, of implied dissolution and cynicism? For all the due orders of behaviour nothing was quite *defined* here. I confused chauffeurs and valets and tutors and maids and beauticians with the persons who employed them. Some of the guests had light suntans or midway complexions I couldn't place – Armenian, or Mauritian, or South American. The vast salons were real and solid, and yet not a part of the world outside. Quiet voices travelled long, long distances through the public rooms, down pink- and fawn-carpeted corridors. Frequently I'd find I was staring into a double-distance reflected in mirrors, and there *I* would be too, but shrunken, at some entirely unexpected contiguous angle. Phrases of chamber music would seep from behind me, which might have had a logical explanation – a palm court quartet may have been practising in a room secreted behind panelling or mirrored doors – but I could never be sure. Sometimes it felt like Marienbad in three dimensions. I was free to wander about the public spaces, without belonging and without understanding, and yet nobody requested me to leave.

The rooms opened out into the gardens, to admit the pristine lawns and clipped shrubbery and pruned palms. The sea light softened the vertical angularity inside. Everything was rendered in a luminous but discreetly pale palette. There was no occasion

for sharpness and stridency, for the obvious. Surfaces hinted
at their depths and concealments.

One or two of the guests may well have been film stars. The
others gave their movements the same studied, deliberate air, as if
they were meaning to represent life at this careful, expensive, vital
distance from it. The amount of space around them emphasised
everything that they did. In the dining-rooms and lounges, their
voices, with as little apparent effort as they could manage, were
required to cover comprehensive tracts of air space, to an
accompaniment of rhetorical (but never hoydenish) expressions
and gestures. It was a very dramatic manner of existence.

In the Café du Prince de Galles a pianist would be playing
classical-style versions of old Broadway show-songs on a glass
grand piano. 'On Your Toes', 'It's De-Lovely', 'The Gypsy In
Me', 'My Funny Valentine', 'What Is There To Say?', 'There's
A Small Hotel'. Afternoon tea was the most perfect imaginable,
more English than any to be had in England. There were
smoked salmon sandwiches as well as cucumber and mayon-
naise chicken, savoury anchovies on toast, strips of sweet
toast sprinkled with cinnamon, tiny hot potato scones straight
off the griddle, a selection of cake – Battenberg, Dundee and
dry saffron – and a choice from a dozen blends of tea.

The café resembled a foreigner's vision of a London club
in its décor – with the singular exception of that marvellous
glass-cased piano. There were leather tub chairs, and sofas
and wing chairs in florentine-patterned fabrics, leather-topped
brass fenders at the open hearths, hunting and horsey prints
on the panelled walls, wooden standard lamps, and a queer
assortment of carpets on the woodblock floors – a mixture
largely of oriental rugs and tartan runners. The place was
cosy and enclosing, especially for its regulars. The waiters in
their striped, wing-collared, brass-buttoned and swallow-tailed
footmen's uniforms observed a precisely calculated balance of
affability and deference, and the café's habitués were made to
feel uniquely comfortable and privileged.

*

It was to the Café du Prince de Galles that I tracked them down.

My wife's companion must have been fifteen or twenty years older than her, although it took me a while to penetrate the disguises. Striking rather than pretty, she dressed in trouser suits and wide-brimmed straw hats, which – worn indoors as well as out – seemed to be her sartorial 'mark' in that age when public personalities were all required to have their gimmicks. Dark glasses in fashion frames such as the kind she sported were in too common currency to be distinctive, but they did an effective job of covering a good portion of her face. Those came off once she was inside the Prince de Galles, however, unless cigarette smoking at any of the other tables caused her to advertise her disapproval.

Marina remained faithful to her Persols, but now eight years on she favoured shorter and skimpier dresses in glossier materials. Her bare legs were still shapely and supple. She wore white and navy shoes with medium-high heels, while her companion preferred flat, strappy boutique sandals. Marina's hair was modestly bouffant – the middle way appeared to be her instinct now – but sometimes, before an appointment at the hairdresser's perhaps, she tied a sturdy floral bandana round her head. Her earrings were the jangly, spinning sort of the day. Several times I saw her with a curious African-like silver halter suspended from her neck, lying as a gleaming crescent on the moderately tanned skin of her upper chest, between her shoulder blades. Her friend sported a gilt – or probably gold – chain or two studded with pearls, and a heavy gold and pearl clasp bracelet. Marina carried a pale red handbag with bamboo handles, to the other woman's unapologetic outsized Kelly bag in ostrich skin to tone with her cream ensembles.

Even in that town of eminently watchable late-season visitors, it was noticeable how many heads turned as the couple promenaded past. Marina would otherwise, I felt, have given the appearance of purpose and destination, having those legs to stride out with, but the older woman took her time and proceeded languidly. Marina had to hold herself back, sometimes in response to the woman's asking her to, in a very faintly twangy Americanised variant of the Queen's English. Her remarks may have been instructions: I doubted if they were straightforward comments, because Marina wouldn't always immediately respond, she might even look down to measure her steps on the pavement. The older woman would then look irritated and tetchy as she followed behind, but her expression became more neutral once – as usually happened – Marina found some pretext for slowing and pointing something out and drawing back to her companion's side.

I followed them on a good many of their walks, observing them from a distance. Most afternoons between three and four they took some air in the town before turning for the Prince de Galles. Either they ambled along the streets and arcades where the best shops were, or they strolled in the Jardin Exotique where sprawling tropical plants and vast cacti provided an almost surreal backdrop. There they moved among decorous young schoolgirls in smocks, nuns in grey habits and soaring white sculpted wimples, and those ubiquitous dallying lovers who made no show whatsoever of botanical curiosity.

I watched how the pair reacted whenever the heads turned. I drew the conclusion that their failing to notice was steadfast resolution not to see and to be seen not noticing, and that they were playing out insouciance. I wondered just how much in fact they remained aware of. What about *me*, did I fall within their range of vision? I tried to take more care how I proceeded about my stalking on those sultry afternoons of the so-called 'dull' season.

My one advantage was that I now carried my own disguise, my beard. It was full, and as much grey as dark brown. People who remembered me without had been for ever telling me how it aged me, but gradually they'd started to forget. On my forays about the town I was glad to be provided with a defence against recognition. The figure I saw reflected side-on in shop windows was a little stooped, prematurely sober and introspective, the greying product of back-room literary life, a bachelor in all but legal status.

Round and round and round the town. When I recall it, when I picture it all to myself now, I can believe they must have been leading me a long and merry dance.

Subtly Marina has changed, to seem again an archetype of the age she's living in.

Her hair is fair rather than blonde. She picks back loose strands from her face in an abstracted way that is also very sensual. With her eyes she has been able somehow to highlight the greenness of the irises. Her lipstick is coloured between red and purple. Her smile continues to be a little askew. She has kept that clean jawline; the chin is still well defined, a little more forceful than I remember. Her nose is engagingly small, slightly retroussé and most definitely erotic in the same way that I recall. Her teeth, I'm able to see in the Prince de Galles, are just as irregularly regular as they used to be.

She has become modern all over again, and without sacrificing herself to voguery. Her ingenuity in defining herself anew is less than straightforward, since what she seems to have done is to make her appearance coincide approximately with famous young exemplars' – the fresh Dorléac, Deneuve, Karin, Fonda – and not to copy a pattern from a source. She shares those women's spirit, perhaps because she has some money and the confidence that results from that, because like them she retains the chief uncopiable qualities of privacy and enigma.

On a display counter in the cosmetics boutique of a department store I recognised the label on one of the bottles, the same yellow and light blue label I used to see from the bed in the flat, when I'd watch her sitting with her back to me at the dressing-table.

I bought a bottle and had it gift-wrapped. I took it back to my hotel, the box inside its yellow and silver paper with trailing blue ribbon. I considered for a while before deciding and taking it with me to the Prince de Galles. I handed it to Jean-Pierre and instructed him to please present it to the younger of the two *Anglaises* without telling her who had given it to him.

I watched from the second room as Marina received the package and placed it before them both. She only opened it after they'd eaten and drunk and folded their napkins. She stared at the contents, at the label, then absently turned the bottle round and round in her hands before, at last, unscrewing the crystal top and putting her nose, that small sexy nose, to the lip. After eight years she may have had to remind herself what it would smell of.

Her companion snatched up the box in its torn paper. She looked inside for a message. Marina was giving the impression that it didn't matter to her whether there was one or not. But I'd seen her confusion at first, laying the gift in the palm of one hand and seeming to test the reality of the object with the fingers of the other hand. She flipped the bottle over, tilted it upright again and removed the stopper, to dab the glass plug on her neck, behind her ear-lobes. She feigned to notice nothing as her companion dropped the empty box on to the table with the most elegant disdain.

I went into Van Cleef & Arpels.

The diamond Trenor had told me about, 'The Star of the Desert', was displayed in a glass case recessed into a wall. It rested on a bosom of the palest buff suede. I bent at the knees to peer closer. The staff in the shop deduced from my appearance that I wasn't a prospective purchaser, and politely steered a path about me. Meantime, through their crossing reflections in the glass, I studied the richness of colours slanting in through the sides of the stone. I looked for some glimpse of the desert, a memory in one of its facets of its origins, but I could see no more than that exquisite spectrum of light like a perfect abstraction: angles of vision that led in the end only to more interior angles.

Later Trenor saved me the additional onus of work it would

have taken. To him it was like air to breathe, an oxygen high. His résumé carried a first-person bias which convinced me of its accuracy.

'Before she met the Maharajah she'd been low profile for a while. I suppose I just forgot about her, I'd stopped wondering whatever happened to her.'

He had a conveniently discriminating memory. The woman who had once broached with him the matter of her (spurious) family tree – presumably my Mrs Eglantine – had faded from recall because she'd failed to meet the minimum standards of social pedigree. Now *this* woman, who better satisfied his requirements, had been salvaged from the ignominy of oblivion.

The story he now found himself able to tell, blank periods notwithstanding, started in the early thirties.

'She'd taken up with a real-life baronet's son. Afterwards she surfaced in Manhattan. She used to call herself *Lady* Courtney there. She wasn't ever a ladyship, but she did very well, whoever she was. I saw her a few times, but not to speak to. My friends talked about her. Apartment on East Eighty-third Street. Accounts on Fifty-seventh. A smart Lincoln car, and her own black driver. The sort of courtesan Proust would have approved of. A demi-mondaine. Then that finished, and she came back home. Maybe she'd got into some sort of trouble. But things went well in London too, after a bit. She'd dropped the "Lady" business. I suspect it may have been her I encountered just after I came over, in thirty-eight. Her hair was a different colour from "Lady" Courtney's, and her nose was thinner. But I thought I remembered the eyes. Anyway, I wasn't quite sure. I kept bumping into her, over the next five or six years. She crossed between groups, just like me. Sometimes she didn't like to let on, and avoided me. During those years I guess she was with three or four men. She had a country place, I've learned. Norfolk, I think, or Suffolk.'

'Yes,' I couldn't resist saying. 'I know.'

'Oh.'

'I'm sorry. I've interrupted you – '

'In those days you could pick up a country pile like that for quite a reasonable sum. I suppose it could've been financed by selling an apartment in Upper East Manhattan. But I never got to see it. We were ships-in-the-night kind of thing, familiar faces in other people's rooms.'

Once into his tale he had no difficulty summoning to mind the woman's tangential social course.

'We never even got to talking. We nodded. I was sort of a Yankee at the Court . . . And she was the type of woman who became some man's obsession for two or three years, but the men always conveniently belonged to different circles of acquaintances, so she'd only have the risk of an accidental encounter once in every long while.'

His recent investigations had been exhaustive, but no doubt pleasurable.

'That's who it was after all, with the Maharajah. She'd met him in Beirut, and maybe she hadn't calculated on his coming back to London. At any rate, here she was – with him – and so she was just making the best of it. Most people supposed it was a fling, but someone in the know assured me it was more serious than that. Maybe she had her claws into him, but *he* liked to stir things up too. He'd given her the diamond by then. They got married in Switzerland, where his family couldn't get at him. But that took her into the international set. And because *I* am but a humble Anglophile, I guess I just lost touch with what was happening – '

He paused. I realised that, ever the self-dramatist, he was pacing his story. I waited for him to continue. Never mind that he had failed to identify her from the newspaper photograph light years ago.

'They made off east, though. Patched it up with the family and disappeared into some sort of oriental happy-ever-after land. Supposedly. But they showed up in their old fleshpot haunts every so often. They were just – '

He paused again. I saw a metaphor coming, delivered in his best innocently throwaway radio manner which – because unlikely to be carried off with half the flair by anyone else – gave him his unassailable edge as a broadcaster.

' – they were just another revolving satellite star in a smart, glittering galaxy of them. Another galaxy from mine. But I was quite content with mine, I had – I had scope enough for adventures. You know?'

Trenor had been opening up to me of late. However, I think that was because he had an instinct he would soon be returning, for good, to America. Later, when he had gone back, I discovered that a new society magazine had approached him with an offer to become its deputy editor. The proprietors had premises in New York, Boston, Chicago and San Francisco: it was to be a job with a high-flying, high-profile portfolio. Imposing doors would be opened to admit, at the right price, a man of his cosmopolitan but respectful airs and – to American tastes – his refined, authentically languorous Anglicised graces. His London life was coming to an end, as was – coincidentally and necessarily – a distinct phase of my own.

That was later.

On France's Riviera – as I was – in that last resort of all, I had practised the words that I might say to Marina, but altering them every time and not really able to tackle the matters that concerned me most. In my mind I even rehearsed the intermittent clearings of my throat. But it was all to no avail. I lacked the resolve, to speak and to confront my abiding ignorance about why she had left me and why she had wanted to marry me in the first place.

I blamed it on the heat. On the lassitude of the season. On my not having sufficient physical presence to signify, in Van Cleef & Arpels or anywhere in the town. I blamed it on the 1960s even, just because it wasn't the decade before.

I was a coward at admitting to myself that I was a coward, and not smart enough to have deserved keeping her.

The woman, Marina's partner in the life they led, still called herself the Maharanee of Randagarh when it was useful to her, but to many it would have been an intimidation.

Trenor's continuing investigations were to confirm that the Maharajah, boasting the title but a comparative indigent among India's five hundred princes, had been killed in the Nyasaland flying-boat tragedy, when most of the passengers and crew were drowned in the Shire River. His mother, under her elder daughter's thumb, had contested the will, and his English-born wife had been accused in an Indian court of unduly influencing her husband to favour her in preference to his family. That point was never established, but the verdict that was handed down – courtesy of a judge who had often been entertained in the past by the dowager Maharanee and the deceased's father – reduced the wife's share of the inheritance to half. That was still too much for the plaintiffs, but the English widow gained some approval in the press by agreeing to the adjudication. Perhaps she had simply been daunted by the prospect of an appeal in the Delhi courts, and in public she let herself be seen as having settled to the inevitable with an imitation of good grace. At any rate, the general presumption at the time was that the re-declared terms of the will provided the Maharajah's widow with sufficient funds to live in some comfort wherever she might choose to set up home.

They weren't staying at either of the big hotels, or in any of the others in the town. Home for the season was a rented property in one of the older pine-lined avenues: a structure built in the 'English' style but which resembled nothing I had retained any memory of, top-heavy with criss-crossing brown beams and cream plasterwork and a soaring chalet-like decorated gable in the middle of the roof. It was a medium-sized house for the locale, four or five bedrooms perhaps, but given pompous pretensions. The garden extended to half an acre or so, and was heavily shadowed by its trees, Chile pines and hemlocks and incense cedars. The name on the high, narrow gate read 'Villa Calypso'. In my mind I saw bone-white sand and heard crashing blue surf. But the house I was standing viewing from the pavement was hunched and sombre, a refugee from a northern suburb, and all I could hear was the silence of the garden, the stillness of the trees and the curious absence of birdsong.

This, I discovered from the postman, had been the English women's home for the past four or five months. He delivered letters with London frank-marks, and if he ever encountered them they would speak to him. (The older woman, Mademoiselle Court-Nei, was quite fluent in the language, although she talked Parisian.) Their neighbours knew little about them, but in this vicinity privacy was respected. The owner lived in the west of the country, and if he could find someone willing to pay a high rent for such a long lease he wasn't going to interfere. The postman had seen a car at the front gate once, no, two cars, on two different occasions, even though the women used taxis: so they must have got to know some of the people in the town.

He imputed nothing. I don't think he meant to. I felt guilty afterwards, as if I had been dredging further beneath the surface than I had any right to. But I wouldn't have cast so deep if I hadn't imagined I had a reason to. I was trying not to suspect, in precise thoughts and words, what I had a gut sense I had a proper justification to suspect. I was holding out in some part of my mind for the best, but also questing to discover the worst, as if *that* should permit me to savour the bitter feelings I had all along suppressed.

If I could have it all out, I fancied I might be able to cleanse and sanitise my system of Marina, to be rid of her once and for all.

But that was to assume that I finally, in my heart of hearts, wished to. I doubt very much that I did. I can recall the days of my marriage now, in very nearly the same spirit as I felt I was living them, unprejudiced by what was still our future time ahead of us. In France also I was reliving them, in that self-same spirit. I understood that I didn't want to lose our past. If my recollections could only be faithful to *my* experience, then at least there might be competing truths in our shared history: mine, and what I was *not* privy to. In that case I could be absolved from the compulsion to make conclusive judgments. There would have been differing realities – the life I had known with Marina, and her hidden life which I hadn't – and those in the end (most expediently for me) would prove to have been, to be, of equal veracity.

I haunted the Avenue Raspail.

To save money, and since I was so seldom there, I moved out of my hotel into a pension.

I knew I was on the point of doing something momentous either way. The choice was mine, I told myself, my own sole responsibility. I had been brought to the very edge of events, which was where I had always meant I should be one day.

The diamond had been removed from the showcase in Van Cleef & Arpels. A chatty member of the staff I spoke to in a bar told me it had been taken to Paris and sold. There had been a number of big diamonds on the market recently, which meant – I gathered – that more customers could be satisfied but that prices weren't as competitive as formerly. A buyer wouldn't balk at a couple of hundred thousand dollars, and less so the seller probably. The money could be swallowed up soon enough in a town like this one, the man added, if you weren't careful. But an object like that could maybe become a burden to you, if you weren't sentimental, and – look at it this way – the money could buy you your compensations, for a while . . .

I was following the pair as they strolled along the Boulevard Edouard VII.

They stopped outside the furriers, Lillemark de Copenhague. The older woman pointed to one of the coats on display in the window. Marina pointed to another. They each took a few steps back on the pavement comparing the coats.

It was another warm day. When they stepped forward again and advanced to the door – the woman sweeping ahead, Marina seeming a little restrained in her wake – I knew it must be with the intention of a purchase.

They emerged half an hour later empty-handed but were seen

off with obsequious respect from the door by a pin-striped man, a woman assistant, and by her assistant, who stood clasping a ledger.

Later the couple lingered outside a superior travel agency with a poster of Davos in its window. The woman preceded Marina inside, and they came out a few minutes afterwards, holding between them an unfolded airline timetable which carried the Swissair emblem.

They went into the Louis Vuitton boutique. A wardrobe trunk was opened and closed for them by an assistant. A shop log-book was consulted. Different sizes of suitcase were removed from the shelves, and two gaps were left when the women returned to the front of the shop.

In Hermès a saddle and silver-handled crop were delicately removed from the display arrangement in the window.

In Ferragamo a choice of shoes was spread out on the floor around them both. Six or seven pairs were repacked in their boxes, and stacked in two piles on top of the counter.

At tea-time they walked past the Prince de Galles. Marina turned to look inside, but her companion – with a spring in her step I wasn't used to seeing – didn't stop. She led the way instead to the Avenue Eugène, which for the cognoscenti served as a short-cut to the Hermitage Hotel. Marina was vaguely attempting to idle, but her companion the Maharanee was impervious today, determined that there should be nothing to drag down this auspicious, spendthrift afternoon.

Five months after his letter from Forte dei Marmi which had precipitated my Riviera visit, when he was in New York and I was back in the kingdom of hackdom, Trenor wrote to me with his selection of two story-lines for Christmas out of the dozen I'd sent him. He included a photograph he'd cut out of the *New York Post*. It showed a famous ice-cold Finnish film actress meeting the American press on board the liner SS *France*. She was wearing the second wedding-anniversary present from her Canadian industrialist husband. The newspaper called the renowned diamond 'The Wilderness Star', which (Trenor pointed out) presumably was a mistranslation of 'The Star of the Desert'. It had also been known as 'The Rose of Petra', according to the deadpan report. A few weeks previously the actress's equally renowned wealthy husband had bought his trophy from a leading Parisian firm of jewellers, which had acquired the item through one of its provincial offices. The diamond's recent provenance was held to be Middle rather than Far Eastern, but that may only have been a politic claim by the dealers.

It was a considerable enough distance of the world's circumference as it was, I felt, to Hollywood from New York from the Place Vendôme from the southern French resort, irrespective of – ? – Syria, or Angola or Sierra Leone or the Ivory Coast or who knew which African badlands.

Sometimes Marina went off alone in the afternoons walking, before she made her way along the boulevards and avenues towards the Prince de Galles. Various fancy cars dropped off her companion at the door, but none was a Bentley Continental, so Marina was indifferent.

Idling in the Parc Orsini beforehand, she would consult her watch at frequent intervals. Even though she was wearing Ferragamo shoes she would kick at little pebbles on the path.

She was drawn several times to a dell, to a sort of grotto, some twenty feet high and sculpted on the outside in the form of a giant face. It was possible to stand in the oval of mouth with its two projecting teeth overhead. Like the nostrils of the flattened apish nose, the round eyes above the creeper-clad cheeks were windows of sorts, deep holes admitting daylight to the dark and dank interior. Arching tracery eyebrows met in carved whorls over the lichened bridge of the nose. As the shape of the rock determined, the face inclined a little backwards and up, and the gaping mouth – wide enough to hold two adults and a dog or three boisterous children side by side – seemed to be screaming at the sky.

The sight of the montrosity set deep in its wooded hollow had startled me, even frightened me at first, but I had become more used to it. Marina would lean against a certain tree's mossy trunk and stare at the shocking ridiculousness of the object, stare and stare.

The last time I saw Marina, from the shade of a plane tree, she was standing at an upstairs window of the Villa Calypso. She stood as I had always remembered her standing at the sitting-room window in our little flat in Sebastopol Street, apparently lost in something more abstract than the view.

Her arms were crossed over her waist, or her hands played with the novel shortness of her hair. At one point she turned her head and called something over her shoulder. Then her eyes returned to the present outlook, to the angle of quiet road and a wedge of the garden where no birds seemed to sing.

A little later a car approached, along the avenue. It slowed as it passed the house. When Marina saw it, she lifted her hand and waved. The driver pointed, towards the next intersecting avenue. Marina nodded, and the driver continued on his way. When the car had gone she leaned back, picked up a pastel cardigan, and tossed it across the room to where, I supposed, her companion was waiting to catch it. Something must have been said: Marina, still keeping watch at the window, shook her head in a preoccupied way.

A couple of minutes later the front door opened, and the one-time Lydia Courtney emerged. She descended the steps, buttoning the cardigan with one hand and holding a white leather shoulder bag and her customary straw hat in the other. She fixed the hat on her head before she reached the gate, so she might be protected by a measure of disguise. She tipped back her cuff to consult her watch.

She turned left, letting the gate clatter shut behind her. From the right, only a few seconds after the gate closed, the man came walking briskly along the pavement. The woman didn't look back at the sound of footsteps but kept her eyes diplomatically trained forwards before she remembered to look into her bag for her sunglasses.

The man turned in at the gate, but knew how to open and close it noiselessly, without betraying his presence to neighbours. The front door was drawn back as he climbed the steps on tiptoe. I glimpsed – just – the lopsided smile on Marina's face. The man sidled between the door and jamb as if he was used to such furtive arrivals. The door closed. Behind the grillework, through the patterned glass panel, I thought – I was almost sure – that I caught the shadow of an embrace. But the figures retreated, the shadow faded, and I was left to the discomfort of my speculations.

A businessman of some quite well-to-do type. He'd had an anonymous appearance in keeping with his manner of arrival. He had known to leave his car parked in a street nearby, at a prudent remove from his destination. Wariness in deception was his motto. He was well practised in this commercial game of ritually requited lust.

I walked off to the echoes of my own heels on the pavement. I tried to lift myself forward up on to my toes, as if I was conscious I might disturb the two occupants of Villa Calypso, respectively at their business and their play.

I was sitting in the Prince de Galles. The weather had turned chillier, and a fire was lit. I was sitting waiting for *les Anglaises* to show, for what would prove to be their final appearance.

I heard their heels and retreated behind my newspaper.

The heels stopped outside, on the pavement.

Two pompous Frenchmen – or Swiss – passed into the room and I couldn't hear Marina and her companion for the crescendo of their voices as they approached.

One said to the other, 'It's those two again.'

'Respect please, Claude.'

'I'm sorry. You have an interest, I forget.'

'*Had*. It was the first year she came out here.'

'Which one?'

'Sixty-two, I think.'

'No, which woman?'

'Which do you think? The younger one.'

'Bloody vampire, you are.'

'In those days it was a hotel room.'

The two men walked past me into the back room, apparently to avoid the couple.

'They're grand enough now.'

'A thousand francs, if I remember.'

'Good value?'

'That part? I think so.'

'What other part – ?' The man laughed.

His friend spoke quietly, almost tenderly, with nostalgia.

'Afterwards she stood at the window. Pulled up her hair and let it down – '

The other man laughed again, but his friend ignored him.

' – stood and looked. And sang a song.'

'She did *what*?'

'Sang. In English.'

'What about?' Bet you you can't remember.'

'Yes, I can.'

'What, then?'

'Trains – '

'Trains?'

'Trains at midnight. In – in empty stations. A ghost. Or something – '

Their voices faded. From the opposite direction I heard high heels in the hallway. Then a few seconds later the shoes turned and left again.

Out on the street, voices – the women's and the staff's – called out last goodbyes. *'Bon voyage!'*

Indoors, and very close to me, a coal split in the grate of the reproduction Robert Adam fireplace. The coal collapsed, consuming itself in its fossil fire. A cascade of sparks whistled up the chimney, and I watched them briefly dance, a dance as old as myth and stone, before they vanished into that blackness.

A rattling tea trolley was approaching from somewhere, and meanwhile life went on.

I picked up my newspaper as a reflex and – only momentarily

– panicked at the fretwork of print, before I remembered how to read. I entered a story, and it was easy because it wasn't mine. In the inky forest of words I started to lose myself, in that familiar charm of faint knowledge and self-forgetting.

SHORT STORIES

GREGOR'S GARAGE

In the early 1960s our families were neighbours on a cul-de-sac, in an affluent suburb of Glasgow. We were all only-children.

My own parents were English, but already at eight years old – in kilt or tartan tie – I considered myself a Scot. Helen's mother was a widow, struggling with the upkeep of a Victorian house and also trying not to fall too far behind the fashions in the magazines.

Gregor's parents were supposed to have had a blazing row in Rogano's Restaurant, and it seemed that they could only shut doors in the house by banging them. Most often I glimpsed his father with his head buried in a medical magazine; I once found one of his empty whisky bottles sticking out of a beech hedge. It was said that the youthful Mrs Fletcher-Kiel had a separate account at the fishmonger's for flowers and sometimes gave lifts in her Citroën Ami to young male hitch-hikers.

Gregor knew precisely how much money was spent on him; he would tell us on the walks uphill from the prep school he and Helen and I attended. The more an object or item of clothing had cost, the less he liked it.

With just one single notable exception, that is – the one-seater, working scale-model of an Alvis convertible, fitted with a lawnmower engine and a set of bona fide, roadworthy white-wall tyres. He said the car was too 'dangerous' for anyone else to take the wheel, but that didn't stop *him* racing across Lindenwood's sloping front lawn as fast as the engine, belching smelly black smoke, could propel him.

The Alvis was kept in a wooden construction like an oversized kennel. Inside, there was just enough room for either the car – or for the three of us to huddle together, knees and elbows touching. Painted above the double doors was the incontrovertible mark of proprietorship: 'Gregor's Garage'.

We played as a threesome for no better reasons that I can think of now than physical convenience, a sense of exclusivity which the cul-de-sac encouraged with its high hedges, and also because the fact of our all being the same age seemed like some directive of fate.

I wasn't comfortable with Gregor's tight eyes, however, nor with the strength in his shoulders and arms. I was much more at my ease with Helen, who had inherited her mother's instinct for seeing the best in people – and an accompanying vulnerability which (without understanding so at the time) I suppose I wanted to protect her from.

As for myself: I spoke with an English accent, and at school I was considered abler than my age at arithmetic and composition. I tried to play down my scholastic ability sometimes, but I wasn't averse to using it as my trump card when I (mistakenly) thought that supplying answers to homework could help to make me better liked among the Picts.

I envied Gregor the Alvis. Speed gave him a rogue glamour. He drove the car faster and faster, and while Helen and I knew the stupidity of that, we were left on a perpetual knife-edge of excitement ourselves: would he overdo it one time and crash the thing?

He finally realised, though, that by not letting either of us ride with him, there were always going to be two camps: himself, and Helen and me. Whenever he drove past and saw the two of us with our heads together, as if we were in cahoots, his brow wrinkled darkly to a scowl. After that he would usually tire of the famously expensive car and suggest we do something else: climb a tree, or look for conkers, or play hide-and-seek.

Mostly we stayed in *his* garden – and, when it rained, sheltered in the summerhouse or the greenhouse. It was as if he didn't want to turn his back on the actual house itself and its mysterious life, in case it changed in some respect in his absence. I would often see him looking, over our heads and past us, towards the windows and the shapes distantly visible through the shadows on the glass.

By an ironic coincidence Helen's favourite game was playing 'house'. Although he didn't like it, Gregor let her have her way. We would throw travelling rugs over the low branches of a tree or between two folding wooden clothes-horses. But he bored more easily with that than anything else, and if he lapsed into one of his moods he would kick at the clothes-horses until they collapsed on themselves. To me such behaviour was worse than rude, it was unforgivable: maybe Helen thought so as well, but I saw how his sudden violence thrilled her too, it made her eyes shine and her mouth almost smile, and all the more so when she begged him to stop, stop, stop, and he wouldn't, right leg thrashing away like a piston.

At school we were in the same class but sat in different rows and had our own confidants. Back in the cul-de-sac we were a trio, but sometimes awkwardly so.

One day I couldn't find Helen, and Mrs Monteith wasn't there to answer the doorbell when I rang it. I walked on to the Fletcher-Kiels' and up the gradient of gravel driveway. Something hit me on the back of the neck, and I looked up and saw Gregor in the fork of a tree, holding a fistful of chestnuts.

'Looking for your girlfriend?'

I was annoyed, but – even more than that – I was embarrassed.

'You're wasting your time, she's not here.'

'*You* told me,' I said, 'there weren't *any* conkers left.'

'Well, there are.'

'Yesterday you – '

'I've just found them.'

'They couldn't have grown in a day.'

'We're going out,' he called down in the drawly way his mother spoke, with which he terminated conversations, 'in ten minutes. To Killearn.'

'Oh well . . .'

I put my hands in my pockets and went back the way I'd

come. On the potholed private road some sixth sense caused
me to stop by the hedge and look in. Between the leaves and
through the fretwork of twigs I was able to make out that the
doors of Gregor's Garage were opening: forearms and calves
and knees and then a face appeared – Helen's – and I stood
staring at the object she held suspended from one of her hands,
a giant gleaming glory of a chestnut knotted on a string.

Helen didn't mention her private visit to me, and I was too
proud and too afraid of a rebuff to enquire.

For a while after that – but only temporarily – Gregor
seemed better disposed towards me. He made me a gift of
some chestnuts: medium-sized and irregularly shaped. We had
duels and he played as if he had a wager on his life. My conkers
exploded like shrapnel. One day he asked me, very politely, to
explain long-division to him, and I did, but when he couldn't pick
it up and I shook my head at him as if he was a turnip-head he
said Helen had told him that only this summer I'd wet my berth
on the night ferry to Denmark and that now he knew why I
never let them see myself on a bicycle, because I hadn't the
knack of getting up on to one with a crossbar.

I had meant those to be confidences between the two of us,
Helen and me. Not the most awesome of secrets, but cautious
offerings of trust.

I pictured Gregor's methods to myself, how he must have
arm-twisted or hair-pulled them out of her.

Why, though?

It came to me in time, several years later.

Because he envied me, for those mental facilities he did not
have himself. He wanted to keep me in childhood, frozen in that
condition, when in fact a boy in our class already had the first
dark tracings of a moustache on his upper lip and we all longed
for our first day in uniform long trousers. He must have hated to
think that anyone might speed past him, get 'there' – to puberty,
to some acknowledged success or other, to wherever we were
all bound in the future – before him.

*

Once I heard Helen's screams from my bedroom and I ran to look for her. Gregor's car was tearing round Lindenwood's garden and there was Helen squatting on the bonnet, eyes tight shut and hands clutching the wheel arches.

I pursued them. For a few seconds I thought she was actually *laughing* through the screams. It was then that I flung myself at Gregor's shoulders. I wrested him out of the driver's seat and the car went somersaulting down the ramp of lawn. Helen was thrown off and in the process sprained an ankle and an arm falling. She started shouting at me from where she lay, and I couldn't understand why I deserved her anger.

'But it was *his* fault,' I said.

'*You* made us crash, stupid.'

'I only meant to help you.'

'Well, you *didn't*. You didn't at all – '

Her mother came hurrying up the gravel drive in high, sinking heels and a goatskin coat which even Helen, upright and trying to hobble on one foot, noticed and was disconcerted by. Gregor's father was found at last, and – doctor's bag in hand – he appeared, with his breath smelling sour, to attend to Helen. Gregor had managed to commando-roll clear and, unscathed, now stood staring at Mrs Monteith's breasts beneath her jumper, primed as they were like perky missiles in the silos of a crossover bra.

When he was eleven Gregor was sent south, to Dorset, to a prep school that had a name for cramming. After that he was despatched to an illustrious public school near London.

In his teen years he would very rarely come home, if he still thought of Lindenwood as his 'home' even. In the holidays he stayed with friends and their parents in ritzy foreign resorts, and took summer jobs crewing on yachts.

In Scotland, termtime lasted longer and began sooner, and early one September Helen said she'd been aware of being spied on – by 'guess who' – through a gap in the beech hedge as she walked home in the burgundy uniform of her Miss Jean Brodie establishment for young ladies. She told me about it the following day on the Milngavie bus out of town, and she didn't seem as unsettled by the incident as I thought she was bound to be. That year was the second last for both of us at our schools, and I observed how she was becoming much more her own person, with her own ideas and secrets: hiding her eyes behind a pair of very dark glasses on the bus journey home and causing heads to turn, pinning her skirt in at the waist after classes in such a way that she'd have taken a couple of inches off the length when she joined the chocolate-and-gold-blazered boys waiting at the bus stop on Great Western Road.

In Gregor's last year at boarding-school his parents bought him a Triumph Spitfire, and occasionally we would hear it between terms, disturbing the peace of the cul-de-sac at two or three o'clock in the morning. After he'd left school a rumour went about that he'd joined a motor-racing équipe; his mother denied it when she was tackled in the fishmonger's about her son's prospects, but later the very same week she made arrangements that all her shopping orders be delivered directly to the house in future, and indeed she was seldom again spotted by any of us walking those all too public thoroughfares of Milngavie.

After school, I embarked on an accountancy course in London, worked harder than I'd thought I would have to to get through, and more or less immediately landed a job with a big oil company. Several years down the line a more senior position fell vacant in their Edinburgh office and I was approached to fill it. I decided I had little to keep me in the south, and I accepted the offer.

In Edinburgh there were three years left to run on a company flat in the New Town, and I lived there in the interim.

Every second or third weekend I drove the fifty or so miles to Milngavie, and then the same back again. Quite by chance I happened to cross tracks with Helen, in a rhododendron glade near Mugdock Loch. She was walking her mother's cocker spaniel and I was walking my parents' Dandie Dinmont. Instantly her hands flew to her make-up, mine to my widow's peak of blowaway hair . . .

The dogs circled one another, and – conversationally – Helen and I adopted much the same ritual. She had modern good looks, I was thinking. Less a case of pretty-prettiness than a matter of attitude, a positive approach – colour-toning and a clean-cut Peter Pan hairstyle to emphasise that frankly determined straight nose and clear jawline. When she'd asked me to explain about myself and I had, she told me she was living in Glasgow, that she was joint partner in a fashion boutique.

'It's playing at a job, really,' she said. 'But it did get me away from home. Barring Sunday dog-walking . . .'

We continued to meet after that, not by accident but by design. I was entertained to tea at her mother's a good few times, and I saw and heard how garrulous Mrs Monteith had become with the years. The talk was mostly of all the eligible men she might have married in the two decades since her husband's death.

As she listened, Helen's mouth would twitch at the corners with embarrassment and her shoulders grow tense. I knew she disliked the brazen romanticism of it all. I felt immensely sorry for her, and also nostalgic for the young woman who'd had to get by on little more than blithe hope and about whom I'd nearly forgotten during my time in London.

Eleven months after our re-encounter, and 'in a whirlwind' as her mother described it, Helen and I were married.

We made the necessary adjustments to the flat in Edinburgh, a very *recherché* nest in which to aspire to wedded bliss. But all too soon Mrs Monteith took ill – psychosomatically? – and we found ourselves returning to Milngavie more often than we had intended. Helen's mother and my own parents, conspiratorially or not, insisted on keeping for us each Tuesday's *Glasgow Herald*, with the pages of property advertisements awaiting our attention should we but choose to peruse them . . .

What happened next seemed somehow fated, or so we convinced ourselves at the time. The Fletcher-Kiels' old home in the cul-de-sac came up for sale. The current owners, a couple called Dawson, had let the garden get on top of them, and the house itself when we inspected it – seeing into all its once forbidden rooms – was only in so-so condition. The estate agent insisted it was too good a chance to let slip, and we hummed and hawed; at the same time Mrs Dawson took a particular fancy to Helen, who was pregnant, and she persuaded her husband – quite why, I can't say – that we were the only people who *suited* the house, it might even have been built for us. The upshot was that the offer we finally made, which was markedly lower than the agent's asking price, was the one the Dawsons accepted.

And thus, with such unexpected ease, the innocuous-sounding Lindenwood became ours.

It took us a couple of years to make our own impression on the house. Likewise the garden required a lot of back-straining attention. But we achieved results in the end, and we had no regrets.

Sometimes at night, though, the house seemed to be dwelling on its own past, when the rooms – in the shadows of lamplight – became less our own; and when I'd scraped down and repainted the facsimile garage on the bottom lawn for our daughter Catriona's future use, not properly bothering that the dampness had warped and buckled the wood, it was impossible to keep the red letters of 'Gregor's Garage' from shining through my four, five, six layers of green emulsion.

I loved Helen very much, and often told her so, and especially now that she didn't work I stinted at nothing to provide her with every material advantage of which I could conceive. Occasionally, however, it was demonstrated very plainly to me that she felt overwhelmed by my solicitude, and even stifled by the comforts of our home. She would suddenly rise to her feet in the middle of a conversation, read her watch, and say it was time for the dog's walk, and it would be understood between us that my own company was not being sought.

She might be away for a couple of hours. When she came back, pink-cheeked, she invariably seemed in a better frame of mind, more reconciled to life, eager first to find Catriona and then content to let me kiss her welcome back. I fussed around her, made her something to drink or eat, stoked the fire as if to me the walk had been a small and intrepid odyssey.

Some evenings, however – unlike those when I watched her literally gasping for air – all she wanted by contrast was the privacy of the lamplight, the hush of our rooms, our distance in the darkness from prying eyes, the oh-so-familiar harmonies of domesticity.

'Look who's here,' Helen said to me, and she sounded quite displeased about his presence in the house. 'Gregor Fletcher-Kiel . . .'

It was a Sunday morning, and I had just returned from my elder's duties at church. In our sitting-room I stood in my flannel business suit and shook hands, giving mine into his grip.

After thirteen years I wasn't able to recognise him. His nose was now Roman and patrician – a car crash on the track, he said – and his thinning black hair, cut modishly long at the back, was flecked with grey.

Helen's mouth, shiny with lipstick, was prim and narrow. She must have guessed, as I had, that he had been drinking.

'Thought I'd have a look at the old policies. You know?'

He smiled, charmingly and warily.

'Told the taxi driver how to come. God knows how many wrong directions I gave him. And buggeration, who do I find when I get here?'

It was our sixth year in the house, I started to explain –

'Snug as bugs by now, I expect?'

We listened to a brief but meandering curriculum vitae. We learned that he owned a sports car dealership in London (the 'West End') and Oxfordshire. 'Italian jobs. Dream cars. You know?' He said he might be looking for somewhere to open up in Scotland, since there was patently a gap in the market.

'Wouldn't you do better in Aberdeen?' Helen said – a little curtly, I thought. 'With the oil money?'

'Well, Aberdeen folk would probably come down here.' He spoke in an expensive, placeless, rather drawly accent – or absence-of-accent. 'And it's the oil people like *you* I'm after, Ronnie.'

Helen must have filled him in before my arrival. And only *she* ever called me 'Ronnie'.

I told him that that sort of transport was well out of my price range unfortunately.

'Too bad, too bad. Although this ole pile here must have cost you – '

Helen's mouth drew straight as he downed his whisky. (The best malt we had, I noticed.) Then she stared – very hard – at Catriona, who had just walked into the room: stared without blinking, almost as if it was a shock, as if she had completely forgotten about her and now certainly didn't care for her to see this specimen of adulthood. But Catriona quite happily turned her back on the three of us and left, running for the garden, for the green-painted hideaway beneath the trees we called 'Catriona's Den'.

'Could we get a car without a roof?' Catriona asked me some weeks later, eyeing what the company indulgently provided me with for appearances' sake.

'A convertible?' I said. 'Why would you want a convertible?'

She shrugged. 'I don't know.'

'I don't think they suit our weather very well,' I told her. 'Don't you like the car we've got?'

She stood at the window, considering but not replying.

'What would *it* say?' I asked her. 'If it could hear you?'

'I didn't mean – '

I thought I heard a crack in her voice. I held my arms out, for her to run into. I wrapped them round her waist and lifted her high.

'If we lived somewhere hot,' I said.

'The desert?'

'None of our friends has a convertible – '

Just as Catriona was going to speak, Helen appeared, soundlessly, at my shoulder. She put a segment of tangerine into Catriona's mouth, then another into mine.

'Before you brush your teeth,' she told Catriona, taking her from me and whisking her away. 'And so, sweet lady, goodnight and let us off to Bedfordshire . . .'

*

I had a meeting arranged with some Americans from Aberdeen: in Perthshire, at Gleneagles Hotel.

I drove on there, foot hard down on the accelerator, after making a detour into Glasgow and dropping Catriona off at school. It was an instance of the more haste, the less speed, because when I reached the hotel, I discovered I'd quite inexplicably left the papers I needed at home.

I owned up, apologising profusely. I said, it took seventy minutes to drive one way, should I go back? The Americans agreed, quite willingly. 'It's okay,' they assured me, 'we can get ourselves in a round on the Queen's Course meantime.' We had drinks first, then I took my leave of them.

Going back, I hit road-works just after Stirling and didn't reach Milngavie until nearly lunchtime. I parked in front of the garage doors and looked in the side window to check if Helen's car was there. It was, but it wasn't alone.

I'm an amateur when it comes to car-spotting, but a few weeks afterwards I found the model photographed in *Autocar*. A Ferrari, if I remember correctly, a Dino (was it?), certainly scarlet and indubitably roofless: although which manner of convertible it was, with which sort of hood – lift-off or foldaway – I would hesitate to say.

Luckily I'd left the papers in a presentation case in the vestibule, so I didn't have to venture into the house to look for them.

If Helen heard my arrival and departure she was never to say. Our sitting-room was at the back (so she might not have heard), but our bedroom was at the front upstairs (so indeed she might). I purposely didn't look into my side-mirror or windscreen-mirror driving away.

That day as I tried to get up speed to overtake on the motorway, for the first time I was conscious that the car was underpowered. I kept slamming my foot down on the accelerator and revving, but it was a devil to get moving. I pressed the horn hard whenever my impatience got the better of me, which only rubbed other drivers the wrong way. I almost collided twice, and the escapes were close things. I think I wanted to cry but I was too angry. Perthshire had never before seemed so greenly, anciently indifferent to the sufferings we mere and callow mortals visit on ourselves.

Only once, maybe four months later, did Helen nearly give herself away.

She took a black eye. She told me – without looking at me – that she'd fallen against a door. Which door? I asked. She couldn't think at first. Her mouth had swollen up too, and I wondered if that was how Gregor preferred 'love' or whatever it was to him: by dispensing hurt and pain, as others bruise with kisses, and by denying himself the happiness he craved either because he knew he was undeserving or because he was afraid of making himself vulnerable to another human being and letting his heart speak.

Now we're honorary Texans, residents of our new home town, Houston. The oil money is supposed to have dried up, but the money-well never quite does.

My job boils down to representing the interests of a British conglomerate. As a family we enjoy – as the word is – 'enjoy' a rarefied existence, in a house with a twenty-five-yard indoor/outdoor swimming-pool, sunken jacuzzi-baths in three bathrooms, and a state-of-the-art white kitchen like an operating theatre. With a surgeon's skill Helen and I each excise with scalpel-precision whatever we wish to be absent from a conversation. Milngavie is seldom referred to; Catriona now talks with a mid-Atlantic twang, and is already – precociously – 'into' soft rock and muscular young tennis players.

The criss-crossing highways here are like a planet-scape, and I'm constantly amazed. I drive a mid-range Mercedes coupé, and Helen a souped-up BMW 3. But these roads are really made for the super-supercars, the dream machines. They're to be glimpsed now and then in a day, even faster than my Merc, outpacing Helen's matt-black toy. Maseratis, Ferraris, Lamborghinis. They move up on you undetected, like stealth-jets, they're there for an instant – and then they've gone, to wherever they're bound for: although I sometimes suspect their speed is for no true purpose, all they do is travel endless unvarying loops of glittering, twenty-first-century Houston.

I read recently, one of the big dealerships of European sports cars here is closing; they're going into powerboats instead, nothing priced at less than half a million dollars. The automobile business is now up for sale, the trade advertising is being pitched at those who will recognise its profit potential and – coincidentally – last week Helen told me that on the rich pickings from Mort's dental practice the Stavners are building a forty-metre pool for themselves with boulders and plants and an underwater sound system, so . . .

. . . so she's been a bit restless of late, taking her swimsuit with her when she drives off, eyes shaded behind her newest Armani frames, to investigate the construction work at the Stavners', who are almost our best friends in Texas. But I've noticed that she brings the costume back bone dry every time. I've noticed other things too, how on her return her gloss lipstick is perfectly in place and there's a faint trace of Scotch on her breath and she's still wearing her dark glasses as she gives me a quick peck on the cheek and goes through the house calling out – with a hint of urgency in her voice – our daughter's name.

PRIVATEERS

'Up' or 'down' was Miss Armitage's dilemma, do I move up the house or down?

'Down' she decided at last, into the basement. (Call it a 'garden flat', it sounded better.) That way she'd be spared the heat in summer through the roof tiles. From the windows beneath the railings and street level she would be able to keep a watch on who went in and out of the house, her lodgers and their friends.

So the removal men came and Miss Armitage made her retreat downstairs. As much as possible was crammed into the warren of small rooms. She hardly had room to turn, there was so much furniture (inherited from her parents, mostly) and every surface so crowded with knick-knacks. But Miss Armitage didn't think of the awkwardness, even when her elbow banged on a cabinet door or against a table, or when her hand sent an ornament flying. Instead she pictured her furnishings and gewgaws in the surroundings that to her mind became them best: not here in the basement, nor in the dark and modest, suffocating rooms of the house upstairs, which had been her parents' – but in large, light-filled rooms, in superior houses, her objects the possessions of people she chose to think now had been her friends, in the long-ago days when she'd still believed, hope against hope, that the world might be Alice Armitage's oyster.

In the little sitting-room of the basement tea is already waiting on a tray. The cups are fine bone china. The tray is laid with a cloth embroidered with Alpine flowers. The tea is Formosa Oolong. Some packet biscuits are fanned on a plate. Miss Armitage has put out the good Hester Bateman silver teaspoons, one in each saucer, and a third in the sugar bowl.

The young man who rings the doorbell, always on cue, is Mr Finch. He talked about himself once, but Miss Armitage has more or less forgotten all he said. He occupies two rooms on the second floor: at the back of the house, because he is a fellow (Miss Armitage believes he may have mentioned) of limited means. However, he is smartly turned out each time he comes to see her for tea, in a charcoal flannel suit, and he wears his hair short, which is how Miss Armitage considers young men ought to look. She appreciates his courteous attention to his appearance. He may have told her what his line of business is: but she has seen him sometimes from her scullery window in the middle of mornings and afternoons, wearing his other, very modern 'casual' clothes as the newspapers call them, so she thinks his occupation must be one which allows him quite a bit of free time.

He is very polite, Mr Finch, as Miss Armitage wishes everyone in the world would allow themselves to be. He always sits where she bids him to sit. 'I'm so glad you could come,' she invariably says by way of welcome; but the surprise in her voice is unnecessary because these twice-weekly afternoon tea visits are a custom, they've been taking place for several months, she forgets just how long.

Miss Armitage forgets a lot, of what is current and here-and-now and to do with the house and its running, and of what appears in the newspapers and on the television set, which she prefers (most of the time) to keep covered with a tartan rug. But there is another life inside her head, containing the version of the past she keeps specifically for these afternoon teas, and in that respect she has excellent 'recall'.

Some word or thought will act as a trigger, and the mechanism is activated. Mr Finch has to do nothing except sit and listen, sip his tea and nibble at a biscuit and hear his hostess embark on her major and minor readjustments of the past.

In the stories she offers to her favoured lodger, Alice Armitage is quite a humdinger of a young woman. She goes to dances and her mother shows her off, her two older sisters pass on their diplomatic advice on the one great subject, 'Men'. She is lunched, wined and dined, and taken to tea-dances; she spectates at Cowes from the bow of a yacht, she watches the polo mounts from the stand at Hurlingham.

Her life as she reconstructs it in those other decades is gracious and thankfully hemmed in with all manner of social ritual.

In her basement, her 'garden flat', Miss Armitage no longer has on show the framed photographs of her family, now all delivered to their Maker in the hereafter. The photographs have been relegated to the gloom of drawers, locked from view; the too familiar faces are forbidden from sharing in the splendour of Miss Armitage's accounts because she knows they wouldn't understand, not without the gift of imagination they were lacking in life, their expressions wouldn't show her any sympathy.

Yet her intentions are only of the best. In her (revised) version of the past her father receives the reward that was due to him – he doesn't just manage, he *owns* the muslin works; her mother doesn't lose her fine looks, they don't fade, and she continues to draw the eyes of handsome strangers across crowded public rooms; her sisters are given the alternative husbands they always deserved to have, an MP and a Harley Street surgeon, both with prominent social connections.

Miss Armitage explains to her tea-time caller that why she herself didn't marry was owing to a positive embarrassment of offers, because she couldn't decide in the end which one of all her suitors she should make her graceful surrender to and accept.

The speaker's attention occasionally returns to the young man in the charcoal suit seated opposite her, she focuses – but as if from yards away, not feet – on her Mr Finch from upstairs.

He smiles, sips his tea, and looks appreciatively round the over-furnished sitting-room.

When Miss Armitage is especially tired and that past time she has been telling her visitor of is making a ringing in her ears

– so that she feels she's under one of the glass bell-jars on the mantelpiece – at that point she'll grant a nod of dispensation, like a duchess, and the young man will rise to his feet, then begin his customary perambulation of the room.

Miss Armitage is aware, vaguely – as she lies back in the chair and closes her eyes, opens them blearily, closes them again – she is aware of what Mr Finch is about. She realises that her memory, or the lack, isn't wholly responsible for the little losses of things that she keeps making in the course of the week: a teaspoon, a paperweight, a piece of ivory, the silver letter-opener, the wee jade dragon from China. With the *things*, because they belong to the perfect past she has collected around her, her mind *is* engaged and doesn't let slip, it remembers, records. She isn't the one to blame this time, not entirely.

Nor, she thinks, is the culprit, Mr Finch, who's sometimes her only visitor between one afternoon tea and the next in the week. Occasionally she thinks that she sees something sorrowful in his face, and that that's why he gives her his time and listens to her, because his own life has not been the most satisfying sort; he too has had his chances but they've been snatched away at the last moment. She recognises that look, it makes her sad for him.

Leaning back and with her eyes closed, Miss Armitage continues her story, her stories, of her desirable, imagined past. Country weekends and London jaunts, picnics and riding to hounds. She remembers what the ladies wore as she stood and watched them, from the careful distance she was required to observe; she recalls word-perfectly the exchanges among the men as she homed in and listened, from her discreet and respectful distance, as they drank from stirrup cups on frosty mornings or studied the form of the sculls on the river.

Somewhere nearby, in the sitting-room of her basement, Miss Armitage also hears the young man: engaged in his deft, light-fingered work. He never interrupts her, he lets her polish and refine her details, arrange her stories as she wishes them to be. He is very considerate, very quiet. Her Mr Finch.

She cares to think he is not like some of the other tenants

in the house, clumping up and down stairs and playing their records too loudly and sending bathwater gushing from the overflow. Discretion and consideration have gone to the four winds apparently, and Miss Armitage is very sorry about it. But Mr Finch offers her back silence, and tact, and a kind of submission that gratifies her heart.

It doesn't even matter about the bits and pieces that are here one day and gone the next. Anyway, Miss Armitage knows, their life and purpose belong elsewhere. She was left the majority of her possessions in relatives' wills, and while the objects have been with her she has given them more 'appropriate' histories than those they had. In the days when she went out for walks she used to pass antiques and bric-à-brac shops and it would occur to her that no one can know a blind thing about what sits in these windows: their pasts are secrets, you buy something and it's up to you to *give* it its history.

Or perhaps it was the other way about, she'd started to think of late, since her move downstairs into the basement: really the object owns *you*, and discovers its new owner whenever *it* feels the need of another life.

He always lets himself out, Mr Finch, and so quietly that she hardly even hears the soft clicking shut of the door.

Miss Armitage sits on over the gas fire, she dozes maybe. Usually her caller has brought her something, a gift: a few flowers, a half-pound carton of chocolates. She smells the flowers from her armchair, anticipates the taste of the chocolates. She imagines a garden seen somewhere, over a fence or a hedge or in a magazine; she tries to remember the name of a *chocolatier* whose window she used to stand looking into, once upon a time, when the streets of London had style. In her mind's wanderings she's been admitted to the garden, she's a guest at a weekend party, everyone is waiting to say 'hello' to her; or a man, a square-cut handsome man, is buying her chocolates in the shop with the white marble walls and floor – a whole box of chocolates, and asking to have it wrapped in gold foil and tied with red ribbon.

At another level of consciousness Miss Armitage knows that upstairs the house is filling again with its young, throbbing life. A different sort of noise may cause her to jump, she hears footsteps passing up on the street, keys or a stick being rattled along the area railings. Sometimes – so she remembers – when she's been up and about on her feet and has twitched the net curtain back, the person she's seen hasn't been any of the other faceless and nameless ones who belong to the transient company of Number 28, Belvedere Street. She'll have chanced to catch a glimpse of her Mr Finch, not in his nice suit but dressed in his 'casual' clothes, and he'll have had his arm around someone, the same person every time, an up-to-the-minute young woman with a mane of frizzy carrot hair. Whenever it's happened, the two of them have been laughing together, laughing their heads off.

Miss Armitage supposes that it is love, the lucky couple's happy abandon – timeless love. Safe and secure again in the familiar hold of her old, worn armchair, she spares kind thoughts for all in their situation, imagining to herself the glorious, blissful adventure love must be.

WALKING MY MISTRESS
IN DEAUVILLE

So . . . this is Deauville.

Clack, clack.

Clack, clack.

Those stupid heels! These bloody duckboards!

Today she has clipped on my new leash. From the Hermès boutique. She said to the assistant, 'I'd better not tell my husband about this!' It was a joke, but it's not the sort you come out with in Hermès. Not that *she* would know. Anyway, it gave her the orange carrier bag to swing, and she scooped me up under the other arm, waited until the doorman obliged, and with that we swept out of the shop.

There's a shih tzu with the same leash; it twigged with me that every time she slowed she was trying to get a look at it. The leash, that is. She doesn't go for long-haired dogs. A moderately hirsute schnauzer possibly, because I saw her having an eyeful the first time we clapped eyes on one another, when they came into the pet shop back in Paris, she on his arm. They weren't married then, but maybe buying a dog was one of the preliminaries in the process. Anyway, the schnauzer in the pen two along from mine looked harmless enough, like a TV ad moggie, but then it barked when she put her hand out. That's *your* big mistake, I told myself. Well, it mightn't have been such a mistake after all; I was only four months old then, though, and I thought I knew it all. When they came to my pen and she did the same – stretching out her hand – I just blinked and blinked at those big fancy stones gleaming so fetchingly on her ring. 'I never thought of a *dachshund*,' she said. Her older, portly, balding companion didn't look very sure, but I knew *she* was taken by me: three weeks in the shop had taught me to recognise my chances. 'And she won't moult . . .' 'Oh, our little chap's a *"he"*, madame,' the owner corrected her, in that winsome way he had. Maybe it was the use of the 'madame' that had her smiling, though. And the man who was with her, holding her other arm so tightly, *he* smiled too, as if the prospect – of being wed – was quite an enticing one to him. She squeezed his elbow, and they nuzzled closer, and the owner undid the catch on the side of my pen and lifted me out. While he showed me off I was a very paragon of a well-bred, well-disposed pedigree – which was some way short of the truth – whereupon the man holding the woman's arm reached into the inside pocket of his jacket (shiny navy alpaca) and pulled out his chequebook. The woman ooh'd and aah'd on an instinct, and the business was attended to with several flourishes of a gold-plated fountain pen. The schnauzer started barking again, and the woman made a face at it, and her companion smiled at her, and the shop owner grinned at both of them. He could well afford to, because I expect they were ripped off something rotten, in the vulgar parlance. But the buyer – I've discovered – knows all about 'ripping off' and exploitation, and he was only getting as much as he deserved. Anyway, you don't go to twee canine boutiques in the 16th *arrondissement* and expect to pay no more than the odds.

So, we travelled back to the Avenue Kléber, the three of us, in the silver Mercedes coupé. It was only a few blocks away, but the woman had said she didn't have the right kind of shoes on for walking: well, they were just like the ones she wears when we negotiate these duckboards of Deauville beach, so I guess she was lying. She'd carried me from the shop holding me clutched against her bosom, and I could feel her heart quickening: maybe she'd spotted someone she recognised and wanted to avoid him – it must have been a 'him' – and wearing high sling-backs was just an excuse. However it came about, I found myself travelling home with them in the style with which I was soon to accustom myself, soothed by taped music and propped up in a bespoke cane basket, in the back of the intimate cabin aromatic with perfume and cheroot smoke and the newness of soft white leather upholstery.

The apartment was rather – well, common. I could only judge that later, from others in the building I saw into. Like the car, there was too much newness: I sank into the pile carpets (which admittedly was better than sliding about on the woodblock surrounds), and the velvet curtains had a suffocating, airless smell of something-or-other, their expense perhaps. Some of the furniture pretended to be antique, but wasn't. Of course my own so-called 'pedigree' was as fake as anything there, and so I dare say I fitted in quite neatly with my surroundings.

I don't suppose I was bought on a whim. I think she had me most cannily foreplanned as an addition to their lives. She had her own brand of cleverness all right. For instance, she must have known it wasn't likely that my purchaser would succeed in holding out against her charms. If the proof were needed . . . one afternoon when he wasn't there but she was, his wife showed up uninvited: a stocky woman with thick ankles who was trying too hard to be fashionable, and – I saw her glancing wide-eyed in the mirror as my mistress fixed drinks – who was hardly able to believe of herself that she was wearing these strident neon colours. That visit convinced me a divorce and a remarriage were fated to happen. But it took me a little while longer to realise that these were only initial formalities to a more tangential design of my mistress.

After the Happy Day, if he tried to call her from his office on the phone, I was her excuse for not being at home.

Sometimes of course she was, and the ringing would continue for a couple of minutes while she sat at the dressing-table calmly making herself up or stood at a window looking down on to the street or picked me up and held me against those heaving breasts inside her georgette camisole. When another type of urgent ringing – the doorbell's – split the silence of the flat, she would suddenly forget all about me – I'd be dumped on a chair – and she'd run in her exotic undress to answer it.

Her visitors were always men. I recognised them from the walks which I was a pretext for, really strolls, when she sauntered along the boulevards gazing in the boutique windows, watching her reflection and letting me do much as I wanted. Occasionally male passers-by found themselves tangled in my leash, or it was they who took the initiative, feigning to be interested in me and asking if I was 'pure-bred', if I had a suitable temperament for the city.

When they came up to the apartment later – at a certain arranged time – they didn't forget me: they brought me bonbons and biscuits, from Fauchon and Lenôtre and Hédiard because they must have known my mistress recognised good taste even if she didn't have a God-given aptitude for it. To them I was like a talisman, dare I say, and I merited my votive offerings. *She* worried that I might get fat, and she rationed me, because – I like to think – she saw there was a certain dependence developing between us, that went beyond the merely pragmatic. We had a deal in common circumstantially, and maybe from that she imagined we had a spiritual bond too: I had come into this apartment on a bank cheque, and so had she, and we were both high-priced, and we both conveyed a vague aura of caste – even though my past was a forgery, and I'd heard her confessing on the phone one day to an old friend that she'd had her accent overhauled in Lyon and her nose and jaw reconstructed in Vichy.

She was always buoyant and smiling and her skin glowed after her sessions with her callers. They left – with any offers of payment they might make politely refused – and she came in to play with me on the sofa or on one of the pile carpets. She told me how handsome I was, what a sweet nature I had, and also how 'discreet' we both must be, how careful, so very *very* careful . . .

He has brought us here to Normandy for the season, her husband and our provider. To Deauville.

We stayed at the Royal for a while, then he took the villa where we still are. For most of this past month he's been anxious, edgy. He tells her I was a mistake – a 'cringing, poncy, brain-dead mutt' he calls me when she's in the bathroom, which is the only time now when she can get away from him. He's always watching her, eyes riveted, meaning to miss nothing but somehow lacking confidence in his amateur sleuth's skills.

Occasionally he hurries back to Paris for an overnight, but otherwise he uses phones a lot – in the villa, in the car, even when we're outside he's never minus the mobile harness-model with the telescopic aerial. He's cryptic about his business in front of her: but she once asked me when he was called away to Paris and I had jumped up on to the bed, what the hell was his *real* game? She knew about the landlording and the money-lending . . . 'Drugs, is it?' She seemed so serious that evening; she carried my basket into her room but let me remain up on the bed when I made no effort to move. Her hair tumbled down, she peeled off her eyelashes, and gradually her accent reverted to what must have been its primitive form.

She told me at a certain point of no-return, in a confidential tone of voice she kept for me alone, that her mother would surely have liked me. Until not so long ago, she explained, her mother had had a café out near Bastille; until, that is, our lord and master – before my mistress got to know him – bought the block, closed down the café, and paid a derisory sum in recompense. The two of them had met because she'd gone to see him at his office, to intercede for her mother; she'd called her a hard-done-by woman, and taken-advantage-of, yet *he* had replied quite cogently, insisting it was a fair price, showing her the books and letting her compare figures. 'Money, money, money, oh he left my head spinning . . .'

Then followed the next stage of the story. He had become intrigued by her, fascinated; forgetting about his office work, or abandoning it, he had stalked her the length and breadth of Paris for several weeks. Maybe she should have resisted: but in that teasing, fraught interim a shrewder idea had occurred to her, and accordingly she'd let him take her up.

Bits and pieces he was to buy her she later sold, and she

passed the proceeds on to her mother, just as she had hatched the plot with herself to do. But at last the ex-*patronne* found out where the money was coming from; she was horrified to discover, her neighbours somehow cottoned on too, and for her that was the end; she was so overcome with shame she threw all her daughter's belongings still in the house out on to the street and told her she would have nothing more to do with her, not ever again.

My mistress duly returned to the man. In the unfolding of time she married him; by the ceremonial vows taken in law she intended to disprove her mother, to try to show that her newly acquired husband wasn't what she had all along claimed he was. Consequently she'd tried to believe the best of him. 'Really and truly . . .' However, the trouble was that – so it transpired – there was no 'best', no moderate 'good' either; not even the word 'indifferent' was applicable. 'Not a damned hope . . .' It was a pity about his former wife, of course, but she'd since heard from someone who'd set eyes on her that she had a new bounce in her step these days, striding out like an unfettered widow.

And now – with a shifty husband she didn't trust or feel she wanted to be 'physical' with any more – she was left with all her true and genuine affection untapped, the surfeit of stuff in her that wasn't pretend. It was too soon to let go of her youth, she told me, even if her mother and her husband had so long ago forgotten theirs. Her spring had only just turned to summer. (She abstractedly twisted the gold band, her wedding ring, on her fourth finger.) Every life has the capacity of offering love, she said: it's love after all which survives us, by which we're remembered, which is the essential and immortal element of ourselves . . .

Now you-know-who is in Paris again – for a week or so of 'meetings' this time – and it turns out, by no coincidence, that we're being followed around Deauville, she and I are being trailed.

As usual she's looking for consolation, but it has become a

more dangerous divertissement. I've worked it out for myself: which isn't bad going for – quote – a 'brain-dead mutt'.

He wears burgundy loafers with tassels: expensive-looking soft kid, so he's probably good at his job, this hired shadow we've acquired, whose speciality (I presume) is The Unfaithful Spouse. He's vigilant, most professionally wary, and not quite invisible. When I strain on the leash and turn round in a crowd, I'll see the detective's shoes between all the intervening legs, and they'll be pointing in our direction. But on the boardwalks, he's nowhere to be seen now: twice, at the weekend, he did pursue us, along the Planches, so I suppose he's taken to using binoculars instead, from afar.

I don't know how much *she* knows. I tug so hard on my leash in the town, she must more than suspect. Whenever a man draws close – someone with an eye for her of late not-so-subtle sort of glamour – I've taken to barking a very loud warning to her. She has stopped correcting me for beastly manners. Sometimes she scoops me up and looks into my eyes and I catch the alarm in hers. She shivers even through her cashmere sweaters. She shakes her head, but with concern.

This afternoon she turned off the street into a travel agency, and approvingly I trotted in behind. She asked for a timetable of flights to Nice-Côte d'Azur and details of pet transportation. We came out. I had shoes on my mind, and tugged at my leash outside a shoe-shop. She looked in and saw some flat-heeled town walkers. Better than those damned awful stilettos, I'm trying to tell her, better for running in.

Then I jerk my head round on my Hermès leash, bought with *his* funny money. Twenty yards away there are the private investigator's tasselled loafers. So I bark. 'It's all right, Rufus,' she tells me, 'it's all right. Just a few days more.'

She shivers again. The woman in the travel agency informed us it's been an excellent summer in the south, that the weather is set to last. Cannes is chihuahuas and clipped poodles, worse luck, but I anticipate we'll have the good sense – my mistress and I – not to want to make ourselves too obvious, for a while at any rate. Not until, by our telepathic will and with the aid of a tangled leash, a collision with a man's legs ensues on the

Croisette. Then and there, on the sunnier side of that salubrious thoroughfare, the rich stranger will pick himself up, my mistress will dust down his (silk? linen?) jacket sleeves and trouser thighs, and – as coy apologies but eloquent eye-contact are exchanged between them – we'll start all over again.

THE SIEGE

This afternoon she's a few minutes early and up in the bedroom she turns on the television set.

There's live coverage of a siege in an airline headquarters in Stockholm. Mug-shots of the five terrorists appear on the screen, then holiday snaps of some of the forty-two hostages. A reporter is asking people in the streets of wintry Stockholm what they think of this state of affairs, here in their own faraway city.

She leaves it on while she slips out of her dress. It crosses her mind to put a call through to her office – she has left instructions about an important client – but she decides it would only take an over-inquisitive telephonist to throw an unhelpful spanner in the works of this weekly 'arrangement'.

He hears reports of the siege on the car radio. A spokesman for the terrorists is interviewed, on a telephone line from the airline building, then the hostages' relatives are asked questions.

Momentarily he catches sight of himself in the driving mirror – the image he has to adjust to every time: a man with thinning hair, blue cheeks, a thickening jowl.

He doesn't think to turn over channels to some music. He isn't really listening. He looks about him and is seeing the spot from the window of another car at the tail-end of the fifties. His father is driving and he watches him from the back seat, a man with thinning hair, blue cheeks, a thickening jowl. His mother sits beside him in the front. For some reason she has hardly spoken since they left home. This is his half-term from school and it's an excuse for them to spend a couple of nights in a hotel. But the mood doesn't seem the proper one, and he has a premonition that the rest of their weekend together won't be so very much different from this.

Then she thinks, why *shouldn't* I call the office? Why shouldn't I do exactly as I like? Why should a telephone operator decide for me?

But 'freedom', she is also aware, doesn't come free. It costs, and – if you're wise – you never stop paying for the precautions.

The irony is that he looks like his father when it was his mother he cared for.

Loved.

He'd cared for his father hardly at all. He was only the role model on which nature had predetermined he was to be based.

She sits at the window in her bra and pants and watches as the car covers the length of the driveway, to the hotel's entrance portico beneath.

She withdraws behind the curtain, not for modesty's sake, but because she realises he will look up – their room is always the same one – and he will presume she is sitting there because she is waiting for him.

Along the ridge of the dunes grow the umbrella pines, looking like the serrated edge of a saw from a couple of miles away.

With the window open he can smell their tang.

Approaching the hotel he is making a dozen journeys, in dazzling sunshine and through a leaf storm and with snow dancing in the tracks of his headlights. The building appears as it always appears, seasonal embellishments apart, suns spinning in windows or leaves spiralling or snow frilling the balconies. It's an eccentric imitation of what was probably the architect's muddled memory of a Swiss or German spa hotel, with a high green roof and two gabled towers at either end (both towers have a clock, but each clock face tells a different time) and a fussily mathematical arrangement of balconies.

He studies the middle windows on the second floor, counting in from the fairy-tale tower on the left.

She pretends to be busy in the bathroom when he opens the door.

She sprays perfume behind her ear lobes. Cristalle. Not one of the perfumes *he* has given her. He can think what he wants to about that.

He looks out at the view as he undresses.

His work has taken him to most countries in Europe, to the States and Canada and the Gulf and Singapore. He has seen landscapes and skylines in their multiple variety, enough to sate him for views from windows. But wherever his journeys take him, it's the memories of other places, nearer and more familiar but long ago, which occur to him.

He daydreams them on taxi journeys and sitting waiting in air-conditioned company offices and eating solitary meals in hotel coffee shops or watching a girl undress in his bedroom, and even after the exhaustion of lovemaking in a foreign climate they can't be forgotten but return to him in his sleep. His wife's voice crackling across a couple of continents into a telephone receiver turns into something else inside him, a pain: not of guilt or remorse, but rather the ache of time forfeited and lost.

Standing in front of the bathroom mirror she pulls down the straps, undoes the catch, and watches her breasts in the glass as they fall out.

In the office the men clients' eyes drop to them, poised beneath her shirts and shifts. Sometimes the women's eyes look too.

She isn't sure what their fascination is with her breasts. She stares down at them. They are neither large nor small, but they sit pertly, invitingly perhaps. Her nipples are neat, compact, pink.

She's noticed how men go to her breasts first, after her mouth and neck. They have always seemed to her too practical-looking as objects and artefacts to be attractive, too much connected with babies and the act of suckling. How can men dissociate *her* breasts from their mothers'?

But maybe, she has realised, that's exactly the point – they don't?

He had come here with his wife, once, before they married.

As they'd driven over, he'd been thinking, maybe it's the wrong place to be bringing her? He hadn't stayed in the hotel since those school-holiday weekends of forced politeness. He'd hoped his mother's presence wasn't going to get in the way, a memory clutching at him: a disabling hand on his arm, preventing him.

But maybe, he'd realised, that's the whole point, it's no accident that here we are, in the province of my past time.

She is listening to the news of the siege with half an ear.

At one time she mightn't have thought it possible for her to be in the situation she now is. The physical situation that is – alone in a room in a hotel, with a man, on a weekday working afternoon.

She doesn't believe it means a great deal more to her than that. She isn't defined by being in this situation.

She doesn't feel herself *obliged* to be here. She can walk out whenever she chooses to; she is a modern woman, all she has to do is put her clothes back on, pick up her bag, find her car keys.

But . . .

He watches her slithering out of her tights. He closes his eyes, he *listens* to her, through the Swedish from the television set.

In the fifties women had a sound: the shimmering sibilants of silk stockings fastened to suspenders, thigh grazing thigh – rustling taffeta and crepe – thin, pointed, clacking heels – bangles jangling on wrists.

Being with him – *choosing* to be with him – what this is in fact is the very assertion of her independence.

*

No other woman has managed to sound quite like his mother, with that effortless harmony of parts he remembers her for.

She knows he's thinking of someone else. Someone he's known. She can tell, there's a look.

Too bad.

She lives in the present. 'Presents,' plural: different, simultaneous presents. The office – outside – the people in the next room – the people in the television studio – the citizens of distant Stockholm – his wife at home, Anna.

Other people carry the past like an anchor.

Her mother was broken by it, although she pretended it meant nothing to her. She'd never discussed it with her children so it had only lived inside her, festering there. 'I hate your father,' she should have told them, or, 'I love him still, I'd forgive him if he walked in that door.' Instead she'd kept it to herself and she'd died over with every new day that came to her.

He traces the perfume to the exact points where she has put it on.

The first time they came here together they went swimming.

Later, she smelt how the beach girls used to in his indulged, indulgent adolescence, burying him in sand, laughing and calling encouragement to each other, their hair falling down and covering their faces and tickling him so that it was no grave displeasure – none at all – to be buried in sand till only his head and neck were showing. That was the time of the group, when you didn't want to be apart from it, 'the girls' or 'the boys', dealing so tentatively with each other like two cautious, diplomatic armies.

Then she had tasted salty. He had licked the gritty flavour from her lips.

Things have got beyond that point now. Maybe it means their days – their afternoons – are numbered.

He isn't happy to think it, nor is he as sorry as he might be. He has refined his extra-marital emotions to the minimum.

Carefully, tenderly, he slips both his palms beneath her

breasts and wishes – as he always wishes – that these few moments in the routine might last until they've yielded all their pleasure of anticipation.

Other men have done exactly the same, but she doesn't think of them, not individually. It is a collective sensation. Sex is a collective, even abstract experience for her.

If she had roots in the soil, in the earth, if she felt ripe inside and had the conscious want of a child, then it might be otherwise. But she lives her life with steadying concrete beneath her feet, and children frighten her with their whelp cries and staring, remembering eyes.

It has almost ceased to matter, 'with whom': it has *almost* ceased to matter . . .

While he is kneading her, she tries to imagine his wife. Anna. Sometimes, in the dark, wives are clearer to her than their husbands.

This affair seldom encounters darkness. They eat afterwards and they drive home separately with the aid of headlights, but she knows she will look back on it in time to come – when and if she cares to look back – as 'the afternoon affair'.

One afternoon they heard the news of a siege on television, and did the necessary with the voices on 'mute' and the flicker from the screen patterning the ceiling and walls.

That afternoon when he caught sight of them both – his father and the woman, in a city street where they shouldn't have been – it was what he noticed about her, her breasts, supported on one of those superstructures of the time, shaped under her turquoise dress and pointing forwards like torpedoes. He stood watching them and wondered if his father did it like this because he was imagining how it used to be, walking the same street with the woman who would be the mother of his children.

This woman wore seamed nylons and kept smoothing her skirt. Her knight companion was holding her elbow.

His mother had brought up a family and didn't have breasts like torpedoes (if she had ever had them), but maybe this other woman in the turquoise dress wasn't supposed to resemble her very closely, she was to be something else, a kind of caricature of a woman, over-the-top and almost too much to handle. Almost.

The teenage boy stood in a shop doorway watching them passing in the glass, imagining those breasts out of their slings, how they pleased in the ample flesh.

He never complains about his wife to her, as she has known other husbands to do. Anna's being such a mystery fascinates her, makes her even more of a mystery.

Sometimes she thinks she herself is only the connection between the different absences and gaps of knowledge, like holes, in her own life. His wife is one of those voids.

They have their gender in common, but that is all. Anna took the traditional option: she went for the new.

Now isn't the time to ask him all about her, but she will.

'Tell me . . . tell me about Anna . . .'

So, why does she need to know?

Sometimes – it's crazy – it's as if it's easier for her to imagine she's one of those other women she knows so little about, than to be the harlot who takes their husbands in adultery.

She only has to remember her mother – one of the wives – to remember all that she isn't.

But her mother lost out in the end.

Maybe, subconsciously, what she's engaged in now is avenging that wrong her father did them both?

He stretches out on the bed beside her and covers her left breast with his hand. He massages it lightly.

In summer, in the dunes, his mother would wear a yellow swimsuit and for the rest of the year whenever she dressed up to go out with his father he would see the mark where her skin took its easy deep tan to, and no further. Dressed up and doused with perfume, swishing past in taffeta and French silk stockings, she fascinated him, she *inspired* him: if for no other reason than because she had survived the experience of them all, husband and children, and she was still looking as she did at the end of it.

It was only later that he discovered she'd also been doing it for someone else: a man she wrote occasional letters to, whom she'd known twenty years before, whom she'd turned down to marry the father of her children. By chance the man caught sight of her and recognised her while she was waiting in an airport departure lounge to fly off to meet his father and he was sitting beside her, the dutiful son, keeping her company. Somehow he immediately intuited the situation, and he thought, how odd if it had been like this, *this* greying, middle-aged man for my father instead of the greying, middle-aged one I have: and would I have been born myself, or someone else? The man was perfectly charming, he explained he was waiting for 'Joan' and the situation was only betrayed by his mother being able to say where his wife was – on her annual solo holiday in Portugal – without having to be told. But that was all, that was as much as had come of it, the moment was over and gone. Or so he'd always presumed.

As he climbs on top of her she's thinking of the company client receiving the instructions she's left for him in the office, and she's watching the colours from the television screen dribbling across the ceiling.

And then she's thinking of Anna at home. Doing what? Cooking, perhaps. But Thursdays are her husband's business evenings, so she probably isn't cooking.

Doing the shopping for the house? Gardening? Repairing children's clothes?

She used to watch her mother and she would vow, 'Never, I shall never . . .' Her mother had belonged to a generation which didn't have the opportunity. She had had the opportunity offered to her, on a plate, and she'd decided very early on, I was born for this. I don't let this one go.

> Sometimes.
> It's easier. Or not.
> *You* have to make the going, that's the
> Bloody shame of it.
> The sweat.
> The grind.

Sometimes,
Though,
It's like reaching beyond.
Everything meets.
Everything clicks.
The great *click*!
Love flows.
Flows.
Too much for himself.
For everyone.
All times, where they were,
Stranded.
Rescuing, saving.
Bringing back, bringing
Home.
Love.
Joy.
Stupid word.
Bloody stupid.
Joy. Sometimes
Joy flowing.
A stream to catch them
All,
Float them off,
Carry them,
Reach beyond.
Beyond.
To . . .

It's a nice room. Very nice. She can hear the sea, just, through his breathing.

The sea. Doing as it is wont. Humouring them today. The gentle, lulling, turning over of its waves.

But not freedom. What of the pull of the tides, the moon-power? The sea, contained by its shores. Repelled by its rocks, defied by its islands.

The sea. Freedom/not freedom.

*

He lay his head on her breasts, between her breasts, in the dip, the slide.

He lies there like a child.
The only child she will have.
She looks up at the drifting coloured light on the ceiling. Ripples of light.
She won't say anything. He has never come to her private, secret place. That is out of his reach. It has been reached before by others, a few times. Just a few. They have come to it together, she and the intrepid, athletic explorers in her past life that she is so reluctant to consider.
Reached that faraway land of tropical heat and waterfalls. The high cliché country. Ridden there on their splendid sex.

There was Sophie, there was his mother, there was Gill, and Viv, there might have been a sister if his parents hadn't decided that two sons constituted a sensibly sized modern family.
He hears them through the flesh of her breasts, through the bones of her chest, beneath his ear, in the running of her blood and her milk. Voices, giggles, the sounds of nylons, georgette, sateen, rayon, disappearing heels.

The sea.
She turns her head and looks to the source of the outer light.
She closes her eyes.
The sea, the sea . . .

Later, he lifts his head.
She is sleeping, in a different day to his, and now, he realises, would be the moment to take his leave. But it would probably only be to return another time, with her or with someone else, to hear the sea, smell it on warm skin, taste it.
He props himself up on his elbows, then eases himself off the bed.

In Sheratons and Marriotts, plugged into the cable films, faxing facts back to base he is a late-twentieth-century hologram man, in as many places as he is required to be. From the windows the view is different every time but really it is always the same, ring-roads and copper-tinted high-rise office blocks and the tough, resisting scrub that grows on the edges of deserts. Away from England he calls home and charges it to expenses: in the background – as if it's from the next room (except that the hotel rooms are soundproofed to exclude intimate sonic intrusions) – he can hear children's voices, music practice, cooker alarms, even, once, a car backfiring in the road. But it isn't to that he is listening, not properly, not to the details: he is further away and longer ago, the house is a new one, the children are running through the echoing rooms, no cooker alarm goes off by mistake, his wife is exploring the kitchen arrangements with a shrewd, canny eye he hasn't expected in her, just as his mother stood in the kitchens of their different houses for the first time taking in the situation, calculating with the part of her brain that didn't have anything to do with the evenings of dressing up to go out and the quiet corners of afternoons when another man than her husband must have trespassed into her thoughts.

She wears a Japanese designer because she is the sort of woman who dresses as she chooses to.

He still wears his city suit, because in that he is most like his 'other' self – and because, in the event of anyone ever chancing to catch sight of him with her, he can argue the all-excusing claims of 'business'.

They might pass as a married couple, even early on this Thursday evening, but she believes she doesn't have a wife's docility, and he knows he is more alert and wound up than he ever is with his wife. He has a habit of hurrying her about the foyer and public rooms with a hand placed on the small of her back and she wishes he wouldn't, but it is a manner of propulsion they have become used to and they can perform it – to all intents and purposes – like a marital ballet. He is comforted by that, while she has begun to blame herself for allowing him.

Sometimes they eat in the hotel. On other evenings they drive in the car to an over-priced restaurant nearby, converted from an old barn. Tonight, on the evening of the siege in distant Stockholm, they eat in the hotel dining-room: at a different table from the last time, which was different from the one before. (They don't want to draw undue attention to themselves. And too much custom stales.)

Being shown to the table they hear two elderly women tut-tutting over the television news, asking whatever is the world coming to?

They sit down; the menus are handed to them.

She suddenly enquires.

'Is your wife a good cook?'

He raises his eyes. He looks puzzled.

'Or maybe you haven't thought about it?' she asks, in a voice that sounds sharpish to her ear.

'I suppose – yes,' he says, 'yes, she *is* a good cook. But . . .'

He closes his mind to it. It's not what he wants to think about, at this moment.

'Lobster,' he suggests, seeing the word on the *à la carte*. He doesn't particularly like or *dislike* lobster, but the word instantly conveys a picture to his brain and from his childhood he remembers live lobsters crawling about inside wicker pots on a quayside, watching them as he stood with his parents – year after year – waiting for the little ferry from the town to the resort, to carry them through the safe channels between the sandbanks like whales' backs.

'Lobster?' she repeats. 'Is that what you're having?'

She doesn't want to eat the same as him, on a principle of sorts. She doesn't want to be *seen* eating lobster if he is to eat lobster.

'Lamb,' she says, for no reason.

'Do you think it would be good?' he asks. 'Maybe I should
have that?'

Lambs, springtime, green grass, sap rising, hope on the
wing.

'No. I'll take the – the sweetbreads,' she says. He has
told her he doesn't care for offal. It seems the only choice
she has, sweetbreads, so properly there is no 'choice' left
to her at all.

'Oh no, not offal.' He shakes his head. 'No. *I* shall have . . .'

He remembers the quayside and the so-so taste he didn't
adjust to till he was in his middle thirties.

' – lobster,' he says.

Sweetbreads and lobster, they tell the waiter. With some chilled
white wine, please.

While they wait they discuss what they see around them in
the dining-room: the newly completed Fifth Avenue-chic decor
(she doesn't like it, he doesn't mind), the clientèle – a curious
mixture of the staid and adulterous, and never the twain mixing
– and, beyond the heads, the views of early dusk through the
window.

When the food arrives, they eat gratefully. The lobster is
salty fresh and tastes of the sea; the sweetbreads have been
cooked simply, with some sorrel, as she likes them best.

The lobster requires dextrous handling, she has a finicky side
salad, so neither of them has very much cause to speak. He
doesn't want another question about his wife, and he wonders
– not for the first time today – why she is so interested, if
she secretly hopes to be a wife herself. She doesn't want to
have to answer another of his questions about her job, or the
colleagues she works with: that life is separate from this one,
and she wonders why he is so interested, when he doesn't
really *listen* to the wary answers she gives him. Does he need
to believe in their difference and apartness? – that it makes for
some sort of danger to them both? Does he need the stimulus
of an imaginary intrigue afoot? Oh Jesus God . . .

*

Leaving the dining-room they pass a news-tape machine. It announces that the siege continues, but they don't stop to read it.

They walk out into the garden.

'I have to go back,' he says. 'Anna is having a party for the children.' He smiles. 'Lots of washing-up, I expect.'

She shrugs unsympathetically.

'Use paper plates,' she says.

'They'd probably just eat them!'

She smiles, relieved she'll never have children, so she will never know if he's exaggerating or not.

At least the children's party provides them with the excuses they require, to finish the afternoon and evening.

There is always a pattern; or, rather, there are two patterns. Sometimes he spends the night in the room, sometimes it is she – it is never both of them together.

Tonight *she* will stay and try to forget her important client and whether or not he received all the instructions she left for him. She will wake in the morning to a skyful of light and the distant rumbling of the breakers.

They walk along one of the gravel paths.

Neither of them speaks.

Their situation eludes them both.

He doesn't seek danger, but – instead – more security than he has: he is wanting to find in her, a stranger, his own past.

From her own experience she fears becoming anyone's wife – an abandoned wife like her mother, who had to bring her up unaided, without the help of any man – and she needs to remind herself continually of the strangulation of marriage.

He wants her to be an empty page for him, the silence of recall, and she tries to catch him glancing at his watch, checking that there are no give-away crumples in the creases of his clothes.

Neither knows how it will end, although it must. They each hope for a clean, very final conclusion. It's most unlikely there will be any anger. They may even arrange to meet every so often for lunch, to show there are no hard feelings on either side. For him the affair will already be a peripheral memory he is trying to recapture in another bed, with another woman, and on her part she will be confirming the wisdom and no-nonsense practicality of her own independence. He will always be a man at the sweet mercy of the women in his life, and she will always be a – considering, self-justifying – person apart, her own woman.

Or something like that.

She leaves the lights off as she watches his departure from the bedroom window. The television picture colours the room, and the words muddle about somewhere in the middle of the empty space.

The car radio, which he forgot to switch off earlier, crackles as he turns the ignition key. Voices come up. It's the news, that same bloody siege.

Coincidentally television and radio are both dwelling on the same aspect of the drama. The relatives are being interviewed again, or it's the two tapes being re-run: the interviewees sound tearful, hopeless.

They each hear, in the bedroom and in the car. *She* is embarrassed by the emotion in this oddly theatrical ritual taking place in a cold northern country, and she wonders what it is the gunmen are fighting for. The woman radio correspondent turns her attention to the 'freedom fighters' but *he* has picked up the word 'home' from a sorrowing Swedish mother and, in his head, he calculates how quickly he can get back to Anna and the children and the kitchen festooned, like a little Christmas in April, with streamers and balloons.

MIRROR, MIRROR

Richard told her as he drove them there that he'd passed through the town the week before and he'd seen the mirror hanging in an antiques shop.

'I was putting off time,' he explained. 'Someone from Taplowe's had the car phone number and rang and said could I make it quarter to four, not three.'

He quite often got about in the car during his working week, and she envied him his superior knowledge of Buckinghamshire after their sixteen months here.

They parked the Saab and walked along the famously picturesque High Street with its photogenic grass verges and cobbles. Richard opened the door of a shop with a bow window; a warning bell buzzed.

He never dared to buy anything for the house without consulting her first. He trusted her aesthetic judgment as he didn't his own. His upbringing had given him very little self-assurance in that respect. He had always been clearly in awe of *her* very different background: boarding-school, a home her ancestors had occupied for nearly three hundred years, four canteens of crested silver, the several items of 'good' furniture her great-grandparents had inherited and clung on to (unfortunately scuffed and worn but what did that matter when they were bona fide – Hepplewhite chairs, marquetry tables, a couple of Japanese lacquer screens, Persian rugs), the gimlet eyes of family grandees in half a dozen oil portraits. Sometimes, it was true, he did have a 'feel' for an object encountered in a shop or a saleroom; but at other times, she would have had to admit, he conspicuously did not.

He pointed to the mirror hanging on the wall, but she had already spotted it. They had agreed one would nicely suit the rather dark dining-room in their own home: placed opposite the window, it would throw back some valuable daylight.

The surrounding panels on this mirror, he had reported to her, were painted. Venetian scenes, late eighteenth century. But it wasn't those she was attending to as she walked across the shop. She was focusing on herself. The wavy glass didn't help, but *it* wasn't wholly to blame. She felt she was surprising herself, for once not being able to prepare and preen before studying her reflection. Now she was looking sourly at what she was confronted with: herself as others must see her. Rumpled skirt, a too visible midriff beginning under her green waxed jacket, impossible flyaway hair. Her knees and ankles were kept out of the picture, thank God. In her youth people would refer to her as being 'big-boned', which even then she'd sensed was their choosing to make the best of her bad lot. For some reason, girls – 'gels' – with her approximately rural background weren't expected to know how to dress, how to show themselves to proper effect. Because it was a tradition, she had merely obliged: and at the age of twenty-nine, this was the result.

She tried to concentrate on the painted surrounds to the glass, but couldn't. How deep had Richard had to look beneath the surface to discover her potential, this suavely handsome husband of hers who had duly become a client of his father-in-law's tailor after an introduction, who wouldn't have looked out of place featured in a magazine lay-out on the well-groomed male. At twenty-seven years old and with an older sister and younger brother married, she had started to panic that no one was going to lift her down from the dusty shelf. But then, at what had felt like the eleventh hour, Richard – her shining white knight – had presented himself.

Not that he had ever laid claims to being a rescuing knight. The castle in their story was her family's seven-gabled honeystone house and the seventy-six prime acres of Oxfordshire arable; she had been a princess and he the pauper, to judge from all that distinctly embarrassing respect he had paid her then (and still, on public occasions, did now). And yet, finally, he'd also had the courage and steel to propose to her, and to ask her father in the old-fashioned way for her hand. In part – she had seen quite well at the time – it was because her circumstances exercised a kind of numbing magic over him; partly because *he* saw quite well that she wasn't drawn to all those dyed-in-the-Aran-sweater-wool Hooray-Hugos and Chinless Wonders her schoolfriends had too predictably succumbed to. Richard was quiet, sensitive, enterprising, bourgeois, amusing, practical, romantic, and something of an enigma.

It had been an unlikely marriage, but it had survived the first two years and certain persons' forecasts, and now here they were.

Richard enjoyed antiques shops. He invariably asked her for advice about what he should buy his mother for birthdays and Christmas, and she complied, no longer telling him *he* should decide. If he pointed to this or that, and she suggested one of them was preferable to the other, he immediately recognised the object's virtues which he had been so uncertain about a few moments before.

This mirror, if they bought it, would be for themselves. It was expensive. But Richard never stinted on the house and its furnishings: he was thought highly of in the company and by fellow accountants outside it, and he didn't hesitate to give his attentive superiors and the London head-hunters a guided tour of their home whenever they entertained them to dinner.

The mirror . . . Again she was unhappy with the version of herself she was standing staring at in the crinkly glass. She didn't think she could live with the outside of that person and have it constantly in the house ready to waylay her. And there were little spots on the margins of the glass, specks the colour of rust, the size of damp marks in books. They could have the glass replaced, of course, a new piece cut and fitted: yes, quite possibly . . .

She reached forward and tilted the heavy gilt frame. She was going to turn round and propose they did change the glass when she looked over the reflection of her shoulder in the mirror. At the back of the shop, in the second room, the owner – a trim middle-aged man with a sunbed tan and too evenly grey hair

– was saying something to Richard. She moved the frame an inch or two to the right and chanced to see – effected in what seemed like a couple of seconds – Richard removing a business card from his wallet and pushing it into the breast pocket of the man's shirt. The gesture must have taken nearer five or six seconds to complete, though, because Richard's hand appeared to linger a fraction too long over the pocket, almost as if he was fingering the material. The two of them smiled at one another, then Richard turned round.

She instantly felt flustered, clumsy. The mirror clattered back against the wall. She knew Richard was watching her, and she looked away, hoping he couldn't see the reflected track of her eyes, that he'd think she had only been paying heed to the mirror.

He walked through without making a sound in his hand-made shoes she would go with him to buy, to lend him confidence with the assistants. But damn all that now.

She tried to steady her breathing, to control it, to give the appearance of normality. In – out, in – out.

In the crooked mirror glass she saw the colour firing her neck.

'I – I'm not sure,' she said. 'If scenes of Venice are – '

'It was just an idea, Roz.'

He didn't sound disappointed, not at all. Very occasionally they would debate the merits of a piece, but that wasn't to be with the mirror.

She felt she ought to be speaking in its defence. But for Richard, smiling again, the matter was finished with. The mirror was history.

Or . . . The thought occurred to her: or it might have been that the mirror was no more and no less than an excuse for them to drop by, so that he could reacquaint himself with the premises, to initiate the process they had begun in other antiques shops, of becoming 'regulars' whose tastes and fancies the owners would learn to become familiar with in time.

They walked back to the car and got in.

She watched Richard's fingers, long and supple ('artistic', her mother had called them when he was wooing her, also making the best of what she had too much tact to tell her she considered a not very satisfactory business). Even the insertion of the key into the ignition lock became a graceful exercise. Following her father's example he had equipped himself with a signet ring for his little finger: but it wasn't engraved with his initials, it was inset with a green stone, which she felt wasn't really the 'done' thing. The signet ring was one purchase he hadn't consulted her about. Maybe it had been a present from a relative, or from a friend belonging to his old life? – but in that case, why shouldn't he have told her? He hadn't volunteered any information at all about it. And she had never enquired, God alone knew why. She would have found it impossible to discuss the matter now, to ask him to fill her in, after holding out with her ignorance for so long.

She was feeling tired, tired and confused. She laid her head back on the headrest. Brightly, quite chirpily, he suggested they have tea somewhere. She told him, in as normal a voice as she could manage, that her stomach was playing her up, it was unsettled, rather queasy – which was true enough.

He immediately flashed a look at her, his eyes wide.

'"Queasy"?' he repeated.

The brightness and chirpiness had evaporated, although he too was feigning normality.

'It's the motion of the car maybe,' she said, sounding to herself a deal less than convincing.

It wasn't the reason she saw that he feared. Another subject they never discussed was having a family of their own. He had vaguely commended they wait until they'd put down their roots, and she had merely agreed, being undecided in herself whether or not she would be able to pass the Good Mother test. In the meantime they were scrupulous about taking precautions, on the one or two occasions in a week when there was even the infinitesimal risk of an accident.

On the way home they stopped at a filling-station for petrol.

There was no sign to say that it wasn't self-service, but a

young man in red overalls stepped nimbly out of the office and
crossed the forecourt to attend to them.

'What motoring used to be like!' Richard said after he'd given
him instructions.

'How did you know – ?' she asked.

'"Know"?'

' – that you don't have to fill the tank yourself?'

'Oh. I came in last week.'

The youth had smiled as if he'd recognised him through the
open window. *Him* in particular. When Saabs, after all, were
two a penny hereabouts.

'Did you?' she said.

Richard opened his door and got out. She watched him
oh-so-casually raise his arms above his head and stretch, as
if they had just travelled dozens of miles, not the two or three
from the town. How lean he looked with that leisure-centre
physique: how careful he was at home about what he ate, always
liking to know in advance what she had on the menu for them
both, fussing almost as much as on the increasing number of
evenings when they entertained his business colleagues, even
recently some big noises from London and someone from the
New York office.

He louchely pushed his hands into his trouser pockets and
walked round to the far side of the island of petrol pumps, where
she couldn't see him. She heard him whistling, tunelessly.

What caused her to look there and then she was never to
comprehend – but it just so chanced that she glanced into the
side-mirror on her door. The boy was replacing the nozzle in
the pump. Simultaneously he must have caught sight of Richard.
He smiled in his direction, and she thought it was the most
disarmingly coy smile she had ever witnessed. Hardly a man's
smile at all.

The long coil of black rubber tubing was hitched into place
and then the figure walked out of the mirror's heavy-duty plastic
frame. She couldn't remember which switch on the dashboard
adjusted and re-angled the mirrors. Where she wasn't able to
see, money was being transferred – she heard the jingle of
coins – and four or five seconds later Richard reappeared. He

pulled his door open and lowered himself into the seat. For a split second he lifted his eyes to look in the driving-mirror, then he – elegantly, as ever – turned the key in the ignition lock. They rolled forward. In the office, the boy stood watching them: or maybe not watching *them*, because she glimpsed through the reflections of the pumps and the canopy that he was holding a comb and slicking it back through his hair.

Her stomach felt worse than squeamish. Topsy-turvy, churning. Sick. She was trying not to think, not to think, not to think. She wound down her window. They passed the first lit interior, in a gentrified cottage. At school, she suddenly recalled, they'd had the strangest French *enseignant*, from Paris, who carried a pochette about with him and wafted trails of pungent after-shave. Richard went to work with a black lizard paper-case and had a penchant for a certain subtle kind of Givenchy talc he'd discovered, which she bought him on her days up in London at the Knightsbridge shops with her mother.

She leaned her head back and closed her eyes. She saw the scenes of Venice on the mirror, the panels on the right-hand side, the paint flaking away but the midnight revellers still unmistakable as they gathered under a sickle moon, their faces and purposes concealed beneath their carnival masks.

She opened her eyes and swivelled them to the right, just in the very nick of time to see Richard repositioning the windscreen mirror with his hand. He had been looking at her, his eyes were moving off her. She turned her head on her neck to face him. He half turned his, a semi-profile that had always put her in mind of Ryan O'Neal. He smiled, inevitably, but his mouth was betrayed by his eyes, which told a different, fraught story.

She said nothing. She was trying not to think, not to think. She closed her eyes again.

The last thing she saw was the oval of emerald (although he claimed it was something else, only semi-precious) on the ring: the wrong choice for the gentleman he aspired so hard to be. The richness of green caught the fading Buckinghamshire light. In the cabin's slow, silent gloaming as they drove, the stone glinted – with all its mute opulence – like a knowing, very sly eye.

TABLE TALK

She reposes in her painted image high on a wall of the restaurant,
above a mirror, among pewter and copper Art Nouveau-ish
flourishes, very nearly at ceiling level, directly beneath a plaster
frieze of stylised laburnum flowers.
  She is depicted in a woodland glade, resting against a tree.
By some acrobatic feat, she has one arm propped against a
branch while lying semi-recumbent at the tree's base. She wears
a gossamer-thin mauve gown; it doesn't end at her bared feet,
but drifts off into a bank of moss and quiet foliage. One shoulder
is left creamily exposed, and the dress is decidedly décolleté. In
the long and slender, possibly over-sized hand of her right arm
(which is not the one draped over the branch) the woman holds
a shallow champagne glass. Her head is tilted coyly towards the
suspended arm and trailing left hand, some auburn hair falls on
to that dress of semi-transparent, spidery fineness. Her mouth is
almost smiling. The eyes are simultaneously wary but inviting as
they gaze down into the room.
  Those eyes have seen so much, while the woman's form
remains so perennially young. Wisdom has accrued to her
as a right, along with the patina of tobacco smoke and
general high living. She is beyond it all, in one sense,
and yet in another continues to be an intense and rapt
observer. She has seen and heard the gamut of emotions,
witnessed the confabulations and aphonies of otherwise untold
personal histories. She is the protectress of confidences and
indiscretions, custodian of confessions and secrets. She is the
room's good genius.

Drink with me! Make merry, make light!
  It's deadly serious when you're living it, but from another angle

– viewed from the ceiling, from hereafter – it has a comic aspect, believe me.

Drink with me! If you're paying out of your own pocket for what you imbibe, forget the cost of it. If you're *not settling the bill, take whatever comes to you and accept what it costs you with good grace – oh, it* will *cost, though, be warned, because nothing in life is ever free.*

So high above you, it is my privilege to regale you with my wisdom – so-called – you who raise your eyes from your plates to look up at me. Preferably you should be doing so over the rim of your glass, so that we can anoint this confederacy, do the rites on it.

Santé! Prosit! *I'm watching, I'm listening. Act your parts. You'll forget that I told you, of course – but be of good heart, it's a play upon words, only a capriccio after all.*

Well, maybe.

But whom does *she* see? My mohair and high wrap-collar aren't fashionable but they're comfortable. So she knows I make up my own mind, and don't follow the magazines, and that I prefer softness to rough. I have told her that much without having to speak a word in my defence, while she – prattling away – has really told me very little. Her clothes are impersonally up-to-the-minute, as the High Street decides, and there is hardly a clue of her individuality anywhere. Except perhaps in the voice, which is more localised than she may think, under the nasal delivery and honed hotel reception-desk vowels. Wherever she learned to talk, her jobbing days are surely behind her now, or suspended.

It's usually at parties that they declare themselves. Or rather, they insinuate themselves, they weave their winsome way about their quarry and don't realise in their relative innocence that *they* are the mantis prey. I am Ignored, which means of course that they know only too well who I am, the wife, and so they go to great lengths to avoid me. They don't sidle up to Geoff; instead they circumnavigate him, like little bobbing craft. They must be giving off distress signals, because I can recognise when he's ready to get up steam for a rescue mission. If I didn't know the signals by now, I should be even more of a fool than I am.

The high collar is a diplomatic choice: it hides my neck. I had the chins seen to, but the gullet provided them with problems. 'Scarves?' the surgeon suggested, and I realised he was being serious. Polo necks are a little passé, but I manage. Best of all is a tight little nelson collar and, tucked into it, a rich silk square. The trick is *not* to have it looking like a surrogate bandage, but quite casually done. I have become, in time, a passable mistress of disguise.

But it's I who will be here when it's over and done, my dear. Madame Defarge by the guillotine and a Greek chorus rolled into one.

Geoff will give you what . . .?
    Rich meals. Fine views of Brighton or the Devon Riviera, from the windows of a luxurious hotel room. The cash to ride wherever you care in taxis.
    Believe it or not, I never had any of them. Others before me were pampered – he had means, I should tell you, even then – but for his own reasons he didn't want me to become inured to that way of living.
    What he must have feared most for me, for the woman he wanted to marry, was complacency.

You can't believe I'm doing this, blithely slogging it out with you over two courses, but I *am* doing it. I can't believe it of myself, but all I want to do is live well. Eat healthy food, refuse to take into my body any part of an animal or fowl that has had a miserable life, to be honest and above-board and not to be two-faced about anybody or anything, even those I dislike most. To think of the mother planet in her plight, to use only unleaded petrol and ozone-friendly aerosols, not to poison the garden with chemicals or forget to return bottles to the bottle-bank. I save newspapers and used postage stamps and zinc cans for collection by charity volunteers, and sometimes I assist them. Oh God, I mean to be a good woman, I really do, the best woman and wife it's in my capacity to be.

So I came here, not travelling by myself in a gratuitous car or in a money-no-object taxi, but by public transport. On an exhaust-spluttering bus.

Why? you fail to ask me. For what end?

To remind myself, I suppose, of what I need not be.

That's *not* how the business began, these lunches *à deux*, because then I was much less curious about your kind than frightened of you. Yet that first lunch with the first of my husband's mistresses didn't turn out to be the scarecrow job I'd imagined – I was all psyched up to throw my accusations at her – and I ended up pitying her instead. I saw into a life which circumstances had rendered so different from mine that her actions became perfectly reasonable to me. And that has been the case all the way down the line. Some of you want an older man's protection, some simply want a good time and a brief oblivion, others are out to wreak revenge on the whole of the male species. One girl confessed she had a criminal record, and another told me (a little apologetically) that nothing ever gave her greater delight than to try to break up a marriage. I listened, and a few times I gave advice, because I was asked. Two had already been to psychiatrists and learned their lesson well: blame everything you can on the past and, as far as possible, load all the responsibility for what went wrong on to somebody else.

'Oh my God,' I'm squealing, 'I'm so sorry . . .'

By mistake she gets the juice of my tangerine segment in her eye.

She copes nobly, with only two flutters of the left eyelid.

It's impressive; she would do well at any of the get-togethers with Geoff's business colleagues. She would make a super-cool embassy wife, seated at one end of the dinner table while grenades are let off in the streets of their Latin American posting. On second thoughts, her voice is a little too much south London, and I doubt if any self-respecting ambassador's wife would ever wear her fingernails silver and *quite* so long.

But she means well, I think. She is struggling pluckily through for my sake. She is pretty much as I expected. Upwardly mobile but not as sophisticated as she pretends. Moderately bright, bosomy, as honest as she can permit herself to be. With the exaggeratedly nice manners of that class who look to their betters. Seven out of ten for looks.

She corresponds to form, although she doesn't realise it. Let the poor girl be spared the stun prod of too much home-truth.

Let it be a game to her, and to all of them, while I appear to pretend and make light.

I smile, and she's deceived, and she prattles on, about everything except Geoff. The consensus of opinion seems to be that I'm not quite in my right mind, but that I'm harmless. Presumably they decide that it would be unwise, cruel even, to tell Geoff about our preliminary lunch, that what he needs are his illusions about me. I remind them after all of what age does to a woman, and at least he picks girls with a vein of feminine sympathy in them.

This is me. I'm not proud. I have a thin, gaunt neck. I treat myself in fancy restaurants. I smoke too much, although I try to be a good woman. I also drink more than I should, but if I get tipsy I wreath it in smiles. Under these nails – false nails – I've others, my own, bitten and bitten away, right down to the little pads of raw flesh.

Don't take him.

Don't entice him from me.

But I talk in a different way from you, I have instinctive good manners, I can hold forth on more or less any subject because I read a lot, I read too much. I can suggest to you by my air, by my demeanour and deportment, that I have seen the world. Oh, I've watched water flow under a great many bridges.

He is my husband, and – the fact of the matter is, Debbie – I shall never find another if you tempt him too hard. If you forget yourself, I shall be the spirit that comes to haunt you down all those lost years you imagine now you've got taken care of in your head.

Yours will be a fancy life for a while, with some useful personal introductions thrown in, but if you should go any further than that I shall call in my debt. We have to render an account for everything. And I have paid prodigiously with my humiliation.

The terrible price for living is death, my dear, and on my bad days I can believe I'm the clarion call. But let us be cheerful, let's have another drink, here's to us. The price for loving is waking from the dream, but you're hardly older than what, a teenager. You'll be right as rain again before you know it, youth is as tough as steel armour.

Nothing could have given her more pleasure than giving birth when she did, to a daughter.

For Ian the novelty slowly wore off, but hardly so for her. *She* had the responsibility, and how happy she was for it. Claire was growing up healthily and – thank God – averagely, according to the Dr Spock scenario then in vogue, and by the time she started primary school she was acquiring prettiness too.

She helped Claire with her homework. She suggested to her teachers at parents' evenings that there could be *more* homework in this or that subject. She took pride in Claire's good marks for the prep exercises, even though she never did quite so well in class work.

Ian took the decision that she should be sent away, first to a junior crammer, then to a boarding-school. They were recommended to both by his business friends, who assured them that they were the right choices.

Maybe they were. 'Right' was a fuzzy sort of word, though, in the circumstances. Soon she had too much time on her hands not to question the validities of others' words that were spoken so simply, so glibly.

With Claire's new friends' parents she felt, suddenly, a clodhopper. Ian seemed to notice also, and – worse – so did Claire.

At home she imposed even greater standards of tidiness on herself. She took a cookery course, and as a consequence overstretched herself when she gave dinner parties. She quite lost the knack of cooking the basics straightforwardly. Otherwise she read, books about archaeology and British history, and suggested trips on Claire's exeat weekends and in the holidays to National Trust properties.

She guessed these excursions were undertaken on sufferance, but Claire had acquired a certain falsity at her fashionable school which obscured her actual feelings. Her attractiveness now had older boys and young men turning their heads, and in herself – for a time – there was mingled pride and concern watching her daughter.

But while concern remained, the pride was to be diluted. Gradually – what she could never have foreseen happening – a degree of irritation was admitted to her system, followed by the first stirrings of jealousy. Claire's life was opening out in front of her: how could she not envy her the gamut of possibilities, the spread of cards in her hand? For her own generation there had been the cheating promise of better days to come just after the war, but these had died on the vine, and everything had reverted to how it had been in the age before: chances were at a premium again and whatever opportunities there were the men got. Marriage had been the inevitable rite of passage for a young woman in her situation, educated past the age of fifteen (to seventeen and a half) but without the encouragement to pursue book knowledge any further.

The next generation was into self-expression and finding themselves. She could see from this distance – in 1992 – the ridiculousness of the clothes they'd worn in the seventies, but that apart she thought it hadn't been a bad time for Claire and her contemporaries to be young. The ego came into play later, in the succeeding decade, which had been all about self-improvement, and by then her envy had weathered to what she'd cared to acknowledge even less – bitterness.

Claire had chosen not to marry – if it had ever been a likely option for her – and a series of young men were fitted into the framework of her working life. She would select them just as girls with her own so-called 'advantages' used to aspire to do in the marrying days – promising professionals with good incomes and social connections – but with Claire they would drift in, stay around for a while, and then as suddenly disappear again.

It was just possible that there had been an 'accident', to explain Claire's absence of six weeks and a subsequent holiday in a French spa town. Nothing had been said at the time, no reference was made to the interlude now, but as a mother or simply as a woman who could fear pain for her body she had always had her suspicions, that *something* had gone awry. If so, the choice was *not* to have a complicating baby as a claim on her, but to dispose of the circumstance altogether. She had watched Claire with children since and noticed the ironcast resolution with which privately she would be putting them right out of her mind.

She was fully aware that Claire *tolerated* her and that now she let her see so. Not so long ago she had been subtler about it, with that highly perfected skill of dropping a glance at her wristwatch in the crack of time between one second and the next, or as she was brushing a crumb from her cuff or picking a thread from her skirt. (Skirt, never trousers. Above all her daughter was feminine in her appearance, taking a market value of herself in the England the New Tories had made.) Now, in her middle thirties, the only difference in the sort of company she kept was that most of her men friends were married. Older single men couldn't be trusted in this age of immune-deficiency systems, and if she jeopardised a marriage in the cause of fellowship then – it seemed – so it must be.

A mother and child.

But not, surely, her mother's daughter.

They did have certain memories in common. In her own words as she retold them they became too sentimental. When Claire decided to remember, she thought she detected a certain edge in the recollection, a suggestion of blame on some account. What they ought to have been sharing they ended up giving their two separate interpretations of.

She sometimes felt that Claire was reacting to expectations about producing a grandchild: within a marriage, of course. She always tried to keep these as far from the conversation as she could, but Claire – to judge from the shrinkages of her mouth and her eyes between their lids – seemed to hear reproaches even in the silences.

After lunch – one of their not very frequent lunches – they inevitably traipsed off to a gallery to 'take in' an exhibition. They went at Claire's behest, not her own, and she felt for herself it was a duty done, to make up for any awkwardnesses she'd helped to cause in the confinement of the restaurant. Yet it was rather hurtful to have to be excused by a parade of Inca pots or Shaker furniture or Erté stage costumes. Even that hurt, though, could only be a little after-echo following the sterner emotions of the previous two decades.

Of course it's only one side of the story. And half our lives, she would think, are lived in the dark, in confusion and ignorance.
This is their first time here, in this restaurant. Probably it will be their last too, because Claire has the sensitivity – no, not that: the *canniness*, rather, inherited from her father – to see when they've been overcharged for what they receive. They will split the bill, and she will pretend that Ian's money is her own to spend as she chooses. Claire could easily pay for them both, and did offer to do so years ago when these lunches began, but she also knows the extent of a mother's pride. They both read about this restaurant's revamp, in the same magazine as it turned out, and it is conveniently sited for where Claire wants them to go afterwards, to an exhibition of new Hungarian photography.
The restaurant is smarter than it needs to be for her own purposes. But Claire is dressed for anywhere, and requires *her* to make the effort too. So they cannot be shamed, just because they're not business colleagues or lovers using the premises to impress. On two or three other days in her week Claire entertains on the marketing firm's expense account –

entertains other PR types like herself, ad-men, media folk of all hues – and there is something in her manner, a brittle determination, which tells her mother that she won't go in for fake subservience and that she will drive quite a hard bargain.

Claire's is the story of an age, of a generation who had it both ways. A teenage vision of love 'n' peace circa 1969–70 and, twenty years later, a Coach black leather 'Wall Street' briefcase and gilded plastic money.

Whatever would the cool cats of 1959–60 have had to say of this dog-eat-dog world?

Elevated on one wall, chronologically well out of her era but boozily adhering to it despite, a flagrant woman reclines.

Claire noticed the painted panel first. But for the past few minutes she has ignored her, just as she will ignore children in the street and the unbalancing sentiment of memories.

A temptress, needless to say. *'That sly come-hither stare . . .'* But the artist's creation victimises herself too, because this is no more than one expects of her. The brimming champagne glass fools nobody. For the woman who holds it is an empty vessel. *'It's wicked witchcraft . . . and strictly taboo . . .'*

'I saw the photographs on television,' Claire says. 'I try to catch that arts show late at night.'

'They *do* put it on late, don't they?'

'It's all to do with TV ratings, I expect.'

Claire has a pragmatic, professional-sounding explanation for most things.

'They know who'll make the effort to stay up for it – '

'But it *is* late. Half past eleven sometimes – '

'You could record it, couldn't you?'

'I . . .'

'Isn't that why Dad bought the video box?'

'It's remembering to switch the thing on – '

'It's just finding the time,' Claire says. 'To play the tapes back.'

The day their very first television set had arrived in the house they'd delayed lunch and sat down together, the two of them, to watch *Picture Book*: side by side, perched on the cushion of the one wing chair, Claire offering her hand to hold with the excitement of the acquisition, hunching forward over her knees. All the world was waiting, theoretically, to be beamed into their sitting-room. With their fast pulses touching, they had held their breath, hands cockled, both of them poised – no less – at the edge of their known experience.

Time had changed pace when he entered his fifties. Previously they had been on the same side, so to speak. Then he started to sense the falling-out between them. Time went on ahead at its own speed, and faster than before, when once it had been as comfortable to him as a shadow. He saw properly for the first time that it was a finite commodity, sparing with itself, and inclined – wherever it could find an outlet – to follow the centrifugal principle of self-drainage.

The simple fact was that there was just too little of it.

The consequence being . . .

He watches the young woman he has brought here to share his table. Her name is Veronica. They are almost strangers to one another. Everything is perfect.

He may, at some point, tell her about his wife: that he has one, although they have lived apart for three years. But he seldom brings her to mind, so why should he compel her on Veronica? He realised at fifty-two that there was no point in Maureen and he both turning themselves into the other's hostage: so he made the proposal that they shouldn't wear one another down any longer but go their own ways, and he suspects that now as then Maureen can't find the charity in herself to forgive him.

Meanwhile Veronica is watching, not him but her weight. He doesn't blame her for her self-concern. She has recognised – long before he did – that you need to take a long, hard, appraising look at yourself.

He didn't appreciate until he turned the big Five-O that life is impermanent. He and Veronica met, although neither is very inclined to culture, in an art gallery, and it seems appropriate now: that they should have been drawn to one another among marble images of beauty, cold and unreal, and surrounded by paintings they were too familiar with from their reproductions.

In his fifties his friends started, out of the blue, to die. One dropped dead on a golf course, another tumbled down a staircase *running* between appointments, a third's lungs packed in. There were too many grey-haired heads at the funerals, too much talk of physical ailments and medical insurance.

Now he calls in at a leisure centre a couple of times a week, but only for some gentle toning-up exercises and principally to keep in touch with the regulars there. He has resisted hair colouring sprays. He isn't tempted into the designer pens in the menswear departments of stores. He still runs a staidish car with high ground clearance. He looks his age, and he acknowledges there is no proper way of 'acting' it except as intelligence and feeling can contrive with good grace between themselves.

Veronica. She is the first girl called Veronica he has ever met, and there should be room for one in every life. So this is she, the one.

She has an insouciance, a lack of urgency, that intrigues him. She doesn't seem to hear the sifting sands of time, time's winged feet. But nor does she seem to have any plans: and no designs on him. She gives the impression that everything she does is of equal significance. Picking a main dish, choosing a dress, finding a parking space, making an appointment at a breast-screening clinic, fixing a loose thread on her hem, ringing up about a stolen credit card, choosing a new lipstick, selecting a hotel for them both. She juggles time about in her diary, to take a couple of hours off work. She knows a lot about eating places, this one and that one, and he wonders how often she's been 'squired' there (the term dates him) and by whom. But the mysteries about her beguile him, and eclipse the metaphysical sort, for which there is the whole of eternity to dwell on. As things stand – sitting at their corner table, one on one (as the modern term is), at twelve fifty of a Wednesday afternoon in the early prime of her life and the gathering sere of his – he is living as fully as he accepts that this particular man with his particular history can, at the speed of experience and no slower, without scope for anticipation or backward-looking.

After the art gallery on that first accidental date, a rainy Saturday afternoon, they went off to a superior champagne bar on Great Queen Street. Bossa nova music was the fashion again, and she told him all he needed to know, out of the blue, from the Lloyd Loom wicker chair beside his, as he drank to forget something or other, that – as a technical point – the beat of that Rio music is played at exactly the same tempo as the human heart's.

Perhaps she was here to see the old place again. To prove to herself that she had the financial means. Perhaps. Even so, old habits die hard, and whom should she have bumped into in the lobby of the Marriott Hotel off Grosvenor Square but Mr Herbert Merrill?

She knew she looked different now, although not to Mr Merrill, who was a recent acquaintance. Thanks to some crucial surgical snipping, she was unidentifiable with her old London self. The waiter had asked her if she was American. She'd told him, 'When I'm on this side of the pond, yes.' But otherwise, she meant, I am as English as . . . She summoned them up again, a litany of images that stocked her dreams . . .

Anchovy toast and angel cake . . . Morris Minors and morris dancers . . . Punch and Judy . . . chintz loose covers . . . winkles . . . Malvern water . . . Your Hundred Best Tunes . . . Harrods' Sale . . . ghost trains . . . Patience Strong and Marjorie Proops . . . fox-hunting . . . Charles Dickens . . . mackerel skies and buttered prawns . . . afternoon tea (of course) . . . turned-away eyes . . . Judith Chalmers and Valerie Pitt . . . tennis club dances and cricket teas . . . Agatha Christie . . . bullying off and scrumming down . . . Gilly Gilly Ossenfeffer Katzenellen Bogen by the Sea . . .

*

I am early, so Mr Merrill is not late.

I always tell the time by Cartier time – I have three watches – and it's four minutes left till one o'clock. I hope he isn't digital.

'I wonder – might I order? A whisky and rye, please. *No* ice. Thanks.'

I've always had dreams, like Jacob in the Bible. Big, bright epics of dreams. Now I trade in them, dreams.

When I was a child, my favourite dream of all was about a rich aunt. Swathed in furs, trailing perfume like chiffon scarves. Every growing girl should have a rich aunt, to show her how to wear perfume and make the best of herself. Every boy deserves a wicked uncle, who'll show him the alluring mystery of women and give him his first swig of a cocktail.

If there were rich aunts and bad uncles, girls and boys would grow up knowing how to respect one another.

That's how I see it.

Until I was twenty-two, I remember my life in monochrome. I remember sleeping badly, and having to keep my dreams for the daylight hours, and doors banging and voices raised and longing for an unknown relative to appear from the opposite end of the world, from Australia or New Zealand, and to take me away for a day. But all the days went by in shades of grey, and there was no surprise visitor from sunny Down Under, no sudden illumination, no antidote to the tedium and all that was too hopelessly matter-of-fact about my life then.

I was born, I believe, with a capacity for affection. A talent even.

No one properly wanted it, until I was twenty-six and in the thick of a marriage that was – as they say – heading nowhere.

Affection was Reggie's problem too, a prodigal surfeit of the stuff that bypassed me and was channelled the only way he knew how, into his Tuesday and Thursday and Saturday afternoon deceits.

For him it was American women who enticed. They drew him like a honeytrap. His ideal was Grace Kelly. But East Coast new brahmin beauties were hard to find in London, and he had to lower his sights. He swooped on all and sundry, so long as they were American, female, adequately curvaceous, approximately white, and young. I never could understand the fascination: I thought it must be like collectors and their manias, why should someone happen to choose postage stamps or coronation china or motorcycles.

Reggie had chosen girls.

I knew all about it, I smelt the evidence on his clothes. Shrill American perfumes and talcs, the sort I imagined chorus-girls wearing, and tobaccos that somehow didn't seem English, but woodier, more organic, sweeter maybe. Americans, he'd once told me – although I wasn't aware he meant his women friends – Americans are different from us: when they speak their characters carry up to the surface, compared with the English they're naïve and they tell you what they're thinking: they're not like us, he meant, because they don't live behind their dignity, their fronts.

I got to know what was going on, and I gave nothing away. Maybe – it's only a hunch of hindsight – he would have preferred I had, because I suspect some of the clues I picked up on were just *too* obvious. Instead we played such an elaborate, genteel divertissement together, of tacit complicity in ignorance. I would pretend I noticed nothing, and he would pretend – with their perfume clinging to him – that he had no secrets. All it *was*, of course, was deception. If he'd had more of a nose and could have smelt for himself the cloth of his jackets, maybe we wouldn't have got into such straits. But his family had long been deficient in the olfactory department, nasal sensitivity; apparently it was a fluke of their genes.

Did I say – I was born, I believe, with a capacity for affection: a talent even.

No one properly wanted it, until I was twenty-six, in the thick of what passed as our marriage.

It was a chance encounter with a stranger that finally unplugged the blockage, undammed the deluge.

Our paths crossed in the Savoy Hotel where I was killing

time before a dental appointment. We happened to meet in the American Bar – ironically enough, although he told me he was Canadian (accents foxed me in those days). He was lonely in London, it came out: but then, I admitted to him, so was I. He had a wife and family in Toronto. 'That's nice' was all I said about *that*, and I brushed the details under the pile carpet.

At the end of his stay in London, when all his business was done – and *our* most agreeable business was done too, I realised – he presented me with an opal bracelet in a plush box. I had to tell Reggie I'd been left it by an ancient and newly discovered great-aunt I'd somehow forgotten all about. I told him with such assurance, as if I'd been lying like this all my life.

Reggie died when one of his women friends burst her string of pearls in her excitement. The pearls flew everywhere, and when they tried moving the wardrobe to get under the rug Reggie's heart, tragically, gave out.

It was the saddest time, of course, and very busy, what with the funeral, and maintaining the stoic front. And at the same time I was deeply envious, because Reggie hadn't died with *me*. Just a few minutes before his heart attack in that not-quite-anonymous hotel bedroom in Kensington he had probably been blissfully happy, in a state of sublime forgetfulness.

I sold up the house. I went off to Paris for a few days. And there it was, in my own cramped and airless hotel room in the wrong *arrondissement*, that I had my inspiration, like a bolt from the ether, like a grotto vision.

I took a taxi all the way to the Louis Vuitton shop on the Avenue Marceau and spent fourteen thousand dollars in a morning, 1958 prices. I rekitted myself in *haute couture*, at Givenchy and Balenciaga, and I knew that wherever I might find myself thereafter I wasn't going to see a woman wearing anything identical. Of the money from the house sale, I was left with almost ten thousand dollars, ample for the liner ticket from Southampton. I sailed on the *United States*, in the second-top category of accommodation, a small stateroom suite.

And so it was that the Lady with the Lamp welcomed me, with her right arm upraised in salute, just as Reggie had been received by his succession of fancies. Up on deck I smiled at this new irony – if that's what it was – and shed a few tears, of course, and then I looked round to find a fragrant, swarthy man at my side, speaking over the fur collar of his cashmere coat. Removing his silk glove and pointing with his index finger, he indicated the glass building he owned a share of, and asked me if I would permit him the honour of transporting me uptown to my hotel in the limousine that would be waiting for him?

I came to America in the wake of Audrey Hepburn. But I was also told, several times, I sounded like Vivien Leigh: and maybe I carried myself like her too.

Later Miss Hepburn took Breakfast at Tiffany's, and so – in a manner of speaking – did I. After my good friend with the fur collar to his cashmere coat and the chauffeured white Cadillac Eldorado, I found other good friends in New York City with Anglophile leanings. It was courtesy of them that I rented my apartments in the Upper Seventies: never settling for long, keeping in motion like a counter in a board game. I liked the variety, paying only three months' rent in advance, never unpacking but living out of the Vuitton trunks and cases, hardly coming down to earth some days. I served my gentlemen friends Fortnum's tea and buttered English-style crumpets and a choice of Tiptree preserves. I watched the skies and saw how the weather in that great town – green storm-clouds and gunmetal snow packs and gilded sunsets – how the weather flavoured all our dealings. I loved it: I loved not knowing my future, not knowing from one month to the next.

It was Mr Kandor who said I needed an American name. He decided to call me 'Sioux'. 'Why?' I asked. He waved his hand at the afternoon tea, which I knew he enjoyed. 'What I keep thinking,' he said (and I quote exactly) 'is this, you're some damn beautiful Sioux Injun and you've come raiding, right up into the heart of this city.'

I couldn't decipher his tone. The remark had me puzzled for days. If he felt it was a raid, I thought, why did he tolerate it? But the point was, of course, that he *did* tolerate it, my Mr Kandor. And it was then I started to think, maybe they all want to believe they're a little bit in danger with me, in hazard, that they're a victim – a willing victim – just as I am with all of them.

Men and women, it isn't a game for amateurs.

What I've done – I believe – is to create, round about the centres of their lives I'm excluded from, my own pleasant haze, my own fond atmosphere. The memories I inhabit afterwards are vague but happy ones. They know that I'm a plus, definitely not a 'downer'. I guess that could stand on my headstone, and it would be something I'd lie beneath proud to think on.

Whenever I've felt myself ceasing to be content with the arrangement, because I sense the contentment between 'him' and me isn't quite mutual any more, I've taken my cue to move on. No hard feelings, except a couple of times, but on each occasion – it should shame me to say – an Englishly enunciated word in a hairy ear about the potential embarrassment to the neglected lady-wife did the trick.

I have travelled their awesome land from sea to shining sea, coast to coast, from pillar to post. The fall colours of Vermont, the moon-valleys of Arizona, the oilfields and dustbowls of Texas, the clammy swamp heat of Missouri, the wheat ocean of Nebraska, the Rocky Mountain snows of Colorado, the glorious days and sudden nights of California. I have been received royally, by outstretched arms, and I've never had to carry more than my Vuitton jewel-case from an automobile to a train or an airline check-in desk, paid labour has attended to the other thirteen items. I breeze in and I breeze out, elemental, seasonal, smiling (I hope), making up for all the lost time in my life, the dry as sawdust years. But I hardly ever remember that, not from where I am now.

Mr Merrill is talking to the *maître d'*. He wants a quiet table, please, at the back of the room.

Mr Merrill and I were introduced in Bemelman's jazz bar at the Carlyle. But oh, he hopes for the burden of something or other to be lifted from his shoulders. He has broad shoulders, although they droop. I persuaded him to take a daily swim at the Athletic Club; it does wonders for the heart and blood. I may be around just long enough to notice an improvement. He told me he is divorced, but a sixth sense tells me he isn't, not yet. (Years ago I learned that apartment blocks and hotels should have two quite separate entrances, because private detectives in this line always come singly and they're too corpulent as a rule to try to be in two places at the one time.)

Mr Merrill too loves English accents. He's said to me I remind him of – Joan Fontaine. Which dates him and me, but maybe he was thinking of how she was in *Rebecca*. Or Vivien Leigh, he said, back at his apartment on Park Avenue South, seeing me pucker and maybe hoping for some of Scarlett O'Hara's wilfulness, in moderation of course, but enough to require him to tame me. Men and women, it's no game for amateurs.

On my last day in New York a child, a little girl, watched me coming up in the UN Plaza Hotel elevator. She watched me nobly bearing the weight of my Blackglamma coat, although this woman is no legend. I'd sprayed myself with Amazone in the back of the yellow cab, and I smelt chic. There was a mirror in the lift and I caught something, not for the first time: the evidence of the years. I've always looked younger than my age: but that day maybe the hardness of concrete on East Fifty-seventh Street where the shops are, or the jolts in the cab over to the East River, or the weight of my coat with the temperature climbing, they were conspiring to show me something I didn't want to see.

The child perceived differently though, and I thanked her with a smile that had her mother looking anxiously for a moment, but then relaxing *her* mouth to a smile too. The little girl saw to the simpler version beneath it all: someone who hardly touches the ground, even in full black mink, who breezes in and breezes out, trailing perfume like chiffon scarves. When *I* was a child, I want to tell her, my favourite dream of all was about a rich aunt. Rich aunts and wicked uncles: they cannot tarry, they scarcely touch ground because once they were afraid but now they fuss with their angels' wings, they mean to scatter happiness like pollen and be excellent propagators.

*

Mr Merrill is not late, I am early.

He walks across the room smiling. The name 'Sioux' which Mr Kandor gave me amuses him, when what I remind him of – he has said – is of wooded walks by the Thames in London. That is hardly possible, I told him, geographically speaking. But maybe, I added, London has changed since I was last there, and they have uprooted some of the concrete and planted trees and shrubs instead and lovers can stroll by a clean, clear blue Thames and be in Arcady.

Now, being here, we shall discover.

Mr Merrill signals to the waiter. The waiter nods. I shall clear a space for Mr Merrill on the little sofa beside me and on whisky ryes this won't seem so far from Arcady. Imagine we're twenty-nine storeys up on Park Avenue South, with the wailing sirens of distress on police cars sounding like the cries of sea birds, winging the downtown streets by sonar.

The last time I smelt another woman's perfume on his large-pored, hirsute skin. And he has no wife, officially.

All he knows to call me is 'Sioux'.

Somewhere I read, in a magazine like the *Geographic*, American Red Indians work so well on skyscraper construction sites because they have no vertigo, no terror of falling.

O Lord, return to them their city, those pitiable Injuns. When I get back there, Lord, deter the tenderfoot, the interloper. Preserve those steely canyons of New Amsterdam for the sure-footed who have stepped through fire.

He found her address, with ludicrous simplicity, in the telephone book, under her husband's name of course: G.S.A. Pearson.

Driving past the red door he'll imagine, to suit himself, that behind it unhappiness is rampant. Discontentment slops around, in such excess that they don't know what to do with it as it goes swilling through the sedately appointed rooms at high-tide breach.

And there she is. Vivian. Not behind her red door, but in the restaurant.

Fear and trembling!
There she is, in the living flesh, after how many years.

Ten minutes later and he found the very same thing was happening as had happened all that time ago. Queasiness, palpitations, fixed vision, a metal band tightening around his head. He felt there had been some vital shift in his internal balance, his brain was tilted askew. None of his physical functions had the precision they should, he was only approximating to himself.

Thirteen years before he had watched from behind a boxed yew as her husband of a few minutes proudly led her out of the church, her arm inside his. A peal of bells. Confetti flying. A 1920s Rolls-Royce crossed with white ribbon waiting on the road.

She has filled out a little, or maybe it's the effect of the jacket's broad shoulders. Her complexion is as clear as it was, her hair still blonde but cut short. Her mother is rather thinner-faced; then he imagined it a severe face, now it belongs to a woman not sure of where she stands – or sits. Once he read pride into its expressions, but – he only understood later – he had been a novice at the business of translation.

Vivian talks. Her mother listens, then offers an opinion. Vivian looks away to consider. Her mother plays with the cutlery in front of her. Vivian says something in reply. Her mother asks for it to be repeated. Vivian shapes the words, patiently. Her mother doesn't respond in words but nods her head.

He hopes he is too far from them in the room to be seen. But the point is, of course, that he is further from them than that, years and years away.

He has often wondered about the colour of it, that red door. That specific shade of red. Why *it* should have been the choice. And *whose* choice had it been, Vivian's or her husband's?

Its redness burns and sears out of the soot-streaked frontages. Perhaps there have been complaints at its appearance, and the irritation of it rankles. The house shrieks at him that it doesn't mean to belong to the other houses in the terrace. Their respectability has only become a front. The red door blows the pretence apart: their interiors duly explode, and doll's house furniture goes hurtling through the balmy evening air.

The violence of the scene satisfies him, at his hour of driving home (sevenish) and even more at this juncture of his life when he frequently experiences the pincer grip of circumstances and, with it, the tightening throat that proves his own helplessness to do a goddam thing about it.

Strictly it isn't the quickest way home for him. But speed is another false modern god. There are more important considerations, that haven't to do with convenience or even with facts.

At most – when the traffic lights are against him, and traffic is heavy – he sits in his silver Rover and watches the red door for a virtually uninterrupted eighty seconds. It is always, invariably, closed. Somehow a red door can seem more finally closed than any other colour of door would be.

At their table in the restaurant they continue their discussion, mother and daughter. It's being done rather tiredly, and not in the best of spirits. At one point Vivian pouts, and of course he remembers.

She lights a cigarette, which is new to him. Always when she thought she was being thwarted, she was most unselfconscious and – to him – at her most attractive. Unfailingly she would be the one of her group who looked away last from a shop window, as if the least certain about the reflection of herself she saw there in the plate-glass.

Now, in the restaurant, her mother has her back to the mirrored wall, but Vivian is taking on the challenge of the room, because she has other things to dwell on. Whatever they are discussing is clearly a matter of moment. Vivian sighs, and blows out cigarette smoke. Her mother raises a wine glass to her lips, spills a little on to her blouse, but fails to notice.

At home they had tactically located mirrors in the public rooms. It was a woman's house, he recognised at once on his first visit. A talcumy smell, a pair of white gloves on the hall table (it was that period of history still in their suburb), a hat on the seat of a chair, too much pollen in the air, Victorian water-colour views, the *Noël Coward Songbook* open on the piano, a choice of four teas for him to drink (he only had to say which he wanted).

He was inexpert at the art of mirrors, but they must have allowed Mrs Bentham and Vivian to see everything, more than he could and maybe much more than was really there.

Vivian's father had died so long before, for her there was no memory even of a man's presence in the house. There were photographs, but the man they showed was a very polite intruder dressed in the clothes of another age.

She might have grown up to continue to believe men were secondary creatures, but the opposite was the case. She and her mother embarked on a rigorous selection policy of suitable male friends: only of the social sort, and not confidants or loiterers.

At the very beginning he was considered eligible by dint of an accident. There were two (unconnected) families called Whelan in the suburb where they lived. *He*, Nigel Whelan, was at the grammar school and regarded as one of the brightest in a bright form, with the prestige of a university scholarship already won. Tom Whelan – with a boarding-school background rather than an education – was dim but good-natured and bound for a relation's thousands of acres of sheep-grazing in Queensland. They were both training for the local Under-21 rugby team, and were both invited to a Hallowe'en party at the club. Vivian Bentham was also there, with special dispensation from her mother who knew some of the organisers' wives. So it was that he first made her acquaintance, and it was there that Vivian also met Tom Whelan and must have become a little confused between them, which confusion she passed on later to her mother when she couldn't quite distinguish in her post-mortem of events. When an invitation reached him six weeks after that, in the hectic run-up to Christmas, he guessed that Mrs Bentham may not have understood or recollected properly but that she had included him on a party list in the festive spirit of gracious condescension.

*

By the time Mrs Bentham realised her mistake it was too late, he had been admitted to their house and seen Vivian in her element. She winked at him over dinner, and nodded to him behind her mother's back to show where to place his index finger on the fork.

She insisted he be invited again, in spite of the mistake. She couldn't credit he had read so many books and played down his learning as he did; she gave him a newspaper crossword and he completed it in twenty-five minutes flat. His knowledge awed her, in that most complacent of suburbs, and maybe it started to make her more self-aware, about how he might be viewing her and her mother in their home. He showed her, referring to books, why he liked certain paintings, and she opened a magazine and showed *him* a photograph of Robert Wagner and asked him if he had ever spotted a resemblance between the actor and himself. Each time he was granted an opportunity to see her he found himself unaccountably nervous and knotted – while exams, for instance, were water off a duck's back to him – and shamblingly uncoordinated with inattention, pulling the paper doily away with a sandwich and dropping the sugar-tongs between his knees on to the Wilton.

Vivian Bentham induced in him a fear he'd never experienced before: a dual fear of her paying him too much notice, and of her not paying him enough. Quite often he walked Hollybush Avenue under cover of darkness, in the interludes between invitations, when he could imagine he might never be invited there again. He remembered *My Fair Lady*, Freddie Eynsford-Hill haunting that street where Eliza lived under the professor's too watchful eye. He didn't feel like waltzing round lampposts, because this seemed to him all too intensely serious. Callers of his own age came and went, a good number of them, by the front door and before the evening grew too late. Vivian and her mother waved them off from the top step or (when it was chillier) from the sitting-room window, and he tried to read degrees of favouritism in the hand-sweeps and finger-wiggling. The two watching faces gave nothing away, though, except sometimes a kind of lassitude with the whole business. At other times, when the curtains remained undrawn, the two would talk – quite volubly, to guess from their motions – and he wondered if all was as well as it might be between them.

When the evenings turned lighter, Vivian removed the bicycle from the back of the garage – her father's Triumph, with a cross-bar – and rejoined the Landsdowne Tennis Club. That was his real undoing, because she chose the more expensive of the two clubs in the suburb, while he and the set he went with made do with the comfortable scruffiness of the Coronation. In the end he did defect, without the others and paying more for the privilege than he could strictly afford. But by then, irony of ironies, it was too late. Vivian, lovelier to his eyes than ever, had already been drawn in, to the luminous centre circle. He meanwhile was relegated to an outer ring about her orbit – and a rumour did the rounds, emanating from some members of the committee, that a rookie from Coronation Gardens wasn't quite to be trusted. His former company and the present treated him alike, as the most blatant and treacherous kind of social climber.

Anyway, there were new players in the game by now, and one in particular called Rupert Naysmyth, who had a habit of regularly cheating by overstepping the line on his serves but who was thought too much of a good egg to have done so except by accident. He was a so-so player himself, better than Naysmyth and not a cheat: however, from his end-court he wouldn't have been able to make any impression. Vivian was always conspicuously, strategically unalone on the pavilion balcony; he knew she watched him, he would catch her out, yet she smiled far too vivaciously for him to bear looking longer, which must have accounted for the habit he'd never indulged in at the Coronation, of gazing down at his sandshoes. All the time, though, there was a storm of butterflies whipped up in his stomach, his shoulders were rigid and his knees shook. How could she not acknowledge the effect she so evidently had on him, how could she seem to let it mean so derisively little to her?

In the end it was Rupert Naysmyth's best friend who claimed her. The foot-faulter might have been taken aback at first, but

a little later he shrugged it off, in a shockingly casual way for
a purported good egg. Graham Pearson had gone straight from
school into business, and was being groomed for some cushy
billet in the family printing works. As for himself, the wrong
Whelan, he kept glimpsing those old-fashioned white gloves of
Vivian's mother in his mind's eye, and he wondered, how odd,
that the future now decreed itself according to a chemical stink
and the mess of printers' ink.

Mrs Bentham failed to see him once in Stanton Street, and he
knew it was deliberate. Vivian was coming out of the bank one
morning and they nearly collided; he was too tongue-tied to
speak straight, and her shrill smile was all over the place, eyes
moving at speed in and out of focus. He felt himself wrapped in
her exotic perfume . . . A car horn's blaring distracted them,
and automatically she lifted her arm to wave, Pearson called
over, something hearty and excluding, and she had to go. Her
smile faded but her eyes as she turned were staring into his,
staring a fraction too long, and he realised with another left
hook and right dealt to his weakened constitution what all
along he'd only hoped, no more than dared to hope, might
be the tragic truth.

In the end he didn't have the courage to pursue her. And she,
he surmised, must have presumed that he wasn't interested
enough.
     They failed to make themselves plain to one another. And
for such simple, inexcusable and everyday reasons the course
of their lives was determined to two quite contrary, arbi-
trary ends.

Vivian lit another cigarette, chain-lit it from the one before,
oblivious that there should have been fear and trembling
anywhere in the room. Her mother's mouth contracted dis-
approvingly. Vivian saw the gesture and ignored it. She placed
one elbow on top of the table and considered her hand in
front of her face. She spread the five fingers while her
mother stared at them, a rich man's wife's creamy white

fingers, with grateful awe. Vivian spread them wider, quite calmly, scrutinising each of her shiny, crimson-varnished nails in turn.

In the end he hadn't had the courage. And she, he surmised, must have presumed that he wasn't interested *enough*.

They had failed to make themselves plain to one another. And for such simple, inexcusable and everyday reasons the course of their lives had been determined to these paradoxical ends. He re-routeing himself – home to wife and children, the long way round – and she painting her front door the melodramatic vermilion she had, not requiring to read his art books to know that scarlet was the traditional colour of the martyrs, sacrificed in gore to the barbarians.

The two women had been widowed within eighteen months of one another.

They had first met nearly twenty-five years ago, sitting at adjoining desks in a Pitman's shorthand class. In an atmosphere of casual friendships theirs had seemed closer than the others which sprang up around them. When they'd gone off and found jobs – the first hurdle – their friendship survived; indeed it was fortified, with more than they'd had before to confide to each other. They both married men of potential within the firms they worked for, they both stopped working in the same year for the same reason, themselves pregnant, and they both – again purely by chance – gave birth to three children over the next six and seven years.

From their separate suburbs they kept up. Once every eight or ten weeks they would meet for lunch. Several times over the years they had, of an evening, involved their husbands, and attended a concert all together. But both men were the workaholic sort – with their own businesses now – and not very versed in small chat or in culture, so that the evenings had fallen rather flat. At least the two women had tried, however, and that made them feel a little less awkward about eliminating Lawrence and Hugh from their future social calculations.

Although they cared for one another, that didn't mean they were necessarily pledged in all matters to the truth. The truth, in fact, proved somewhat dull, to Helen as for June: at any rate in the Sevenoaks and Chorleywood versions respectively. They didn't expand on it greatly, and it was a harmless enough exercise surely. One might have seen a shimmery silver dress in a shop window and shied from it but in her retelling of the story she tried it on, bowled over the assistant, and bought it. The other had spotted Gregory Peck coming out of a hotel on Piccadilly, and while she had merely stood on the pavement gawping like everyone else, her account allowed the film star to raise his hat to her and say 'Good afternoon!' Helen might have driven past a hitch-hiker who'd drawn her attention, but in her story of the event she gave the girl a lift and put into her mouth something or other she'd heard on the radio. June had seen a television crew shooting a drama in Amersham, and in her refashioning of a simple incident they had included her as an extra, a face in a crowd scene, 'but you never know, probably I'll be cut out.'

It amounted to nothing so much perhaps. 'The Women' were a slightly different matter, however. Each had simultaneously, in that infamous seventh year of her marriage, focused her suspicions on a *someone*. For Helen it was a girl her husband employed in the book-keeping office; in June's case it was the younger wife of one of her husband's business colleagues whom they entertained. Each Woman became a sister siren to the other, while remaining – for the wives – the definitive 'One'. Neither Helen nor June took invention to the point of declaring that Anything had actually Happened, but suggestion was sufficient to unsettle each of them in the other's telling, with pauses left between the words which the listener could infill with her own unsavoury mental picture.

In effect they mutually alarmed but consoled at one and the same time. It was as little and as much as they could do to redeem a situation which straddled, as none of their other subjects did, the suddenly fluid, unstated divide between a fact and its potentiality.

And somehow she, the woman painted on the panel suspended above the other dining heads, was part and parcel of the problem, the debate between other people's actuality and private imagination.

After their husbands' deaths within a fateful (and fatal) eighteen months' period – one from a coronary, the other as a result of liver cirrhosis – they had upgraded their lunch rendezvous. They each knew they deserved it.

But what they liked least about this location – and there was little else about it that had not taken their fancy – was that sly, quaffing baggage overhead, resting so shamelessly on her laurels. Each viewed her through narrowed eyes, and each was set remembering.

The crazy thing was, that the former book-keeper had travelled two hundred miles from her fancy job to be at Lawrence's cemetery funeral, dressed like a mail-order catalogue model. The other craziness was that at Hugh's cremation the business colleague's wife had burst into tears while his widow had been unable to; the stifled sobs of an immature woman had accompanied the coffin's hydraulic exit behind the tasselled maroon velvet curtains.

All that had been only too factually, incontrovertibly true.

The painted woman continued to loll above them, glass in hand, raised to toast or carouse. The longer the face was looked at, between tensed lids, the more inscrutable it became. A woman ought to have been more – more *open*. To the man who'd painted her, she had been a creature of his own fuzzled fantasy. To these two fresh widows his representation showed a she-snake, a devious arrant little schemer of the very first order.

From their not inconsiderable private pensions they had graduated to sea-bass steak and venison noisettes. They now drank Chinon or Sancerre reds.

It would have been so perfect without the woman. But without her, there might perhaps have been less.

They could fix on her, in that ostentatiously furtive way that they found themselves doing. She seemed to have concentrated into her person *their* past – or rather, the vague mysteries they have spirited out of that past. When they began their innocuous game, of course there was always the risk that it might turn out to be not so innocuous in some respect: everything was fine while they could cause the mysteries in their mild fictions to happen, while they could at will introduce their characters and dispose of them. The danger lay in the characters' deciding for themselves.

The reclining naiad had made herself what she now so brazenly was, a third at their lunches. How curious it was that from whichever corner of the room they both looked, she seemed to have her lazy harlot's eyes trained most specifically on *them*.

They had each had their suspicions inevitably about the verisimilitude of the other's stories, excepting the matter of the Women. But exchanging them every five or six weeks as they now did was different from living every day with them. Conveniently, because it hardly mattered, they had allowed themselves to believe, with artistic licence, in the silver cocktail dress and the old-fashioned, gentlemanly courtesy of Gregory Peck.

It was with the one-time book-keeper and the ex-colleague's wife – and with their microscopically detailed accounts of every nuance and gesture which might be given a 'certain' interpretation – that they'd become confused, by the subject and its presentation. Somehow they had made their alter egos *too* credible, and that hadn't been the initial intention at all. Their Women had become oblique criticisms of themselves, because they were described – scurrilously – as being everything to a vulnerable mere male's eye that they, Helen and June, recognised with mingled pride and envy the two of them were not.

They had come to give their creations too much life perhaps. The creations *were* them, in as much as they could imagine quite well – each from some dark recess of her brain – the worst that those harpies might be capable of.

She hovered over them, louche imbiber and wanton hussy. Her invidious thought-process was the sort drawn in comic strips, contained in a cloudlet rising from a trail of bubbles. But in practical terms she was fully as large as life, and – unlike the material of most comics – she was definitely no joke.

Money gilds. It excuses, makes bearable those who wouldn't deserve attention in a world where all were fair. It enfolds and removes one from the public's grubby touch.

Money means that the rich and their acolytes travel – always – in cars. Taxis by comparison have a particularly germy-feeling atmosphere (reminiscent of ear- and mouth-pieces on the receivers of old black bakelite public telephones), and they are to be occupied, on sufferance, only *in extremis*. He has never been one for the village hall camaraderie of buses or the hellish forced bodily intimacies of the London Underground. So, as Pangloss would have it, all is for the best – if you have money, that is. (Oh, he *has* read – whatever was to hand, even Voltaire – waiting in drawing-rooms furnished with yards of leather-bound books on the instruction of interior decorators.)

'Walker' technically is a misnomer, 'delayer' and 'time-killer' being more applicable when it isn't actually a 'door-opener', 'umbrella-raiser', 'carrier-of-parcels-in-the-wake-of'. Some of the women he has accompanied have had very bad feet, or sciatica flashes, or dodgy backs, or creaky hips, so what *they* require is a 'stroller-with' or 'propper-up', a 'hobbler-alongside'. But he has often been told that he has just the right manner. Usually, when an assumption is made by innocent onlookers, it is that he's the son of whichever woman he's with at the time: one of those prematurely bald, pudgy men who could be any age in middle age, with a heavy beard-line on flour-white skin and jowl scrapes on their shirt collar and a gold signet ring on a fat, hammer-headed fifth finger and fashionably framed spectacles and, peering vigilantly out through them, two small beady eyes, like dark currants in an under-baked bun.

As God is a witness, he is perfectly aware of his corporeal limitations. All the stuffy, overheated rooms and the passing in and out of cooled and conditioned air-systems haven't helped his skin or his colouring, and he wears a copper bracelet on each wrist to keep at bay the rheumatism he seriously thought for a while might be infectious, so often was the subject spoken of by those rich women who are his life. (Superstition takes a dastardly hold in such fetid, thick-pile carpeted, heavily draped accommodations as the ones he frequents.)

This, in an alarming nutshell, is the actuality of Mr Ferdy Latimer, born 1953.

He is what he is not because he loves men but because he is afraid of women.

When he watches men's bodies in the changing-room of the sports club he belongs to, the majority of them are a turn-off. A few – younger ones – can precipitate a moderate erection afterwards, thinking about them in the privacy of his small flat, but his fantasies usually concern them making vigorous love to their wives and girlfriends. From his adolescence on, his dreams of lust have always been so: intensely voyeuristic.

He finds gay magazines do little for him, they are too brutish, an embarrassing and ungainly excess of animal. *Playgirl* appeals rather more, since male sexuality there has been sanitised, also customised, for women, for frustrated women caressing their de-luxe bendy vibrators. Those young naked bucks belong to the ritzy, glitzy, soulless gilt-and-onyx rooms of Los Angeles, where they work out and tend bar or drive delivery vans and dream of being actors, where their credited 'perfect dates' pliantly have love made to them on the strength of a pina colada, on warm beaches at sunset or by the glowing embers of a ski-lodge fire. That is the sort of sex he can take, at the end of his right arm, imagining the skilful covering of those once eligible women of good parentage whom Mother directed him towards, now fallen into hasty marriages or gathering dust on their shelves.

The thought of female genitalia has never excited him, not at all. What curiosity he had was 'satisfied' by the purchase and perusal of a magazine called *Climax* in his twenty-sixth year. If the memory of the contents still turns his stomach queasy, those ageing instruments of tackle minus jock-straps which he views being talc-dusted and deodorised in the changing-rooms are no heavenly vision by contrast. Some force him to turn his eyes away and leave him pitying the sheer *absurdity* of the browning, uncomely, inartistic utilities that pendulate apologetically – to left or right – between those thundering upper thighs.

He may be afraid of women, but he can't let them alone – in a manner of speaking. They fill his thoughts day and night, they obsess him.

He knows *them* better than they know themselves.

He discovered his calling in life four years ago. He had been working as PA to a financier of doubtful sexual leanings, who had introduced him to his older widowed sister-in-law. She was well set up in a flat in a Regent's Park terrace, and lived by her dog-eared diary, packed with luncheon- and dinner-party engagements. The company which attended those occasions – brunches, at-homes, soirées, after-theatre collations – was more or less interchangeable, but the dismal fact of her own situation was that she had no one to be seen arriving *with*. Men's wives didn't take kindly to unaccompanied women, especially if they were more attractive than themselves. Of course there were a few widowers of her own age about, but they were much in demand and frequently proved fickle, and – anyway – wasn't there something a little 'obvious' about it, as if you were contriving to pair yourself off or (more likely) *had been* paired off by others in their calculations? – the Walking Dead syndrome. Oh no, much better with the arrangement whereby an obliging younger man – sociable, never stuck for an opening gambit and a closing line, with a good memory for faces and names and jokes – led you on his proffered arm. A camp follower, could one say: and didn't that make *you* appear somehow *ironic*, your own best defence, which was no bad thing in a demanding and (if the newspapers were to be taken on trust) grasping, violently disposed world.

In the four years since his very first introduction, Ferdy Latimer had been walker – on word-of-mouth recommendation – to a string of women.

Now he might go out with each of his four different women, his current stable, in the week. Sometimes one objected to another's demands on his time, but that was the way of it, he let them know. The premise of engagement was his spreading himself (in yet another manner of speaking) so thinly. This didn't stop generous presents being heaped on him. Indeed the harder he played to catch and pin down, to 'own', the more foolishly his clients behaved.

He was sincere, though. *They* knew how things stood – that he was to a limited degree public property – but he for his part was loyal and dedicated to each of them, so long as they would allow him to feel he wanted to be so. He meant to make *them* feel the best they could about themselves. He certainly did nothing to encourage competition between them, or tension, or friction. Everything was kept pristinely platonic – although some of them adored *double entendres* – and no advantage was ever, *could* ever, be taken.

He didn't feel guilty in any respect, that he might be leeching off his women. He was confident that he provided them with a service, wholly celibate and conducted professionally to the best of his capacities. He never forgot appointments; he always gave his most wherever he was taken – lunch, tea party, cocktails, formal dinner – although the presence of another walker could be intimidating, unless they were able to spark brighter by vying to outdo one another in joke-telling and name-dropping. (Not – when he dropped names – that he wasn't wholly reticent as to the habits and histories of the women who had engaged him in the past. Ferdy Latimer was, he knew – and he was duly proud of the fact – a byword for courteous, smilingly effected discretion.)

Today – this lunchtime – he catches a man's eye, because this too is part of his professional technology, the ability to spot from afar and home in. The man is exactly the sort one would expect to be interested in a Mrs Livingstone: not quite up to it financially, or socially, but sexually ready for the challenge. Mrs Livingstone is a sexual woman, although she isn't keen to admit so in words. When she's with him, she behaves

and dresses very nearly like a man in drag, everything is
a melodrama. But – he guesses – she longs for it: how she
aches for it.

He is instantly jealous. He envies and resents the man his
potency as a beast of the field. For the man, the feeling just
rises from his gut, it's body clockwork, it doesn't have to be
justified and apologised for. For himself it's enough to bring on
one of his paler brown moods – burnt sienna, to match it on his
emotional shade card. Mrs Livingstone is being far too careful
not looking in the stranger's direction to notice the effect the
business is having on him.

This is the negative aspect of Ferdy Latimer. He knows he
can't show himself at his best under these conditions. He is
confronted with the brute fact of heterosexuality at its most
galling: a silver-haired, sunbed-tanned man in his sixties with
willing feelings for a woman, and an earthy woman for whom
charm alone won't satisfy. The two of them seem engaged in
a conspiracy against him. All his famous ready wit and skilful
recall cannot save him now.

This calls for some drastic action, and instantly.

'You were saying to me the other day,' he launches in, 'about
wanting to find a new diet. I think I know just the one. A doctor
I'm on good terms with – '

They discuss that for a while. Mrs Livingstone loses some
of her confidence.

He lets her catch him looking at the crown of her head. She
is sensitive about the thinness of her hair there, which she has
lavishly combed out to disguise her fears. She's so caught up
thinking about it that she swallows a mouthful of wine without
realising and it goes down the wrong way. She splutters some
back out on to the table's linen cover, her eyes water, and
her companion is aware the ogler is watching her rather more
critically.

She can't recover her composure, so he places his hand on
top of hers on the cloth, where everyone can see. He has
reserves of physical strength when he requires it, and she
is unable to withdraw her hand. If I don't look like a toy-boy
lover, he knows, I look all too much like a son: a veritable

cuckoo in the nest should any fool be contemplating moving in on us.

Of course, it's also a case of protection and deliverance, thus he can justify it to himself. A wealthy, unattached woman such as Mrs Livingstone needs to be guarded from marauders and from her own most natural instincts. *I shall be rewarded with cash, in the car back to Regent's Park, because she will be embarrassed at having shown herself up and because she is really willing me to forget, to scrub the business from my bank of memory. We can all so easily deceive ourselves, into making a selfish act selfless, into rendering some self-preserving circumspection as a deed of vast generosity.*

And eventually the man across the room turns his attention elsewhere.

They both feign not to have noticed, Mrs Livingstone and her companion.

Things brighten again at their table when the man, the ogler, gets up to leave. Mrs Livingstone relaxes, she swells, because to be rid of that witness of her discomfiture means she can start again, seeming to be the person she means to be: expertly coiffured, size fourteen, seductive and elegant, each walking step shadowed by its complement – the manly solidness of shoe touching ground, the comforting click of a steel heel-tip. You have to be special to be wanted, and he will have to be an extra-special man to replace this amply proportioned shadow that's so convenient and solatus to her (at two full days' notice of an engagement) and to offer instead the literal, sterling substance.

She's been gone for at least three minutes. Three and a half, nearly four. 'I have to go to the loo.' The remark had suddenly popped out, between the first and second courses. 'Yes,' she'd replied to her too brightly, 'yes, do.'

The chair was pushed back, scraping on the floor.

'Don't worry, Cathy. I'll keep your place for you.'

It was a joke. But for a second or two, she was certain, Cathy's face took on an expression she wasn't wanting to see.

There was irritation in it, and maybe a cruel condescension.

Cathy's reaction to the joke delayed her those few moments, until she remembered and geared herself up to start the journey across the room.

She sat watching her progress in the wall-mirrors while dabbing at her mouth with the white linen napkin. Her eyes stared and she was aware of nothing else. Just *that* singular person, that one particular body.

Only when Cathy turned the corner, past the panelled screen which led to the Ladies', did she realise how intently she had been watching. Her eyes smarted from the effort of concentration on her movements, the coordination of shoulders, elbows, buttocks, thighs, ankles. It dawned on her that she must have been seen watching, in her jealousy to fend off other eyes with the protectiveness of her own.

She lowered hers to the table-top. She refolded the napkin and placed it in the empty space of pink cloth between her fork and knife. The wings of her nose itched with embarrassment. When she closed her eyes she saw not the napkin or the cutlery but the pulling of the black jersey dress over Cathy's mobile hips and bottom. She lacked the courage herself to wear skirts so short, but Cathy had the long legs and the wiry slimness and, of course, she had the bravado. A tight black dress and a red matador jacket: sheer flesh tights and black shoes with high pencil heels. She had been with her when they'd bought the outfit and the shoes. Encouraging her when she sighed that it was too expensive, siding with the pushy assistant who knew at a glance who did the clothes in the shop justice and who did not. When Cathy stepped out of the changing-room she could only smile at her with admiration, like the assistant beside her. A few moments later, having settled the bill with her own Visa card, she reverted to the 'self' Cathy was turning her into. She narrowed her eyes and scanned the shop for the evidence of any other woman's – or man's – attention. Briefly she caught sight of herself in a mirror, mid-head swivel: tight-eyed, prim-mouthed, tense-shouldered, and – least believably of all to her – one hand bunched to a fist by her side.

*

Lesbians, everyone knows, don't have happy endings. How could *she* disprove such an assuredly proven truth? Everything must unravel, dissever into – the usual, of course – anger and recrimination and bitterness. They would walk off, not into a contented sunset, but – raging – in their quite separate, one-hundred-and-eighty-degree distinct directions. The conclusion would be utterly final, kaput, end of story and triple-underlined.

She doesn't make the mistake of thinking of Cathy as *the* Other. Certain persons exist, the chemistry of whose personalities with yours could produce an approximation to joy. Some women sought the perfect one, and their lives turned into morbid sagas of mood swings, of disappointment and strenuously willed fits of optimism in which they became less and less able to trust. Their notions of 'perfection' became, not more practical, but more rarefied and impossible because of all it had already been proved not to be.

Was the rashest but wisest policy, therefore, not to confide in 'personality' at all, but instead to search out the most vacant vacancy, the blankest blank? To find a white internal space, as sheerly white as the cloths they used to have here on the tables, on which to realise, as through a projector lens, the opera bouffa of your desires and dreams?

There is an uncomfortable gap of years between them. She was fourteen when Cathy was born in a faraway city, a suburban schoolgirl with her own head full of the tennis club and the daily treacheries of her own body. Boys were already closing in on her circle, but she found them all the same – gawky, wavery-voiced, narrow-minded, and very foreign to her. Another two years on, the boys were filling out and she was aware that she wasn't feeling on their account what her friends did. She pretended, though, and let a few boys kiss her, but they smelt of Benson & Hedges and mouthwash and stale deodorant, and the thought of discovering the shark-belly whiteness of their bodies left her cold. By this time she could better control her own body, so that it didn't betray her, but her mind as a consequence found itself seething with uncertainties. She pitied boys for having to do the coming on, for having to labour with the load of those unaesthetic genitals she examined in museums with a student's impartiality when they were exhibited in sculpted marble. The boys saw that she pitied them and were irritated and maybe it was they who had started the rumours: because she could surely have kept her cover among girls, maintaining the camouflage of feminine timorousness for the male. The rumours spread, and went on spreading.

At the tennis club late one evening a sturdy girl called Sonia Dimmock staged a splay-legged fall on the grass banking behind the laurels, which required her getting down on her knees in the soft gloaming to help her, and it was from that point that she knew how what was euphemistically called her 'private life' – of the emotions, of carnal wants – was determined.

She stares at the minute hand of her watch.

All her adult life she has been afraid that she might not be able to hold on to what she doesn't want to lose. She has tried – tried – never to buy loyalty with money, with gifts. She has tried to give *herself* instead, to offer enthusiasm and as much fun as she feels her own rather inward character has at its disposal. She has offered back interest, concern, but not – not ever – her prying curiosity.

With Cathy she has worked to make herself look younger, to be more youthful in her attitudes. It has been easier, admittedly, to deal with the externals than with the interior life. The shift dresses and swashbuckler belts are hardly second nature to her – she has seen too many fashions come and go, into the second half of her fourth decade – but she has made the effort to fasten on a modern, now-is-now(ish) image. ('Image', not 'attitude'.) It will never become habit with her, but the glory of fashion is that it cannot permit itself to become so. Onward and on, and on.

A pair of women are looking at her. About her own age, but dressed in very nearly a different generation's clothes. A square-cut Chanel look-alike outline for one, and a Laura Ashley pallid chintz print for the other.

They wear wedding rings.

For several moments she preoccupies them. But it isn't long enough to distract them from the serious business of eating. For them it's a luxury to have food prepared, even to be paying what they must be paying for it.

She looks away, in case they start to discuss her and she imagines she's lip-reading their verdict. She doesn't want to catch the word that she dreads, the L-word, which could only be ruthless poetic injustice. *I suppose we should pity her*. She thinks she could take anything – even Cathy's walking out on her – anything except that.

Four minutes have passed.

Is there a back entrance she could have left by?

She sits staring at the nearest panel of mirror, into its frozen glass interior, into its ice heart.

She could go on sitting here for ever, or possibly for another minute, but these are the only two possibilities.

Her stomach has shrivelled to a tense, aching sac. This isn't how she wants to live, but this is also the sum of it. She looks hard into the mirror, into that snow floe country. She fixes her eyes, she concentrates them into a glacial stare. The other faces reflected become blurs, their colours run.

For these moments the fear intensifies, to constricting panic, to a terror that might devour her. What if this is it? What if Cathy never comes back?

Then, for all she knows, the vertebrae of her back will collapse like dominoes. Her nervous system will fail, blow out. She'll melt to the floor. As if she's been zapped in a sci-fi film. There'll be nothing left of her.

But . . .

She blinks at the shapes in the mirror, at the disorder that is only another pattern after all. This is how she lives. She is defined by this, by her tenterhooks tension, by living so close as she does daily to the drop. Here is the unmaking but also the making of her. Submerged in her but by no means obscured, there's a vein of prime, redoubtable pride: pride for the truth of her own nature, which neither guilt nor shame can wish out of existence. She sees so with clear, undimmed, unsentimental eyes, that are as hard as the surface of the mirror itself: intelligent, restive eyes of ungentle, ice-blue glass.

This is me, this is me.

That bloody song, 'I am what I am . . .'

What I am, I am.

How could she possibly have wanted it to end like this, on the melodious back of supper-room wisdom, with the kitsch flourish of a seventies torch-song?

But then she hears the heels and her head shoots up. She can feel her heart expanding, gladdening in her chest; it's packed in so tightly behind her ribs that she can only snatch at the air in little half mouthfuls. How ridiculous, what a cliché, which is the reason why she knows it to be the absolute truth.

With every girl she has acquired a modicum of their looks and some of their mannerisms. She is quite a repository by now. When she can be beady-eyed-objective about herself she recognises it as vampire love. But all love involves cloaked inventions, velvet-gloved intimidation and soul-sucking. All love is looking for a private mirror, for an opportunity to believe in yourself through the 'other' – your own capacity for inclusion and influence – so why shouldn't it be as honest to locate it in your own gender?

Cathy smiles, but oh she is – not sly but – evasive. Her body is how she might have wanted her own, but she becomes confused whenever what Cathy tells her of her own experience fails to match with hers. Suddenly they're not a unity, and sex isn't a bonding but a second-best, a consolation prize for trying. Unlike in marriage, though, there is no stake-all obligation. The quest can begin again, and again. At the time it is performed in all deadly earnest. This is no catch-as-catch-can exercise, her resolution is the out-and-out pursuit of nothing less than the archetype.

The delay isn't explained. Nothing is said about it, by either of them.

This is less opera bouffa than a dumb-show, a mime.

Cathy opens a pack of Marlboro and shakes out a cigarette.

She tolerates the smoke, because she must. Cathy knows she will offer no comment, on the cigarette or on the five minutes that have just gone by.

Or . . . perhaps she was telephoning?

She looks at Cathy's index finger, the dialling one, helping to hold the cigarette rigid as she lights up.

Indeed this is a savage game, played in the name of love. But the idea of it – love – is no more substantial than a word whispered in the night. Than smoke. It won't allow itself to be purloined by anyone.

She watches the cigarette, and she winds her thoughts round that index finger of Cathy's, until they're taut like threads. Such as, who is cat and who is mouse in this subtle, unending pursuance? Such as, how can zesty hope so suddenly turn tail on her, to such a shrinking quivering little thing?

I have beautiful hands.

I can tell myself that without immodesty. It's my trade after all, my calling, that I should exhibit these hands to the world.

I take the greatest care of them, of course, but they had to be fine and elegant hands to begin with, otherwise the agency wouldn't have taken me on.

I'd never heard of a modelling agency that only dealt in the bits and bobs, but there's as much money there as anywhere else, and it's money that keeps the world turning smoothly on its axis.

'Your hands . . .!' They didn't even give the rest of me a second glance, or not much of one. It was the hands.

I'd need advice, manicures, but they recognised the potential. They already saw me holding an object to the camera. My rubbing the palms and backs with lotion – stroking a pedigree cat – caressing a bar of chocolate. Anything but putting them in hot sudsy washing-up water, which is murder apparently, and something they warned me about with serious faces:

like cracking the skin on the knuckle-joints with too much swimming-pool chlorine.

'Your hands are just like an actress's voice.'

I've been the hands of some very famous women, and mainly they've been actresses. I seldom get a chance to meet them. By the time I'm called in for my shots in the ads, they're back home in Los Angeles or away on their film lots.

Their voices are played back on tape to me or I'm shown a studio video, sometimes I'm wearing a similar dress or even the same towelling robe. That's so I get the 'feel' of who they are, although I already know very well. But it does help, as to how I play my own little scenes with my hands which I'm sacrificing – money considerations notwithstanding – to the myth of their talent or beauty.

It's just unfortunate for them that they don't have the hands for it, even though they have so much in other respects that I do not. With certain voices my fingers get fluttery, with others I let myself be more assertive and in control. Either way I touch whatever I'm required to touch with what I make-believe might be their mannerisms, in the spirit of the women themselves.

They need me, wherever they are – in their magazine homes perched on the sides of canyons, or in their air-conditioned trailers on the sets of movies and TV mini-series. They realise it, some of the time, and equally they try to shut it out of their minds. But the fact – if not my own true and actual situation in Muswell Hill – is there in front of me every time they lift their hands in front of their faces, to do even the simplest thing. I have the touch, the feel, of their lives – velvet, brocade, satin, sun-shield cream, car leather – and I can experience it with no more than the echo of their voices on playback inside my head.

Just occasionally I like to see my hands where others can see them too, in a restaurant that isn't a studio mock-up, with four solid walls and a ceiling. On a crisply laundered pink linen tablecloth, wielding the heavy gleaming cutlery the way even one or two of those soap queens don't have the know-how to.

They've bought me the meal anyway, indirectly, so I only have to act it out for them, as if they're the ones sitting where I am, in restaurants that wouldn't disgrace their fame. Zoom in on hands . . .

I am here courtesy of those Janes and Joans and Stephanies. But they enjoy their full glamour courtesy of such humble likes as yours truly.

Mum knows who they all are. Dad thinks it's a bit of a poncy lark, never mind that I park a 205 GTi outside their door in Gospel Oak. He has a rough labourer's hands, even though he's worked indoors all his life. Mum's are thin and rather fretful, but they taper, and she has longer than average fingers although not as distinctively so as mine.

My first job in this line was as a duchess's hands on a TV ad for furniture polish, and it went to Mum's head and she told all her friends, she even phoned Aunt Vi in Melbourne especially. She sits looking at my hands, and Dad does too ever since I told him I've taken out insurance on them, maybe because he thought I should have gone to the firm he's a clerk with. I've seen Mum looking at all three pairs, and I know she's thinking what I'm thinking, how come the daughter's got hands like this with a father who has hands like that?

Mum's are ladylike, but she couldn't have got them on to an agency's books. She sees me sitting at the tea-table wondering. She has an enigmatic look then. She seems to me sunk deep down into herself, and she is quite alone, even though we are sitting here at the table with her. I want to bring her back when that happens, but at the same time it's as if she's keeping me from her, she doesn't want to be brought back.

Meanwhile Dad's looking at my third finger and asking himself why there's no sparkly stone or gold band there, and Mum is putting the same question to the back of her mind because she knows the foolishness it surely is – and *was*, to the women who knew no better – to make a match too soon only for the sake of making one, because all of a sudden time has become much too much too pressing.

I could learn to talk like a duchess – the young aristo sort who get themselves photographed on the Nigel Dempster page. There are elocution coaches who can put everything that's wrong to rights, even some with computer data that dissect your speech and show vowel-pronunciation patterns on a little green screen.

I could diversify, expand, become my own one-woman enterprise. I should call myself 'Famous People's Hands Limited'. I should scour London for models. I'd eat out with my business clients on expenses. I'd have a chance to socialise occasionally with those big names whose bits and bobs we are. They would know very well we share a professional secret, that they ought to be affable with me, introduce me around.

I see it all, when I have the confidence of my lunches en route between the studios and home. The woman whose hands I now am, to whom I currently belong, took a flight yesterday evening back to LA, carefully avoiding having to meet me, maybe not caring two cents anyway. These hands she ignores will fight back. I haven't frittered away my time in those long delays between takes and setting-up, sitting about in the vanishing perfume trails of those women who depart in nothing so ordinary as taxicabs, but hire-car Granadas and stretch-Mercs and those hunchback Daimlers I've seen slowly gliding over the mews cobbles. I have the measure of the business, I'm coming to think; I have the span of these ten digits from straight *distingué* thumb to long, narrowing little finger.

They lie on the cloth before me, quiet and at rest, like – oh, like graceful fauna fronds or like the momentarily languorous tail accessories of some streamlined urchiny creature of the deep brine. To be frank, they sometimes look a shade fantastical to me. They have an aura, of command, quite of their own. I like the idea of it, it amuses and slightly amazes me. I follow in the tail's wake, and the fronds and folioles guide the plant to the light.

The hands beckon in whichever direction. The fingers, as that other ad puts it, they'll do my walking for me.

Her son has never married, but he does have girlfriends. They don't last longer than eight or nine months usually, a year at the outside.

Before she had to deal with them, she didn't fully understand the concept of jealousy. Over the years, however, she has feasted well on it, gorged and sated herself. Alistair knows the effect the girls will have on her, and it may be that he takes some pleasure in her discomfiture. But she sees what he perhaps, and certainly the girls, cannot. That they are facsimiles of one another, as close to Xerox run-offs as humans can come to be.

He thinks she is offhand with them. But the truth is, she can't really be bothered repeating *herself*. She can't believe that her behaviour will be held against her when she knows that, once it's over, she'll never see the girl – once young, now a year less so – again. He always covers the same ground, indeed, but he never retraces his precise steps: once it's over, it *is* over.

So, it finishes every time. Her jealousy becomes no less, though, and how she suffers in the interim.

She is making up now for all those years of her own marriage, after the fifth or sixth, when she'd appreciated how unlikely it was that any other woman would be properly – or improperly – interested in her husband. By then Hamish had become too predictable and dull, incurious, quite guileless too, and she had experienced the initial pulses of distaste, the first early purling of scorn for such a sorry narrowness of imagination as his.

In Alistair she started to see the potential she tried to believe had once fired the – now sputtering – spirit of her husband. She encouraged their only son in everything he wanted to do: his tennis, his skiing, his jazz lessons on the tenor saxophone instead of classical, his amateur theatricals, even helping to restore the local railway station. Everything which the suburbs had offered, Alistair had taken advantage of. He had grown up tall and healthy, with good hair and teeth, and with a sociable disposition: that is to say, he remembered jokes to repeat at people's parties, and he knew how women responded to charm, the Omar Sharif sort of charm, and he had the knack of bringing men out of themselves without threatening their precious sense of status. He had been all she had ever hoped for, and even more, with a clairvoyant gift for anticipating her own wants and satisfying them, making of them the little pleasures with which she came to stake out her married life. Unlike Hamish he knew exactly the sort of music she liked to listen to, what her favourite flowers were, the colours her eyes preferred, the feel of which fabrics, the tastes of which foods, the prose of which novelists. It was uncanny how often he could tell her what was in her mind. Lying in bed at night with Hamish, trying to get to sleep, she would imagine Alistair lying in her womb with his senses primed, truly more her own child than his father's.

Andrea is the latest. She has the current 'look' about her – her hair is cut how morning television presenters have theirs cut, full and puffed out, leonine, with the ears and earrings accentuated. Black hair, as her own was before it greyed in less time than a calendar year. All Alistair's girlfriends have slender wrists and hands, as people used to compliment *her* on having in the days before some of her knuckles knotted and her wrists started to swell and stiffen in draughts. They have neat ankles and tidy feet, in preferably flat shoes, which she so often used to tell Alistair were more sensible for women, never mind more 'U': 'Remember, Alistair, the higher the heel the lower the class.' Her son is not a man for the larger-boned woman, or for those who don't know how to present themselves: on certain afternoons when he used to join her from school in his uniform – an aeon ago now – they would sit in the restaurants of department stores to watch the mannequins parade between the tables as they treated themselves to a full set tea apiece.

In his adulthood he has always chosen girls unafraid of making exotic choices from the menu of whichever restaurant he has taken them to for lunch *à trois* – the girlfriend seated between Alistair and herself. She, like he, can appreciate their faultless manners. They have all spoken in the same neutral, accentless way that he does, which he learned when she decided that, at ten years old, her gifted son should attend elocution lessons. Whenever they all three get talking at lunch, she will find there is actually plenty to fill a conversation. The girls have a knowledge of tennis and skiing – as she once had herself, to keep up with Alistair's enthusiasm, but unlike her they can play one and do the other. They too, in common with Alistair, enjoy jazz; they each have a clear recall of all the plays they've seen in theatres since their childhood, they can identify the flowers in a posy vase on a table; they admire the wisdom of this or that hue used in a restaurant's colour scheme; they unexceptionally prefer fish to meat; they are all able to put a title to at least a few books written by her own favourite authoresses, Françoise Sagan and Mary Wesley.

'Andrea,' she has to remind herself. '*Andrea*.'

Over fourteen or fifteen years, since the first, the women have stayed constant, apart from the little vagaries of fashion which hardly count in a final perspective. While she and Alistair have grown older – even *his* hair at thirty-six is flecked with grey, but becomingly (his father's brown hair simply lost all its colour, it was drained away so that now it is an old man's white) – the girlfriends have remained the same age, about twenty-five or so, the age she herself must be in Alistair's first memories of her. They are by no stretch of the imagination fragile, but they are certainly ideal. 'What a perfect young lady for Alistair,' the women in her circle say if they should cast eyes on his present favourite. She will nod in agreement with their verdict most heartily. But her friends, as is their wont, can indulge in airy, incidental speculations on the future when the facts of life actually pertain to the past, which – in the suburban tradition – is guarded from the knowledge of others by beech and privet, by gates with tightly sprung latches, by secondary glazing and strategic sprays of dried flowers and reeds placed on the sills of windows thought too open to public view.

Jill / 1.15 / Q's B'o.

He checked the entry in his diary under today's date. He

was in the restaurant, in the bistro end, sitting at a table for two. It was now (he glanced at his watch) twenty to two. But, so far, no sign of Jill.

He turned to the front pages of the diary and found her office phone number. He pushed his chair back and stood up, looking round for the telephone. He cast an eye over the clientèle as he walked towards the back of the room, to see if they'd missed each other.

She wasn't at any of the other tables.

His new leather soles slapped on the chequered floor. In a mirror he caught sight of himself. He looked much less confident than he always imagined he did. In his mind's eye he always wore a smile, an easy expression on his face to inspire people's trust.

Under the telephone hood he lifted the receiver and dialled. The number rang. A receptionist answered. He gave the extension number, and he was connected.

More ringing.

There was no reply.

He tucked the receiver under his jaw, positioning it closer to his ear and mouth. Still no reply.

He held on. After a couple of minutes he replaced the receiver on the hook.

He walked back to his table, preferring not to look at the uneasy, unsmiling man shadowing him in the mirror. He pulled in the waist of his jacket as he sat down on the chair. He stared at the entry scribbled on the page. Jill / 1.15 / Q's B'o. He closed the diary and returned it to his inside pocket.

He lifted his glass, tipped his head back, and swallowed.

He caught the bistro *maître d*'s eye alighting on him for a moment. *Stood up, M'sieur? C'est la vie, non?*

He consulted his watch. 1.46. The little second hand was spinning as if it was possessed. 1.47.

Whenever he had lunch in a restaurant on a weekday it was invariably with clients or with his colleagues. They discussed business. If he had no reason to stop work except to go out and eat by himself, then he didn't eat.

Suggesting to Jill that they meet for lunch hadn't any precedent in his recent life. Even his brief affairs had always been kept for holidays, or an occasional long weekend: hardly 'affairs' at all in fact, rather a bachelor's 'encounters'. He had many friends (their addresses and telephone numbers filled seven narrow-spaced pages of his diary), he allowed them to plan his evenings and weekends for him, and that was just how he liked it – with the result that there was almost no time left over to focus on specific individuals with any amorous intent.

The sexual encounters he did find time for were in the way of an obligation, a concession to what the rest of the world did. He'd originally met Jill because he'd agreed to drive her down to someone's house for a weekend of (supposed) country pursuits. En route out of London on that Friday evening they'd got held up in traffic and he'd been able to concentrate on her as he felt he hadn't done on anyone for years.

After the weekend, he continued to concentrate. They met at friends' supper tables. Arranged to have a drink together. Went to a film they both wanted to see. Saw a second film. Tried a new pizza place. Then a mock-speakeasy with food. And a sushi bar. She visited him, he visited her. Evenings were their thing, maybe a couple of times a week. Bed, briefly, but not (yet) breakfast. And so it had gone, diaries and business trips permitting, for the past ten or eleven weeks.

'Let's have lunch,' he'd suggested to her. 'Through the week.' Now he'd forgotten the reason why. Maybe something to do with a momentary mellowness brought on by a warm evening: or a mad impulse to knock one day out of kilter with all the others, to make just this one afternoon seem like a dangerous adventure of indulgence – Jill, 1.15, Q's B'o, a table for two, an overflowing in-tray on his desk, the fax machine grinding in its corner, the pair of phones in his office ringing to distraction . . .

He caught himself about to look at his watch again, and told himself 'no'.

He pulled down his cuff.

Even with Jill, he'd been living by the clock. They both

had clocks beside their beds and on their cooker fascias; luminous green digits recorded the flight of seconds on their video recorders and on their car consoles.

The *maître d'* had placed him at a table next to a screen, not along the mirrored wall. Perhaps a first impression had suggested he was an adulterer, hence this discreet refuge from prying eyes?

He'd looked at his watch again before he realised what he was doing. It was the habit of a lifetime, like a nervous tic. That's just how he was. He liked every moment to be accounted for, he liked to believe each second and minute served its function.

Why? a voice inside his head suddenly asked him.

He shifted his eyes away from the table, trying to ignore the voice and its question: *Why must every moment be accounted for?* He looked across the room and saw – surprise, surprise – only himself. Himself staring back out of a wall mirror and no one else with him. A single man in a business suit and the crown of his head just starting to go bald.

Why? the voice persisted.

He swivelled his eyes towards the door – to the propeller fans turning on the ceiling – to the waiters in their black waistcoats and long white aprons busying themselves behind the bar.

Why?

He spotted the woman painted on the high panel, knocking it back. He lifted up the wine glass and tipped his head backwards and swallowed.

Why?

He put down the glass. He twisted its stem between his right-hand thumb and forefinger.

Well, why the hell NOT?

He let go of the glass.

In that crowded restaurant he closed his eyes. He looked into darkness.

What are you so afraid of?

He opened his eyes again and saw his hands laid flat on the table-top.

I am afraid – I am afraid – of not believing anything.

He knotted the fingers of both hands together and leaned forward intently on his elbows, seeing only the cradle of his fingers.

Afraid. Afraid of not believing that there is a point to living this life that I do, with every moment accounted for. Afraid of learning that the whole business is just like this, sitting at a table by myself waiting, and that the rest of it – the activity – it's only a kind of blur, a cover. Counting the minutes and seconds so that I don't see the days and months and years escaping from me. Filling in every spare moment: like daubing plaster on the cracks of a wall and not realising that the building is structurally unsound. Afraid of stopping in my tracks and hearing my own breathing under the others' voices and laughter.

Afraid of loneliness.

Afraid of putting these questions to myself and answering them with such bloody, killing earnestness.

He looked over at the tables on the mirrored wall of the bistro. This time one of the single men was staring across at him, as if he was recognising one of his own kind. Another man in a business suit, balding crown, eating alone, a rolled newspaper for company, with an empty hour in his day to fill.

He creaked back in the cane chair and turned his head away, taken aback by the thought of what the other man was thinking. He faced forwards, towards the window and the traffic moving in the street.

'*M'sieur*!' A voice spoke at his shoulder. '*M'sieur*, would you like to order now?'

'No,' he said, pushing his chair back. 'No, thank you. I'm afraid my guest hasn't – '

The *maître d'* brought him his coat. He handed the man several coins for a tip and received a bow from him.

He manoeuvred past and walked off, wondering how his stock must stand in future if a client should chance to bring him here.

Over the heads of two departing women exchanging family talk he glimpsed in the mirror a sombre, sober thirty-three-year-old who might have passed for forty-five.

He pushed through the revolving doors and stepped out on to the pavement. High white clouds scudded across a drying blue sky.

Now it was back to work . . .

He was buttoning his coat when he heard the stabbing of high heels on the pavement behind him. He turned round.

It was Jill.

She called his name. She smiled. She ran a few steps more, then stopped.

She looked at him. In the solemn silence he felt himself stiff, unsmiling, inflexible in his fitted businessman's topcoat. A look of puzzlement crossed her face, then concern. The concern turned to alarm. The full gamut of emotions in a relationship seemed compressed into those few seconds as he watched her.

She spoke his name again. Then one of her eyebrows slowly lifted.

It was that gesture – doubtful, perplexed: perhaps ironic, even amused – which settled the matter for him.

He felt his mouth straining at the corners. The smile broke and seemed to be splitting his face.

Her alarm vanished. A smile spread across her face, like the image of his own.

She walked forward and clutched his arm.

He breathed in her perfume and wrapped his arms around her.

'I'm so sorry,' she said. 'I had a *pile* of things – '

'It's all right.'

'I just couldn't help it.'

'I understand.'

'What's the time?' she asked.

'I don't know. Two-ish.'

'Have I kept you?'

'I'm supposed to be seeing someone at three – '

'Stay a while, Peter. Please.'

He stood, committing this moment to memory. The two of them embracing outside the restaurant. A periwinkle blue sky, a jet miles up in the ether making white vapour trails. Jill in her fur hat, like Anna Karenina, in a camel coat with a fur collar and black boots with narrow heels.

Behind her, customers were walking out through the revolving doors. He watched them as he continued to hold her. First, two women shoppers with their prematurely pinched, rather unhappy faces; they looked as if they were trying too hard to make conversation, old school friends holding on to lost time. After them one of the single men appeared. He raised his newspaper aloft to hail a cab. One stopped almost immediately, brakes squealing on the road. The man climbed inside. The taxi rattled off at a rate of knots with its single passenger. Spiriting him away, like a black gondola of loneliness . . .

Jill looked up at him.

'Who are you watching, Peter? What is it?'

'I once read a short story. About a woman during the war, in blitzed London. Looking for a lost lover.'

'Yes?'

'She hailed a taxi.'

'She did?'

'She got into the back and the taxi rushed off.'

He paused.

'And – ?' Jill prompted him. 'What happened?'

'It was very strange.'

'How was it strange?'

'She tried to tell the driver where she wanted to go but he wouldn't listen. She banged on the glass. The taxi was travelling too fast for her to jump out, you see. She couldn't make out his face. And then finally, he did look round . . .'

'What happened then?'

'End of story. With her staring at this – but we weren't told – Her lover? The devil. A skeleton?'

'Where was she being taken?'

He didn't reply. He vaguely shrugged his shoulders. Jill shivered into her fur collar, with cold or with fear perhaps.

He turned round, so he was facing in the same direction as her. He folded his arm tight around her waist and held her close against his side.

'Let's walk,' she said, cheering.

'Yes, let's.'

'Walk anywhere – '

'And keep walking.'

'You're not needing to get back?' she asked him.

'Of course not,' he said, and leaning towards her he placed another kiss on her cheek, with a gentleness this time that seemed quite new to them both.

She eats alone.

It is an art. A quiet but accomplished one.

There is art in how to handle a fork and knife. Surgeons are the most deft and delicate of cutlery-users, she has noticed.

Her solitude is no disadvantage to her now. Her life has developed to this point. Long ago she would sit watching, she and whichever man she was with at the time, and they would seem pitiable, those other figures – of either courage or dejection, or merely embarrassment – who ate alone.

She knew this restaurant several existences ago, long prior to the present one. It had the same name, but it was new on the scene. Every evening there was a clamour and crush to get in.

A band used to play on Friday and Saturday evenings, and couples turned on a small hardwood dance floor. The chef was French – no, not French, *Belgian* – and all the rage. The brightest people came, the *shiniest*. This was the place – out of all London – to be.

By now eating alone is no tribulation to her. The secret is, if not to blend in, then to make yourself as little conspicuous as possible.

She has become quite adept at gauging the 'feel' of a room. It is simpler to judge in the evening, when romance usually takes over. At lunch people are often less at their ease: too *awake* perhaps. Too many reasons have brought them – frequently on business-account expenses – for them all to be sharing a common mood. For her, as a watcher, the atmosphere has much to do with the architecture and décor.

The restaurant, dating as she knows from the early twenties, aspires to be one in *fin-de-siècle* Paris. The designers didn't do a bad job of it. Her grandparents brought her shortly after it opened, when she must have been six or seven. She was always to have a reliable memory, and she has never forgotten.

It was not to be one of her haunts later, though, when she was being taken about by young men, and then during the war. It would have been wholly suitable, she believes now. Rather rarefied, and other-worldly, slightly old-fashioned. Then, at that time, she didn't want to be in some of the places where she was entertained: modernly self-conscious in their appointments, quite thrumming with voices, the 'in'-spots. Love ought to have been treated a little differently. And it had, truly enough, been exactly that . . .

Love. She can recognise the emotion in strangers, every permutation of it, from fifty yards. It can't disguise itself from her. Nothing is more real to her after all these years.

She had her marriage to confirm it for her. She also had two quiet affairs, which she took great care that her husband should learn nothing about. She wouldn't have wanted to hurt him, but – equally – there had been more affection contained inside her than one recipient alone could have dealt with.

Where she sits she imagines it is all happening again for the first time, two or three years before she made the acquaintance of the man who would become her husband. It was never so very different after that first occasion. She can feel the constriction which the excitement of anticipation – a sixth sense – used to cause, tightening her ribcage and putting her stomach into spasm. A flush would pass across her chest. The lobes of her ears would tingle and feel impossibly sensitive. Then she would know that she was ready to receive the full revelation whenever it might strike.

Sometimes she can believe it still might happen, that the intervening years of widowhood and old age haven't occurred, that she is waiting for one of those men who conveniently filled her middle age, claiming some business connection with Richard but never specifying quite what. Or longer ago, she has arrived too early to rendezvous with another of those clandestine dates who drained her resources, mental and physical, as a child might have done. Or yet longer ago, she's waiting to see if Richard will really show up after all; or else if the man whose invitation she has accepted is a match for that other one she has guessed she will one day marry.

She knows better than to look into any of the mirrors, in case she disappoints herself. Like this, *inside*, she is – merely – herself as she always was. A woman with an adventurous disposition and – could it have been? – a too loving heart.

She opens her handbag.

From its maw, from beneath the three tubes of pills and capsules prescribed for taking every day, from beneath a lace handkerchief given to her by a great-niece, from beneath a powder compact and a lipstick and emery boards, from beneath a scuffed lizard purse and battered ostrich note-case – from beneath all this junk that's so necessary to her, she extracts a photograph. A small square black and white photograph with a white border, now faded and marked but still quite legible. It shows a young woman – in her very early twenties or thereabouts – seated at an open mullioned window. It seems to make all the difference, it always has, that the casement of the window behind her should happen to be ajar. Her cousin Willie had positioned her at an open window because he had decided that that was the most appropriate placing for the person he judged her to be. Beyond her – through that wedge – is daylight, fresh clean air, and (just out of focus) a prospect of lavish seasonal fecundity: free nature insinuating itself into the more stolid indoors life. Such a small detail – the crack between a window casement and the wooden jamb – could be made by Willie's sharp eye and mind to signify so much.

The young woman in the photograph smiles, she can't help smiling. It radiates her face, which is turned in quietly exultant profile. She's smiling at that prospect on such an intensely

summery summer's day, at all she sees there – which is
nothing less than the whole world laid out before her.

At the door on leaving the restaurant she felt a hand touch
her arm. It was gently but firmly done. She didn't look round,
not immediately, but allowed the hand-hold to support her. She
was grateful for it. Its strength gave *her* strength.

She stood gazing out at the street, at the incessant shiny
activity, the inane speed of all that motion. She blinked. The
sunlight was too strong for her. She remembered someone
saying, at one of those fraught and frosty parties to which
childless widows are invited en masse supposedly to be
cheered up by one another's company, why had London
become so competitive? Driving, getting on to a bus, hailing
a taxi, even crossing the road, they were competitive acts,
done in contention against other people. Why on earth did
that have to be?

'Excuse me, madam . . .'

The voice spoke at her shoulder, quietly but authoritatively.

For a moment she heard another voice through it –

'You – you left this, madam.'

But no, it wasn't. Not Richard, not Willie, and neither
Leonard nor Alec. The man standing beside her, she realised,
was an employee of the restaurant. What was the name given
to his sort? She considered . . . puzzled it out . . . 'Junior
Managerial', was it?

'I found it at your table, madam.'

She looked down to see what he was holding out to her.

'I'm sure it *is* yours, madam.'

A photograph. A square black and white photograph. *The*
photograph. Of course, of course –

'I couldn't help noticing, madam, what a good photograph it
is.'

The likeness. Of course, of course.

'Might I guess – it's your daughter?'

She stared at him.

'I . . .'

He started to redden.

'I mean – your granddaughter.'

She continued to stare. Such intensely blue eyes, beneath his fair eyebrows, with the sun shining directly into the irises. But blue eyes like these – as blue as Richard's were – they're always the weakest, that is the sorrow of it.

She didn't speak as he returned the photograph to the flat of her hand. She opened the clasp of her handbag and slowly, tiredly, looked for a space inside, in its once cavernous hold now crowded with so much medical wisdom supplied by the chemist's dispensary and with the fripperies of vanity bought at the cosmetics counters in department stores. As she brought the sides of the bag together to close it, she saw the girl looking up at her, still smiling. It was only naïve optimism, of course – or worse, wide-eyed brown-eyed damned stupidity. But no, she didn't want to believe it, of that exultant young woman on the summer day of all summer days, turning to face a garden of fragrance and insects, with all the world laid out before her.

They had come here because they'd said they would, on their fifth wedding anniversary.

The odds had been against their marriage lasting so long. Both their mothers had imagined that they weren't an obvious match for one another. The truth was that they had each presented the other with a challenge. Neither he nor she was a giver-in; each had a little too much pride for that. But nor were they intransigent, either of them: they had gone on believing they had too much healthy pragmatism in their natures ever to become so.

The marriage would *not* have endured without some skilful manoeuvring from both parties. Each continued to be receptive to the other's essential wants: alternatively expressed, each understood the psychological but eminently practical need that the other fulfilled. She had always required his financial security, and from the outset he had depended on the social fillip of her education and the abundance of little graces provided by breeding. It was essential to both of them that the marriage should continue working, and if such a fundamental instinct wasn't attributable to individual self-interest, then a joint concern for their success as a social organism – 'the Lesters' – surely did have much to do with the determination they shared. Neither of them had exactly *mellowed*, but as temperament went they had learned to trim their cloth. Mutual accommodation – within limits, and excepting some too humiliating compromise – was their working philosophy for the union.

Then suddenly it all goes wrong. How simply it happens. She's been enjoying herself; the day is proving so out of the ordinary she momentarily forgets, and blurts out that long, long ago she was brought here.

'By your parents?'

'Oh no.'

He tries again. 'A relative?'

'No. No.'

'A friend?'

She smiles. She realises as she does so that she's smiling in a silly, wobbly way.

She nods her head.

'A woman?' he asks.

She doesn't nod or shake her head.

'A man?'

She continues to smile.

'Yes,' she replies.

Then it has to come out. Who he was, why they'd come. But it was such a long, long time ago, and really – really there had been nothing to it, she suggests, or hardly anything, it was over before it had a chance to begin.

'But he brought you here?'

'Yes.'

'It must've been expensive?'

'I don't know. Yes, I suppose so.'

'He wasn't interested in you?'

'I wasn't . . .' She pauses, with fateful consequence. '. . . interested in *him*.'

'You came, though?'

'I came, yes. But – '

'You didn't enjoy it?'

'Not really.'

'You hated every minute of it?'

'No. Not exactly – '

'Hated only some of it?'

'That's not what – '

'You're remembering it now?'

'*No*, Mike.'

'So why did you mention it?'

'I just – '

'If you hated it. We could have gone somewhere else instead. Anywhere else.'

'*You* wanted to come – '

'I wanted to do what *you* wanted – '

'You thought you knew best where – '

'Don't I?' he asks.

She is going to reply, but she hesitates.

'About restaurants?' he says.

'Yes,' she admits to him.

Her tone of voice, she hears for herself, is suddenly wearied.

'What does that mean?' he fires back at her.

'Nothing.'

'C'mon, I know you well enough – '

She starts to shake her head.

'I don't get you, Lizzie.'

'No, I don't expect you do.'

'Meaning – meaning what?'

'Men *assume* they know. They will always assume.'

'Ah. Plural now. A generalisation, is it?'

She foolishly stays silent.

'"*Men*", Lizzie – ?'

She turns one of the lilies in the vase. It's too delicate, however: the head snaps off the stalk, but so gently that she doesn't realise for several seconds.

'Men and women,' she says at last.

'What? What's that?'

Did she really say it? She can't be so sure. She crumples the waxy lily head tightly in her fist.

'What did you . . .?'

They come from their two worlds. The difference is far more profound than just social. It's as wide and deep as gender. At thirteen she was sent away to a school to be among girls. One of three brothers, all *his* best friends had been boys. Their home lives had presented them with the spectacle of the stereotypical sexual roles society expected of a married man and woman, a father and mother. But something – something flawed in both of them – had prevented them from ever quite *believing* what was enacted (or mimed out) in front of them. The worst – she sees it now, as unbeknown to her he also does – the worst that could have happened was that they should have attracted one another, that – so to speak – their own two particular molecules, his and hers, should have collided.

She puts her elbows up on the table – one cardinal rule of her boarding-school education broken – and cups her chin in the palm of her hand.

They were only words. But words were what had preserved them this far, after the rages and following the conversations in the middle of the night that seemed to put things in a better light, when all the time they were lying flat on their backs on the mattress – expensively open-sprung, his side firm and hers medium – in enveloping darkness. The words had seemed capable of spelling away the rancour and hurt. They had put their faith in the words, the vocabulary, as they could do in nothing else.

It had been words too, long long ago, the first time she'd been brought to this restaurant. Something so silly, when she'd mistranslated from the menu – *poire* for *poivre*, pear for pepper – and her companion had laughed, giggled rather, and she'd persuaded herself she heard a sneering tone to it: when – so she was to realise a couple of years later, and far too late to repair the damage – when quite possibly all it had been was Andrew's nerves, wanting too much for this dinner to work. He'd brought her for a meal he couldn't afford because . . . There and then the words had dried up on him as he'd tried

in the stilted silence to explain / so that he hadn't finished /
so that she'd let herself put the direst interpretation on his
piscine gasping for air . . .

Now, seeing the place again, she guesses why the Pollingers'
son invited her *here*. Because he'd wanted to find the surroundings that expressed best his hopefulness, his unselfish pride in
her. It had had to be somewhere very special: even out of his
orbit. Maybe, she sits thinking now in a denser, more opaque
silence with a Siberian iciness to it, maybe if anybody could
have converted her from infidel to believer, it would have been
Andrew Pollinger, and that was the occasion – evening into
night – when her evangelisation ought to have begun.

This is an afternoon his daughter will remember. All her life
she will remember, trying to remember more.

From the future she will have lost the details of so much.
Except that it wasn't a hamburger restaurant, although that's
where she would rather have been. That a shower came on,
and they had to look for somewhere quickly. (He couldn't
have afforded to deliver her back home soaking wet.) That
the kitchen in the restaurant specially made up a strawberry
milk shake for her, so the situation was partially saved. She
drank the milk shake but didn't eat very much. The drink was
better than nothing, though, because her father wanted to put
something into her stomach.

He had never been very knowledgeable about nutrition. But
he didn't mean his daughter to have a memory of a hamburger
restaurant, pricey and trendy or not. He knew all about the
way town centres were going, turning into a succession
of too brightly lit dispensaries of factory-made fast food.
There was always something fraught about those eateries
– neatly turned-out uniformed staff with an eye constantly
on the clientèle, on the look-out for transactions of illegal
substances in the lavatories – and maybe she too had picked
it up from her father, that the bright lights were deceptive.
For the two of them it might have been that *any* place would

have proved to be one of secrets and the unsaid, of shaded areas of morality. She must have been able to tell from his forced cheerfulness, from the effort not to appear to her – even to a four-year-old child – listless or angry, although what he recognised himself to be (and only too well) was a defeated man.

They were having to pretend for ninety minutes – the length of a film – that the situation was quite different, to a soundtrack accompaniment. The tinkling of glass and ringing of cutlery. The genteel collision of bits of crockery on the cloth-covered tables.

Her mother wanted her back permanently because she had plans – to marry again, for one thing – and *he* had the choice of fighting for his child or not. He had chosen not to play tug-of-love, as the newspapers call that war game. He mistrusted himself perhaps, as he loved Sophie too much, to believe that he had any feasible, realistic capacity for choice in the matter. Her mother wanted to begin all over again. He, by giving her up, was proving to a child – as no one else in her life might ever do – how absolute and ambiguous true love is.

She could surely see it, at four years old. In the way he stirred and stirred his espresso coffee with the spoon and didn't take a single sip of it. Now he was watching her, staring through her as if he was trying in the minutes left to get right inside the very soul of her.

All the soft lights and refined chatter had fallen away, until there were only themselves, islanded here, and two turning to one.

In the future he would hear about her, very occasionally, and see a photograph or two, and hope for a birthday or Christmas card that would never come, and although he might have other children none of them would be as she had been, the first one. *They* would have a too ready access to love, and undervalue it, not realising that it finally proves itself by dint of what it surrenders, by the extent of its self-denial. *They* would have everything, so how could they possibly be able to appreciate just how ambiguous and how absolute such true love is?

Daylight outside. Inside, a glassy gilded stage-setting. But the emotions, although disguised, are too urgent for theatre. No actor would have had the technique to stir a cup of coffee so abstractedly and endlessly, with only minutes left. This is real life, all too real. An afternoon out of the sum of afternoons, not in a plastic and vinyl hamburger restaurant but in the classiest, most timeless location he could find for them in a shower of rain.

All her life she, like he, will remember – at four years old she is remembering it now – trying to remember when she's forty and older than her father was when it happened, needing to recall more and more, every tiniest detail that she can.

I try to catch a resemblance between us, myself and the woman who floats above our heads. In the mirrors I see people looking at me, then at the panel, and I know what they're thinking. *Well, that would make a neat photograph, wouldn't it? 'Age' rapt in vain contemplation of 'Youth'.* So I act for them, I ham it up a bit, and they won't have any recollection that I trod the boards for nearly sixty years to earn myself a living, that I was brought here to this same restaurant after my first night in the West End, to celebrate my success.

The people who watch me see – as my audiences in the theatres always did – only what they want to see.

Sometimes Mother comes as a ghost to view herself, which is how we find one another.

We aren't together long enough on any occasion for the mother and daughter relationship to become what in the common experience it surely is – a source of discord. She disappears into the mirrors, to move behind the glass. I look for her, and now and then I think I can find her behind my dejected reflection, but more usually not.

When she's there I try to see her for what she was, before she became my mother: a well-brought-up girl who rebelled against the cause of home and hearth. It didn't matter to her that she was married when she met the man who would paint her. She spent whole afternoons in his Kensington studio in the pose of nymphs and naiads. Later, when she'd returned to the other life, he transplanted her to a landscape of trees and ferns and mossy banks, to the mythical champaigns where she also belonged.

What a shock it must have been for her husband the first time he saw the image of his wife in a public place. Or could he not believe it? Or – I wonder – was it not such a shock to him after all? The mind becomes very versed at resolving itself to the inevitable. He may have judged it a not exorbitant price – his possible social embarrassment – if the consequence would be that he was able to keep her his wife.

Whose daughter am I? Her husband's, or her immortalist's?

The meal always plumbs to such solemn depths. The coffee tastes of the question, and of my own uncertainty. There is no one to ask because Mother is at her most elusive when she comes to me here. When she was alive, at home, she could be imperious, or cussed, but in this restaurant, in another age, she is doubly insubstantial.

Her mouth makes words, but she doesn't speak them. I watch her eyes watching from the elevated *mise-en-scène* that marked her metamorphosis from wife to *bonne viveuse*. Recumbent on her woodland bier of lichen and leafy tendril, shaded by boughs and cooled by the proximity of lapping water.

And the sky. Ah, the sky! The essence of all blue-wash summer skies. It's glimpsed, through dense foliage, but the implication is that it vaults eternally, too remote to protect us and too incorporeal to be an imprisonment. Really it's nothing – refracted light, the tenuous blue deception of colourless aerial gases – but where would lovers and philosphers be without it?

Believe it, if you can. Whether it's zero and doesn't exist, or is the intrinsic round in which is held everything our lives are and that we might wish them to be.

OYSTERS AND CIGARS

She turned over from a dream – running along a country
road frothy with wild flowers – and woke to the dazzle of
a sea glare.

For a few seconds she couldn't think where she was. Then
the mattress creaked under her, and the sound confirmed
that she had lived these moments before. First waking to
sunshine, brilliantly sharp through primrose curtains, then
trying to remember.

The sunshine came straight in off the sea and coloured the
wood of the window-frame like – like sticky honey. It oozed
out from there on to the walls but gradually faded back to
the pattern of the wallpaper, a mathematical trellis of climbing
roses. At home the walls were plain matt, pastels so pale and
inoffensive that now she couldn't bring to mind which colour
– pink or green or blue – belonged to which room.

They only had to live in *these* rented rooms for three weeks
of the high summer, so the wallpaper didn't matter. There
was no danger of their becoming people who liked patterned
wallpaper, not in twenty-one days. She thought the background,
and ignoring it, must somehow make them concentrate more on
each other, her mother and herself.

On their holiday they spent most of the time together, except
when she was dragooned into a game of rounders with her
beach friends (as her mother dubbed them) and except for the
occasional chats on the esplanade wall with whoever were this
year's confidantes. The two of them had always been as close
as it was possible to be, as her mother's friends would for
ever make a point of telling them. The past couple of years
had changed things a little, inevitably. Firstly her mother had
started working, and she'd had to think about her job. Then

she had left home for her first year at boarding-school. But the changes weren't serious ones. Being on holiday now meant that they had three terms' worth of catching up to do.

Between the school sports day and packing the car to leave London for Suffolk they had filled one another in. On the journey down they had listened to Flanders and Swann on the cassette-player, and her mother had sung along to the sad song 'The Slow Train' as she could never resist doing, and they might have been making the journey in any other year, away from the motorway and heading for the coast along the red country roads still flanked by high hedges, past cottages with roofs of straggling thatch and pink plaster walls.

She would keep a look-out for the old road signs, almost lost in meadowsweet and long grass, which told the distance in measures chiselled in stone. She would watch for her first glimpse of the sea. Then for a while they would return inland; briefly the terrain became hillier and more wooded before the last flat stretch opened out in front of them – the fields turned stridently green, yacht sails passed behind trees, the wide river snaked slowly between banks of mud and reeds to the sea. She always wound down her window for a first sniff of salt, the brine, and kept her eyes peeled to spot a curlew or a sandpiper.

Now lying in bed she could hear the shore birds, gulls and kittiwakes, perhaps a tern or two. Their tall, gaunt, pebbledashed Edwardian semi stood on the Parade, with nothing but a low wall between them and the beach of banked shingle. Fifty yards away from the house was the sea. The fishing boats puttered in just after dawn, the catch was unloaded and the gutting begun on trestle tables set up outside the wooden work huts. Black-headed scavengers wheeled overhead, waiting to snatch at the debris, but usually they'd gone – fed and shrieking – by the time she properly woke. She always had an approximate notion of the time from the amount of light in the room.

Now the amount of light was increasing rapidly. The ugly pale wood wardrobe stood out from the wall in full 3-D. She knew that it must be seven o'clock at least.

She reached out for her watch. The rattan table on its spindly splayed legs rocked as her fingers fumbled across its surface.

She touched the buckle on the strap. She retrieved the watch and held it above the table, its face on a line with her eyes. The light was quite enough to see by. The hands told her ten past seven.

Already time was pushing her into the swim of the day.

Leah found her mother already up and about, as she always did on the first morning. She would be sitting in the bay window of the upstairs sitting-room – in the sunshine usually – making a shopping list of what they needed. They always brought a cardboard box of groceries with them, but the point of a holiday was to live differently, eating holiday fare.

This time she was in the kitchen.

'I was thirsty,' she said, removing the tea-bag from the mug and dropping it into the sink. 'Would you like something, darling?'

Leah shook her head. Their first breakfast was always an event: like an Arthur Ransome tiffin. It took a while to remember where to find all the cutlery and crockery.

Her mother smiled, then sipped at her tea and swallowed. She placed the mug on the draining-board and reached sideways, picking up her dressing-gown from the back of the chair.

Leah watched as she slid her arms into the sleeves. It had always happened that on holiday they didn't stand on ceremony, they would walk about in their nightdresses, and it didn't matter if she saw the outlines of her mother's breasts and the heavy shadow between her legs. Leah had been planning for their mornings in the kitchen, deciding she would leave off her knickers beneath her nightdress as she didn't like to at school, and even though her own nightdress was Chilprufe and scarcely hinted at anything underneath. She had wanted to be in the same boat as her mother: notwithstanding that they'd had their Private Talk on the evening before she left for her new school eleven months ago, she hadn't thought that that would make any difference to their holiday. But her mother was wrapping the dressing-gown about her waist and pulling at the sash; her eyes seemed more serious than her mouth, which was trying to smile.

'Will you want tea?' Leah asked. Real tea, she meant.

'When?'

'When we have breakfast.'

'Oh.' Her mother lifted the mug from the draining-board. 'I wasn't thinking.'

They always used a bright red Alice-in-Wonderland pot you needed two hands to hold. For breakfast the brew required three and a half teaspoonfuls of the loose tea, and very fresh boiling water filled up to the level of the top of the spout. That was the ritual.

'Actually I'm not so hungry at the moment,' her mother said. 'But *you* have something.'

Leah felt her brow crinkling. Breakfast for one, eaten alone in front of the other, was an impossibility.

'I'd just like tea too,' Leah said.

'Tea it is, then.' Her mother didn't encourage her again to eat; she sounded almost relieved that the business had been simplified – no cereal packets, no milk rings left on the table by the jug, no toast crumbs.

'I could live on tea,' her mother said, lighting the gas and removing the lid from the dormouse pot while Leah filled the kettle from the cold tap at the basin.

As the water heated, Leah positioned herself behind one of the old pine chairs. She placed her hands on the back. The slats weren't any protection to her modesty, but then there wasn't much to be seen through the fabric of her nightdress, even if she'd had full daylight behind her. She needed something to do with her hands, however, she felt they were untidy, flapping weights. Her mother's hands were fine, bony, purposeful, never at a loss. If they had nothing else to do they would push back through her hair and tidy the roll at the back. They could always seem busy. Leah was beginning to appreciate such things, living only among girls and women, being initiated in her first term into the lore of skin lotions and moisturisers, how not to chap knuckles or chip nails or let the corner of your mouth fray to a cold sore. She had discovered so early that a farmer's daughter might have unblemished, tapering hands and a girl with a titled father have thick wrists and stumpy fingers, so that nothing in life was quite to be predicted.

When the water had boiled and been drawn and the pot filled, she watched how her mother's hands wrapped themselves tightly around the hot belly of the pot: as if she was a potter pressing wayward clay.

'Was your bed comfortable, Leah?'

She sat down on the chair; she nodded.

'Yes, thanks.'

She wondered why she should have used her name, when there were only the two of them.

'I woke very early,' her mother said. 'I lay listening to the sea.'

Leah nodded.

'Maybe I dozed off again,' she continued, 'but I don't think so. I thought I'd get up. Hearing the sea, it's made me thirsty.'

Leah nodded again.

'I must get a new swimsuit. I'll look in the Fo'c'sle.'

The pot was lifted, with two hands required to support it, and the spout tipped into two mugs. Without a mesh strainer, Leah saw when it was already too late –

'They had some nice ones last year, but maybe the fashion's different.'

Leah placed her arms on the table and leaned forward. She pulled her steaming mug towards her.

'They did a feature in the newspaper,' her mother said. 'On swimwear. But I don't think I liked *them* so much.'

Leah looked into the tea, as if a pattern was to be glimpsed preparing itself among the leaves that always escaped. Then she realised that there weren't any, strainer or not: that her mother had used a tea-bag. She hadn't thought that there was anything to be had in the grocery box *except* loose tea. Unless her mother imagined now that this way was more convenient?

She cast her eyes along the shelf and spotted a packet of

Jackson's Darjeeling loose tea. It must have been taken out of the box last night. Since she had gone off to school, perhaps her mother had used tea-bags more often.

She watched her mother stand up to fetch something and happen (?) to catch sight of herself in the square mirror next to the printer's calendar of Flatford Mill. Her eyes quickly scanned the impression; then they angled across the mirror and swivelled out of the wooden frame, towards where she sat on her chair watching.

A second or two later they both smiled. Her mother put down the mug of tea on the bread-board. Leah lifted her elbows from the table.

'I think I've had enough tea,' her mother said. 'But *you* drink up.'

Leah swallowed from her mug.

'I must get changed. I should have done it by now anyway. What a *slovenly* mother you have.'

Get changed for the first breakfast? Had her mother really forgotten? The first breakfast was always informal, as if they were camping or on a boat: Swallows and Amazons stuff, Coot Club, Picts and Martyrs.

'Actually I might have a bath,' her mother said. 'Is that all right? Do you want to go into the bathroom first?'

Leah shook her head.

'There should be enough water by now. I hope they've had the plumbing looked at.'

Last year the pipes had sounded possessed during the final days. The whole house had quaked as the water thundered down from the tank in the attic and the old metal jumped and rattled behind its wooden casing. They had scarcely been able to hear one another speak and her mother, in high good humour at the situation, had invented an easy-to-learn sign language for them both, which had left them both doubled over with laughter.

'We don't want that hassle all over again, do we?' her mother said. She slopped the tea into the sink. 'Well, I can phone the agents.'

The mug was replaced on the plastic drying-rack.

'Never mind,' she said. 'We're here to empty our minds. To forget all that.'

She turned round from the sink and smiled. She retied the cord and the dressing-gown pulled tighter over her hips.

Leah had begun to appreciate better at school the virtue of slimness, which had hardly occurred to her before. She hadn't had to think about it previously because the woman she knew best hadn't appeared to change with the years. At Christmas-time, with so much temptation on offer, she had started to wonder what effort of will it took to keep yourself looking the same person. She'd heard it said of some of the mistresses at school that they lived 'on their nerves' ends', and since those ones were mostly as thin as rakes and beanpoles it had struck her that her mother might be afflicted in the same way. But her mother didn't fret and fuss about little things as they did. So she preferred to believe it was the effort of will that stopped her from putting on weight, and that she wasn't without a little pride: the right sort.

Leah smiled at her. She wanted her mother to approve of her. At the school commem she had seen the other parents watching them both. Some of the mothers seemed to have the wrong sort of pride: the waists of their dresses were too tight and straps showed through bodices, their wedding rings had stuck on their fingers and too much jewellery jangled on their pudgy wrists, and they looked down their noses at everyone else. Her mother had borne it all with smiles: like the premature widows, she too – although a divorcee – had cultivated a second, more mature version of 'youth' and walked with a born-again spring in her step.

Is this where she wants to be?

A *good* restaurant, of course, since he means to impress her. Lunch is a new stage in their brief affair.

Maybe the question is, does she want to be in this particular place with this particular man?

Christopher has no great disadvantages, so far as she can tell. He is no more materialistic than her last was, who was in the same line, corporate finance. She wonders why she was attractive to Phil, and is even more so now to Christopher. She has the most normal of jobs in their world – public relations – and yet she's been told you could only guess from her clothes. Apparently her manner is . . . a little distracted, also a little wary, which makes for a strange combination. Maybe she offers them all a challenge?

'Some oysters? Leah?'

As he says it, she's reading the name on the menu. 'Ikness Oysters.' She blinks at it. Very carefully she smiles.

'Yes?'

She considers.

'You know what *they*'re supposed to do for you?'

She nods her head.

'I'd love oysters,' she says.

She lifts her eyes and watches him over the top of the menu. He's smiling at her. He's interpreting her decision as he wants to, as a seemly lunchtime statement of the erotic. It's not how *she* means it, though. But misunderstandings must happen: Christopher and she are a gender apart, after all.

She shrugs, with her own quiet smile, as if, really, it doesn't matter so very much. He seems content with that reply, with the self-deprecation.

'Oysters it is, then,' he says, and his conspiratorial smile stays in place.

To him they are a legendary food, infamous since his schooldays. She imagines him then, imagining himself ordering oysters in the dining-room of the hotel in the small market-town close to the boarding-school: ordering them in that scene of his illicit dreams for a woman of his mother's age probably, and not at all like herself.

'All right, Leah?'

She nods.

'Oh yes.'

Herself. A woman offering a 'challenge' only appeals – so she concludes – after a man has played the field and found himself with a lack.

She drops her eyes to the menu, to the list of main dishes, but she loses track among the lines of print. The pianist is playing 'La Mer' and she feels herself suddenly stranded, beached, among the mullet and brill and bass. She also feels herself smiling: at the title not at the tune, at the coincidence of this of all images. She hears it first – the sea – and then it gradually takes some appropriately fluid shape in her mind's eye, through the music, through the other voices and his loaded silence, through the net curtains and looped drapes and double-glazed windows of a restaurant in the very centre of a city.

'Just another half an hour in bed,' her mother said. 'I want to finish my book.'

Leah tried not to look disapproving.

'You can have a look around, can't you? And report back. What's what.'

Leah nodded. Her mother pulled her dressing-gown even tighter about herself. And that was that.

Well, it *is* only eight o'clock, she argued on her mother's behalf, getting up her speed on the esplanade.

And her mother had had the drive down yesterday. So maybe it was excusable. Even though a long lie-in had never happened before: in fact they'd been actively discouraged in the past. Up – breakfast – get washed and dressed – then outside and get on with it.

Hmmm.

In the old days she used to smell frying bacon from the houses on the Terrace, but nowadays everyone took muesli and/or bran and wholemeal bread. It had become that kind of clean-living, *thoughtful* place.

She could see only a couple of other people in the distance. The upper part of a man's body appeared above the bank of shingle; a woman was walking a black labrador along the esplanade. Both were moving away from her.

Instead of bacon, the air held a confusion of smells, which

she slowly disentangled: brine, fish, tar, vegetation, creosote, but most of all what would remain for her always the ineffably fresh essence of unoccupied, unused summer mornings, which – the habit was never to leave her – she would get up before the rest of the world to savour.

From the esplanade wall she watched the oyster boats. They didn't stop at the beach but travelled ten miles or so further down the coast to a small harbour. Even so they were called 'Ikness Oysters'

Those occupied pride of place in the window of Ginger & Daughter, Fishmongers, on Crag Street. Leah would anticipate her mother always stopping to look. Last year she'd asked her, could they buy some, and her mother had told her they were only for special occasions: the question had seemed to persist after she'd answered, though, lightly clouding the air for a few days, and on their last Saturday her mother had bought half a dozen and they'd feasted themselves from a picnic hamper on the beach as the hottest sun of that holiday started to decline in the sky. Wielding old forks, they'd split and opened the rough, blistered shells. Squashy and gummy, the raw flesh had tasted salty, and a bit sour and of no particular flavour, only of fish and sea, but they had been remarkably quenching as they slithered whole from her mouth into her throat. Her mother reminded her of the question she'd asked another year, did the oysters contain pearls, when she'd told her they were a different sort, that pearls are some kind of bacterial infection, an *imperfection*, that you never knew when you might just crack a shell and strike lucky with one.

And to come, a shark steak for him and turbot with scallops and spinach for her.

It's all going very well, isn't it? On the other side of the room the oysters are being served from an old-fashioned fishmonger's slab. Lengths of weed and sea foliage draped hither and thither add the spoiling inauthentic touch.

She stares, and knows she is staring. Not at the oysters. The waiter's shirt-sleeves are rolled back in the vague way her father used to roll back his, halfway along his forearms and with the unlinked cuffs hanging down. How strange to be reminded, and now, sitting at a table with this confidential stranger. Such a minor detail, and yet how vitally inseparable from the too little that she remembers of the man.

At first, when she was six, she had thought her father was dead. It was the easiest thing to believe then, at the time.

She had grown up accepting that in a sense he *was* dead, because his faraway existence so evidently had nothing to do with theirs. He had another wife, and another daughter, and a son, and they all lived abroad, in Canada. Her mother had told her no more than that, though, and because nothing else was ever volunteered and because the photographs of him had disappeared she didn't enquire.

At thirteen going on fourteen she could bring very little back to mind, and she wasn't sure if her memories were really of what had happened or what she had wound round about whatever it was she did actually remember.

Already her early childhood was a mystery to her. She couldn't approach any closer, so she had to take it more or less on trust. It was also, she was beginning to sense, the bond between her mother and herself: what they chiefly shared was all their life lived alone together.

And anyway, the girl will one day remind herself when her luncheon companion inevitably makes his little joke, isn't the lustrous pearl embedded in the oyster flesh really no more than an aberration, the most beautiful flaw?

The plates of oyster shells have been removed from the table.

Leah can taste their brininess still. She is here in this restaurant and she is meanwhile somewhere else entirely, where her companion cannot follow her.

He is watching her carefully across the table. She feels she is performing for him rather like a marionette. Is that what he is thinking? – or does he not even realise? It seems to her to be a very important point to establish, but she doesn't see how she can.

For the moment she lets it go, places her hands flat like starfish on the blue cloth, tastes the blue saltiness of the Ikness sea. She listens to the pianist, to 'Aria' fading into 'Stranger On The Shore', and she hears from this distance the shingle, shrieking at her as it is sucked under by the breakers.

Then she noticed. The telephone was on a different table from the one it had been on last night and the flex had coiled round the front left castor of the button-back chair. Her mother must have been calling when she was out on her recce.

She dropped on to the sofa. The cushion was as soft as ever and she sank into it; the back was stiff, rigid, prickly horsehair. She reached up with her elbow and laid it awkwardly on the high arm. It was best for sleeping on, the sofa, but she wasn't tired. Not at all. She had only been up for a couple of hours.

From downstairs her mother's footsteps sounded on the worn, threadbare staircase carpet. The same treads creaked that always did so. A few moments later she walked into the room, still wearing her dressing-gown. She stood smiling generally at the furniture before the smile came to rest on the sofa.

'We must get some flowers for in here.'

Leah nodded instead of speaking.

'*You* could pick them.'

Leah nodded again.

'It's *you* who knows all the places to go.'

They grew beside the bridle-paths that skirted the fields of corn and barley. Red campion, blue meadow cranesbill, heath dog violet, yellow ragwort, purple Venus's looking-glass, there were clumps of thrift in the dunes, and white sea-spurrey near the marshes. It had become her job to collect them on their walks, posies they would arrange on the kitchen table or on the mantelpiece or on the broad sill above the middle landing.

'I was thinking – '

Her mother stood at the bay window, pulling the curtain as far back as it would travel on its rail.

' – you could hire a bike this year, couldn't you?'

Leah watched her mother's fingers smoothing the curtain's flimsy material. The pattern was flowery, to sort of match the chintz covers: a wild garden of unidentifiable blooms, against which any posy would have paled to insignificance.

'At the toy shop. *They* have bikes, don't they?'

Leah continued to watch. Then she sensed that an answer was required, that her mother was being purposefully patient: but that she mightn't remain so.

She spoke before the smile had a chance to narrow.

'Yes.'

'It was an idea. We've always passed them – the bikes – outside the shop. Only I never thought before.'

The sash of the window was pulled up, squeaking. With that thin glass protection gone, Leah listened to the quiet roar of the waves washing on to the shingle. Fainter but still recognisable, she heard the screaming as the pebbles slid down the ramp, dragged back by their own mass and weight into the sea. It was the rhythm of all their days and nights in the town. The first dog-walkers crunched along the shoreline in time to it; the night-anglers – sheltered behind windbreaks, setting their rods by lantern-light – dozed off on their camp stools lulled by it.

'The sun's up there!' her mother said. 'Somewhere.'

Leah mumbled a reply.

'It's just high cloud,' her mother confirmed for them both. 'It'll disappear.'

Leah nodded. The sky had its habitual glare. Ships appeared motionless on the horizon.

'Did you see anybody? When you were out?'

'Anybody' was whoever came during the same three weeks as themselves, or who sufficiently overlapped. 'Regulars.' A friendship could be taken up after twelve months and put aside when the holiday was over and somehow it could survive on so little, from one year to the next. An August friendship was a particular sort: it didn't go too deep, and so it didn't carry a potential of harm if it should fail for any reason. It was a kind of skating over the surface, and if you didn't take it too seriously it could work quite well.

On her walk she had taken note of the cars parked outside certain houses. Most of them she recognised, or else their contents, and she had begun to compose the mental map by which she lived during their annual three weeks in the town. The group she belonged to had a nucleus of girls her own age. She wasn't able to foretell how the past year would have changed them. Three had been at the same school and were going on to different ones, and she didn't know how well they would fit back together again. But it was a compact town and, if they had all come back, they wouldn't be able to avoid each other. The tennis courts were the outer limit of the town proper, but that wasn't the spot to escape people: and the bridle-paths were intersected by other bridle-paths, which surely meant that there was nowhere which could *not* be reached by escapee and stalker.

Her mother got herself dressed and ready.

Leah watched her as she stood in front of the bathroom mirror with the radio turned on to talking voices. She seemed about to open the quilted zip-bag where she kept her toiletries and cosmetics, then she appeared to change her mind. But she stood looking at herself with the sort of attention Leah would have expected only at home, on one of the evenings when she was invited out to visit friends.

The quilted bag was new. It replaced the sponge-bag, which she'd let her play with in previous years. On the car journeys down she used to open and close the clasp and take out a lipstick or a jar of moisturising cream for closer inspection, then replace them in the washable plastic hold. The quilted bag had pockets, she knew, and inside zips, and the lining was made of some clever absorbent fabric.

The bag was replaced on top of the shelf beside the cabinet. Leah watched as her mother turned on the taps, leaned forward over the basin, and dabbed her face with lukewarm water. While she stooped forward splashing herself and as the music played, Leah ran up the three treads of staircase on to the second landing, opened the airing cupboard door, and pulled the top towel off the pile. She shook it out and returned to the bathroom. She touched her mother's arm.

'Oh. *Leah* – !'

Her mother jumped, quite literally. Leah took two steps backwards.

'I didn't hear you. You nearly gave me a heart attack.'

Water was dripping from her face. Leah handed her the towel; she pressed it against her cheeks, watching them both in the mirror over the basin. She slowly mopped at the wet skin, on her nose, her chin, the line of her jaw, her neck, then – again – her cheeks.

Unless one of them was in the bath, they always used to wait while the other washed her face and neck and under her arms. Her mother would be wearing a brassière and knickers, and Leah loved the intimacy, the confidentiality, since she knew no one else ever saw them like this. There were just themselves, and it felt to her like a secret.

'Hey, can you switch the radio off?'

Leah turned the left-hand knob on top of the set. The music evaporated; silence swilled about the room for several seconds. Her ears adjusted to it slowly, and then to the magnification of the single sounds: the drips from the taps, the gurgles inside the chrome tube as the towel was replaced on the stand, the leather creaking on her mother's new shoes. She even heard her mother's smile determinedly pulling back over her teeth, into her cheeks.

'Right! That's done. Now I'm ready for anything, I think.'

The surprise of her appearance in the bathroom was forgotten. The taps were turned tight off.

As Leah moved to the door, a hand pulled her hair out from under her collar and smoothed down her crown.

'Have you combed your hair?'

'Yes,' Leah said, turning her head to look back.

Her mother seemed to be debating the truthfulness or otherwise of the reply. She *had* pulled a comb through her hair, but quickly, and before her walk, not since. So 'yes' was the truth, but from a couple of hours before.

Her mother still kept the smile in place on her face. She might have been going to ask her to please comb her hair again. Leah paused, waiting to be told, but the request wasn't made.

Leah watched as her mother took a last look at herself in the cabinet mirror. Her eyes were suddenly serious, even though her mouth hadn't lost its smile.

Leah turned away before their glances could cross in the glass. Through the window on the landing she saw the town waiting for them: the inviting stretch of promenade, the picturesque muddle of rooftops and the network of lanes that was such a puzzle to strangers, washing pegged out early on a line and cheerfully waving in a back yard, hardly a cloud in the sky to bother them, a Union Jack on the hotel's flagpole unfurling in just enough breeze to give the day its lift.

It's only thirteen years ago. But also half her life.

'You're *sure* you don't want any wine, Leah?'

She nods her head.

'Yes, thank you. Quite sure.'

'Just mineral water?'

'Oh, there's mineral water and mineral water. You hardly ever – ' She holds up her glass. ' – get the chance of a German one.'

It's her favourite sort. It had seemed – alarmingly – to be a very bright omen.

He toasts her. She reciprocates, not quite so confidently. '*Prosit!*' she says – and has to repeat herself.

She sees, over his shoulder, the approach of the waiter, bearing their orders. To her companion's thinking, she can sense, the meal is swimming along nicely. Very nicely, indeed, thank you.

She sips at her water. She prefers that the jury should continue to deliberate and stay 'out' on their little *amourette*.

In the newsagent's her mother turned the carousel of postcards, but didn't pick any out. Instead she bought a long concertina letter-card. Usually she wrote the minimum, and only for politeness's sake.

She stopped outside Huffkin's.

'I might go in,' she said. 'For a coffee.'

In the mornings they served only coffee or tea, not soft drinks, which had always kept it off their itinerary before.

Leah was momentarily nonplussed.

'Would you like to get yourself something in the Sundial Yard?' her mother asked her, not looking at her as she opened the purse in her basket. 'A Coke? Or an ice-cream?'

She picked over some coins in her hand.

'Then we could meet up? In the Fo'c'sle – '

She transferred the coins into Leah's hand.

' – and you could help me pick a swimsuit?'

Leah lifted her eyes. Her mother's face was bright, full of easy good cheer.

'You could tell me what's the fashion? What suits me best?'

Leah stepped sideways on the narrow pavement, closer to the wall. A couple were trying to walk past.

'Oh, I'm so sorry,' her mother said when she realised.

The young blonde woman managed a blunt smile. Leah watched the man stare at her mother with the concentration people betray when they try to remember where they've seen someone before. Her mother noticed too, for an instant, but let her own attention be absorbed by a car driving past, a red BMW.

Leah dropped the coins into her jacket pocket.

She peered through the window, into the coffee shop. Mostly they were elderly people at the tables. There was no one there as young as her mother.

The purse was returned to the basket and the folding letter-card laid on top of it, and a see-through black biro on top of that. The tables inside Huffkin's were broad enough and solid enough to write on, while those at the Sundial were set outside on cobbles and because they were metal never kept steady, so that drinks predictably spilled. (Her mother had joked one year that it was probably a ploy to encourage you to buy something else, to make up for what you'd lost in spillage.)

'All right,' she replied when her mother asked how she felt about the arrangement.

'And I'll have my coffee. The coffee's best in here, you see.'

Leah nodded.

'It's a pity they do nothing else. No soft drinks. They just lose good business.'

They said goodbye.

Her mother straightened her collar before pushing on the door and making a face at the weight. The bell rang and they smiled at one another.

Leah turned round and started walking.

Further along the road, on the other side, was the toy shop. A number of uniformly green bicycles of assorted vintages stood outside, propped against the windows. They looked as if they would be difficult to ride with such high gouged saddles. She wondered if they would have a choice of sizes inside. Her mother seemed determined she should try, and had mentioned it again as they passed. She didn't have strong feelings either way: it simply hadn't occurred to her that she should become, as her mother put it, 'mobile'.

Oh, now it's gliding past, this lunch that loomed like a formal asseveration, an avouchment of the state of things between them. She let herself be persuaded to come, and it was as easy as . . . as riding a bicycle. Now she's as comfortable as a passenger in a car that's driving into dusk. Oh, she catches her breath at the simplicity and effortlessness of it all!

And all the while time passes. Nothing between them will ever be quite as this fine lunch has been. They will know too much about one another in future, or rather they will think that they do.

II

Her ice-cream was brought outside to her. In fact they were sorbets, an unexpected addition to last year's menu. She had chosen a scoop of lime and another of lemon.

She wasn't very hungry, but always on the first day their eating pattern was thrown for six. She wasn't even sure that she *liked* sorbets. They didn't seem to be much more than frozen coloured water. But ice-cream would have 'sat too heavily' as her mother might have said. For some reason her stomach already felt weighted, and queasy. As the morning had worn on she'd been conscious of her skin and how sensitive it was to the touch of whatever came against it. The tops of her legs beneath her skirt throbbed, as if she had been running, too far and too fast.

She tried to ignore the sun breaking the cover of the clouds, she tried to ignore the heat inside her head that was making her scalp itch. With the edge of her spoon she pared several slivers from the two sorbet balls and lifted them to her mouth. She felt the sensation of cold on her lips, then on her tongue. The chill numbed them for a few moments as the sorbet melted on the floor of her mouth. The liquid trickled down her throat and she swallowed.

She saw herself watching from the opposite side of the courtyard, reflected in the side-window of an antiques shop. She immediately turned her eyes away, towards the car park and the promenade beyond, and the top pillars of a wooden sea-groin sunk deep into the shingle. Then she looked down at the artificially heightened colours, green and yellow on her plate; she scraped some more shavings of ice on to the tip of her spoon. As she put the second much smaller helping of sorbet into her mouth, she found herself glancing across the yard from her chair again, towards the antiques shop window.

She crossed her legs without realising and hit the pedestal

base of the tin table with her foot. The table rocked and the glass dish almost skidded off the top. She shot her hand out just in time to prevent an accident and a further embarrassment. A couple of the other tables were now occupied and she felt herself reddening. She wished she hadn't come, that she'd walked out to the strand instead, past the martello tower: she hadn't wanted an ice-cream, or even a sorbet. Or she should have taken a cup of coffee at Huffkin's and forced herself to gulp it down. But then she could only have carried that off (maybe) on one morning, and if her mother had suggested tomorrow that they go back there she would have had to admit that she was only pretending, that coffee gave her coils of pain in the pit of her stomach. Even the bland, watery sorbet seemed to be having an unsettling effect on her: the sensation of sickness hadn't passed yet.

In a minute or two, when everyone had forgotten she'd kicked the table, she would get up and leave. She would go and find her favourite perch on the flinty beach wall, and maybe she would see somebody she recognised and they'd be able to pick up their friendship again, where they'd left off last summer. By this time tomorrow she would be back into the old routine, she wouldn't need either to drink coffee in Huffkin's or to come here to the Sundial by herself and be obliged to make an impression on a dish of dayglow citrus sorbets.

Sitting tight, she waited until she sensed that the group at the next table were preoccupied. She shifted her eyes leftwards to look at them. A boy of about her own age, or just a little older, sat on one side of his parents; a younger girl – his sister presumably – was seated with her back to her. The boy straddled the white plastic chair side-saddle, as it were: with his body angled away, even though he had turned his head and was listening to the conversation between the adults.

She tried to catch the drift of their words, but couldn't. The woman, the mother, was shaking her head as she spoke. The man, the father, was looking at his cup and saucer on the table-top and quietly smiling to himself. The girl's arm rested on the table-top, her hand cupped her chin and she was gazing sideways, into the café, as if she was bored or miffed.

Leah was so taken up watching her that she was unaware
for several seconds that she in turn was being watched from
the table. Something did alert her, though – an instinct that
came to her through her primed skin – and she glanced to the
right of the girl.

The boy's eyes were on her. His attention wasn't accidental;
he was studying her. Most particularly *her*. It was a look she
couldn't remember having encountered before, certainly not
directed on herself. It was tense, and secretive, and daring, all
at the same time. And somehow she already *knew*, although the
precise thoughts would actually come to her a couple of years
later when she had been subjected to a number of other looks
very like it: that the giving of attention so concentratedly, with
such focus, is meant to be Significant. He, the observing male,
is declaring some point: that he simply can't help looking, and
that he is making himself vulnerable above all by not trying to
conceal the compulsion.

The complexities and paradoxes will only occur to her in the
time to come. At the moment, in the Sundial Yard, she has
to cope with the novelty of what is happening, the shock of
it, and that isn't easy for her. The contact of their eyes may
have lasted no longer than three or four seconds in toto, until
she forced herself to look away, but the intensity of it was, is
– is to be – unforgettable.

In the interval between uncrossing her legs and getting,
very shakily, to her feet on the absurd cobbles, a door bangs
somewhere – a house door or a shop door or a car door – and
she will always remember the sound, of all the morning's trivial
details to pick up on. It is the door of a familiar, comfortable
room closing behind her, a place that was perfect because she
never thought beyond it, which time and perspective will tell
her – not to beat about that particular bush – was a fleeting
condition coyly and unsatisfactorily called 'innocence', taken
from her before she could know and appreciate what it was
and quite impossible to return to.

Cheese, they've agreed, although she didn't mean to after the turbot. But he has recommended the Derby Sage, and the Dymock: or the Gigha. How does he know, though, unless he's more intimate with the place than he has admitted? Whom else has he come with when he hasn't been entertaining in the business line?

She smiles, without quite meaning to. Really she is too intent remembering, too abstracted. Which isn't – as he must have judged – the point of the exercise: her sitting here with him in this expensive eatery.

He says her name, in that most familiar way he has.

'Le-ah.'

She manages another smile. It carries them, just.

Then it's behind her, the Sundial Yard, although she knows it isn't really.

She's running to put distance between them, even if she has to sacrifice her dignity in the process. She runs sprouting flames, great bellowing wings of fire, she runs for the quenching sea.

She holds her glass of aerated spa water to the light. Its coolness steels her hand. She is composed, and she's at a loss to know why. She deserves to be more agitated. Men customarily induce a suspense in her, but now she is like . . . like a victim lying soft and low beneath a vampire's shadow.

She smiles at the shameless hyperbole. Christopher deserves better of her. He may be an innovator after all, transforming her out of the person she has been for so long: ever since that one auspicious morning of an August not to be confused (Heaven forfend) with any of those simpler others that preceded it.

She had begun by walking along the top of the esplanade wall with her arms of flame halfspread, but the ice lying in her stomach had taken away her confidence. Anyway that was a child's game.

So she returned to the red tarmacadam, which was curiously deserted for midday. None of last year's crowd was about. The people she did pass she read at a distance before turning her eyes from them as they approached. She assumed an appearance of abstracted detachment, involvement in her thoughts. Which was true to a degree.

The ice wouldn't all melt. Her stomach still felt cold. *Froid*, as the French say, *kalt* as the Germans do. She was taking both languages at school and it was in her mind to continue with them when she grew up: a mistress had said that's where their futures lay, in the European Community. She believed everything else Miss Holte told them, so why not that too? Her father had sent her some postcards from countries where he went on business, but that had been very long ago, and now they didn't hear from him.

She definitely felt dizzy, and she had to stop for several moments. What on earth was happening to her?

She was still trying to get her balance when a hand clasped her shoulder and she jumped. She looked round and saw a Mr Happy smile hung across her mother's face.

'You *were* far away – '

Leah felt her mother had been ready to laugh. She only shrugged in reply.

'Who – who did you think I was?'

Leah shook her head. No other answer suggested itself to her.

Her mother kept her arm on her shoulder and turned her in the direction of the starkly plain house, still a couple of hundred yards away.

'I prefer this end, I think. Don't you, darling? To the top of the town – '

Her mother looked up at the balconied fronts. Some were glazed in and furnished with cane seating and table lamps and potted yukkas. Behind, there were shelves of paperbacks and sea paintings in old frames. Where the verandahs remained open, swimwear hung over the wooden balustrades to dry.

'But – '

Leah listened to her mother clear a frog from her throat.

' – but probably they're bigger inside than they look.'

They walked along the flat, with the strides of their legs accidentally synchronised. Mysteriously the chill of lemon ice persisted, and Leah felt herself shiver. Her mother noticed too.

'Are you cold?'

'A bit . . .'

'Here.' Her mother took the cardigan from her shoulders. 'Put this on.'

Leah stood still while her mother arranged the jumper around her shoulders as she had worn it; she knotted it on her chest, over the swellings.

They started to walk again, more briskly. Leah dipped her chin and jaw into the soft lambswool and cashmere. The jumper was new, she didn't remember it. There was a trace of perfume on the neckline.

And then she caught, on one shoulder, pungent and unmistakable . . . the aroma of a cigar.

Very definitely a cigar.

She found the spot where it was strongest.

She undid the loose knot to nuzzle her nose closer and saw, two or three inches from her mouth, a strand of dark tobacco.

Then another. And another.

Her mother must have been sitting very close to a smoker somewhere – not in Huffkin's, which didn't allow it, but longer ago, back in London – there must have been a collision of some sort.

Smoking was banned in their own home. Just about the only memento of her father which had been passed over in the great clear-out following his defection were the colourful foreign matchboxes he'd bought to light his Senior Service cigarettes, which he'd always given to her and which she kept in the Lego tin. Her mother had forgotten about those, with their illustrations of East European national costumes and Scandinavian cities and Canadian butterflies.

Always Senior Service, and never cigars. Cigars, his daughter would realise better when she was an adult, must have been anathema to him, 'vulgar' and self-made while he preferred to think of himself as a modern and honest man.

At school she'd heard some of the 'Old Stock' girls – daughters of Old Girls – referring disparagingly, as their mothers must have done, to the *nouveaux*: the daughters of tradesmen and get-rich-quick financiers. It was true that now they were worming their way in everywhere. Her friend Diana's father was one, but – in truth – she rather liked their home: over-furnished by a department store's own 'interior design consultants', containing nothing more than a couple of years old, warm and comfortable and padded like a nest, with robust air-conditioning which meant you hardly even needed to step outside. Mr Brunton didn't smoke because, since he worked so hard, his doctor had forbidden him to.

Leah sniffed again. It was a rich aroma, of restaurants and leather upholstery. In a room it must be more noticeable than perfume. It smelt stronger than the sea.

She left the dark strands of tobacco where they were. She let a few moments pass before she turned again and looked at her mother. She continued to be preoccupied by the clapboard houses which had been home to grizzled sea captains of yore; she was held by those naturally thrown together, attractively casual, slightly chaotic rooms. They were spaces where families lived: there couldn't be any mistaking their purpose. Mobiles were suspended at bedroom windows, urchins and crab shells and dead starfish lined the sills, hallstands were a clutter of frivolous and serious hats and golfing and city umbrellas, the dogs were the inevitable golden retrievers and dalmatians.

Leah watched as her mother gave herself to the rooms, those intimate intimations of the domestic, with an expression compressing her features which might equally well have been envy or fearfulness.

'Leah?'

'What's that?'

Throughout the meal she has drifted in and out of the conversation. It's what seems to charm him about her, also amuse him – her intermittent unavailability.

He removes a small cigarillo from a slim packet.

'Do you mind?'

She quite starts with surprise.

'If I smoke – ?'

This is new. Somehow he has managed to keep the fact from her, that he indulges.

'It's just when I lunch,' he says, as if he can follow her line of thought.

'Ah,' she replies.

'I won't if you – '

'No, no.'

She shakes her head.

But oh God, she's thinking. She knows he's been making further plans on the strength of the oysters. She hasn't planned on cheroot smoke too. This complicates matters. Suddenly she spies a blueprint imposed on this previously meandering, unthreatening little affair between them.

In a degree of smiling panic she looks round the room, trying to spot a resemblance in one of these other women to her mother. She couldn't be here, of course. Now she and Malcolm, her stepfather, spend most of the year in Madeira, in their fancy flat that reminded her when she first saw it of a most elegant birdcage, of something Diana Brunton's parents might have rigged up for themselves.

For some reason both of them – her mother and Malcolm – decided independence to be worth surrendering for the sake of social definition: freedom mattered less than establishing the parameters of 'you' and 'me' and the construction of a new entity, 'we', even in Madeira. Nothing would ever have been the same again, and it wasn't, it isn't. She has been slowly detached by the pressure of their kindness, their respectability, their joint pose as parents.

Everything before that seems to her to have been natural, without claim or presumption acting. Until Huffkin's coffee house and the so-called 'Bistro' in the cobbled yard of the Sundial. The boy's look from the tin table did it, demanding her to think of herself in quite a new way, to 'be' for the benefit of another.

Now Christopher is looking at her, and she supposes they're

bedroom eyes. They're also calculating possibilities from the image, from her presentation of herself. She can help to publicise and promote other people in her job of work, she's for ever being told so, but with herself she doesn't know where to begin.

He lights his cigarillo. Neither one thing nor the other, a common-or-garden cigarette or a fat cigar. He is too placating maybe as a personality, a man for the middle way. But he doesn't like to let a problem in business defeat him, and he is applying the same principle to her.

He watches her through the plume of smoke. Everything in her life has led her to this point. She could get up and go, she knows. But she wonders what it can solve. She can walk and run, but it's always 'from' and never 'to'.

She leans forward on the table-top, supporting herself on her elbows.

'A penny for them,' he says.

She smiles and shakes her head.

'Maybe I don't need to ask?'

'Maybe,' she says, 'you don't.'

He thinks he knows. He imagines he understands so much about her. Of her solitude, maybe he does. She could tell him, go back to the beginning.

They go no further back than a month, that is their history. It is as far back as they need to go with their new authorised version. Her mother too must have seen in time that she had to start a new story before the old one refused to let her go. Possibly she has ended up not quite believing in either, but that is exactly the point.

She, Leah, smiles vaguely. He, Christopher, will translate the smile – through his eyes, to his brain – as he translates it all. Smoke gets in the way, a little. He blows at it as if he's master of the situation. The pianist is playing 'Pigalle'. She mouths the words without singing them; her companion joins in, humming the tune softly, in a different key although he may not be aware.

Never mind 'wanting'. She won't think now of her studio flat at the day's end, waiting for her in smothering darkness and silence. For the moment the nicely bustling, sunlit restaurant in dog-day August will do as well as any place, this is where she means to be, this is where she means to be.

DRIVE

19.48. Anthony will be home. He'll have looked into the garage first, seen the car's not there. 'Gone to Polly's, she's poorly again.' Sisters have their uses. Will he guess it's a lie? Polly would kill me. I could pick up a hitch-hiker, just to hear a voice talking at me, not those plastic radio voices, they're so bland, it's like verbal masturbation. Never mind that Tom and I were speaking all afternoon, round and round, and coming to no conclusion. Will Anthony phone Polly and find out I've been nowhere near again? If you hate a man enough you leave him, but I don't leave Anthony, I don't even hate him, all I feel is indifference, or *don't* feel. So I stay with him, and that solves nothing. Christ, it's this tiredness. The to-ing and fro-ing. And the world goes on singing, those same godawful silly love songs as before . . . And always 'Anthony', why not call himself 'Tony', but I married someone else, not this man, he's a counterfeit. It's in his eyes, though, he's on to me, and deep down he's laughing. 'With all your false, silly young woman's expectations, what a bloody fool you were, as much as you'll make of yourself for your fancy man, whoever he is . . .' 19.49. 52, 53, 54. But I can't believe in Tom without Anthony, and I love him more because of my husband, Anthony's faults and failings drove me to Tom in the first place, I see Tom through Anthony's weaknesses, so maybe I don't really see the whole of Tom as he is, but how I need him to be. 19.50. 10, 11, 12, 13. Thence to thither. From Tom's bed, looking at my dress where I left it, draped over the top of the wardrobe door, my empty shoes racing each other across the carpet, the drift of my underclothes on the dressing-table, and all it ends up being is . . . mediocrity. The middle-way, driving myself home, and it's nothing and nowhere, this is between love and loathing, I'm no adulteress, this is a film, driving a car in a film, windscreen mirror widescreen. Mediocrity is eternal, it never ends, it means being in two minds and driving forever. Unless I crashed the car, but Anthony would only suppose I'd done the deed for him, sunk to such despair. 'You have to leave Anthony, tell me you will.' 'Okay, Tom.' 'When . . .?' But he knows Anthony can't fathom all of it, my mystery, and maybe that's what keeps Tom true to me. He spoke of him as 'Tony' by mistake, and what day was it Anthony pretended not to notice I'd forgotten and worn the yellow dress Tom bought me. Suffering to no end at all, except to keep everything just as it is. The year will run down, and the evenings swoop on the afternoons, and I'll be driving on main beam. Tom-Anthony-Tom-Anthony-Tom-Anthony. Dazzlelights. 19.53. Witchery. 32, 33, 34. Just watching the road, it'll hang on so little, my safety, a mood like will o' the wisp, my balance, the memory of unshaven Anthony first thing, whistling 'Happy Talk', through his teeth at the breakfast table. Or. Or Tom promising me, next time he'll buy us a dozen Quimper oysters, a bottle of something special, Clos du something, du Papillon, '84, or '85 is it, and the engine running, up into fifth, the engine like this, unhampered and sweet, and all it'll take is losing my confidence just for a moment, mediocrity for miles and miles, I'm pushing the accelerator into the floor, opening up, letting roar, letting rip, faster than sound even until I'm out of thought range, look, I'm that tiny mote on your horizon.

CROSSING THE ALPS

Mr Plummer – aka 'Ballcock' – had stopped drinking and was growing a moustache.

I doubted the first, but had the proof of the second. He should have attended to the moustache-growing during the long summer break, but he wasn't the most organised of the masters who taught us, even equipped as he was now with a wife. His getting married had been the sensation of the previous school year. A tall lanky man of fifty with round shoulders and a bullet-shaped head wasn't a likely candidate to have his nuptials done, to plight his troth, and other such schoolboy smutteries.

'When did he ask her?'

'It just popped up.' (Laughter)

'What's wrong with her? Is she a dwarf?'

'Someone must have put her up to it.' (Laughter)

'What did the bishop say to the actress?'

'There you have it, dear. That's about the size of it.' (Laughter)

'Did you hear about the castrated Russian ballet dancer called Nokabolov . . .?' About the prostitute who kept eating oranges . . .? She liked to peel the skin back and squeeze out the juice . . .

We were in our sixteenth year of life, at an unhealthily competitive boys-only day school in Glasgow and adrift in a morass of sexual innuendo and dodgy info about how big and how often, stranded between *Penthouse* centrefolds pored over in the bogs and a common homoerotic compulsion. After someone told us he'd heard that building workers are permanently erect and ready for it, heads would pass between textbooks and the denimed crotches negotiating the scaffolding on the thrusting new office building rising across the street. Evidently crotches were called 'baskets'. I was afflicted as my peers doubtless were: the third eye would insolently obtrude through the folds and tucks of Y-fronts and struggle in the darkness of regulation flannel trousers kept frantically zipped as high as the catch could reach.

The moustache was hormonal too, in some way, and enviable to most boys of fifteen. It was turning into quite a thick, sturdy accretion. Someone wondered if that meant . . . What it really meant, I appreciate now, was that Ballcock wanted to change his appearance for his new wife. Or perhaps she had done the wanting, and he had obliged, even though the moustache would have to be grown mostly in term-time. It did help to make him look more worldly and, simultaneously, more elusive: a wedge of sandy-coloured bristles he could hide behind but which also gave him the air of a habitué of lounge bars, or even cocktail bars, the sorts of rendezvous in films where raffish men and lonely women – or lonely men and racy women – go to meet, by contrived chance.

In fact the moustache grew in quickly, but when it might have seemed the proper length and breadth and thickness for a schoolmaster to start snipping, to keep it tidy and controlled, he continued to let it grow. The style would have suited a dago very well, a Latin – but not a Latin *master*. Spivs had very thin, pared moustaches, and yet I felt my clean-shaven father would have considered such a profuse moustache – a cross between the boffiny Mr Pastry on early television and Frank Zappa without the Zapata trailing ends – the sign of a less than trustworthy personality. What is the point, would have been his response; why is the man trying to disguise himself, what does he have to conceal under his bushel?

None of us, even sharing a classroom with him for six periods a week, was to discover the final answer to that riddle.

The rank and file of the Carthaginian army had a wholesome respect for Roman arms, as the former war was not yet forgotten; but they were much

**more alarmed by the prospect of the long march
and, especially of the passage of the Alps – about
which stories were told dreadful enough to frighten
anyone, particularly the inexperienced.**

It was Mr Plummer's first year of marriage, and it was our
first taste of Livy.

Livy was hard-going, because so dull. Were schoolboys
supposed to be so bellicose by nature that the minutiae of
a guerrilla war would be bound to enthral them?

More interesting to me were the occasional rumours that went
around concerning Ballcock's marriage. That every so often he
arrived at the school by seven thirty of a morning, because he'd
left the house at first light. That he would ring home two or three
times in a day using the phone in the General Office, sometimes
dropping the receiver down on to the telephone quite suddenly
and risking the ire of the battle-axe senior secretary. That he
and his wife had been seen having words one lunchtime at the
back of Adelmo's coffee house on Sauchiehall Street. That he
bought chocolates from Fuller's and flowers from the stall at
Queen Street Station. That – was there a connection? – the
handle of his briefcase had been strengthened with string as
if the bag had been violently wrenched out of his hand.

**'What sudden panic is this,' Hannibal said, 'which has
entered those breasts where fear has never been?'**

At that time we lived, my family, about twenty miles to the
north of Glasgow, in an overgrown commuting village in fine
country beneath the Campsie Hills. A 'through' single-decker
bus made the journey every hour from town to Balfron. Those
of us who didn't get regular lifts home from school either trekked
to the bus station or on games days waited at the West End
stops where the drivers knew to collect.

The regulars I saw went to four or five of Glasgow's single-sex private schools, and I was familiar – to varying extents – with a number of them, from the local tennis courts or from my sister's Pony Club socials. The first thing we did was to pull off our compulsory caps and berets and stuff them into our briefcases and satchels or coat pockets. Then we either talked, sensibly enough, or it might coincide – among us boys – that we were all in a silly, sexy sniggering mood together.

Sometimes, though, when I had a ton of homework, I made my way to the back of the bus, took out my books and got started.

Livy was the least of it, but he too was laboured over on the route out via Anniesland and the salubrious suburbs, Bearsden, Milngavie, Strathblane, Blanefield and beyond. Hannibal persevered, past the riding stables at Kilmardinny, past the numerous golf courses and the high reservoir at Dougalston. Gradually he came to seem appropriate to the journey, especially on the days when I had compulsory Corps or rugby, and had to travel home later, without most of the usual company. Hannibal and I endured the travail of the distance – he and his army negotiating the Ebro and the Rhône, mine done in the stuffy, rolling blue bus belching exhaust behind it – and we suffered together in our adversity.

'Then . . . none of you thought of the journey long, though it stretched from the setting to the rising sun; but now, when you can see that much the greater part of the distance is already behind you . . . when, finally, you have the Alps in sight . . . now, I repeat, at the very gateway of the enemy's country, you come to a halt – exhausted!'**

'Livy? What a creep! We did him last year.'

She dumped herself down on the back seat beside me.

'For O-levels,' she said. 'I'm doing Highers now. Not Latin. I got bored stiff of it.'

'Weren't you any good at it?'

'I said I got bored of it, didn't I?'

She spoke sharply. But immediately afterwards she smiled. I was confused. She continued to smile at my serious puzzlement.

Of course I knew who she was. But she hadn't ever spoken to me before, she hadn't deigned to speak. A year's difference in age was a most definite distinction: pride and deference were unspoken tenets of behaviour on the bus. Boys could chaff with girls, but they must be of one another's age. The girls were comparatively more sophisticated for their years than the boys, but the boys had to begin the business, to initiate, so that their necessary courage – a euphemism for their frequent rashness – helped to even out that fundamental imbalance.

I was out of joint on two counts: being younger than she, and having *her* talk first to *me*. Also, and worst of all, she was easily the most attractive girl who made the Campsie run. Someone had told me she dyed her long hair so fair, and I lacked the evidence to tell. But having her sitting beside me, that was the information that was pounding away inside my head: she dyes her hair, she knows how to make herself fair. She had the appearance of a glamorous model in a shampoo advert, especially the way she shook out that hair. It looked and smelt so clean and fresh.

Livy dropped to the floor that first afternoon. I bent down to pick it up. My face was within a couple of inches of her legs in their black tights. The narrow skirt of her slate grey uniform was hitched high up her thighs. When I'd retrieved the book and pulled myself up straight again, I felt my face red and hot. I could also feel my cock reacting, complicating matters as it uncurled, unfurling how it did when I opened up the fifth-hand dog-eared nude centrefolds in my bedroom at home with the door locked.

I dropped Livy on to my lap. She looked down at it, then tapped the maroon board cover.

'Those bloody elephants,' she said.

I nodded.

'Somebody wrote in a crib for me. I got him to. Our teacher knew the Penguin – the translation – so that was no go.'

I nodded again.

'I could bring it for you.'

'Could you?'

'Maybe,' she said. 'If I can remember.'

I watched her profile against the demure Switchback Road bungalows outside. I wondered how it was possible that she *could* ever remember. I was surely insignificance itself.

The bus pitched on the descent to Canniesburn Roundabout, by the hospital gates. I found she was tilting against me. My cock jerked, and I thought it was going to tear through my flannel. I rammed Livy down on top of it.

She didn't speak again until we were in Milngavie, with the afternoon walkers visible on the airy reservoir ramparts. She sighed. I didn't know why. Something to do with me, I supposed. (Now – today – I can hear a terrible sort of tedium in the exhalation. She is suffering just as much as Hannibal, God knows.) The bus driver revved, exhaust chundered out on to the incline. She *is* beautiful, I was thinking – and never more so than when she distances herself like this. Far too beautiful to be sitting beside *me*.

She turned and smiled. Compassionately, mercifully. As if somehow she could comprehend. That this was how it was. Both of us in service to our bodies. She with her looks, me with my embarrassment. She dyes her hair, I had the sudden insight to recognise, because beauty is a compulsion too, being distinguished and apart imposes the onus of appearing always so, her finding means to make herself even more so.

Hair dye might have been cheating, but (I can only find the words to frame that original insight now) she had to try to believe herself – what? – believe herself *unassailable*.

'What do you think the Alps *are*? Are they anything worse than high mountains? Say, if you will, that they are higher than the Pyrenees, but what of it? No part of earth reaches the sky; no height is insuperable to man.'

Her name was Fiona McFadyen. She didn't tell me, and must
have presumed that I had ascertained as much for myself already.
Nor did she tell me what I probed further, behind her back, to
discover, that her father worked for an oil company and was
often abroad, which left her alone at home with her father's
sister, her aunt, while a brother (a real crackpot, someone
said: army-mad, and in disgrace after some incident in Balfron
Main Street with an air-gun) was having the rough corners
knocked off him at a supposedly prestigious boarding-school
in the north.

She had more than a touch of the Françoise Hardy's.
Shoulder-length hair: the same oval shape of face, with the
same mixture of the aloof and the vulnerable in its expressions.
The alternation between the two sorts was quite sensual enough:
but her mouth had a clear-cut definiteness few other girls' did,
and her nose was very slightly tilted, making Hardy seem a little
more like Shrimpton. For the journey home she wore lipstick:
a pale purple shade which she could have denied possibly,
claiming it was the cold weather's doing, but I myself was in
no doubt about the shiny waxiness of her lips. Once I saw the
traces on her top teeth, but only once, so her hand must have
been quite steady through habit. The lipstick accentuated the
shape of her mouth and stressed even more the contradictions
between artifice and knowingness on the one hand and on the
other – I don't know what to call it – a kind of voluptuous
childishness, the way those lips (neither too full nor too thin)
parted, the way the moist tip of her tongue hovered between
the serrations of her teeth.

'Moreover, the Alps are not desert: men live there,
they till the ground; there are animals there, living
creatures. If a small party can cross them, surely
armies can? The envoys you see with us did
not, in order to get over, soar into the air on
wings.'

We continued to meet. Sometimes she would only look up the length of the bus from the longer of the two side-on seats at the front, the one without boys, studying me yet acknowledging me with the merest motion of her mouth. But at other times she was her other self, she would collect her things together – not *too* hastily – and come up and join me on the back seat. I regularly left my male company with the pretence of homework so that she might. I always took Livy – now annotated with her inattentive translation – out of my bag, because that was our contact.

'I've got a Mont Blanc fountain-pen,' she announced to me once, and of course I caught the Alpine reference. 'My dad bought me it.'

She had told me that her mother was dead. But I'd previously heard from others that Mr McFadyen was divorced. Whatever the truth about it, the man was devoted to his daughter but unable to deal with her. She had told me herself that she stayed out however long she liked. Since they lived on an isolated back road, it must have involved her being driven about in cars. She had about her an aura of glamour, of speed, of enigma.

One afternoon I presented her with a Toblerone bar. She stared at the triangular-sided cardboard container in my hand, not seeming to make the connection.

'What's this for?'

'Livy,' I mumbled. 'You know – The mountains – '

'Chocolate'll bring me out in spots,' she said.

I spluttered an apology. I had been trying to elevate myself to the dignity of being her occasional travelling companion. I was only too conscious that the function marked me out, that it was a supreme honour. I was cut down to size again in a moment.

A few seconds later, though, when I was able to look at her, I found that she was smiling at me. I was confused all over again, only worse than before. I fired, down to my chest, and the book went slithering between my legs and dropped to the floor.

I bent down. I thought as I did so that her legs were deliberately moved nearer to me. I pulled myself up suddenly. My elbow brushed against her left breast.

I stared the length of the aisle and noticed one of the green blazer-wearers staring back. Not at myself, but at Fiona.

It might have been the look of someone who'd never chanced to set eyes on her before, but I knew that that was far from being the case. I had always associated her previously with certain boys of her own age: she would seat herself side-saddle on the long seat at the front as they drifted on at the stop where she and they waited, and she would exchange banter with them or not, encourage them by the tone of her words or else defy them by her silence to sit opposite her. The back seat had been too *louche* or too swotty for her, since – ironically – both sorts used it. The front seat was breaking convention, for a girl. But no one had followed her to the back, as if they were afraid of a rebuff. She turned all the routine expectations on their head. Other passengers would study her as she made her way languidly up the aisle, no one sure if she was wayward or if she was the vision of clear skin and long fair hair that she appeared to be, like that television advert model.

I was eliminated from the stare of her contemporary. He only had eyes for her, and I was banished – I supposed, and with some relief when I saw the intensity of his expression – to the margins of consideration. But in that respect too I was a naïf.

'Has anyone ever told you,' I heard her ask, turning to me, 'that you look just like Sacha Distel?'

I thought she was joking. Those were the days just before Sacha Distel became rather a camp commodity for some in Britain, almost in the Engelbert Humperdinck league. She was meaning the man who got written up in women's magazines, whose records were played on the channel no one would have admitted listening to, the new Radio Two.

'Well, you do,' she announced to me and to our end of the bus.

I didn't have to answer her in words. The helpless blush on my face must have said it all.

The nature of the mountains was not, of course, unknown to his men by rumour and report — and rumour commonly exaggerates the truth; yet in this case all tales were eclipsed by the reality. The dreadful vision was now before their eyes: the towering peaks, the snow-clad pinnacles soaring to the sky . . . all this, and other sights the horror of which words cannot express, gave a fresh edge to their apprehension.

Ballcock's wife would be waiting outside the gates for him at the schoolday's end.

She wasn't at all what we were expecting her to be. She was thirty or so, not exactly pretty but not plain either, very thin, with a modern, possibly undernourished face framed by shoulder-length brown hair. Her eyes filled the face: alert, vigilant, surely too careful (apprehensive?) to be happy. She had long slender legs and narrow ankles, and favoured high heels. She strutted, steering herself by using her shoulder bag as a rudder. She invariably wore her coat open, so that whenever she was spotted putting off time near the school she looked half perished with cold.

Did she have a job? What was she? We wondered about an office clerk, assuming something modest but decent enough. A secretary even? Or an assistant in a shop? She was too pallid to be behind the desks in any of the travel agencies round about, too whey-faced to be advising on holiday adventures. Someone suggested barmaid, and we laughed. But I observed how she could stand about for long periods, on those late afternoons when I hung around the corridor windows, waiting for the moment by my watch when I'd set off for the bus station, venturing out into the wind and the damp. Sometimes she stood under a little lilac umbrella, but she didn't shelter. It was as if she was positioning herself to be seen. Only occasionally did she look towards the school buildings, but at

all times she was visible *from* the school. She would smile in
a briefly ingratiating way on each occasion that she stood back
to let someone whom she hadn't appeared to notice pass by
her. It was a barmaid's, or a waitress's, smile certainly. She
could conceivably have been a librarian, at the other spectrum
end, and possibly I didn't care greatly one way or the other.
She was a fixture, and I was conscious of her in a not very
concentrated fashion chiefly for the reason that her timetable
and mine coincided on those afternoons when I waited for my
'off' and when Ballcock, up in the eyrie of a staffroom, breezed
through our ink exercises (we knew he never took them home
now) and (a wholly new habit with him) dusted the chalk from
his suit jacket and trousers and took the sleeve of his gown to
polish his shoes to a shine.

**This Alpine stream [the River Druentia] is more
awkward to cross than any other river in Gaul; in
spite of its volume of water nothing can float on it,
because, not being contained by banks, it is split
up into a number of constantly changing channels,
where the shallows and deep potholes, dangerous
to a man on foot, shift from day to day; add the
stones and gravel swept down by the rapid current,
and it is clear that anyone who enters it will find a
foothold by no means firm or safe.**

I wanted to ask Fiona which buses she took home on different
days of the week, but I shied from the question. It was a
matter of luck whether we were on the same one or not.

On ordinary days I took the bus from town, and if she was
waiting – or not waiting – on the pavement six stops later,
then I knew or didn't know. More exciting to me were the
sports afternoons, when I travelled home from the playing fields
one stop after hers and couldn't know until the bus stopped.
Perversely, *because* it excited me so much, I sometimes took
a green and orange corporation bus out on ordinary days and

got off to wait at the stop by the playing fields for the blue single-decker Number 38 to roll into sight. If I thought I saw her on it I would run after it. If she wasn't, and if the bus was actually catchable, I would let it go and try to persuade myself I couldn't have reached it after all and wait for the next, hoping hard she would be on *that* one.

I heard that remarks were being passed round about me. Very few questions were put to me directly, since no one liked to dignify even a rumour. But I knew I was under surveillance. The sly attention was flattering to me. My credit rose with myself.

My afternoons were passed in conjecture – would I see Fiona or not? If she *was* on the bus, she would be sitting on the longer of the front seats, behind the driver. (I discovered she was able to see herself reflected in the round fish-eye mirror if she craned forward at a certain angle, casually affecting to be straightening her tights at the ankle or rubbing the ball of her foot.) I never presumed to join her, but hesitated momentarily or smiled before continuing to the back seat, or as far back as I could go. Usually she would follow, at her own speed: sometimes not until Anniesland, or even Temple, three stops and half a mile away.

She would weave her way down the aisle with an elegant sailor's roll to join me. I always made quite sure that there was room beside me by spreading myself. She would yank off her grey beret, drop her bag on to the floor and flop down on to the seat. The different bits of her settled in sequence, breasts last of all. She would shake out her hair, first over her right shoulder and then the left.

The regulars from the other boys' schools would time their backward glances so as not to seem concerned. Some were defectors from different buses or from the train to Milngavie, a few uncomfortable in their uniforms with their height, breadth of shoulders, shaved moustache shadows and nascent beard lines. Their attention for the sports cars that roared past or the office girls sitting in other buses were no more than very minor interruptions, very temporary distractions.

Hannibal took only fifteen days to cross the Alps, but five months altogether to march from New Carthage to Italy. Livy seemed equally ponderous about it, as if he knew that Scottish schoolboys nearly two millennia hence, living on the line of the Antonine Wall on the empire's outermost boundary, would experience a protracted agony emblematic of the great man's.

In class one day someone asked if Hannibal was black – a 'negro' – and Ballcock, looking uncomfortable with the disclosure, replied that he had been a half-caste.

Fiona lent me her book so that I could take down all her crib, but eventually I reached the point where her rather absent-mindedly copied translation ran out, where – she said – the Latin mistress had got as fed up as they all were.

As the bus trundled along Roman Road in Bearsden we saw where the university archaeologists were digging to the foundations of the bath-house on the wall, in the neglected gardens of some Victorian sandstone villas which were to be demolished so that blocks of flats could be built.

The elephants were only a part of it: I remember sections about Hannibal in Apulia and Hannibal in Nola. Livy may only have occupied us for a segment of that year. Did I have Fiona's company for months, or only weeks?

My memory clock is confused. The habit of meeting her on the journey became so serious, so vital to me, that I lost track of whatever else fringed it, I can't now set the experience *against* anything. Sleet fell, and she pointed out to me the raked banks of daffodils on Great Western Road, but both occurred within the concentrated middle span of the same season, spring. The months – or weeks – are so telescoped, and I see a series of blurred essential images, yet I can almost believe that time, like hope and ambition, rolls around us like virgin territory; it reaches in its pristine splendour to its mythical horizon.

At the head of the column were the cavalry and

elephants; Hannibal himself, with the pick of the infantry, brought up the rear, keeping his eyes open and alert for every contingency. Before long the column found itself on a narrowing track, one side of which was overhung by a precipitous wall of rock, and it was suddenly attacked. The natives, springing from their places of concealment, fiercely assaulted front and rear, leaping into the fray, hurling missiles, rolling down rocks from the heights above.

During one period after lunch I noticed that Ballcock's hand was shaking slightly. He lowered it to the ledge beneath the lectern's lid. One foot noisily slipped off the bar of the high stool he always sat on.

I had charge of the Green Book, the class register, that week. I took it out to have the attendance sheet signed. I leaned as close to him as I could and smelt it, the proof of his liquid lunch ineptly disguised by Polo mints.

He fumbled with the pen and dropped it. I picked it up and replaced it in his hand, all but pushing it between his fingers myself. He should have dashed off a signature but instead he made the mistake of trying to be especially legible.

I showed the clumsy signature to no one. His condition seemed to have escaped the class's notice, but I suddenly felt a need to be defensive, to verify my own capacity to keep a secret.

Most of the climb had been over trackless mountainsides; frequently a wrong route was taken — sometimes through the deliberate deception of the guides, or, again, when some likely-looking valley would be entered by guess-work, without knowledge of whither it led.

For a few weeks Mrs Plummer was to be seen in the vicinity

of Raeburn Street during school hours, morning or afternoon. If you could station yourself close enough to a window, you easily caught a glimpse of her. She was by herself, dressed in higher heels than before and – unusually for married women during that glum period of dropping hemlines – in a skirt or dress that didn't come below her knees. Her shoulder bag swung by her hip as she strode up and down Raeburn Street. Every so often on her perambulations, and always within clear sight of the school's windows, she would suddenly stop.

Stop and stand stock still. Like a plaster dummy in a department store window. Only her bag moved. Sometimes her arms were crossed, or she folded them across her waist, or one hand was splayed upon a hip bone, or both were raised behind her head to gather up her dark hair. She would hold that position and posture for several seconds, or even up to half a minute. The activity of the street surrounded her. Heads would turn, of course, and cars would slow – but she would continue to be a still frame photograph in a moving film.

At some juncture, though – when she must have felt that she'd made her point, whatever that might be – she snapped out of it. She swung round on her pencil heels – again, well out of or ahead of the fashion for the chunky sort – and went striding off along the street or down one of the cobbled lanes which criss-cross that part of town.

Closer to, as reports had it, she was quite painted.

On the one occasion when I managed to make an approach, in the few seconds' grace I had before she spun round and hurried off on her squawking heels, I saw that it was true enough. But the painting was inexpertly done, and didn't highlight but, rather, masked. She left a little cloud – a vaporlet, a thin nimbus – of perfume behind her; very definitely perfume, which suggests to me now it lacked subtlety, although at that time I didn't know expensive from cheap. I stared at her disappearing back, the calves of her legs, the uncertain gait as she picked her way over cracked flagstones in her stilettos. She lacked the harmony of a woman used to dressing and walking in the way she pretended to do. She was trying to walk provocatively, I dare say – accentuating the activity of her hips, causing them to roll more; flicking back her hair with tosses of her head – but it wasn't very convincing, not a patch on Fiona. I remember smelling a rat through, or under, the perfume trail as she proceeded at a good lick towards the corner that led into Savannah Street. Heads continued to turn and cars would suddenly drop speed as she came into view. She was ignoring all signs of attention, however, concentrating instead on negotiating the potholes and pitfalls on the pavement. The scraping heels were no disclaimer either – she sounded as if she was running away from herself – while she persisted in letting people see only her wholesale indifference to them. It was either wholly genuine behaviour or a very expert double-bluff.

But I was a schoolboy educated on the myths of tarts and randy punters, so how could I have known which? And all the men who watched from office windows and behind the windscreens of cars, they were only myself grown up, the schoolboy versions of themselves unleashed upon the world.

The troops had indeed endured hardships enough; but there was worse to come. It was the season of the setting of the Pleiades: winter was near — and it began to snow.

The inclement weather outside induced a feeling of confinement, by which I mean intimacy, inside the bus. There were still flurries of snow about, until the end of April. Whenever the clouds descended to the height of Dumgoyne and Dumdoyne, the two dumpling-shaped volcanic plugs, we ran into rain on Mugdock Moor. It was comforting to hear the first drops dribbling on to the roof, splattering against the windows; the stuffy warmth blowing up from under the seats and smelling of oil didn't seem so bad then. Getting off in a shower or a downpour was another matter, but I could sprint home from the stop in three minutes if I really put my mind to it. Fiona had further to go, and I'd see her sometimes move up the bus after I'd gone, not to the front where one or two boys would still be sitting but midway up, eyeing – or seeming to eye – the weather intently. I had never asked her how she got home from the crossroads, but that was another element of her mystery for me. I didn't want to know all the truths that might be discoverable about her; I was content to have the perceptions I did have, defined by my remaining ignorance.

For Hannibal there must have been an apex, a peak among peaks to be scaled with those bloody elephants.

For me there was no zenith, no apogee. The best part finished before I realised, before I was equipped to recognise that it was the best. Perhaps it wasn't the best after all, however, if I failed so significantly to notice. There wasn't a worst, so there may have been no antithesis either.

The potential of the situation diminished and diminished, that's all. Perhaps that continuing loss came to seem inevitable to me, but frankly I forget.

What happened was this: we duly gravitated to wherever we were bound.

Unfortunately, however, as in most parts of the Alps the descent on the Italian side, being shorter, is correspondingly steeper, the going was much more difficult than it had been during the ascent. The track was almost everywhere precipitous, narrow, and slippery; it was impossible for a man to keep his feet; the least tumble meant a fall, and a fall a slide, so that there was indescribable confusion, men and beasts stumbling on top of each other.

Then I don't know what happened, except that I didn't see Fiona as dependably often as I used to. Less and less, in fact.

She told me there were things at school she was getting involved with. Or that she had to meet a great-uncle in town, or go shopping with her aunt, to buy someone or other's birthday present.

I kept a look-out, as always, but usually I was disappointed. On the few occasions when I did meet up with her I couldn't work out her mood. Sometimes she looked out the bus's window, lost in thought. Or at traffic lights I'd see her turn a teasing, heartless smile on some driver in his company-owned fleet car. Or she'd sing a few bars of 'Raindrops Keep Fallin' On Me 'Ead', because Sacha Distel had got the song into the charts, and it would bring a more mirthful sort of smile to her face.

I would rather have had to bear that confusion than not seen her at all. But the matter was settled, when she so seldom appeared anyway.

I was left to struggle with Livy alone. Already, though – with the exams almost upon us – he was a fading and receding cause.

The result was a horrible struggle, the ice affording no foothold in any case, and least of all on a steep slope; when a man tried by hands or knees to get on his feet again, even those useless supports slipped from under him and let him down, there were no stumps or roots anywhere to afford a purchase to either foot or hand; in short, there was nothing for it but to roll and slither on the smooth ice and melting snow.

I used to skip maths sometimes, I hated it so much. No corner of the school was safe for bunking off, with the prefects on a kind of favours-on-commission basis for hauling in miscreants.

It was less dangerous to slip out by the side gate and make for the mews lane behind Raeburn Street or, better, the network of alleys that began at the stage door of the Saint Mungo's Theatre. I could put off the forty minutes without too much difficulty by walking about looking purposeful, even if I was only repeating

and repeating myself, sometimes retreating with a paperback
behind strategic high walls, into dingy dustbin yards.

A few times I encountered one of the construction workers
from the office site. I suspected he was doing a bunk too. We
exchanged nods like conspirators. I remember wondering how
it was that our bunkings-off happened to coincide as they did,
but I only thought about it *en passant*, as we edged past one
another in those dark places.

We got to talking, just a little. We might simply have been
chancing to spend the time of day in those dreary, dank conduits.
An instinct in common had us turning towards shafts of sunshine
whenever and wherever they fell. I don't know what we spoke
about – a football headline in the newspaper, a car revving
past on the street, something on television, a pop song. He
once offered me a cigarette; I took one, although I'd never
smoked before, had a few frantic gasps, then stubbed it out
telling him I'd finish it later, the smoke on my blazer might be
a give-away. Probably he could see through that quite well,
but he didn't let on.

It was a conversational drift. That was okay. I also had to
think about what I was doing there so furtively in those places,
and I kept my eyes peeled for masters or prefects. Another
time he gave me one of the two Milky Ways in his back pocket,
and watched as I fed the warm bar of sweet chocolate into my
mouth. I watched *him* looking up at the skeleton of scaffolding
and maybe I did sense there was something romantic about
scaling those heights, on a crisp clear day under a blue sky.

Once I thought I caught sight of Mrs Plummer, back to
her old tricks, but I wasn't very sure. I remembered Fiona
telling me weeks back that she wanted to get tickets for
Godspell at the theatre. I never gave a thought to calculus or
trigonometry, which would completely floor me in Stanger's
class. I loved to hear the canvas thrashing in the wind up
on the scaffolding; the din thrilled me. I considered it was
an enviable thing to do, to be airborne on that flighty,
fantastical ship.

'Here, I want to show you something,' my fellow skiver
said.

I shrugged. I followed him behind a wall. He stood with his back to me for some moments. Then he turned round.

His jeans were unzipped and opened. From the split in the dirty denim obtruded something very small, a squiggle of flesh. A cock, of course. But nothing like what had been speculated on as concealed inside the workers' jeans and overalls as they shinned up and down the scaffolding and balanced, wishbone-legged, on the lengths of metal tubing. It looked pale and meagre, and quite sorry for itself. The funnel foreskin caused it to taper away. I was circumcised, so that technically I'd lost something I might have had, but the foreskins I saw in the changing-rooms mostly had an untidy, fraying appearance to me.

When I could take my eyes off it, I lifted them to the man's face. Its expression was beseeching. He was staring at me, wide-eyed, desperate for a reaction and at the same time fearful of it.

I found myself looking again at his crotch, at the gift of something or other he was offering me. He took one step forward, then another. I retreated by the same. I felt my knees trembling. Maybe he saw and made a supposition. He was raising his arms. I should have taken my cue and vamoosed. Instead, fixed by the skimpy little protrusion, I smiled. Smiled at the absurdity of the situation. Smiled maybe with relief, that not all building workers were hung like satyrs.

He started whispering at me – but so softly that I couldn't be certain. *Touch me! Give me a wank! Toss me off!* It couldn't have been myself thinking the words. *I've seen you looking. C'mon, pal, toss us off. Then I'll give you a wank too . . .*

My smile grew broader. It was then he started to swear at me, fucking this and fucking that, and his big hand dropped to cup the wee thing protectively. I did turn, and fled, hell for bloody leather, just as fast as I could. Ran, and ran, and I never looked back.

. . . on most of the peaks nothing grows, or, if there is any pasture, the snow covers it. Lower down there are sunny hills and valleys and woods with streams

flowing by: country, in fact, more worthy for men to dwell in.

Hannibal's light dimmed for me after the crossing had been made and north Italy reached. He shrank in my mind's eye from that gilded hero of legend, tirelessly resolute among the ice wastes of glaciers bloodied by red sunsets, to a not very sane man at the head of a circus troupe of elephants, continually on the look-out for a fight, for a good spoiling and dust-up. Ballcock lost some interest too, and I'd catch him skimming through the remaining pages with his thumbnail to calculate how much was left, how long it was going to take us, would he be able to spin it out? With interminable Cicero on certain days and grammar and unseens on others and home ink exercises on the remainder, he did in the end manage.

The year was running out on us, dribbling away between infrequent little spurts of animation. The temperature was climbing. We were allowed to remove our blazers in class. Short-sleeved shirts were permissible, but not long sleeves rolled back. Ballcock would sit – or perch – at his lectern with perspiration visible on his moustache. Surely the appendage would need to be cropped back – not just lightly tinkered with – if the weather were to turn even better in July and August? That time would once have lain ahead of us like perfect enticement. But now we had the ordeal of waiting for O-level results. A lot of life currently seemed to consist of waiting: waiting to get into the Gartness Tennis Club, waiting to get a nod of recognition from someone who belonged to the 'right' group, waiting for body hair to grow in, waiting for explanations, waiting for a purpose to declare itself, waiting for the mists to clear.

Across the street from the school, the latest addition to Glasgow's concrete cityscape was being prepared for topping out. The building of prefabricated parts had an inert look, twenty years before the mirrored and bronzed flanks of its neighbours would cast critical reflections on it against the colours of the sky. But to us then – in our somewhat less than innocent state – it was modernity itself, on a par with Marc Bolan and clogs and that *Last Tango in Paris*. Now the scaffolding was coming down, with one hell of a racket you could have heard a mile away; the majority of the workmen had moved on elsewhere, taking with them those fabled twenty-four-hour tumescences between their legs.

Seeing their despair, Hannibal rode ahead and at a point of vantage which afforded a prospect of a vast extent of country, he gave the order to halt, pointing to Italy far below, and the Po Valley beyond the foothills of the Alps.

Once I saw Fiona roaring past in a sports car, an MG convertible, with the remains of a gummed L-plate stuck to the chrome back bumper. She was in the passenger seat.

It happened in town, not on Great Western Road by any of the bus stops, and since they were heading in a different direction I didn't suppose that they – she and the driver – were doing it for effect: at any rate, not for the benefit of those who still travelled on the Number 38 Balfron via Killearn bus.

I would have asked her about it if she had come back, but she didn't come back. How could she have, after enjoying speed in an MG? The canvas hood had been down and folded away and the wind was blowing her hair, so that it winnowed about her head. I wondered if her companion could have had any suspicions about its being dyed, whether it even mattered a sod to him at sixty mph, in his low-slung bright yellow pleasure machine.

'My men,' Hannibal said, 'you are at this moment passing the protective barrier of Italy – nay more, you are walking over the very walls of Rome . . .'

I didn't smell drink again on Ballcock's breath. It must have been a temporary reversal only, a stopgap aberration. I didn't know why it had happened, and why it should have ceased to happen since.

One day he walked into his classroom and I saw at once the full transformation. A pair of scissors had been taken to trim back and shape the moustache. For the first time that I could remember he was carrying himself with some confidence, straight-backed, like a man with an understanding of himself and his capabilities, who knows he has affections and that they are returned.

Livy was almost behind us. After the exams we had carried on, but for the sake of form. Ballcock started to while away whole periods talking in quite an entertaining way he had about Roman agriculture or architecture.

He would shortly be losing us. He never kept a class for longer than one year, but in fact he had proved for the most part a very capable enthusiast and instructor. He knew just how much information to disclose at a time, how to break down complex matters into digestible portions suiting our concentration span and powers of retention. I came to conclude later that that had been quite a rare instinct. At the time I had half sensed the fact, as with so much else, but I was too inexperienced to articulate the thought properly to myself. With the mists still left to clear, I lived in a hazy swirl of imprecision. Anything might be possible for the rest of our lives, but for the moment we lacked clarity and focus.

'Henceforward,' [Hannibal assured his men] 'all will be easy going – no more hills to climb. After a fight or two you will have the capital of Italy, the citadel of Rome, in the hollow of your hands.'

Mrs Plummer came to the annual fund-raising fête held in June, a fortnight before term ended. She wasn't immediately identifiable to me: soberly dressed, demure, with her arm linked through her husband's. I could almost have believed she showed the evidence of placid, fulfilled contentment.

It *was* her, wasn't it? We kept having to ask ourselves. It was the woman I'd seen on Raeburn Street, I was very nearly certain, but without the warpaint: it was the height of her, and the same slim girth. She was wearing a longer skirt, but through her tights I did recognise – or thought I must be recognising – the two red marks like scorch burns scraped on the backs of her ankles by the pressure of two tight-fitting shoes. Her mannerisms were collected, middle class. When the sun came out she put on a pair of Polaroid aviator sunglasses, which were the rage then. Ballcock looked as proud as Punch. His wife hardly rolled her hips at all, her heels were fashionably solid and squat and neither too high nor too low.

We were all of us, it seemed, living very medium and, after the earlier little hazards, very safe lives.

That same afternoon I also saw Fiona.

She had drifted into the proceedings – probably gatecrashed, when the two ticket collectors had had their backs turned – on the arm of a sixth-former I knew to come from the south side of the city, from rich and non-gentile Whitecraigs. With his swarthiness and the premature signs of a receding hairline, he looked closer to thirty than twenty. He already had the stooped and oblique manner of a professional – in anticipation, he was the consultant surgeon it was his ambition to be, encouraging a confession by his demeanour and allowing money to pay for his solicitude. Fiona could have been his wife, so accurately did she match her stride to his, so closely did she hold herself to him.

The business was a little outrage. I saw how taken aback some of the staff were: not shocked, but winded briefly by their own excruciating envy. Goldman would land on his feet, having the proper air about him which no one could have *taught* him, and somehow or other Fiona would also, so gifted as she was by nature with her looks and a new complement of grace.

The grace was a further refinement of what I remembered – an impression of elegance, harmony, composure – but she carried it as if she had always known what it was. She was as maxi as the fashions permitted her to be; there wasn't a trace to be seen of her thighs. Her long hair hung down over her shoulder-blades, Janis Joplin style, expensively cut no doubt and now distinctly crimped and a little less fair. She smiled or laughed at the things Goldman pointed out to her while she strenuously ignored what she did not want to see.

At one narrow point in the proceedings, a gully between two tides of human traffic, she was jostled sideways, against Mrs Plummer. The woman's shoulder bag slipped, the strap slithered down her arm carried by the weight of the bag's contents, but Fiona – if she noticed or if she didn't – proceeded on her way regardless, leaving the Plummers in her wake, with Mrs Plummer's Polaroids dropped somewhere upon the grass where feet threatened to tread.

I ran after Fiona and Goldman to observe them. I looked for some small token of recognition from her, although I felt it must give me heartfelt pain to receive it. But she was determined. As she turned, however, at the pillow-fight pole, I noticed what I had seen long ago, which I remembered even from the days before we met.

An expression, decently concealed – an under-expression – of aching, ineffable *boredom*.

It was, and would be, the reverse aspect of everything that was buoyant and attractive about her. The ennui was sunk deep and inextricably into her constitution, from a time before she could recall, from circumstances that were family history and denied to her but of which she had the cost to pay. The situation is clearer to me now than it could possibly have been to me then. A terrible blankness – an amalgam of tedium and an intuitive sense of purposelessness – pertained at the frosted centre of her: a vacuum of response which nothing else closer to the surface could compensate for. She lacked faith rather than confidence, and the want was endemic.

Actual life had never matched Fiona McFadyen's expectations of it, and by this stage she had no firmer certainty than her skill at these minor theatrical performances. Her own ambition might flare on occasions, but usually for a trivial end; and anyway she soon grew tired of every new game, and she would reapply herself – with the cruel and ironic enthusiasm of a true cynic – to the next one.

I stayed on until the sun vanished, devoured not by translucent raspberry-ripple and lime sorbet mares' tails like a Hannibal sky, but by clouds of habitual, west coast, Atlantic greyness. Neutrality reclaimed us. Fiona vanished also, with her new companion, both of them spirited forwards in time – by implication – into respectability and rareripe middle age. I did catch sight of the Plummers leaving, still arm in arm as they headed with the throng for the gates of the sports ground: she was tossing her hair back, as I had watched her do on Savannah Street, and every time she did so the brown hair brushed against her husband's cheek, it skidded on to his neck and shoulder, but he let it, glorying in the thing's happening.

I was touched, and I was saddened. Leaving the playing fields after both couples, I felt that I had acquired a burden of sobriety in the course of the afternoon. Like Fiona's consuming sense of ennui, it must always have existed in me, from long before my birth. But now I was properly noticing it and accepting it – this gravitas, this vague melancholy – for the first and original time.

The clouds didn't part to let shafts of illumination pass through. They stayed just as routinely and inevitably grey as they had been. They looked, not like the peaks of ethereal mountains as clouds will sometimes do, but like packed city snow: or merely like themselves, like the very normality of clouds, like the carriers of drizzle and the harbingers of falling barometer gauges that they are.